"You aren't dealing with a besotted child anymore."

He looked her over. "No, I can see that you're all woman now," he said, "and a beautiful one at that. But I'm not available."

She drew her fan down the side of his cheek. "You haven't given your heart to another, have you?"

"No, I haven't."

"Then you're available." She smiled sweetly. "Who knows? I might just end up with you, after all."

"You can try," he said.

"If I wanted you, Tavis Mackinnon, and it didn't matter how I got you, I could do it." She stopped, and poked his chest with her folded fan. "You would do well to remember that."

"We haven't finished our dance."

"We haven't finished a lot of things," she said, then caught up her skirts and walked off the dance floor.

Also by Elaine Coffman:

ESCAPE NOT MY LOVE
IF MY LOVE COULD HOLD YOU
MY ENEMY, MY LOVE
ANGEL IN MARBLE
FOR ALL THE RIGHT REASONS
SOMEWHERE ALONG THE WAY
SO THIS IS LOVE*

*Published by Fawcett Books

HEAVEN KNOWS

Elaine Coffman

A Fawcett Gold Medal Book

FAWCETT GOLD MEDAL • NEW YORK

A Fawcett Gold Medal Book
Published by Ballantine Books
Copyright © 1994 by Guardant Inc.

All rights reserved under International and Pan-American Copyright Conventions. Published in the United States of America by Ballantine Books, a division of Random House, Inc., New York, and simultaneously in Canada by Random House of Canada Limited, Toronto.

Library of Congress Catalog Card Number: 93-90866

ISBN 0-449-14861-0

Printed in Canada

First Edition: April 1994

10 9 8 7 6 5 4 3 2 1

Can love and peace live in the same heart?
Beaumarchais,
The Barber of Seville (1775)

CHAPTER
❧ ONE ❧

Nantucket, 1850

Two hours after Lizzie Robinson got a bosom, she lost it.

That in itself wouldn't have been so bad if she hadn't had the misfortune to lose it on the steps that lead from the Crosby mansion down to their backyard. Even that might not have been so humiliating if Tavis Mackinnon had not been standing at the bottom of those ill-fated steps at the exact moment the pull of gravity had gotten the best of her.

Just thinking about it made Lizzie cringe. It seemed to her that the problem all began with desire—her desire to have Tavis Mackinnon realize she wasn't a child, and Tavis's desire to see her as nothing but. In Lizzie's mind there had been only one thing that kept her from being accepted as a woman instead of a child, and that was a bosom.

So she got herself one.

Only then she realized that having a bosom did not necessarily mean it would be noticed. By that time the question had gone from *How could she get a bosom?* to *How could she get Tavis to notice it?*

Lizzie had wanted Tavis to notice her bosom. Desperately. She had even prayed about it, saying, "Dear God, please, please, please let him notice my bosom." But that hadn't meant she wanted to drop it at his feet.

Lizzie remembered vividly the day when she had first learned that Tavis Mackinnon was a man who liked a woman with a generous bosom. She had been at the Starbucks' party, doing what she always did at parties— spying. Hiding behind a potted palm in the corner of the Starbucks' magnificent ballroom—which she had thought a good omen, palms being the symbol of triumph and all—she had parted the fronds to stare blankly at what had been the object of her affections for five long years. Tavis Mackinnon.

Tavis was doing what he had been doing for most of those five years. Ignoring her. At that particular moment he was leaning on one shoulder, which he rested in a self-possessed manner against a classically fluted pillar in the Starbucks' Palladian-style ballroom. Whenever she looked at him standing in front of that plaster wall panel with scenes from mythology set within panels of plaster architrave and framed by pediments and swags, she felt transported to Mount Olympus. Truly Tavis was no less magnificent than Zeus himself, for indeed, Lizzie had felt struck by thunderbolts whenever he came into her line of vision.

He was deep in conversation with his two friends and constant companions, Cole Cassidy and Nathaniel Starbuck. After giving Tavis a quick once-over, Lizzie's gaze dropped to the perfectly polished shoes on feet that were crossed at the ankles. Her gaze moved slowly, deliberately, painstakingly upward, pausing at the knees—

one was bent slightly—before moving higher. His legs were long. His arms were folded across his midsection in a casual manner, and for a brief moment her gaze rested upon his hand. His fingers were long and graceful, the fingers of a sensitive man. His middle was lean. His shoulders were broad. In her opinion, everything about him was genuine flawless perfection. But it was whenever Lizzie looked at his face that she saw a vision of heaven.

As she watched, Tavis laughed at something Cole said, and then he turned toward Nathaniel to speak—but to Lizzie, it seemed as if Tavis looked directly at her. Her knees buckled. Her heart hammered faster than before. Her mouth went oven-dry. Her palms began to perspire. Heaven help her, but she wondered what would happen if he ever did more than look.

"Why, Lizzie Robinson, whatever are you doing way back here all by yourself?" Mrs. Starbuck asked, catching sight of Lizzie as she passed.

Lizzie wrenched her head back so fast, the palm branches snapped her in the face. "Well . . . you see . . . that is, I am . . ."

Mrs. Starbuck gave her a knowing smile. "Shy, are you?"

Her mouth too dry to speak, Lizzie simply nodded.

Mrs. Starbuck sighed and got that far-off look in her eyes like grownups sometimes did when they were remembering their own youth. "My, my, don't I know how you feel, Lizzie. Believe me when I tell you that every young girl that has ever lived has had similar feelings whenever the first buds of youth were sprouting. The best thing to do is to get it over with. Stand tall and straight with your chin high. Take a deep breath and make your most graceful entrance. Once you have it over with, and you're with your friends, you will find you feel ever so much better. You try it, Lizzie, and you'll see what I mean," Mrs. Starbuck said with a kindhearted nod, and then moved on.

As soon as Mrs. Starbuck was out of sight, Lizzie buried her head back in the palm branches, where her gaze delighted, once more, upon the person of Tavis Mackinnon, Mrs. Starbuck's words all but forgotten.

Lizzie sighed, wistfully meditating. Was there ever a more beautiful mouth, or a stronger, more arrogant jaw? His nose, she decided, was perfect for such a face as his—looking as if it had been put there and then refined. It was both aquiline and proud. But it was his eyes—the good Lord help her—that made Lizzie want to cross herself whenever she gazed into them, and Lizzie wasn't even Catholic. They were fall-over-in-a-dead-faint eyes if she had ever seen such—not gray and not blue, but storm-swept and lost somewhere in between.

Tavis looked away at that moment, and it slowly soaked into Lizzie's infatuated brain that he and his friends were mighty interested in something that was going on across the room.

Following the direction of their stares, Lizzie saw they were watching Vernelia Carrouthers make a spectacle of herself—spectacles being something Vernelia excelled at—after she made one too many dips into the punch bowl, where some daring soul had emptied an entire bottle of prime Kentucky bourbon. By her fifth cup of punch, Vernelia was having trouble walking. In fact, if the truth be known, she had trouble standing—something the three well-dressed men across the room seemed to notice.

"My God!" Nathaniel said. "She's going for the punch bowl . . . *again.*"

"One more drink and she'll be under the table," Cole said.

"Or Jared Crosby," Tavis added, obviously reading the signals Vernelia was sending to Crosby.

"She's wasting her time on Jared," Nathaniel observed. "Jared goes for a woman with more depth, wouldn't you say?"

Tavis only laughed and said, "Yes, he does . . . in her décolletage."

Then Cole laughed. "Jared may go for depth, but *you* go for the general overall dimensions," Cole said, giving Tavis a healthy poke in the ribs.

"Like 'em big, don't you, Tavis?" Nathaniel replied, using his hands to emphasize just how big *big* was.

Tavis simply shrugged. "Big enough to hold my interest, I guess."

"And to fill your hands," was Cole's reply.

This time it was Nathaniel who laughed, slapping Tavis on the back. "Ol' Tavis has always been a true believer in the ample bosom."

With a scandalized gasp, Lizzie jumped back, allowing the palm shoots to slap back into place. *A believer in the ample bosom . . .*

At that moment, she had looked down at the bodice of her best white dress of figured gauze, seeing for the first time that there was nothing that remotely resembled a bosom behind the intricate pleats down the front. She was certain if the neck had been lower, she would have seen clear down to her toes. It was a sad thing to admit that her pitifully small breasts made a poor showing at best. Suddenly she recalled Mrs. Starbuck's words: *Whenever the first buds of youth are sprouting* ... Looking down again, Lizzie gave a disheartening sigh as she realized the cold, hard truth: When it came to the first sprouting buds of youth, she didn't have so much as a sprig. No wonder Tavis thought her a child. How much time she had wasted giving him languishing looks and adoring smiles. Of course, he would never look at her love for him as anything more than an amusement, a hapless childish infatuation.

Putting her trust in the inspiration of the moment, Lizzie turned away in humiliated defeat, telling herself this was only a temporary setback, nothing more. As she walked to the black lacquered screen everyone knew one of Mr. Starbuck's ships brought back from Damascus, she took a seat on one of a pair of Belter méridiennes that faced each other, preferring the high-backed end of the elongated seat that was farthermost from Tavis Mackinnon.

She wanted to hide. Feeling lower than a grasshopper, she hooked her satin slippers behind the méridienne's cabriole legs and propped her chin in her palms as she began to ponder, weighing what she had just heard Tavis liked against what she had—or did not have, as her case was.

Lizzie frowned with perplexed exasperation when she was momentarily distracted by the derisive sniggers that were directed her way by Caroline and Harriet Weatherby as they passed by. "Tavis must be ignoring her," Harriet said, "or else he saw her first and decided to hide."

As she always did, she ignored their gibes, biting back the impulse to tell smug-faced Harriet that her sister Juliet would have been better off if Dewey Allison had ignored her; then she would have been there at the dance, instead of at home knitting bootees for a baby that would never know its father.

At last, and after much thought, Lizzie released a resigned sigh as she came to one final conclusion: If Tavis Mackinnon was impressed by a woman with ample dimensions, then she would simply have to find a way to ample up her dimensions.

The question wasn't so much *what* to do as *how*. Lips, she could tint with paper. Eyes, she could darken with charcoal. Pinching would give cheeks color. But what would make a flat bosom ample? she wondered. After a few moments of heavy contemplation, the shadow of a slow stretching smile curved itself across her mouth.

The next morning Lizzie was waiting at *Burnell's Store* when it opened. Mr. Burnell seemed surprised when she poked her golden head in his store and a moment later was seen placing a roll of cotton batting on the counter.

"Batting?" Mr. Burnell said with brow-raising surprise. "Why, Lizzie Robinson, I didn't know you had a fondness for quilting."

"Oh, I do, Mr. Burnell. I do."

After that day, Lizzie waited impatiently to be invited to the very next spring social, because she had known the moment Tavis Mackinnon saw her bosom, he would be hers. At last. It was so simple, really. He would notice her bosom, fall in love, ask her to marry him, and they would live happily ever after.

She was partly right. He did notice her bosom.

In fact, he held it in his hand.

CHAPTER
❧ TWO ❧

It was only a few weeks after the dance at the Starbucks' that Lizzie dressed for another dance. She wore a gown of deep purple moiré, piped with green. The bodice was modest, but lower than all her others, with a chastely rounded neck that dipped in the front. When she was dressed, she stood before the mirror and looked herself over critically, first from the front, then from the side.

Flat.

There was no doubt about it; everywhere she looked, from every angle, she was flat. Where there should have been some generously rounded curves, or at least some of the first budding signs of youth, there was nothing. Flat. Worse than flat. Why hadn't she noticed it before? Grown women had ample bosoms. And what did she have? A concave chest.

By this point in time, she was convinced Tavis Mackinnon could have mistaken her for a boy if she hadn't had long hair. *Well, there is nothing to be done about the past,* she told herself, but she most certainly could do something about the future.

8

Down on all fours now, she lifted the brightly colored counterpane on her bed and peered beneath the deeply ruffled lace border, dragging out the roll of batting she had purchased from *Burnell's Store*. Extracting two adequate wads of cotton batting—and one more pinch added for good measure—she rolled and patted them into the proper shape, then stuffed them into her chemise, giving herself the once-over again.

Mount Vesuvius would have been envious. *Why, I've blossomed into a woman right before my very eyes,* she thought, and seeing the proud thrust of her cotton padding, she said to her reflection, "Now, *that* is what I call a bosom."

Shortly after she arrived at the party, Lizzie held her breath as she watched Tavis walk in with his two friends. While the orchestra began warming up, she found a place to stand behind the spectacular stairway that curved down into the ballroom, her small, gloved hand clutching the newel post as she watched him stroll outside with Nathaniel and Cole.

Without wasting a precious minute, Lizzie hurried to find her best friend, Rebecca Field, making her way through conversing guests in the crowded ballroom. At last she spied Becca on the other side of the dance floor. Threading her way through the dancers and ignoring their hot glares, she crossed the dance floor and arrived at Becca's side.

Grabbing her friend by the arm and pulling her toward the door, she said, "Come with me. Quick!"

"What's wrong?" asked Becca, then getting no response, she said, "Lizzie, for Heaven's sake, will you please slow down? I'm losing all the flowers in my hair."

"Think of it as a trail for Prince Charming to follow."

"What Prince Charming?" Becca asked. "You could at least tell me where we're going," she said.

"Out," was Lizzie's only reply.

Once they were outside, the two girls stood at the top of the steps that led down to the Crosbys' small yard. The moon was high and full and round, putting out a fair amount of light, and added to the mellow amber glow of a half dozen or so lanterns strung from the house to the lone tree in the yard, it was more than enough light for them to see the silhouettes of three men standing near a statue, and see, too, the faint dull glow of the tip of Cole's cigar.

"I might have known," Becca whispered in tones just loud enough to be heard over the orchestra drifting through the open doors from the ballroom.

In spite of doing something she was well accustomed to—blatantly stalking Tavis by following him wherever he went—Lizzie was not at ease. Playing the woman was a new role for her and one she was uncertain of, in spite of the beautiful bosom she had sprouted or the feelings of love she had harbored for so long. She was in unfamiliar territory, and it made her anxious and a little fidgety and on edge. She glanced at Becca, who seemed ever so much like a gentle and unsuspecting lamb being led to slaughter, but even Becca's calm acceptance did nothing to lessen her apprehension.

Looking back down the steps, Lizzie took one quick glance at Tavis and felt like she was in a dory with only one oar, destined to row in circles. He was a man full grown, while she was ill-equipped at best—nothing more than a flat-bosomed girl of fifteen, going on sixteen—hopelessly in love with a god ten years her senior. Even with her ample bosom, she knew she was no match for a man who looked like Tavis.

And he did look good—something every woman in Nantucket would be happy to admit. He wore a black evening coat and pants tight enough to raise some interesting questions. Glancing away from Tavis, Lizzie discovered Cole was looking at her in the fashion of one who senses disaster is about to strike and wondering what could be done to prevent it. It angered her that she hadn't taken so much as one step toward them, and already Cole was forecasting gloom and doom. Not *everything* she did ended up in disaster.

With a lift of her chin, and what she hoped was a fetching pose, Lizzie started down the steps, holding the front of her dress aloft so she wouldn't trip over it. This gave the three men below a healthy view of her ankles.

The moment she started her descent, Lizzie realized something was amiss. Her heart thumped uncomfortably as Cole exclaimed softly, and the other two men turned their attention upon her.

Her eyes rounding to a horrified width, Lizzie drew up short, stopping so fast that Becca, who was coming down the steps right behind her, thumped against her. Before Lizzie could think about the untimely slipping of her cotton padding, Becca knocked the breath from her.

She knocked something else from Lizzie as well.

With a soundless descent and a similar landing, the two cotton orbs floated downward and landed two steps below where Lizzie stood. For the smallest twinkling of a second, she had the most fervent wish that the earth would open up and swallow her whole.

In horrified dismay, Lizzie stared down, just as Becca landed on the step next to her. Seeing what Lizzie saw, she gave a scandalized gasp and tried to put her skirt over it.

"It's a little late for that, I'm afraid," Nathaniel said.

"I've heard of women throwing themselves at a man, but this is ridiculous," Cole said.

Sudden as a thunderclap, and just as irritable, came the mocking cackle of laughter. Lizzie's spine crumpled and her body froze. She was gripped with the terrible fear that she might cry like the true idiot she was. Trembling and humiliated down to the soles of her feet, she stood before the three men with all the self-confidence of a wet sock.

"Would it be too much to ask," Tavis said in almost civil tones as he stepped toward them, stopping at the base of the steps, "*what* you two numbskulls are up to?"

"Now, Tavis, don't be so hard on them. Can't you see it's Lizzie who wants to play that game, *I'll show you mine if you show me yours first*?" Nathaniel said before folding over with laughter.

"Well, she sure as hell was first," Tavis said. "Of all the asinine . . ." Tavis clamped his mouth together. With something that sounded painfully close to a growl, he took the steps two at a time, stopping just long enough to pick Becca up and set her out of the way. Then he turned his attention to Lizzie.

Lizzie was looking down, where her stuffings lay as peaked and silent as the pyramids bathed in moonlight. With a muffled curse, Tavis leaned over to retrieve Lizzie's batting. Thrusting them into her face, he said, "Next time you want to play at being a woman, worry more about behaving like one. Stuffing your bosom with cotton doesn't make you a woman any more than a—"

"Careful," Cole said.

Tavis glanced at his friend. With another muffled curse, he shoved the cotton into Lizzie's trembling hands. "Take your stuffings and your mute friend and get the hell out of here, because I'm not going to be very nice in about two seconds."

Lizzie and Becca both turned up the steps at the same time, bumped together, then went at it again, bolting up the steps like a couple of frightened sheep trying to go through a gate at the same time.

When they reached the top of the stairs, Becca shot through the door like her drawers were afire, but Lizzie paused just long enough to turn and say, "I hate you, Tavis Mackinnon. I really and truly do."

"I have lived for the moment," Tavis said, amid his friends' hooting guffaws.

As she turned away, she knew he watched her, his face contorted with laughter, her own cheeks red and burning with humiliation. Once she was inside the ball-room, Lizzie's last words to Becca were, "I wish I could die."

Becca looked doubtful. "God would never be so merciful," she said.

Lizzie ran all the way home, knowing her father was still at the party. As soon as she entered her house she mumbled something inaudible to the housekeeper and fled up the stairs, seeking the sanctuary of her room. Dropping her blue velvet cape on the tufted child's chair beside the door, she threw herself across her Chippendale canopy bed, stubbing her toe on one of the claw-and-ball feet. All in all, it was the perfect ending for a horrible day.

She had never felt so dejected, and now the pain

shooting through her foot brought the tears that had threatened all the way home, splashing down her cheeks. Crying like her heart would break, she sobbed out the pain and despair of the humiliating scene Tavis had witnessed. There was little doubt in her mind that others besides Nathaniel and Cole had witnessed it also—the entire town, more than likely. Well she knew that by tomorrow it would be all over the whole of Nantucket Island—maybe even as far as Tuckernuck or Martha's Vineyard. She slumped in defeat.

To make matters worse, her father was on his way home right now—walking because he was too angry to take the carriage—and she shuddered to think she would have to face him and admit the horrible, shameful truth that she had, indeed, been at it again.

When would she ever learn? For the first time in a long time she found herself feeling just a little sorry for herself. She needed someone to talk to, someone older than Becca, someone younger than her grandfather, someone more understanding than her father. If only she had a mother . . .

Lizzie's mother had been dead for over five years, and never, ever had she felt the pain of Patience's loss more than tonight. *Oh, Mama, Mama, please help me. Wherever you are, please help me. I am so ashamed.*

Lizzie heard the front door slam and knew her father was home, knew he was thinking hard about what he should do. Slowly she pulled herself up and slid off the bed, wiping the tears from her face. Appealing to her mother, she said, *"If you're going to help me, it better be now."* Then she started counting.

One . . . two . . . three . . . Well she knew that she could count to three from the time the front door slammed until her father called her name from the bottom of the stairway.

"Lizzie? Lizzie, where are you?"

Four . . . five . . . six . . . Now he would be looking up the stairs, ready to order her downstairs as he began to unbutton his topcoat.

"Lizzie, I know you're up there, so you might as well march yourself down here right now."

Seven . . . He would be heading toward the parlor by now. By the count of *eight,* Lizzie was already walking down the stairs.

By the time she stepped through the parlor door, her father was red-faced and huffing, looking for all the world as if he were on the verge of apoplexy. His expression said he was thinking about giving Lizzie a stern look, then decided against it. Stern looks never had any effect upon her anyway.

It was no secret to everyone in the Robinson family—including Lizzie—that her father got down on his knees every night and prayed that he would live to see the day when she grew up.

Until tonight, Lizzie hadn't particularly cared if she grew up or not, as long as she got Tavis Mackinnon to notice her. Until tonight, being in love with Tavis had gotten to be such a habit that it was something she did quite naturally and without thinking—sort of like a sneeze. As a result, being hauled over the coals by her father had become quite a habit, too.

Throwing his hands up into the air in his most exasperated manner, Samuel dropped them to his sides and simply stared at her for a moment. Then he said, "Lizzie, how in the name of all that's holy can I make you understand?" Dropping his arms, he faced her squarely and said, "Why can't you grasp what I've been trying to tell you all these years? Child, child, why can't you see?"

"What, Papa?"

"That you don't get a man by chasing him until he drops from exhaustion."

"I *can* see that, Papa. Truly."

"No you can't!" Samuel shouted.

He stood in the middle of the small parlor, his sides heaving like a blown horse as he took out his handkerchief and mopped the shine from his forehead. Both were signs that he was readying himself for the final assault: the fatherly appeal. Breathing deeply, he spoke in subdued tones. "A fifteen-year-old girl has no business setting her heart and hopes on a twenty-five-year-old man. Can't you interest yourself in a boy nearer your own age? How about one of your schoolmates?"

Lizzie frowned. Didn't her father realize it was too late for that? A boy her own age was not someone she could fall in love with, even if it did make her father happy. She loved Tavis Mackinnon. Didn't *anyone* understand that? It wasn't her fault he was a man full grown; a man with eyes as gray-blue and clear as the summer sky above, and hair as black as the River Styx. She didn't have any use for boys her age. And her schoolmates? They were about as interesting as whale blubber.

Still Lizzie didn't say anything. She was accustomed to these calamitous discussions with her father, and she knew nothing she said would appease him. He would go right on ranting and raving until he wore himself to a frazzle.

She looked at her father. Right now his face was as red and bursting as a spring rose. He was a small, robust man with a balding head and the tendency to push his spectacles up on his forehead, only to forget where he had put them. He was what Lizzie liked to think of as homemade, possessing an unpretentious quality, rather like a handmade doll that had everything a store-bought doll had, but none of it possessed a hint of perfection. Samuel wasn't a father figure. He was a daddy. But that didn't mean he understood Lizzie.

"Lizzie, child of mine, what am I going to do with you?"

The question was plain and simple. It was also pure, undiluted rhetoric. For whenever Samuel Robinson started a question with "Lizzie, child of mine," he wasn't fishing for an answer—which was a good thing, since none was forthcoming.

Although the question was directed to Lizzie, there was a strange understanding in arguments of this kind between the two of them, and their dramatic, almost humorous appeal to any bystanders. It was the sort of thing others would never have wished upon themselves, but wouldn't want to miss for the world. It was Don Quixote charging the windmills. It was *The Taming of the Shrew.* It was Father thinking he knew best. It was Lizzie thinking her love for Tavis Mackinnon was destined to be the greatest tragedy of all time, simply because her father did not have one featherweight of romance in his entire body.

Lizzie wanted to take her journal (the one entitled *Reasons I Will Love Tavis Mackinnon Forever*) and hit her father over the head with it. Couldn't he understand? Didn't he remember what it was like to be young and in love? But instead of hitting her father, she counted to ten. When she finished, she still wanted to take her journal and slam him over the head.

A confrontation between Lizzie and her father often

mounted to epic proportions. This was due more to Lizzie's flair for the flamboyant and the melodramatic than with the Bible. Because Lizzie lived life to its fullest, she experienced its agonies and ecstasies with quadrupled intensity. And today she was experiencing the pain of an insurmountable task and one she was devoted to: trying to convince her father that what she felt for Tavis was as real and unwavering as it was enduring. Not only did Tavis fit her romantic vision of her future, but she was certain he was destined to become a part of it as well.

Besides her two younger sisters, Lizzie had six older brothers and one father. Living with this many men in the house made her an authority of sorts. Men, she decided some time ago, were shortsighted creatures with absolutely no capacity for speechlessness over the fog-shrouded beauty of a rainy day, or the sparkle of sunlight dancing over the great, green swells of the Atlantic. No wonder her father had no ability to understand the ways of the heart. Here she was, a child of passion, with nothing in her future but waiting and weeping.

Her father could not understand. Her brothers did not try to understand. And her sisters were too young to understand. Such was a woman's lot, she decided, thinking upon Tennyson's words:

> *Man for the field and woman for the hearth:*
> *Man for the sword and for the needle she:*
> *Man with the head and woman with the heart:*
> *Man to command and woman to obey:*
> *All else confusion.*

Lizzie stamped her foot in vexation. All else *was* confusion. And Lizzie wanted so much more.

To the folks around Nantucket, Lizzie Robinson was

the bane of young girlhood, something like a hurricane, or a pestilence that strikes every few years and will pass, or in her case, grow into maturity. To her father she was the dearest and most lovable witch of a child whose growing pains were half amusement, half heartache. Lizzie was such a poignant mixture of laughter and tears. It was obvious he loved her, this motherless daughter of his, but it was also obvious that Samuel Robinson did not know what to do with her. Lizzie's infatuation for a man ten years older than herself had to stop. Samuel knew this—the whole of Nantucket knew this. Tavis Mackinnon had been a patient man. A man who was fast running out of patience—about as fast as Samuel was running out of ideas.

Giving his attention back to Lizzie, Samuel again spoke in normal tones. "Staying on the trail of a man like a wolf after a wounded stag is all wrong. You can't keep hounding the man. He is plumb worn-out. How many times have I told you that a woman does not chase a man? It simply is not done. It's *never* been done."

"Why not?"

Samuel threw up his hands in exasperation. "I don't know why. I didn't make the rules. It's been that way since the beginning of time. It's always been the man's place to do the chasing . . . if any is to be done. It's in the Bible, for goodness' sake! Can't you understand that?"

Lizzie had her arms crossed and her eyes fixed stubbornly on the ceiling. "No, I can't. There are no rules in love."

Samuel's brows shot up in surprise, then a suspicious look settled over his face. "Who told you *that*?"

"Miss Samson."

"Miss Samson ... *that* rattlehead?" He crossed his arms and gave her a wise-owl look. "Your teacher doesn't know what she's talking about."

"Miss Samson is not a rattlehead. You are just saying that because she's a woman. I'll have you know she's a very smart woman, Papa. She went to normal school. She has a diploma. *I* saw it."

"She may have a diploma, and she may have gone to normal school, but none of it rubbed off on her. *That* woman is not normal."

"Miss Samson is a wonderful person," Lizzie said, in her most mournful tones. "I don't know how you can say that."

"I can and will say it with ease. Anyone who goes about putting wild ideas into a young girl's head is *not* normal. And that includes Miss Samson."

"She didn't put wild ideas into my head."

"Well, where *did* you get them, then?"

"My head came this way," she cried. "I was born with a headful of ideas ... although I must say I don't understand why God saw fit to fill my head with ideas and then give me to a family who refuses to even try to understand them. How could you call all the beauty and poetry inside my head nothing but wild ideas?"

"I'll tell you how. Because telling you there are no rules in love is a wild idea, and Miss Samson is a fool for saying such."

"Miss Samson didn't say that. She read it."

"Said it, read it, what's the difference? And even if she did read it, that just proves there's more than one rattleheaded woman out there trying to stir up trouble. I can tell you right now, I don't know what the world is coming to. I sent you to school to be educated, not to have a bunch of fanciful ideas crammed into your head." Samuel paused and gave her a penetrating look. "Have you been reading that Browning woman again? Is that where you're getting those ideas?"

Lizzie shook her head.

"The Brontë sisters then," he said, "and don't try to deny it. I've told you before, reading the likes of those rebellious women is putting ridiculous notions in your head. *There are no rules in love*. . . . Bah! What a preposterous bunch of poppycock. No one but a woman would think of saying such."

"Those words were written by a man, Papa."

Samuel blanched, and his glasses popped off his forehead and slid onto his nose. Pushing his glasses back up, Samuel choked out, "A man?"

Lizzie nodded. "Miss Samson said it was the English writer John Lyly who wrote, *'Might, malice, deceit, treachery, all perjury, any impiety, may lawfully be committed in love, which is lawless.'* "

Samuel snorted. "It's strange to me that you can remember every word of a long quote, but you can't remember something as simple as staying away from Tavis Mackinnon. And for your information, Miss Storehouse of Knowledge, John Lyly was a *comic*. And Miss Samson is a troublemaker. Understandably so."

"*I* don't understand it, so it must not be so," Lizzie said, quickly.

But Samuel went on as if he hadn't heard her. "Any woman with a name like Delilah Samson *has* to be a contradiction."

Lizzie's face went blank. She didn't say anything else. Neither did her father, but his expression was a mixture of vexation and fatigue. His words didn't appear to be any more effective than water dripping over a duck's back.

Besides that blank expression she wore whenever her father hauled her over the coals, Lizzie had three other looks: charge, retreat, and euphoric. Charge was just that—assertive and ready for attack—and one she used when hot on Mackinnon's trail. Retreat was an expression she used whenever she had to look utterly innocent, something she had to do whenever her father was angry, or Mackinnon looked on the verge of murder. Euphoric was reserved for those rare occasions when Tavis actually seemed to be amused by something she had done. It was an expression seldom used.

Judging from the way he looked at her now, Lizzie knew her father was contemplating her blank look. Perhaps it was that look that prompted him to say, "Elizabeth Amelia"—he always called her by her whole name, Elizabeth Amelia, whenever his ire was on the wane—"haven't I explained to you until I was blue in the face how a woman must wait patiently for a man to be attracted to her?"

"Yes, Papa, you have, but I'd never get Tavis to notice me if I waited for him," said Lizzie.

"Believe me when I tell you this. Tavis Mackinnon *has* noticed you. More than he'd like. The problem is, he wants nothing to do with you. Tonight he explicitly requested . . . no, *ordered* me to keep you away from him. Far away. This means you will not sit behind him in church, cross the street when you see him coming, or wait outside any buildings he is in. You will not write him love notes, follow him home, peek through the windows of his office, or tell any of the young ladies he is squiring about that he has an exotic and highly contagious disease he caught in Borneo."

"I didn't say he *had* an exotic disease he caught in Borneo, I said he *might* have one," Lizzie said.

Samuel's face turned red and he shouted so loud, he came up on his toes. "Mackinnon has never even *been* in Borneo!"

"How do you know?"

"Because he told me."

"Maybe he just said that."

"Lizzie, the man gets seasick if he gets more than ten feet away from shore. That's why he designs ships instead of sailing them." Samuel paused, not because he was out of breath, but because he was out of things to say. Why did talking to Lizzie always end up like he was talking to a blank wall?

He began to wish with all his heart that Patience were alive to tame their unruly daughter. What had he done wrong? How had he failed as a father? Why couldn't Lizzie be like her younger sisters? What made her such an exasperating little devil, when Sally and Meg were such angels?

He picked up his pipe and crammed a pinch of tobacco in it, lighting it and taking a couple of steady draws to calm his jittery nerves. After two fortifying puffs, he still remembered all too vividly the red, angry face of Tavis Mackinnon as he led Lizzie home by the pigtails just last week—informing him that Lizzie had been at it again.

Samuel cringed every time he thought about his daughter hiding behind a buggy to spy on Mackinnon and his two friends as they went for a swim—wearing nothing but the skin the Almighty had given them. According to Mackinnon, he had caught Lizzie—*after* putting his clothes on—and confronted her, only to have her say, "You don't have anything I haven't seen before . . . lots of times. I *have* six brothers, you know."

To which Mackinnon had replied, "Well, *I'm* not one

of them," just before he grabbed her by the pigtails and marched her home.

Across the room, Samuel was standing in stiff silence, just staring at Lizzie as he thought things through. He wished he could be more firm with her, but how could he? Just looking at her, the perfect picture of contriteness, he lost some of his bluster. Lizzie might be an exasperating little devil, but she had the face of an angel with silver-blond hair and eyes of the deepest lavender-blue—just like her mother.

Her face was about the only angelic thing about her, however, for she had a temper that belonged to a redhead, and the stubborn disposition of a mule. For the past three years she had made his life a living hell.

As if sensing her father's thoughts, Lizzie said softly, "I know I'm an awful bother to you, Papa."

Samuel sighed. "You're no bother, child, except when it comes to Mackinnon . . . and that is getting out of hand, as well as being downright embarrassing. Your escapades are drawing larger crowds than the Congregationalist Church."

"I know. I'm truly sorry for . . . for embarrassing you again."

"And well you should be, but sorry doesn't fix it. Not this time. Mackinnon is spitting mad, and I'm two hops behind him."

Samuel looked at Lizzie's pale face. Whenever he scolded her and she became sadly pale and remorseful, he would feel guilty for being so hard on her. As he was fond of saying, "It wasn't her fault her mama had died when little Meg was born, any more than it had been Meg's fault."

Patience's death had been a blow to all of them, but most particularly to Samuel, who was left with nine children to raise. The boys, he could handle, and so far there hadn't been any problems with Sally or Meg, but perhaps that was because Sally was only eight, and Meg five.

The room grew quiet again—a sign that they were at a stalemate. At last Samuel sighed. "Go see to your sisters," he said, dropping wearily into a banister-back chair.

Samuel watched Lizzie depart, then he rocked the chair back on two legs and studied the ceiling. "Dear God in heaven," he said, "what will she do next?"

CHAPTER
❧ THREE ❧

She dyed her hair.

Red.

"It isn't dye," she said to a stupefied Becca. "It's henna. It's as old as Egypt."

"It may be as old as Egypt, but it's as ugly as sin," Becca said, following Lizzie into her bedroom.

The room was a lot like Lizzie, ordinary at first glance, but on closer study, quite unlike any other room. The walls were white and the floors were a warm, polished wood. The furniture was a mixture of well-known names like Chippendale, Sheraton, Windsor, and junk. The style was a cross between classic, novelty, and whimsy. In essence it was a collection of congenial clutter, a patchwork of styles and periods. Clocks, lamps, a mirror, an old oak chest, a Bible box, a washstand with its porcelain jug and basin, all worked in with patterns that vied for attention and furniture that fought for space. It was a mélange. It was as if litter had become a powerful weapon in the hands of someone who knew what she needed to be comfortable. Of all the rooms in the house, Lizzie's room was a private retreat filled with personal belongings that were both cozy and intimately revealing. It was a room at war with itself—a place where Cupids and nymphs chased one another along a border that topped stark white walls, where dried flowers tied up with satin bows rested atop boxes stuffed with seashells, bird nests, and a fragile butterfly wing—and yet it was gracious, unself-conscious, comfortable, stimulating, and beautifully free from rules. It was Lizzie.

Becca closed the door and came to stand behind Lizzie, who was looking at herself in the mirror, liking what she saw. Lizzie looked up and caught Becca's black-haired reflection in the mirror. Becca's eyes were wide with a look that lay somewhere between astonishment and awe. Lizzie wondered how Becca would look with red hair.

"I can't believe you did it. Whatever were you thinking of?" Becca asked at last.

"A change, of course." Lizzie looked at her friend's rich, raven tresses. "Oh, Becca, you can't imagine how dull it is having hair the color of beach sand. Blond is frightfully dull. It's so ordinary . . . like water. Boring. It's unimaginative, you know. When you're blond, you look at yourself in the mirror and nothing looks back. You think of blond and what comes to mind?"

Becca shrugged.

"I'll tell you. Yellow! That's what comes to mind. Yellow . . . the color of bile. It's a jealous, inconstant color, a symbol of adultery, perfidy, and cowardice," she said, almost spitting the words out. Then her voice turned soft and melodious. "But red . . ." Her eyes took on a dreamy expression. "Red is such a magnanimous color, don't you think? It simply takes my breath away. Why, just hearing the word brings so many brilliant pictures to my mind. Scarlet . . . crimson . . . burgundy . . . blood . . . Such beautiful, colorful, imaginative words. Did you know that in heraldry red is said to signify fortitude?"

"Something you had to have a lot of to do what you've done," said Becca. "Red," Becca repeated, as if her mind were so fertile with the implications of what Lizzie had done that she could think of little else. "Red. Blazing red. Holly-berry red. You-have-done-it-now red," she said absently with a shake of her head. Then she stopped, taking Lizzie by the arm.

Lizzie ignored her. "Did you know that in folklore, red is the color of magic?"

"It's also the color of revolution," said Becca. "And I think you may have started one. It's also the color your pa is going to see when he finds out what you've done."

Lizzie looked at herself again in the mirror, holding a bunch of flaming red hair aloft and piling it on her head.

"I don't know how I survived this long with blond hair, when it's so very obvious that I am a true redhead at heart."

"But not quite *that* red," Becca said.

Lizzie looked at her in the mirror. "Do you think it's too red?"

"It is *awfully* red, Lizzie," Becca said. Then, apparently seeing the way Lizzie was looking at her, she added, "Don't you think?"

The piled handful of flaming hair fell, but the determined look on Lizzie's face did not. If anything, it was more determined than ever. "I think it's quite the thing."

Becca shook her head and said, "I don't know. I wouldn't want to be in your shoes for all the sails between here and Cape Cod. Why did you do it, Lizzie? No, never mind, don't answer that. I *know* why you did it. It's because Tavis Mackinnon asked Abbie Billingsley to the dance."

Lizzie pretended indifference. "Why would I dye my hair just because he asked that old whey-faced Abigail?"

"Because Abbie has red hair."

It was the truth, of course, and everyone in town knew it, even Lizzie's father, who, as Becca predicted, was seeing red.

"That's it," Samuel said to his eldest son, Matt. "I'm at the end of my tether. I never thought I'd hear myself admit defeat, but I don't know what to do with Lizzie—short of throttling her."

"What's happened now?" Matt asked.

"Lizzie dyed her hair red, that's what's happened. Harlot-red, mind you, and then she walked up to Mackinnon at the Tattingers' party and asked him to dance. Bold as brass tacks, she was. It nearly put every matron in the place into a swoon, and I don't have to tell you how the young women Lizzie's age took it. Half of them aren't speaking to her, and the other half that are, are doing it only because they're afraid of that abominable temper of hers."

Stephen, another one of Lizzie's brothers, shook his head. "I know Lizzie does exasperating things, but I don't think it's all her fault."

"Then whose fault is it? It certainly isn't mine," Samuel said, poking himself in the chest as he added, "*I* never put her up to dyeing her hair red."

"Aw, I know that, Pa," Stephen said. "That isn't what I meant. It's just that Lizzie needs a woman's influence—someone to teach her the things a woman needs to know. She doesn't act like a properly reared lady because she hasn't been taught what it is, exactly, that a properly reared lady is supposed to know. And there isn't anyone around here that could teach her. It would take a special woman to educate Lizzie, because Lizzie is stronger than half the women she meets and smarter than the other half."

"A lot of help you are—telling me what Lizzie needs on the one hand, and telling me it's impossible to give it to her on the other."

"I said it would take a special woman. I did not say it was impossible. If I were you, I'd send her to Boston, to Aunt Phoebe."

"Aunt Phoebe? *That* Aunt Phoebe? Your mother's sister, Aunt Phoebe?"

Stephen nodded.

"Your aunt Phoebe has been a widow for so long, she couldn't possibly remember the things a young woman needs to know, and she's too strict and straitlaced by half. She's a perfectionist; she's eccentric; she's so ingrained into Boston society, she wouldn't give Lizzie a long look. And if she did, the two of them, having tempers like they have . . . why, whenever they tangled— and they would—it would take a crowbar to pry them apart."

"You haven't seen Aunt Phoebe in years. Maybe she's mellowed some," Matt said.

"Mellowed? *Your* aunt Phoebe? Ha! Even mellowed, she'd be formidable. That woman could make a glacier look warm. Besides, a tart temper never mellows no matter how old it gets, and a razor-sharp tongue like hers only gets sharper with use . . . like a blade put to a whetstone."

"I think it's a good idea," said Matt.

"Of course, I agree," said Stephen.

"I don't know," Samuel said, shaking his head. "If I sent Lizzie to Phoebe, she'd probably shoot me."

"Who? Aunt Phoebe or Lizzie?" Stephen asked.

"Both of them," Samuel said.

Stephen and Matt laughed.

"That might happen, of course, but then Aunt Phoebe might be just the person to change Lizzie. Either way, you'd have your problem solved. If Lizzie isn't here, she can't cause any more trouble," Stephen said.

"Put that way, the idea does have merit," Samuel said. "I'll sleep on it."

It must have been a good sleep, for the next morning Samuel wrote a letter to Lizzie's aunt Phoebe in Boston. A month later, Samuel had his response.

The morning after the arrival of Aunt Phoebe's letter, Lizzie walked into the dining room for breakfast, hearing her father speaking just as she entered.

"Sometimes I think Lizzie is a child of the devil," Samuel said.

"Good morning, *Father*," she said sweetly as she entered the room.

Seeing the amused looks on his children's faces, Samuel cleared his throat and went on with his meal.

"Is Lizzie in trouble, Papa?" Meg asked, her blond curls bobbing.

"She's always in trouble," Sally said. "Mrs. Husey says when Lizzie is about, there is always mischief brewing."

"Mrs. Husey is an old gossip," Lizzie said.

Samuel frowned. "If you cannot say something nice, Lizzie, don't say anything at all."

Lizzie nodded. "Mrs. Husey is a *nice* old gossip."

Samuel looked at the ceiling, mumbling to himself. Then he picked up a biscuit, put it on his plate, and cut it open as he said, "Lizzie, your aunt Phoebe has invited you to come to Boston to live with her."

"Who is Aunt Phoebe?" Meg asked.

Lizzie stopped her spoon midway between her bowl and her mouth and gave him a skeptical look. "Aunt Phoebe wouldn't invite me to Boston if you held a gun to her head," she said. "She fairly twisted my ear off the last time I saw her. Twisted it good, she did, and told me I was the most unpleasant, ill-mannered, ill-behaved creature God ever had the misfortune to create."

"Aunt Phoebe sounds like a wise woman to me," Matt said, laughing and giving Lizzie a wink.

"Who is Aunt Phoebe?" asked Meg.

"I don't know why Aunt Phoebe would have said something like that to Lizzie," Stephen said.

"Maybe she said it because it's true," Sally said. She snapped her mouth shut when Lizzie gave her a quelling look.

"Who is Aunt Phoebe?" Meg asked again.

Samuel looked at Lizzie. "Aunt Phoebe may have said those things, but she *has* asked you to come to Boston, nevertheless."

"I won't go," Lizzie said.

"Yes, you will," said Samuel.

"I will never go to Boston," Lizzie said. "You can lock me in my room. You can make me eat toads. You can starve me to death. I would rather be dead anyway than to go to Boston to live with bony-faced Aunt Phoebe."

Meg looked from Lizzie to her father. "Who is Aunt Phoebe?"

"There is no need to get overly dramatic. I haven't any punishment that exotic planned out," Samuel said. "You will write your aunt Phoebe and tell her you would be happy to pay her a visit, or you will not set foot outside of the house . . . nor will Becca Field be allowed to put a dainty, slippered foot inside."

Lizzie sprang to her feet, knocking over her bowl. "Then I will rot here . . . friendless and abandoned by my own family. I am sorry I've always been such a bother to everyone. I'm sorry I've never been wanted. I don't even think I'm your daughter. I think I was adopted."

"Where did you get a foolish idea like that? Adopted. Indeed." Samuel shook his head.

"If Lizzie was adopted, you could have sent her back, couldn't you, Papa?" Meg said.

"Meg, mind your mouth," Samuel said. "We aren't sending Lizzie back, and she wasn't adopted."

"No, you're just sending me to Boston, which is worse. Why don't *you* go live with Aunt Phoebe?" she said. Leaving this last outburst to vibrate like an arrow shaft in her father's bosom, Lizzie shot from the room.

Meg looked at Sally. She looked at her brothers. Then she looked at her father. "Why won't anyone tell me who Aunt Phoebe is?"

"She's your aunt," Samuel snapped.

All the next day, Lizzie did not come out of her room, and whenever the housekeeper took a tray of food to her, she brought it back an hour later, untouched.

Later that night, while sitting at the dinner table—

which was uncomfortably quiet because of Lizzie's absence—Stephen looked at his father and asked, "How long are you going to allow Lizzie to starve herself?"

"Until she comes to her senses and writes that letter," Samuel said.

"What if she starves herself to death?" Sally asked.

"She won't," Samuel said. "She's got enough mouse in her to ferret out something to keep herself alive."

Meg's eyes rounded. "Lizzie wouldn't eat a mouse," she said. "She doesn't like them."

Samuel threw up his hands.

Much later, after everyone in the Robinson household had gone to bed, Sally and Meg tiptoed down to the kitchen in their long linen nightgowns. Moving about the kitchen in the dark, they packed a small basket of biscuits, fried chicken, and fruit, then they tiptoed back up the stairs, going to Lizzie's room.

Without waking their sister, they quietly eased open the door and entered. While Meg placed the basket on the table beside Lizzie's bed, Sally fished around in her pocket, extracting a hastily written note, placing it on top of the basket.

We love you, was all it said.

Early the next morning, shortly after Samuel left for his law office, Stephen slipped over to the lighthouse to have a word with their grandfather, Asa Robinson.

Not long after Stephen left the lighthouse, Asa, or Captain Robinson as he was known around the island, left, too. On his way into town, he made a detour to stop by his son's house.

Once inside, he briefly spoke with the housekeeper,

then made his way up the stairs, going down the hall to Lizzie's room.

He stood outside Lizzie's door for a moment, his ear angled toward the room. Hearing nothing, he rapped lightly upon the door. When Lizzie did not answer, he tiptoed inside.

Lizzie was sitting at her desk, writing in her journal. She looked sad and much smaller and more fragile than he had ever remembered seeing her. And never could Asa remember Lizzie ever being so subdued.

"How are you doing?" he asked, coming to sit on the edge of the bed.

Lizzie looked up and felt her heart lurch at the sight of her beloved grandfather. *He's the only one who comes close to understanding.* "Hello, Grandpa. I'm getting on," she said.

"I came to visit and missed seeing you downstairs."

"If you missed me, you're the only one who has, I'll wager," she said.

"Oh, I wouldn't go so far as to say that. I hear they all miss you. Matt said Meg hasn't stopped crying for what she said at the dinner table the other night."

"Tell Meg not to worry. I'm not angry with her. She's only a child."

"Why won't you write Aunt Phoebe that letter, Lizzie? You'll have to sooner or later. You don't have the constitution of a person who would commit suicide," he said. "And you know your father won't relent. Not this time. He can't. He made a decision, and the whole family knows about it. He can't back down. He would lose too much. But you could give in. Besides, going to Boston might be the most wonderful thing that ever happened to you. If it isn't, you can always come back home and live in the lighthouse with me."

Lizzie looked up to see the way his eyes sparkled. "It's not like you're signing on for a whaling voyage, or being sold into slavery in China," he said.

"Do you mean you want me to write a letter to that dreadful old woman and thank her for inviting me, telling her I would *love* to come?"

"Yes, because I feel in my heart it would be the best thing for you. You remember the sermon we heard in church last Sunday . . . the one about a prophet not being recognized in his own town?"

"Vaguely," Lizzie said. "It was difficult to pay attention last Sunday, if you will remember, because Mrs. Husey was sporting that new sealskin coat her husband brought her after his last voyage."

Asa chuckled. "Yes, and she almost suffocated from the heat. I bet it was seventy degrees in there . . . hardly the weather for a light coat, let alone sealskin." He paused to look at Lizzie. "I'm sorry you didn't hear much of the sermon, because I see a good lesson there for you. No one in Nantucket will ever give you a chance to prove yourself because they all remember the past too much. You need a change, Lizzie, a fresh start. Go to Boston. Stay with Aunt Phoebe. Don't look at it as punishment. Look at it as an opportunity to refine yourself, to gain the patina and luster you can never get here. And then, when you come back, you won't be like any other girl on the island, and they will all be green-eyed with envy because you have something none of them have."

"Tavis Mackinnon," Lizzie said wistfully.

"That, too," Asa said with an inward smile.

"I suppose I could write Aunt Phoebe . . . just for you," Lizzie said, after giving it some thought. "Actually, I'm not as set against it now as I was the other night. I've really been thinking more positively about it, but didn't know how to go about telling Papa . . . without it looking like I was giving in." She frowned, as if remembering something unpleasant. "I don't like to give in."

"Yes, I know," Asa said, fighting unsuccessfully to hide his smile. "I don't like to be without my hat either, but there are times, like when I go to church, that I have to take it off." He came to his feet, and Lizzie's gaze dropped to the captain's hat dangling from his rough, old hands. "Well, I guess I'd better up anchor and go downstairs to see what the mischief is about. Can I expect to see your smiling face at dinner?"

Her face brightened. "Are you staying for dinner?"

Asa nodded. "I am if you're going to be there." He raised his brows in question.

"Yes," Lizzie said with a resigned look. "I'll be there . . . although I might as well confess that I'd rather face a hundred-mile hurricane in a leaky rowboat."

And Lizzie was there, walking into the dining room at the appointed hour, not holding up the rest of the family, as she normally did.

"I'm glad to see you have come to your senses," Samuel said. "I understand you have written your aunt Phoebe."

"Yes, I've written her," Lizzie said, with an air of exhilaration.

"And I posted it for her," Asa said. "Carried it over to the post office myself."

Samuel looked from his father to the bright countenance of his daughter, taking in her dreamy expression. "What, exactly, did you put in your letter?"

"I said I would be so very happy to visit Aunt

Phoebe in Boston, for Nantucket was never a place where one such as me could express herself. I told her I had shamed my family and been a terrible bother to you, and although I fully deserved to be cast out and sent away without a *sou*—"

"What's a *sou*?" asked Meg.

"It's French . . . a five-cent piece, I think," said Matt.

"Why didn't you just say 'five-cent piece'?" Sally asked.

"Because there is no music in it, but when you say '*sou*' . . . the sound dances off your tongue," Lizzie replied.

"Dances off your tongue!" exclaimed Meg, before turning to her father. "Papa, didn't you say we oughtn't to put money in our mouth?"

"Be quiet, oakhead. She isn't talking about putting *real* money in her mouth. She is speaking like a poet," Sally said.

"I think Lizzie is quite right," said Stephen, who was sitting at the far end of the table. " '*Sou*' does have a nice ring to it."

"You could have used '*farthing*'," another brother, Hayden, said. "I fancy it has a pleasant ring to it as well."

Samuel sat back in his chair, turning his gaze from one child to another, as he thought that somehow he had lost control of the situation again. As he looked at Lizzie, holding the rapt attention of everyone at the table, he could not rid himself of the notion that her punishment had gone awry. Wistfully Samuel thought it was a pity there were no women politicians. Lizzie would make a great one.

Lizzie went to Boston.

Her aunt Phoebe Brewster was far, far worse than she

remembered. Tall, slender, and regal, she had sharp, piercing blue eyes, iron-gray hair to match her will, and long, slender fingers, six of which bore rings. Her diction was perfect, and her accent one that marked her as a member of the Boston aristocracy. Whenever she spoke, she did so with such authority that Lizzie was sure the doilies on the tables flattened.

She was old lace and old jewelry, and adhered to the old way of doing things. She lived in a mansion, and had a fondness for marzipan and high tea served every day at precisely two o'clock. She had two long-haired, flat-faced cats, Robin Hood and Friar Tuck—both of which took an immediate dislike to Lizzie. Her English butler, Peterby, was so old and decrepit, his bones rattled when he walked, and Lizzie wrote to Becca, in her first letter, that she was certain he must have come to America with Columbus.

The moment Lizzie stepped into her aunt Phoebe's parlor, she knew she was doomed. Standing meekly beside her father, she endured her aunt's dismembering stare as she recalled how Samuel had once told her Aunt Phoebe's maiden name was Brewster and that when she married, she married a man by the same name. *Phoebe Brewster Brewster,* she was thinking when her aunt's voice penetrated her consciousness.

"You don't look a thing like Patience," Phoebe said. "Patience looked like our mother. She was a Caldwell and took after their side of the family, but you— although it pains me to say so—are the spitting image of me when I was your age. You are a Brewster, through and through. That bodes ill for you, child. A Brewster, especially the female Brewsters, never had an easy time of it. The Brewster women were always stronger than the Brewster men." She waved a beringed hand. "Weaklings, the lot of them, including my father, God rest his poor quaking soul."

Lizzie cringed. She didn't want to be a Brewster anything, and certainly not anything that remotely resembled or reminded her of this bony-fingered old woman.

"Lizzie, say hello to your aunt Phoebe."

When Lizzie didn't say anything, her father gave her a nudge with his elbow.

"Hello, Aunt Phoebe."

Phoebe barely nodded before she turned her horrified gaze upon Samuel. "*Lizzie?* What an excruciating sound. Upon my word, Samuel, the sound of it goes against one's grain, like a screeching cat."

At the word cat, Lizzie looked at the two sitting on the back of the chair Aunt Phoebe perched on. One was white and had blue eyes, the other was a mottled orange-black with orange eyes. She could tell by the way they looked at her that the three of them were not going to get along.

Lizzie looked at her aunt. Phoebe's gaze flicked over to Lizzie for a moment before going back to Samuel. "You *dare* call this child *Lizzie*, when she has such a fine Christian name? What is wrong, pray tell, with calling her by her baptized name, Elizabeth? Or even Amelia?"

"I hate Amelia," Lizzie said.

"Don't speak until you are spoken to, child," Aunt Phoebe said, giving Samuel a look that said she was still waiting for her answer. "Well?"

Samuel shrugged. "I don't know, Phoebe. She just always seemed more like a Lizzie to me."

"And there you have it," Phoebe said, crossing her hands with authority over the head of her walking stick. "With a name like Lizzie to live up to, it's no precious wonder that she is an undisciplined hoyden and an ill-mannered shrew. You have slapped this child a numbing blow with a name that forces her to behave in the manner of a flibbertigibbet."

Her gaze back on Lizzie now, Phoebe said, "The first thing we shall do is forget we ever heard that horrendous name ... which I refuse to have repeated in my house. The very thought of it is grating on my nerves and lingering on my tongue like a bad taste." Her hand came to the ruffled lace jabot at her throat. "God was merciful to let poor Patience die before she could see what end this child of hers has come to." She shook her head. "Patience always set such high hopes upon Elizabeth. Isn't that right, Samuel?"

Samuel nodded.

"From now on you shall be Elizabeth, or at the absolute worst, Eliza or Liza."

"I am called Lizzie," Lizzie said, "and I like it."

"Be quiet, child, or I'll have Peterby bring in the opium pipe. You shall be called whatever I say you will be called, and you will speak *only* when you have been spoken to."

With a look of dismissal, Phoebe said, "Take her to the kitchen, Peterby."

"If he can make it," Lizzie said, giving Peterby a doubtful stare, for to Lizzie, it couldn't have sounded more final if she had said, *Take her to the dungeon, Peterby.*

After that comment, she received a rap across the knuckles with Aunt Phoebe's fan, just before she said to Peterby, "Have Liddy serve her some tea ... in the kitchen."

"Shall you be taking tea, mum?"

"Yes, I'll take it in the parlor as usual. Tell Liddy to

set a cup for Mr. Robinson." She gave Lizzie a brief look before looking back at Samuel. "I daresay the child's manners would give me dyspepsia."

Samuel shook his head. "And her manners are her best part. I'll tell you now, Phoebe, if I had known I was going to live this long, I would have had fewer children."

Lizzie followed Peterby from the room, hearing her aunt Phoebe say, "We will talk again later, Elizabeth. After I've told your father good-bye."

"Good-bye and good riddance," Lizzie mumbled under her breath. *I don't know why I should expect my father or Aunt Phoebe to understand. There isn't an ounce of feeling between them.*

She sighed and gave Peterby a scowling look. Being young was exceedingly irksome principally because one had to deal with fathers. Fathers. Their capacity to comprehend love was a solitary thing, like a butterfly that lives for a season, then dies. Love was something fathers understood only once in their entire life, and that was when they fell in love. After that, the capacity was lost to them forever. As for Aunt Phoebe . . . well, she couldn't be blamed, not really—after all, she wouldn't understand simply because Lizzie seriously doubted she had ever been in love, and on top of that, she had never seen Tavis Mackinnon.

One had to see a man such as that to understand love at first sight.

CHAPTER
❧ FOUR ❧

Like almost every other woman in Nantucket, Lizzie had been in love with Tavis Mackinnon since the first moment she saw him. It wasn't simply because he was incredibly handsome that Lizzie loved him. It wasn't because his hair was as black as the devil's soul either, or because his eyes were an iron gray-blue that made her knees go weak whenever they looked at her. It wasn't because he had legs longer than a ship's mast, or a smile that made her heart flutter. No, it wasn't any of these things that made her fall in love with him. It was because he stepped out of a rainbow.

She had only been a tangle-haired, eleven-year-old wearing a blue dress and a white pinafore back in 1846—the year Tavis Mackinnon came to Nantucket at the age of twenty-one with his brother, Nicholas.

After her mother's death the year before, Lizzie felt alone and abandoned, unable to understand why her mother had to die and leave her when all the other girls on the island still had theirs. Missing fathers were something everyone on Nantucket Island was used to, for hardly a family didn't have a father or sons—

43

sometimes both—who sailed off on a whaler to be gone for years at a time. Many of them were like Captain Ben Worth, who spent forty-one years at sea and only six years at home with his family, who lived on Liberty Street. Others simply sailed away, never to be heard from again.

Normally it was the mother of a family who managed the home and sometimes ran a business. In Lizzie's case, it was just the opposite. Since she had no mother, it was her father who managed the home and ran his business—which, in Samuel Robinson's case, was law. In spite of having a devoted father, Lizzie felt lonely and left out after her mother died. Her six brothers had one another, and her papa had her younger sister Sally, and Sally had the baby, Meg. But Lizzie had no one; that is, until her grandfather came into her life.

For forty years her grandfather, Asa Robinson, had been the captain of a whaler, and gone most of Lizzie's childhood. Not long after her mother died, Asa Robinson decided it was time to retire. For several years the whaling industry had been in steady decline. The right whales close to home had all been killed, making it necessary for a whaler to be gone for two to five years before he had enough whale oil to make it profitable to return home. So Asa came back to Nantucket that fateful year—for 1846 had also been the year of Nantucket's great fire.

After Captain Robinson returned, he took up residence in the lighthouse out on Brandt Point. As the caretaker there, he could be close to the things he loved most in the world. Lizzie. Ships. The sea.

There were no public schools in Nantucket, and when they were younger, Lizzie's father had taught all nine of his children at home. As the boys grew older, he sent them to the Coffin School, a private institution founded by Captain Sir Isaac Coffin for his descendants. Many Nantucketers were related to the Coffins in one way or the other, and since Lizzie's paternal grandmother had been a Coffin, Samuel enrolled his sons, keeping Lizzie and her sisters at home, adhering to the traditional idea that girls don't need a formal education.

She might not have ever had the opportunity to go to school if it hadn't been for her grandfather. For Asa Robinson was not just a lover of mathematics, he was addicted to it. It wasn't surprising, therefore, that Lizzie, who spent a great deal of her time with her grandfather, inherited a love for numbers. By the time she was eleven, she was calculating figures in the nautical almanac and correcting the navigating instruments of whaling captains. One of the first things her grandfather gave her was a telescope. There were many long night watches from the top of the lighthouse, where Lizzie had her eye stuck to the end of her instrument.

At thirteen, Lizzie was finally allowed to attend a real school. Her instructors found Lizzie to be a bright girl who excelled in math and science.

But she missed the long stretches of time with her grandfather. Often she would walk out to the lighthouse on Brandt Point and spend Saturday or Sunday afternoon with him, listening to whaling tales, or stories about the places Asa had been and the things he had seen. Many a cold, snowy evening she would spend sitting across the table from him, listening to the steady cadence of his voice while watching him weave lightship baskets or carve scrimshaw on whalebone. If love were a galaxy, her grandfather would have been its second star. He taught her to sail, and he taught her to love the sea, but most of all, he taught her hope.

As Asa was fond of saying, "It's stormy weather being a girl."

Blessings come in many ways, and Lizzie knew hers had come in the form of her grandfather. Whenever the two of them would walk down Main Street, her small hand tucked in his tough old scarred one, people would turn to look at them and smile—at the gnarled old man with his seaman's walk and the laughing young girl at his side with a head of curly blond hair and so much love in her eyes.

Sometimes Lizzie would catch a ride out to the lighthouse with Jethro Newton, who had a box of supplies or a crate of brass polish to drop off there, and just as often she would stay with her grandfather for days at a time. At night, when the great light would flash its warning to ships to be wary, Asa would read to her from the diary of his travels or his collection of books.

He had done just that one rainy evening, reading to her from Milton after she had helped him polish the great light.

> *"I took it for a faery vision*
> *Of some gay creatures of the element.*
> *That in the colours of the rainbow live,*
> *And play i' the plighted clouds."*

It had been a natural thing for Lizzie to stop him there and ask him where rainbows came from. "Why do we see them only after it rains?"

Lizzie watched her grandfather close the book and light his pipe, the smoke swirling upward like a picture frame around his weathered face and thick white hair.

"It's a covenant—God's covenant, that He will never again destroy the earth by rain, as He did in the time of

Noah. Whenever you see a rainbow, Lizzie, you must always remember that. A rainbow means promise and hope, and everything has its rainbow, its ray of hope."

Rainbows became something special for Lizzie after that. A few months later, she was walking along the docks with her grandfather and saw a handsome black-haired man come down a ship's gangway. A rainbow arched over him, and she knew he was something special. He was laughing as he disembarked, and for some strange reason he stopped laughing and drew to a halt, his vivid blue-gray eyes resting on Lizzie. Lizzie stopped, too.

"What's the matter, Tavis?" his brother, Nicholas, asked.

"What?" Tavis said, turning to look back at his brother. "Oh, nothing," he said, looking back at Lizzie. "That little girl over there . . . For a moment I thought she reminded me of someone."

Lizzie had never forgotten that moment, or the way those vivid eyes and the man with the beautiful face had looked at her. A rainbow was God's promise, just as her grandpa said, and in Lizzie's young heart, this beautiful man was promised to her.

And in Lizzie's mind, that was that.

Only Lizzie had no idea how difficult it would be convincing Tavis Mackinnon that he was the man God had promised her. "Stubborn and doubtful as Abraham," she would often say.

Over the years, it had become commonplace—sort of a routine set of circumstances—for one resident of Nantucket or the other to see Lizzie in hot pursuit of Tavis Mackinnon. It had also become quite commonplace for the young men around town to tease Lizzie about it, often telling her, "Stay after him, Lizzie. Maybe he'll marry you out of sheer exhaustion. A man can run only so long," or "Hang in there, Lizzie. It's a small island. He can't go *too* far."

Then, as always, laughter would follow, and Lizzie would stiffen her spine and walk on down the street, thinking they were just too provincial to understand anything but their own rustic ways. They were not capable of understanding the way of it, and because of that, the pain of ridicule remained constant.

"Ohhhh, I can't wait to grow up," she said to her grandfather after a particularly painful ribbing she had taken in town.

"Well, you'll just have to be patient," Asa said. "It does no good to rant or rave against time, the wind, or the sea. You gain nothing by slapping at the hand of fate. What is promised, is promised, and comes at its own time." He patted her hand. "Besides, those boys wouldn't have anything to do if they couldn't tease you, you know." He laughed and ruffled her hair. "Don't look so downtrodden. You'll grow up soon enough."

It couldn't be soon enough to suit her, Lizzie thought, looking around at her aunt's creaky old mansion as she followed Peterby, trying to imagine herself ever calling this place home.

"This is your room, miss," Peterby said, opening the tall doors to a large corner room with a blessing of windows.

Lizzie followed Peterby into the bedroom her aunt had chosen for her, thinking it would at least get her mind off her grandfather, which was another reminder of just how miserable and homesick she was.

"If you should need anything else, miss, just ring for

me or the housekeeper, Mrs. Potter." With that, Peterby closed the door.

Lizzie looked around the bedroom that now belonged to her, seeing her trunk and baggage had already been carried up. It was quite a room, she decided. A slender four-poster bed was hung with crisp alabaster-colored curtains, the same fabric used to draw the sunburst pleats that formed a roof over the bed. In front of the window was an English walnut writing desk, and behind the fat chintz sofa stood a coromandel lacquer screen. On the opposite wall, a flamboyant gilt looking glass stood over a dressing table with a fitted drapery skirt of alabaster and pale pink.

It was a room that she would have ordinarily found quite lovely—under different circumstances. But circumstances being what they were, she was prompted to say, "I don't like this room. I don't like Boston. And most especially I don't like Aunt Phoebe . . . or her cats."

Lizzie fell across the satin coverlet on the bed. It did little for her morale to know her own father had wanted to be rid of her. It also made her wonder why—that being the case—he hadn't simply sent her to live with her grandfather in the lighthouse.

He hadn't, though, and what hurt her the most about this wasn't so much the fact that he hadn't sent her to live with her grandfather, but that he had refused to let her say good-bye to him.

"But why can't I, Papa? What would it hurt?"

When Lizzie had asked this, Samuel said simply, "Because my mind is made up, and I don't want to start second-guessing myself, which is exactly what I'd do if I watched you say good-bye to your grandfather."

Lizzie could not help wondering when she would see

her grandfather again. *About the same time you see Tavis Mackinnon,* a voice inside her head seemed to say, but Lizzie knew that might not be the case. Tavis was young, and even if her father did leave her here in Boston until she finished school, Tavis would still be alive. But her grandfather was old and hadn't much time. *Wait for me, Grandpa.*

Lizzie rolled herself into a tight ball, her thoughts spinning backward to relive the last time she had visited Asa.

Captain Robinson lived in the keeper's lodge adjacent to the lighthouse on Brandt Point, just at the entrance to Nantucket Harbor. Nestled down among shifting dunes and sea grasses, the small frame house was dwarfed by the round shaft of the lighthouse, which looked like a windmill from a distance.

Proceeding through the deepening twilight at a gait that was half skip and half canter, Lizzie had made her way through the marshy bottoms that flooded at high tide. She could see the tower, and already its beacon flashed to guide sailors through the treacherous sandbars. Across the stretch of water that lay before her stood the Great Point lighthouse flashing its huge beam—as if bragging that it would soon be getting the new Fresnel lens light to replace the outdated Lewis reflectors. But Lizzie knew the old Lewis reflectors left in the lighthouse on Brandt Point would still do a better job, simply because that lighthouse was run by her grandfather.

For a moment Lizzie pictured the lovely scene in her mind, seeing it exactly as it had been that day, bathed in purple twilight. She remembered how she had been reminded of Longfellow's lovely lighthouse lines that day,

and how she thought that he must have had Brandt
Point in mind when he penned them.

On that particular day it had never entered Lizzie's
mind that she could simply *think* Longfellow's words.
She had to dramatize them. Her artistic sense demanded
this, and Lizzie was never one to ignore any of her
senses, artistic or otherwise. Reciting the lines at the top
of her voice, she had given her creative side full vent.

> *And as the evening darkens, lo! how bright*
> *Through the deep purple of the twilight air,*
> *Beams forth the sudden radiance of its light*
> *With strange unearthly splendor in its glare!*
> *And the great ships sail outward and return*
> *Bending and blowing o'er the billowy swells;*
> *And ever joyful, as they see it burn,*
> *They wave their silent welcomes and farewells.*

She smiled to herself as she remembered how she
had finished with a dramatic leap over a marshy spot,
making her way to drier sand at last. It was almost dark
then, and she slowed her pace, thinking about Tavis
Mackinnon, and making up her mind to be patient and
persevere. After all, trees weren't felled with just one
stroke. "I know what I know," she said to herself as she
entered her grandfather's house.

Asa Robinson was sitting at the table beneath an oil
lamp. With the sail needle in his hand, he scratched
the intricate design of a ship on a piece of whalebone,
glancing up when Lizzie entered. She would never forget the way he had looked at her, as if he was trapped
between laughing and trying to remain serious, as he
managed to ask, "You know *what?*"

Lizzie took a piece of wood out of the woodbox and

put it into the stove, then laughing and hugging herself, she whirled around and around in a circle in the middle of the floor. Suddenly she stopped. "Oh, Grandpa, I know what I know. I *know* I shall marry Tavis Mackinnon. I know it. I have all the faith in the world, and faith is believing what doesn't seem so, isn't that right?"

"Aye," Asa Robinson said, "having faith is like walking in the sunshine when it's raining on everyone else."

Lizzie had thrown off her cape then, and dropping it on a nearby chair, rushed around the table and threw her arms around her grandfather. "Oh, Grandpa, you *do* understand, don't you? That's why I love you so."

The pain wasn't so much in remembering as it was in knowing—knowing her grandfather did understand, and that now she had been removed from the one person in the whole world who did. The scalding burn of tears streaked down her cheeks, and on her first night in Boston, Lizzie cried herself to sleep.

CHAPTER
❧ FIVE ❧

The house Lizzie shared with her aunt Phoebe was a three-story town house of Roxbury pudding stone that seemed to stare out at Beacon Street from beneath the frown of a mansard roof. The airy tracery of a wrought-iron fence, with the swirling images of Persia worked into it, marked the boundaries of the front yard and garden. The house and gardens, like everything about Aunt Phoebe, were immaculately kept. Signs of wealth were evident, but not ostentatiously displayed. Everywhere she looked, Lizzie was reminded of family, position, and money. At first glance, she knew immediately that Boston was going to be nothing like Nantucket.

The main floor of the town house contained five rooms—dining room, parlor, sitting room, and library, plus the kitchen. The dining room was somber and dark, paneled in oak and containing a long mahogany table and twelve Hepplewhite chairs, with a dark oak mantelpiece carved with lions' heads, cherubs, and acanthus leaves that surrounded the fireplace (over which hung a gouache of Lake Geneva, brought back by Aunt Phoebe from her honeymoon in Switzerland). The mood changed abruptly when one went into the parlor, for there the walls were a strong green and the furniture was upholstered in old-gold velvet. A glass-fronted display cabinet lined with green moiré housed Aunt Phoebe's glass menagerie and green Wedgewood pottery. Over the fireplace hung a full-length painting of Aunt Phoebe on her wedding day. Flanking it were two small ovals painted of her husband, the late Charles Filmore Octavius Brewster—one of him wearing a white dress when he was one year old, and the other when he graduated from Harvard at the age of twenty-two. In the library a round, leather-topped drum table that belonged to Phoebe's grandfather stood in the center of a room filled with books collected by successive generations of Brewsters on both sides. It was in this room that Aunt Phoebe's canary busied itself, singing and throwing seed about the floor. "Of all the unmitigated gall!" Aunt Phoebe was heard to exclaim one morning as she pulled birdseed sprouts from the base of her palm tree.

Lizzie was never certain if Aunt Phoebe was galled over the canary's audacity in throwing his seed about, or over the seeds' arrogance in growing where they had been tossed.

All in all, the dwelling on Beacon Street was simply a perfectly kept house made lovely by the disciplined lavishness of a woman who could afford to follow the dictates of wealth and style without worrying about what she spent. The town house was narrow but tall, the rooms square, the ceilings high. Windows were draped with three sets of curtains. Rosewood furniture and graceful Sheraton chairs sat near carved tables inlaid with gold. In the parlor was a perfectly tuned piano; in the dining room, the family silver, ornate and worn from generations of use. Dinner was served promptly at seven, followed by after-dinner calls from proper Bostonians. Mrs. Potter managed the house. Peterby's presence reminded everyone of their station in life. The cook served up perfectly cooked roasts (fashionably unadorned), and a coachman would hitch Aunt Phoebe's one blooded horse to her carriage to drive them to the opera, or along the streets of Boston to make their calls, and to St. Paul's Church on Tremont Street every Sunday.

Life in Boston was at first frightening to her, but soon Lizzie came to see it for what it was: old-fashioned, dull, and quite predictable. Life there had its intellectual as well as its social side, and Lizzie quickly learned she fit in much better with the intellectuals, since her social graces came much slower. This did not seem to bother Aunt Phoebe, who was quick to remind her that they were direct descendants of proper Boston stock—the English Puritans, having both Cabots and Lowells in their family tree—and that it was from this proper stock that had come many prominent educators, writers, scientists, and business leaders.

Over the next few years, she was to receive numerous compliments about her knowledge of mathematics and astronomy, and countless raps across the knuckles with Aunt Phoebe's ivory fan—whenever it was deemed that she had done something not in accordance with good breeding—as her aunt began the arduous task of transforming her into a proper Boston lady.

Phoebe saw in Elizabeth a unique charm, for she was a young woman as resonant with rich color as the rarest painting. She was a flamboyant hoyden one moment, and as sober and soulful as a Quaker church service the next. At other times she would slip into the most abominable theatrical melodramatics Phoebe had ever witnessed. She had the uncanny knack for voicing the exact things people were thinking, but never said. Once, Phoebe wrote to Samuel, *She has a romantic idea about life that I hope to curb, but not dispel.*

She was both woman and child, poet and comic. Her zest for the everyday things endeared her to Phoebe, who saw in the girl something she had been missing in her barren life: the joy of living.

As the years passed, Lizzie gradually became Liza to her friends, although Aunt Phoebe never called her anything but Elizabeth. "There are so many people in me," Elizabeth said to Phoebe one day. "Perhaps that's why I've had so many different names—Elizabeth, Eliza, Liza, Lizzie. Perhaps I should settle for one. If I was only one person, I wouldn't be so complicated."

"Or half as interesting," said Phoebe. "You must remember, Elizabeth, there is a certain amount of charm in having a character made up of so many facets, as long as you employ them skillfully when they are called upon, and manage them with an iron fist when they are not."

It was while living the refined and disciplined life with her aunt that Elizabeth reflected upon her past. She was having tea with Phoebe in the parlor and discussing her upcoming debut into society when she reached for a tea cake, ignoring the arched back and hiss of Robin, who jumped to the floor just as Friar Tuck had done only moments before. She was distracted for a moment, thinking it odd that after all this time, Aunt Phoebe's cats still did not trust her.

"Sometimes I find it difficult to believe I did all the things I did," Elizabeth said, pulling her thoughts away from Aunt Phoebe's cats. "Poor Papa. What I must have put him through. I think every time a child is born it is given a definite number of foolish, absurd things it must do before reaching maturity. That's why we're given a guardian angel ... to protect us from ourselves. I suppose I should be happy in knowing that when I finally did grow up, I was free of them, once and for all," Elizabeth said.

Elizabeth's formal debut and presentation to Boston society was relatively easy. She put her hair up, her white dress on, and received guests at tea. Later she accompanied her aunt to evening parties, where she was entertained by parlor games with the other young people her age. By this time, Elizabeth Robinson's beauty was quite the rage, and for the men not interested in just her beauty, her mind was a major attraction. The moment she arrived at a party, she was besieged by handsome young suitors in satin-lined coats and smart-fitting breeches who requested either the next dance or a moment of her time for thought-provoking discussions. More than once her aunt Phoebe related to her how one young man or the other managed to keep her in his range of vision for an entire evening.

And why not? Elizabeth was, as Phoebe said, "in full bloom—an American beauty rose if there ever was one." She had the fair coloring and deep-set eyes of the loveliest English lass, the graciousness and subtle flirtatious ways of a southern belle, and the sharp wit and intellect of a New York Knickerbocker—all coupled with the practicality of a New Englander, the unpretentiousness of a Nantucketer. And like the women from her native island, she was practical, intellectual, and moral, a woman known not only for her intellect and beauty, but for the force of her character.

During the course of her first season, Elizabeth became friends with another debutante, Genevieve Beecham. It wasn't until the following year that she met Genny's oldest brother, Harry, who was in his fourth year at Cambridge University.

Catching sight of Elizabeth across the room, Genny hurried toward her. "Elizabeth, I have the most wonderful news. Harry is in town. You know how anxious I've been for you to meet him."

"Where is he?" Elizabeth said, looking over Genny's shoulder.

"Oh, he isn't here tonight. He's just arrived, and not in time to unpack and dress for tonight, much to Mama's chagrin," Genny said. "Oh, I do want you to meet him, and soon. I have a fitting at Madame Broussard's tomorrow at ten, and Harry is going riding. I thought we might meet at your house afterward. Harry could take us to Boston Common." Genny took Elizabeth's arm, walking a few feet away where they could speak more privately. "I suppose I should warn you about Harry," she whispered.

Liza looked into Genny's warm brown eyes. "Warn me?"

"Well, yes. You see, Harry is a bit arrogant . . . *nice* but arrogant. I suppose that is because he is so handsome that women are wont to swoon. He is quite the rage in London, and Papa says that is interfering beastly with his studies. It seems Harry is spending too much time in the city with the ladies, and not enough time at Cambridge with the books. When Papa told Harry he needed to find himself a woman with a brain, Harry said, 'Women with brains have nothing that interests me.' "

"What did your father say to that?"

"He asked Harry what he meant by that. And do you know what Harry said?"

"What?"

"He said the more a woman's intellect went up, the more her beauty went down."

That comment didn't chafe Elizabeth in the least, simply because she had heard such before. Many times. "Maybe he should come home to study," Elizabeth said. "Perhaps if he went to Harvard, your father could keep an eye on him."

Genny tossed a glossy chocolate brown curl over her shoulder. "He *was* at Harvard. Papa was so swamped with marriage-minded mamas interested in Harry for their daughters that he decided to send my brother abroad to give us all a little peace."

"I suppose that is why he is so arrogant," Elizabeth observed, "from always having to be on the defensive."

"I suppose you are right," Genny said, then catching her mother's look, she took Elizabeth's arm and leaned closer to whisper, "Mama's giving me the eye, so I must be quick, but I want you to know I'm dying for Harry to meet you, and not just because you're my best friend."

"Then why?"

"Because you will completely disprove his theory, of course, and you cannot imagine how long I've wanted to see Harry set in his place. You have both intellect and beauty, and Harry is convinced it cannot coexist in one female."

"That's absurd. What about yourself? You're beautiful, and I happen to know how intelligent you are."

"I'm Harry's sister, so I don't count. He has to like me, regardless." She glanced back at her mother. "I've

got to go. I'll tell Harry to meet me at your house at one
o'clock tomorrow afternoon . . . if that's all right."

"One o'clock will be fine," Elizabeth said, trying to
pump some excitement into her voice. Truth was, concern for Genny's feelings was the only thing that pre-
vented Elizabeth from saying she couldn't go to Boston
Common tomorrow. After listening to Genny talk at
length about her brother, Elizabeth wasn't the least bit
interested in meeting the overly handsome, under-
achieving, and overopinionated Harry Beecham.

The next day Elizabeth was in the parlor, sitting at
the piano, when Mrs. Potter brought her a letter that had
just arrived from her grandfather. She stopped playing
and ripped open the envelope. She scanned the pages
quickly, smiling when she read, toward the bottom of
the letter, *Although you haven't inquired, I thought you
might like to know Tavis Mackinnon is still as free as an
Atlantic breeze and is frequently seen in the presence of
a number of different local women.*

Elizabeth dropped her hands and the letter to her lap
and closed her eyes, breathing a sigh of relief. If Tavis
was seen in the presence of a *number* of different local
women, that meant he had not focused his attention
upon any certain one. As far as women were concerned,
there was safety in numbers. When Tavis singled out
one certain woman . . . that was the time to become
concerned. Feeling an extra skip in her heartbeat, she
read her grandfather's letter again, unaware that she was
being watched.

Harry Beecham had been shown into the sitting room
by Peterby. "If you will wait here, I will inform Mrs.
Brewster of your arrival."

The moment Peterby left, Harry began pacing the room. The third time he passed by the open door, he glanced up, catching a glimpse of a very fetching young woman in the room across the hall. A moment later, he stood in the doorway of the parlor, his practiced gaze roaming at leisure over the lovely, fair-haired young woman engrossed in the letter she was reading. The setting and the picture she made could not have been better if she had been posing for a painting.

Harry cleared his throat and stepped into the room. "I'm half an hour late. I hope you haven't been holding that pose since one o'clock."

The sound of his voice startled her, and Elizabeth immediately pressed the letter to her bosom as her head snapped up. She came to her feet quickly as she looked at the man who leaned casually against the doorjamb, assessing her with his gaze in a flagrantly impudent manner. Looking around him, she said, "Where is Genny?"

He pushed away from the door and walked farther into the room. "Oh, come now, you don't need to pretend with me. If there is anything I've learned to recognize, it's when I'm being set up. My sister has always been notorious for thinking up ways to throw me together with one of her friends. You see, I never expected Genny to meet me here at one o'clock. In fact, I never expected Genny to meet me at all. That's why I made it a point to be late."

Elizabeth's first thought was that Genny had been far too kind. *Arrogant* was too mild a word for this young man, she thought, her mind still too stunned from the words he had spoken to come up with anything to say in her defense. In her opinion, it was more likely that women swooned from his brassy self-confidence, rather than his handsome looks as Genny had said.

"Allow me to introduce myself," he said, with a sarcastic bow. "I am—"

"Harry Beecham, Genevieve's *august* brother," Elizabeth said.

Harry's face took on a look of surprise. "August," he repeated, as if mulling it over. His gaze swept over her, looking at her much longer than he had the time before, as if searching for something previously overlooked. His face brightened and a lazy, slow-spreading smile curved across his mouth. "I should have expected as much," he said. "I had almost forgotten. Genny said she told you about me and that you called me . . . What was it? Offensive?"

"I couldn't have possibly called you offensive. I didn't know you were . . . at the time."

It was obvious the cut startled Harry, but he recovered quickly. One moment he was frowning at her, the next he threw back his head, consumed with laughter.

"I recognized that laugh," Genny said, coming into the room with Aunt Phoebe. "Sorry I'm late. I had a devil of a time at the dressmaker's, and then my carriage was literally plowed down on Washington Street by a runaway wagon. I had to hire a cabbie to bring me here. The carriage is a pile of splinters. Father will be livid when he sees the damage."

"He will be so happy you weren't injured that he probably won't say a word," Phoebe said, patting Genny's hand. "Now, I'm off to tea, and I don't want to be late. You young people have a good time."

Elizabeth's gaze fastened upon Harry, noticing for the first time how the lamplight turned his wheat-brown hair to a golden color that matched his eyes. "We will," she said, her gaze never wavering. Then speaking more softly, she added, "That is, if the invitation isn't too offensive."

Harry laughed, crossing the room to where Elizabeth stood. He extended his arm for her, showing her his charming side, giving her a devastating smile along with his perfect manners. "Offensive or not, I wouldn't miss the opportunity to sit beside you in a small buggy for the world," he said.

As they quit the room, Elizabeth was thinking Harry Beecham was quite as handsome as sin, and his arrogance was tempered considerably by his charm. He was tall and slender, and his body moved with eye-catching grace. His eyes were warm and every bit as sensual as his mouth—both of which were as likely to show signs of humor as not. His was the kind of face that struck one as friendly, but not too accessible. He was a devil and a charmer, and she liked him right off. If her heart hadn't already been given to another, she could have quite easily fallen in love with Harry Beecham.

It was shortly after Elizabeth met Harry Beecham that Aunt Phoebe had a stroke, and from that moment on, the doctor confined Phoebe to her bed for the greater part of the day. Phoebe's color faded and she lost the use of her right arm. Her appetite was virtually nonexistent, but her mind was as sharp as ever.

The first time Liza tiptoed into her room after the stroke, Phoebe said, "You don't have to slink in here, looking so long-faced. I've had a stroke. I'm not dead . . . and I don't plan to be for a good many years yet."

In spite of Phoebe's condition and Liza's concern for this woman whom she had come to love like a mother, Elizabeth finished her schooling—primarily because her aunt Phoebe would not tolerate any talk of her quitting. "As if your quitting school would suddenly make me better," Phoebe said over tea. "I'll tell you right now, Elizabeth. The only thing that would make me happy is to see you finish school at the top of your class," she said, tapping the side of the teacup with her spoon for emphasis. The tapping and Elizabeth's presence in the room were just too much for Robin and Tuck, who jumped off the sofa and hid behind the damask draperies, which Elizabeth noticed were the exact color of her aunt's mulberry-colored dress. Elizabeth sat back, looking at her aunt, at the enormous brooch that was pinned at a bunch of cream lace at her throat, at the diamonds, emeralds, and rubies that glittered on her still handsome hands. Above a few iron-gray curls, a cap of cream lace and mulberry-colored ribbons hinted at a time gone by. In spite of her illness and the useless right hand, Aunt Phoebe was still an impressive woman, formidable, dark-hued, and full of a vitality that gave her a commanding air.

"Well? What do you say? Are you going to play the fool and stop your studies, or are you going to do as I ask?" Phoebe said at last.

"Was there ever any doubt? You did say I was like you, didn't you?" Elizabeth said, putting down her teacup and coming over to kiss Aunt Phoebe on the cheek, where a few stiff hairs grew.

In the weeks that followed, it seemed to Elizabeth that her aunt was losing some of her luster. Her face was pale, the color of old ivory, and the veins on her hands became more prominent. Elizabeth devoted at least two hours a day to Phoebe, which was usually spent in her room, which Aunt Phoebe left less and less. On this particular day, Elizabeth came to visit earlier than usual, catching Phoebe still in her beruffled night-dress, sitting in her bed, with her cats in her lap, alternately stroking them with her left hand.

When Elizabeth walked in, the cats—who preferred to be under the bed instead of on it whenever she was present—jumped to the floor and disappeared beneath the coverlet. Phoebe watched them go. "I worry about Robin and Tuck," Phoebe said. "About what will happen to them when I'm gone."

"You know I will care for them," Elizabeth said.

Phoebe smiled. "I know you will, but the problem is that they don't care for you."

"They never have."

Phoebe snorted. "They were ever foolish cats."

Elizabeth laughed. "Thank you for the compliment."

"You're welcome. Now, what brings you in here so early? Don't tell me you've discovered a new star?"

Elizabeth smiled. "If that were only true, then I could be as famous as Maria Mitchell."

"Who is Maria Mitchell? The name seems familiar, but I can't remember why."

"She's the woman from Nantucket I told you about. The one who discovered a new comet back in forty-seven."

"Ahhhh, I do remember now. So if it's not the discovery of a new star that brings you, then what?"

"To tell you I'm going to Faneuil Hall, to Quincy Market, with Genny."

Phoebe raised her brows. "Only Genny?"

Elizabeth smiled. "Harry is coming later ... to take us to Blackstone Square. Mayor Rice is giving a speech at four."

"Mayor Rice was ever a talker. What is the issue this time? Are they still complaining about the Irish? Mrs.

Potts mentioned there has been a lot of complaining going on over the Celtic locust swarm that is overcrowding into old North End." She shook her head. "It's useless to fret. Like the poor, the Irish will always be with us."

"I don't know the issue; all Harry said was that Mayor Rice would be speaking."

It was obvious to Elizabeth that her visit and mention of the mayor had revived her aunt's interest in what was going on in the world about her, which always seemed to give Phoebe renewed strength and vitality.

Of late, Phoebe had been losing weight, eating more often, but eating less. She had become sloppy with her eating, and the fact that she could not chew her food properly made her bitter. Often she would throw her spoon in her soup and shove the bowl away and mumble, "All I ever get is soup, potatoes, applesauce, and gravy. No wonder my rings are falling off my fingers." She pulled the rings from her right hand and said, "You'll have to take them off my other hand for me."

Elizabeth picked up Phoebe's left hand and removed the three rings. Before she could ask where Phoebe wanted her to put them, her aunt said, "Now, bring me my jewel casket, and get the key. It's in the inlaid box on the table by my chair."

Elizabeth brought the casket and the key. Phoebe instructed her to open the box. Her aunt dropped the rings into the casket, then closed the lid. "Take it," she said, waving her hand. "I have no use for those things now."

Elizabeth carried the casket to the bureau. "No, not there," Phoebe shouted. "Take it away . . . to your room. I want you to have it."

"Oh, I couldn't."

"I'd like to know why not. I want you to have these

things before I die ... or my memory fails me. I'll never understand you, Elizabeth. You're as giving as can be and do it with such loving grace, but let a body try and give you something ... it's worse than extracting teeth. There is as much an art to receiving a gift as there is in the giving of it. Now, don't deny me the pleasure of giving these things to you. Besides, they would look ridiculous on my cats."

Elizabeth stood silently looking at her aunt, unable to think of anything to say.

Phoebe laid her head back against the pillows. "It's a fine, fine thing that you came into my life," she said. "Now I can rest easy, knowing you will love this house and everything in it as much as I have. . . ." She raised her head and gave Elizabeth a wink as she said, "With the exception of those blasted cats." She laid her head back and closed her eyes. "What shall I do with those cats? Humph! I might have to delay my going a bit, if I can't work something out."

Elizabeth stood there for a long while, with the casket tucked under her arm as she watched Phoebe sleep. At last she turned away, opening the door quietly, noticing just as she closed it that Robin and Tuck were back on Phoebe's lap, completely unconcerned with their future.

Because of her condition, Phoebe could not attend Elizabeth's graduation, but the moment it was over, Elizabeth rushed home. Leaving Harry waiting in the coach, she thanked him for the ride and hurried through the door, catching sight of Mrs. Potter as she went up the front stairs.

"Oh, Mrs. Potter," she called. "I've graduated. Look,

I have a diploma." Elizabeth started up the stairs behind her. "Is Aunt Phoebe in her room?"

Mrs. Potter turned around and placed her hand on Elizabeth's arm. "I'm sorry as I can be, love, but I'm afraid I've got terrible bad news. Your aunt had another stroke this morning. Dr. Worthington just left."

Elizabeth's heart hammered in her chest. Her face paled. When she spoke, her voice was soft and unsteady. "Is she all right? What did Dr. Worthington say?"

Mrs. Potter's eyes filled with tears and she shook her head.

Elizabeth felt her throat constrict, felt, too, the burn of tears behind her eyes. "She will be all right, won't she?"

Mrs. Potter put her arm around Elizabeth. "Love, I'm sorry to be the one to tell you this. Your aunt is completely paralyzed on the right side of her body, poor dear soul. The doctor doesn't think she will ever walk again. God be praised, she hasn't completely lost her speech." Mrs. Potter wiped her eyes with the corner of her apron. "Dr. Worthington gave her something to help her sleep. He said it would be best if you didn't disturb your aunt right now . . . the excitement and all."

The tears in Elizabeth's eyes splashed down the front of her dress, and she felt herself dropping down to the steps. "I feel so horrible," she sobbed. "Here I was laughing and having such a grand time, when all the while, Aunt Phoebe was suffering. I will never forgive myself for that. Never. Never."

"Here now, you mustn't talk like that. Why, what would your aunt say if she could hear that kind of nonsense? You know your aunt Phoebe wouldn't tolerate for a minute your being so sad-faced. Now, would she?"

Elizabeth swiped at her tears with the back of her hand. "No, I suppose not."

Mrs. Potter paused, looking over Elizabeth's head. Then Elizabeth glanced up to see Harry standing just inside the door.

"You heard?" Elizabeth asked.

Harry nodded. "I heard," he said softly, then taking a step closer, he asked, "Is there anything I can do?"

Elizabeth came to her feet. "No, I—"

"Yes, there is," Mrs. Potter said. "You two can go right on living your life just as you were doing—just as your aunt Phoebe would be telling you to do herself if she was standing here right now." With a quick glance at Harry, she said, "Now, why don't you run along with your young man?"

"Oh, I couldn't," Elizabeth said, turning toward Harry and placing a pleading hand upon his arm. "Please understand, Harry. I can't go. Not now."

"I understand. If there is anything I can do, will you send for me?"

"Yes, you know I will."

"I'll drop by tomorrow and see how you're doing, if that's all right."

"Oh, Harry," Elizabeth said, giving his arm a squeeze. "You are such a dear, dear person. What would I do without you?"

Harry smiled, cuffing her lightly beneath the chin. "That is something I hope you never find out," he said, then his expression turned serious. "I would like to be more to you than a dear, dear person. You know that, don't you, Elizabeth?"

"Yes, I know, and I'm sorry, Harry. Truly I am."

The light in his eyes faded. "I'll see you tomorrow," he said, kissing her lightly on the forehead.

* * *

Over the next few years, Phoebe's condition grew gradually worse, and although it had been Elizabeth's plan to return to Nantucket after graduation, she refused to leave her aunt—no matter how many times Phoebe told her to go on with her life, which they both knew meant returning to Nantucket.

Aunt Phoebe was reading when Elizabeth walked in. "I had Mrs. Potter get me a book. I wanted to try my hand at reading, but my eyes are just too bad. I can't make out the words. Maybe it isn't my eyes. They, at least, seem to be taking in the words. Maybe it's my old fool mind that doesn't know what the devil to do with those words once they're there. I'll tell you, Elizabeth, old age certainly comes at a bad time, although I suppose if you live long enough, you'll be revered, rather like the Liberty Bell."

Elizabeth fluffed the pillows behind Phoebe's head, then plucked the book from her hand. "There isn't anything wrong with your mind. And you don't need to read anyway—not when I can read to you."

Phoebe gave her a straight look. "It isn't just my eyes, or even my inability to walk. The next stroke may get me; if not, it will probably leave me unable to speak. There are so many things I want you to know, and I feel now is the time to tell you ... while I still can."

"Don't talk like that. Dr. Worthington says you are doing fine."

Phoebe ignored her and went on to speak what was on her mind. "I met with my lawyers today. I want you to have this house and whatever else I have left when I die. Now, don't look like that. Death is a perfectly natural thing, and I don't mind telling you I'm just a little curious to see what it's like over there, on the other side." She nodded in the direction of her bureau. "Those papers lying there on my bureau are for you. Inside the pouch you will find a complete listing of everything I own. There are certificates for stock in the Boston and Albany Railroad, and Merchant's Marine and Fire Insurance. My account books for Washington National Bank are there, as well as a list of all my interests held by Thatcher and Dewberry, my brokers. I own a little stock in Union Bank, some interest in Suffolk Glass Works, and a wee little bit of Riverside Press. It's all being transferred over to you."

"I don't want it."

"Nonsense, child. I want you to have it. Who else would I leave it to? My carriage horse?"

Elizabeth smiled, but the smile faded when Phoebe said, "I think it's time for you to return to Nantucket. You've finished your schooling long ago. There isn't any reason for you to remain here."

"I won't leave you."

"It's what we always planned . . . for you to return home after graduation."

"That was a long time ago. I've changed my mind now."

"But your family . . ."

"*You* are my family now."

"I'm not fit to be anyone's family," Phoebe said. "It isn't right for someone as young and bright as you to waste away your best years caring for an old leftover like me."

Elizabeth started to speak, but Phoebe cut her off. "I'm tired. I want to rest a bit now. You take those papers with you. I want you to look them over. Promise me you'll keep them in a safe place. Promise."

"I promise."

Phoebe patted her hand. "That's a good girl," she said, closing her eyes.

Elizabeth went upstairs to her bedroom. She placed the papers on her desk and went to sit in the slipper chair by the window, not bothering to light the lamp, preferring to sit in the darkness, where she could be alone with her tears, her sadness, as if that would help her to understand the heaviness in her heart. She looked outside at the darkness, at the stars that twinkled against a black backdrop of velvety night. Out of habit, her gaze went from constellation to constellation, but her mind was occupied with other things.

She had always thought of Aunt Phoebe as part of her future, where everything lay rosy with promise. How different things looked now. Elizabeth felt as if she were a hundred years old. How far away the brightness of her grandfather's lighthouse seemed. In her heart she yearned to return to Nantucket, to see once more the sandy shores of home, to sit in the lighthouse gazing out at the stars with her grandfather. But she had a duty here, and she knew she could not shirk it, not even if it meant losing the one thing she had always loved, Tavis. Her mind made up, she removed her clothes and slipped on her gown in the dark.

When Mrs. Potter came to call her to dinner, she found Elizabeth asleep and looking so exhausted, she did not have the heart to wake her. When Mrs. Potter went downstairs, she told Peterby, "The poor lamb looked as if she needed sleep more than food."

The next afternoon, Elizabeth walked into Phoebe's room and announced, "I'm not going home."

"You can't sacrifice your life here with me. I won't allow it."

"And I won't allow you to drive me away. I decided last night that I was going to stay here for as long as I feel it's necessary. I've looked through your papers. There is plenty here to keep me busy. I met with Mr. Thornton, your broker, this morning. Frankly, Aunt Phoebe, your finances are in a mess. Mr. Thornton said you hadn't been keeping abreast of things as you had in the past, and there are numerous stocks, as well as other things, that should have been liquidated some time ago. I have another appointment with him tomorrow. He gave me several papers to look over in the meantime. All in all, I find the business world quite fascinating . . . enough that I almost wish I were born a boy."

"You've a head for business. I've always told you that. It's always been like that with the Brewster women. It takes brainpower to get by in the world. Unfortunately we women get the brain, and the men get all the power. What a waste. It's one of the reasons I never remarried after Charles died. I can take care of myself, thank you. I'll tell you, Elizabeth, there is nothing more pitiable in the world than a woman who thinks she needs a man to take care of her, to make her whole. As long as you have a few stocks and a little cash in reserve to fall back on, whether or not you're married, you'll always have control of your life, always have something to tide you over. You keep this house and you keep at least some of those stocks. Don't liquidate everything the moment I'm gone. As long as you have this house, you'll always have a place to go, and as long as you have money, you'll be able to take care of yourself. You remember that."

"I will, *if* you remember that I'm not leaving."

"I'll remember it, but nothing says I have to like it. Now, you go find Mrs. Potter and tell her to get out my black cashmere dress. Then go tell Peterby that I want to be taken downstairs for dinner. If I don't get out of this bed, my backside will grow barnacles. It's already getting as broad as a beam."

Harry continued to float in and out of Elizabeth's life, finishing his schooling at Cambridge, then coming back to Boston to go to law school at Harvard. Her father and grandfather came several times to visit, and Elizabeth saw all six of her brothers and her two sisters at one time or another, but she never went back to Nantucket.

Harry graduated from Harvard the year Elizabeth turned twenty-three. It was also the year Phoebe had her third stroke, which, like the previous two strokes, took something. This time it was her speech. Harry turned down a distinguished position with a well-known law firm in New York, accepting a position with his uncle's firm in Boston, and Elizabeth knew this was so he could be near her. Of late, his interest was becoming more and more intent.

She attended a small party at the Howells' shortly before Christmas. Harry was waiting for her when she arrived. "I thought you'd never get here," he said, crossing the room quickly and giving her a kiss on the cheek. He took her wrap and gloves and handed them to the butler. "What took you so long?"

"I read the paper to Aunt Phoebe until she fell asleep."

Taking her by the arm, he led her into the library and closed the door. "Harry, I don't think we should be in here like this. I haven't had a chance to speak to the Howells yet, and my coming in here alone with you doesn't look right. What will people think?"

"They will think you are as lovely as I do," he said, taking her in his arms.

Elizabeth looked into the face as dear to her as any brother's, then pulled back. "Harry . . . please."

He released her. "All right, but give me a moment. I want to talk to you, and I won't be able to once you go into the main room."

"What did you want to talk about?"

"You . . . and me. Your aunt doesn't expect you to devote your entire life to her."

"I know she doesn't. Aunt Phoebe's expectations have nothing to do with it."

"What does?"

"Love. Affection. Understanding. She was there for me when I needed someone wise and strong in my life. She has been like a mother to me. She has given me so much. But most importantly, it's what *I* want to do. This is one small way I can give something back."

"Giving up the prime of your life isn't small in my estimation," Harry said.

Not bothering to hide her irritation, Elizabeth said, "It's my life, Harry. I will live it as I see fit. You aren't my father, and you aren't my husband."

He took her in his arms. "No, but I'd like to be. Marry me, Elizabeth. You know how long I've waited for you."

She pulled away from him. "I've never asked you to wait, Harry. I've never encouraged you at all."

Before she could fathom what he was about, Harry took her in his arms again, more firmly this time, pulling her against him, his mouth angling toward hers. "Harry, I . . ." His mouth cut off her words, his lips moving with an ease that comes with long practice. Harry definitely knew what he was about, for he was

fairly courting her with his mouth, kissing, tasting—
doing all the things a man does to weaken a woman's
defenses. But in Elizabeth's case, it didn't work.

Oh, his kiss had certainly been arousing, and it had
awakened a feeling in her she hadn't felt since the last
time she had gazed at Tavis Mackinnon, and for a moment she almost gave in to that luxurious feeling and
kissed him back with all the fervor in her heart. But that
was the problem. The fervor in her heart already belonged to someone else. There just wasn't anything
there for Harry. She broke the kiss and stepped back. "I
didn't give you permission to do that."

"A man who asks permission to kiss a desirable
woman will find himself constantly disappointed. Kiss
first and ask questions later is my motto."

"You seem to have a motto for everything," she said.

"Only around you," he said. He kissed her again,
lightly, resting his chin on the top of her head. "What
can I do to make you see how much I care for you?
How can I make you love me?"

"Oh, Harry, you could never make me love you. You
wouldn't have to. I love you already . . . as a friend."

Harry, ever the charmer, slapped both hands over his
heart and staggered around a bit. "Stabbed in the heart
with your point," he said. Then straightening, his face
taking on a more serious look, he said, "You don't think
it could ever work out for us, not even if you tried?"

"Harry . . ." she said, reaching out to touch his
sleeve. "Don't you think I know what a wonderful man
you are? Don't you think I would have loved you long
ago if I could? But I can't. I simply can't will myself to
love. No one can."

He looked at her in a strange new way. "You've
never told me why."

"Because I'm already in love with someone else."

Harry looked crestfallen. "Someone else? Why haven't I heard about him? Who is he? What's his name?"

"He is no one you would know. He is . . . he's someone I've known for a long time . . . someone in Nantucket."

"Nantucket?" He chuckled and reached for her, but Elizabeth stepped quickly away.

"Why are you giving me that *I-know-something-you-don't-know* look?"

He laughed. "Because I know something you *don't* know. Whoever this rogue is that has stolen your heart—well, let's just say that I'm not too terribly concerned about some buffoon from Nantucket who hasn't even cared enough to pay you a visit in all these years."

"He isn't a buffoon, and I never said he loved me. I said I was in love with him."

Recognizing that gleam in his eye, Elizabeth turned away. "Oh, no you don't," she said, then hurried from the room before Harry could claim her mouth with another knee-buckling kiss.

CHAPTER
❧ SIX ❧

Elizabeth returned to Nantucket shortly after the death of her aunt Phoebe, and her twenty-fourth birthday.

What had been a wild and undisciplined girl was now a refined lady. Many things had changed in Elizabeth's life, and many of her old ways were gone, or at least tempered. But one thing had remained constant during the eight years she had been gone. Shining like a beacon that guided her from some distant shore was the fact that she was still in love with Tavis Mackinnon.

It was no longer the childish, pathetically inept adoration of a young girl with no bosom and even less discretion, but it was still love.

As it happened, there was a big dance being held on the first of May, just a few days after her return. Elizabeth, her golden-blond hair done up in the latest curls, wore a gown of white tulle, embroidered with gold wheat ears, which the seamstress in Boston claimed to be an exact copy of Worth's latest from Paris.

Elizabeth had always been a beauty, but now she had the presence and style to carry it off. Her years in Boston under Aunt Phoebe's tutelage, her successful debut into Boston society, and yes, even the attention of Harry Beecham all served, if not to remove the tarnish from the pain of her past, then to make her future shine so bright that the painful past was hardly felt or noticed.

Feeling every bit as beautiful as she looked, she went to the dance with her father and her brother Matt. She was as nervous as a schoolgirl, wondering if Tavis Mackinnon had heard she was back in town.

About the time Elizabeth arrived with her father and Matt, Tavis was having a cup of whiskey-laced punch with his friends Cole Cassidy and Nathaniel Starbuck. Just about that time, a brunette across the room caught his eye.

"Now, that's what I call a real beauty," Tavis said.

"Yes, she is," said Cole. "Who is she?"

"I don't know, but I know one thing. I could ask a woman like that to marry me," Tavis said.

"You could, but her family would object," Nathaniel said, breaking into a wide grin.

"Her family?" asked Tavis.

"Her husband and six sons." Nathaniel's grin broke into a full laugh.

They fell into silence, each man allowing his attention to roam the room in a never-ending search for a new and beautiful face.

"Hello, Nathaniel . . . Cole . . . Tavis," said Mrs. Witherspoon, the whalebone in her corset laces creaking as she passed.

"Mrs. Witherspoon," they said in unison, nodding politely.

The moment she passed, Nathaniel leaned close and said, "That a whale should have been killed to provide a corset for that woman is an animalistic affront."

The three of them downed the rest of their drinks and laughed, making their way back to the punch bowl. If they didn't find any beautiful new prospects, they could, at least, get drunk.

"My God! Speaking of beauties. Look at that silver-haired angel," Cole said, coming to a standstill. "She puts every woman in the room to shame."

The three of them stared. "Who is she?" asked Nathaniel.

"I don't know, but I sure intend to find out. My prayers have been answered," Cole said.

"When did you ever pray?" Nathaniel asked.

"The moment I first saw her," Cole said.

Tavis narrowed his eyes. She might be beautiful. She might have been gone for seven or eight years. She might have even changed. But he knew who she was the moment she entered the room.

"That's no angel," he said with his same old cynicism. "That's a witch in disguise."

"You know her?" asked Nathaniel.

"I know her, and so do you," Tavis said. "Don't be taken in by her beauty."

"Say what you will, my friend, but anyone that looks like that shouldn't be taken lightly." Nathaniel let his eyes roam over the silver-haired beauty in the white cloud of a dress. "In fact," he drawled, "I should like to take her with great vigor."

"Introduce me to her," Cole said.

"And me," said Nathaniel.

"You need no introduction. I told you . . . you know her," Tavis said. "That *angel*, as you call her, is none other than Samuel Robinson's daughter." With a low, mocking bow, he said, "Gentlemen, may I present to you the infamous Lizzie."

"Lizzie," they gasped in unison.

Cole shook his head. "I would have never believed it. My God, man, look how much she's changed. She's ravishing and she walks like a queen. How *did* you know it was her?"

"If there is any being in the entire world that can raise the hackles on the back of my neck by simply entering the room, that brat can."

"Brat?" Nathaniel said. "How can you call her that? Witch or not, she's a beauty."

Tavis looked her over. He might have been tempted, if he had not known her. "Unlike you, her effect upon me, I am happy to say, has not changed."

"Well, old man, it looks like *your* effect upon her has. She isn't even looking your way," Cole said.

"She will," Tavis said, his voice brimming with confidence.

"I don't know," Nathaniel said, "she's being besieged with offers to dance."

"She'll not only dance with me, but she'll do the asking, just like she always did," Tavis said.

"And if she does, will you turn her down like you always did?" asked Cole.

"I might," Tavis said, giving her the once-over, "and again I might not. And don't be forgetting. I *did* dance with her on occasion."

"Five dollars says she won't ask you," Cole said.

"You're on," Tavis said.

Becca was waiting for her after Elizabeth finished her dance with Alvin Hull. "Let's have some punch," Elizabeth said.

"Good," said Becca. "After that dance with Thad

Elmore, I can't decide if I should drink it or soak my feet in it."

"I thought you went outside to have a cup of punch with him," Elizabeth said.

"I did, but I didn't stay long," Becca said, then taking Elizabeth by the arm, she leaned close and whispered. "Whatever you do, don't dance with him."

"Why not?"

"When he dances, he's all over your feet. When he stops, he goes for the rest of you."

Elizabeth laughed. "Come on, then. I could use some punch myself."

They started for the punch, but before they reached it, Elizabeth took Becca's arm and steered her off course.

"Where are we going?" asked Becca.

"You wanted punch, didn't you?"

"Yes, but you're going the wrong way."

"No, I'm not. We're having the punch from the other table."

Becca jerked to a halt. "*That* punch is for the men. You know that. We can't have it. It's scandalous. We'll be seen."

"We'll down it before anyone can say anything, then we plead innocence. How were we to know which was which?"

"Because they've put it where they always put it."

"But *I* don't know that," Elizabeth said. "I've been away for a long time, remember?"

"Fine. Then you go," Becca said, giving Elizabeth a push in the right direction, then dropping onto a nearby bench. "I'll wait here."

"Coward."

"Absolutely and unequivocally," said Becca, frantically nodding her head, her glossy black curls bobbing.

Elizabeth ignored the raised brows of several men standing around the punch bowl. Blinding them with a dazzling smile, she dipped in to fill two cups, then carried them across the room to join Becca. Handing the drink to her, she said, "Drink up quickly; here comes Mrs. Witherspoon."

Becca downed the punch in three gulps. Elizabeth in two.

Mrs. Witherspoon was huffing like a bellows by the time she reached them. "My dear Elizabeth, you know a lady must not drink from the men's punch."

"Is that what I've done?" Elizabeth asked, aghast, her hand coming up to fan across her breast.

Mrs. Witherspoon nodded. "I am afraid it is."

"Oh, do forgive me. I was so accustomed to Boston, you see, and the punch there is all the same, since the men retire to the billiards room for their spirits."

Mrs. Witherspoon looked down at the two empty cups. "Well, I suppose there is no harm done, as long as you don't have any more."

"Oh, we shan't," Becca said, doing her best imitation of looking horrified. "Why, I'm shamed, simply shamed."

Mrs. Witherspoon looked sufficiently appeased, and nodding, made her departure.

Standing, Becca and Elizabeth hid their smiles and made their way across the room.

"Surely this can't be right. The Lizzie Robinson I knew would never have let Mrs. Witherspoon stand between her and her affinity for spirits."

Elizabeth looked up and into the grayest blue eyes this side of heaven. "One cup was all I wanted," she said, taking her skirt into her hand and walking away from those heavenly eyes.

Tavis took her arm. "What? No hello for your long-time friend?"

"Hello, Tavis." She forced herself to look at him. He was studying her intently, as if he were taking great pleasure from her appearance, the changes maturity had wrought upon her person. Her body trembled as if cold, but that was impossible, considering the heated flood of knee-weakening warmth that seemed to invade every inch of her. Never, in the years that she had been gone, had she had a man look her over like this—look as if he were trying to see inside her, or at least see what lay beneath her clothes. A fiery tremor rippled down her spine, and she glanced away.

What had happened to all the things she had learned in Boston? Where was her polish now? Or her ability to make artful conversation in awkward situations? One look into his eyes told her he was enjoying this, finding satisfaction in her discomfort. Perhaps it was uneasiness that prompted her to say, "You still look the same. Somehow I knew you would."

A smile touched his lips. "And you've turned into quite an elegant lady. Somehow *that* surprises me."

She blushed, feeling the sudden sting of anger. If there had not been so much truth to what he said, she would have taken issue with his comment. But as it was, she let it go, saying simply and honestly, "I am not the foolish child I once was."

That apparently amused him, for he smiled and said, "I'm glad to see you've gotten over your infatuation with me."

"Did I say that?" she asked, looking at him squarely. "What if I told you my feelings had not changed, only the way in which I deal with them?" She was feeling a surge of triumph now, seeing the way her blatant honesty left him somewhat taken aback. It was plain to see that the memories of the old Tavis Mackinnon were indeed wrestling with the image of the new Lizzie Robinson. She felt the power of it and reveled in its intensity.

Now it was time to exit, to leave him wondering and temporarily speechless. She started around him, realizing he still held her arm.

"Aren't you forgetting something?" he asked.

She paused and looked down at her arm. "Aren't you?"

He didn't release her, but he did ease up on his grip. "Don't tell me you've changed so much that you can come to a party like this and not ask me to dance."

"All right, I won't tell you that. Now, will you release my arm? People are looking. What are you trying to do? Cause a scene?"

He had the audacity to laugh at that. "And what if I am? You thrive on scenes, remember? Scenes and spying were your two favorite pastimes, as I recall. Even now I am distrustful of every palm I pass."

"That was another time, another girl," she said. "It is indelicate and quite ill mannered of you to mention it now."

For a brief second he seemed ready to let her go. But he didn't. The strength of him, the enormous power of those eyes . . . There was nothing she could do. She felt mesmerized, helpless to do more than wait.

There was an unfamiliar gleam in the liquid depths of those blue-gray eyes. She knew he was not going to let her off so easy. He was going to press her, and she knew why. He was challenged by the woman he saw, vengeful toward the girl he remembered. As she looked at him, she realized he was going to taunt her, if for no other reason than to see if she would lose her cool composure.

"Can it be that you've gotten over your infatuation of me so easily?" he asked.

She looked directly into his eyes. "I am not going to ask you to dance, if that's what you mean."

He released her abruptly. "Why? Are you afraid I would refuse?"

"I never gave it much thought, one way or the other," she said. "I already have more requests for dances than I can honor," she said, holding up her dance card.

He didn't even glance at it. Instead, he looked as though he might laugh when his gaze raked her over. "Well, one more shouldn't matter, then. May I have the honor?"

The "No" barely escaped her lips before he took her firmly in his arms and drew her against him, guiding her with little effort onto the crowded dance floor.

Her body went numb. All thought seemed to vanish from her mind. This is what she had always dreamed of, what she had lived for. So why wasn't she happy? *This isn't love,* her heart cried out. It wasn't happily ever after, or the picture-perfect ending to a long romantic entanglement. It was the right gesture but for all the wrong reasons. That robbed her of her joy. She looked at the face she had always held so dear, wishing . . . wishing . . . She closed her eyes and tried to calm herself, willing herself to think clearly and rationally. *Don't read more into this than there is,* she thought. *Don't melt into his arms. Don't lose yourself in those eyes. And whatever you do, don't look at him and smile. People will know you're still in love with him.*

At that moment he leaned closer, whispering, "Your dancing seems to have improved along with your manners."

"While yours seem to have gotten worse," she said,

pushing him back to the proper distance. He laughed, and she felt the eyes of every person in the room upon her. How many years had she dreamed about the first time she would see him? How many times had she practiced what she would say? So much depended upon this first meeting. And yet nothing was going according to her plans. She prayed for wisdom and fortitude, feeling the burn of his gaze on her.

"Is this a new game we're playing?" he asked.

She looked up, catching the unreadable expression upon his face, not bothering to hide her puzzlement. "A new game? What do you mean?"

He smiled down at her, but his eyes were expressionless. "Your feelings for me haven't changed, but your tactics have. Do you think to win my attentions by acting indifferent? You aren't setting your cap for me again, are you?"

She knew her heart's message was in her eyes, that to say what she was about to say would mean she placed her fragile feelings at his feet. "And if I am?" she asked softly.

He hesitated, and for one wonderful second he looked as if he might be moved by her words. But he wasn't. His eyes shuttered now, his voice was hard and mocking. "Cry off, love. You'll never get me, you know."

Her ire raised at his impudence, she said, "Is that a challenge?"

"It won't work, Lizzie."

"No one calls me Lizzie anymore."

He raised a dubious brow. "Really? Which is it then, Elizabeth . . . Eliza . . . Liza?"

"Any of those will do."

He nodded. "It still won't work. You aren't going to snare me, no matter what tactics you employ."

"*If* all I wanted was to snare you, Tavis Mackinnon, I could do it easily enough ... *if* I set my mind to it."

"Set whatever you like, but it still won't work. I'm not the marrying kind. I've seen what marriage does to people ... the men gone on whalers for five-year stretches, the women raising children and viewing the world through eyes bleary from too much opium."

"It's not that way with everyone. . . ."

"Give it up," he said. "I'm a confirmed bachelor. You'll never win. Never," he said with supreme confidence. "Whatever it was that they taught you in Boston, it wasn't enough to lure me into marriage. Give it up, Elizabeth. You can't win. Admit it."

She stopped dancing and tapped his chest with her fan as she said, "I admit nothing. And don't keep throwing that challenge into my face, or I might surprise you and take you up on it. You aren't dealing with a besotted child anymore."

He looked her over. "No, I can see that you're all woman now," he said, "and a beautiful one at that. But I'm not available."

She drew her fan down the side of his cheek. "You haven't given your heart to another, have you?"

"No, I haven't."

"Then you're available." She smiled sweetly. "Who knows? I might just end up with you, after all."

"You can try," he said.

Oh, I intend to. "I might just do that, Tavis Mackinnon. I surely might."

"You sound awfully confident," he said.

"It's not confidence. I simply know what I know."

"Which is?"

"*If* I wanted you, Tavis Mackinnon, and it didn't matter how I got you, I could do it." She stopped, and poked his chest with her folded fan. "You would do well to remember that." She turned away, ready to walk off and leave him there.

He took her arm. "We haven't finished our dance," he said.

"We haven't finished a lot of things," she said, then she caught up her skirts and walked off the dance floor, leaving Tavis Mackinnon to stare, openmouthed, after her.

Becca, also openmouthed, was standing just a few feet away. It did not take a tremendous amount of wit to see that she was completely aghast. "I can't believe you walked away from him like that. How could you do it? How can you even speak to him? He's so divine. Every time I'm around him my brain stops working and I can't think of a single thing to say."

"It's quite easy," Elizabeth said. "Whenever I see him, I always picture him standing there in his underwear with a finger up his nose."

Becca looked shocked, then crestfallen. "I wish you hadn't told me that," she said, "for I will never be able to look at him again without seeing him that way."

"It worked for me," was all Elizabeth said.

For the rest of the evening, Elizabeth avoided Tavis, but she knew that Becca knew she kept him in her sight. When Minnie Woodbury planted herself in front of Tavis, Becca poked Elizabeth and said, "My goodness, will you look at her? Minnie looks like she was poured into that dress."

"And forgot to say when," Elizabeth said.

Becca sighed. "Maybe you should forget Tavis," she said.

"Why?"

"Because you could have your pick of any man on the island, you know."

"Oh, Becca . . ."

"It's true. I've never seen some of these men look at a woman like they look at you. James Woodbury is positively slavering."

Elizabeth smiled behind her fan and whispered, "Slavering is for wolves."

"Well?" Becca said.

"Well, looking is one thing, marriage is another."

"Right," Becca said, glancing around the room. "Maybe we're both destined to be spinsters," she said softly, and Elizabeth knew she was thinking about her own engagement, which was broken last year.

"Me, perhaps, but not you," Elizabeth said brightly, hoping to draw Becca's thoughts away. "Your clumsy friend Jason hasn't taken his eyes off you all evening."

Becca's face brightened. "Really?"

"Would this face lie?"

Becca laughed. "In that case, why don't we walk by him . . . on our way to the punch bowl, of course. We might even see Tavis."

"I won't hang my heart on that star," Elizabeth said. "Tavis has always said he wasn't the marrying kind. I'm beginning to wonder if that isn't true."

"Oh, he tells everyone that," Becca said, "but no one believes it. They just keep wondering and speculating on whom, not whether, he'll marry."

Part of what they said was true. Folks around Nantucket did wonder if Tavis Mackinnon would ever get married. Some people were inclined to speculate. Some even went so far as to place bets. While others simply came right out and asked him about it.

"Hey, Mackinnon, aren't you ever going to tie the knot?"

And as always, Tavis Mackinnon would laugh and say with a shrug, "Heaven knows."

Heaven knows. It wasn't a terribly honest answer, for deep in his heart, Tavis knew he would never marry. It wasn't that he had anything against marriage, or even women, for that matter, for if anything could be said about Tavis, it was that he loved women. *All* women. And that was just the problem. How could a man who loved all women pick just one? It was as if every time he heard someone say it was time for him to take a wife, his first impulse was to ask, "Whose?"

There were times, of course, when one particular girl or the other would catch his eye, and even hold it for a while, and he would squire her around for a time—sometimes even going so far as to think this might be the one—when up would jump the devil, and Tavis would suddenly find himself attracted to another pretty face. Over and over again, it happened this way, but oh, how he enjoyed that delightful interval between meeting a beautiful woman and discovering that she had all the charm of a cod.

Time and time again, it occurred to him that whenever a new woman caught his eye, the marital mist was dispelled. He found as much delight in variety as he did in novelty. He could not help it. Whenever he saw a pretty face, he was like one who labored in the heat of day and stumbled upon a cool spring.

He wallowed in it.

A long time ago Tavis had decided that any man who couldn't stay with one woman for any length of time had no business whatsoever getting married. This was his philosophy, and he stuck with it. "You can be happy with any woman, as long as you don't fall in love with her," he had said more than once. "Once you fall, it's pure hell after that."

In other words, Tavis was a bachelor, tried, tested, and true. This philosophy of his gained him a lot of notoriety—almost as much notoriety as his ability to design ships—and not just around Nantucket, but as far over as Cape Cod, where his brother, Nicholas, had moved with his family. It was a well-known fact that unmarried women (and a few married ones as well) had their eye on Tavis Mackinnon.

But in Elizabeth's case it was more than that. She didn't just have her eye on Tavis. She had her hopes, her dreams, her entire future, pinned upon him.

Life settled into a sort of routine after the night of the party, Elizabeth acting uninterested whenever she saw him, and Tavis seemingly falling into his old habit of generally ignoring her. But there were times that she would be going to this place or that, and she would feel as if someone were watching her. More often than not, she would look up to find Tavis standing somewhere on the fringe, his arms crossed over his chest, his gaze direct, speculative, and steady upon her.

Whenever he looked at her this way, Elizabeth could no more control the delicious shiver that went over her than she could control the love she felt. And as always, she would wonder if his interest in her would ever go beyond speculative looks.

On one occasion, however, he did more than just give her a speculative look.

It was a Sunday afternoon, and as was customary for her and her sisters on a Sunday afternoon after church, Elizabeth, Sally, and Meg paid their grandfather a visit.

Finding it such a warm, sunny afternoon—a welcome sight after more than a week of rain—the girls packed a picnic basket while Asa hitched up his old gelding to the buggy, and the four of them set off across the moors to Saul's Pond.

Once the meal was over, Captain Robinson declared, "It's time for my nap." Reclining on the picnic blanket, he pushed his hat down over his eyes and folded his hands over his enormous old chest and dozed off.

Shortly after their grandfather began his customary snoring, Meg and Sally grew bored with watching him and set off on their own to gather wildflowers, which bloomed in profusion and lay scattered all over the gently sloped Saul's Hills.

Watching the two of them wander off, Elizabeth busied herself with packing up the basket. A few minutes later, she made her way toward the buggy.

What she found there was far more than the buggy and horse they had left behind. The moment she stepped over the last sloping hill and made her descent, she saw him, mounted on his horse, giving the buggy a curious stare.

He dismounted, walking around the buggy, then he stopped. Tall and slim-hipped, he stood with his profile toward her, the sun catching him from the back. When his horse noticed her and snorted, he looked up.

It was hard to ignore those sensual features, the promise of that experienced mouth and softly arousing gaze. Oddly enough, his expression was, for a change, one she could easily read. It was the same sort of expression her father had often worn when she was a child—whenever he was trying to decide between punishing her or giving her a hug.

He was wearing a dark blue shirt, which made his

hair look blue-black. His face was as beautiful to her as it had always been, his thick black brows curving almost wickedly over the intense iron-blue eyes whose gaze never left the scrutiny of her face.

"This is an unexpected, but pleasant, surprise," he said. "I was thinking that perhaps this horse had run away with the buggy."

She gave him a curious stare. "Ran away? Why would you think that?"

He looked back toward the buggy. "Because he wasn't tied."

Elizabeth's gaze went to the gelding standing quietly in his traces. He was right. Her grandfather hadn't tied him. They were fortunate, she supposed, that the gelding hadn't decided to wander back to the lighthouse and leave them afoot. But then she remembered the animal was old, and like her grandpa, was probably a bit forgetful at times.

"Grandpa is a little absentminded," she said.

His gaze traveled over her slowly. "He isn't the only one," Tavis said. "Every time I look at you, I find it hard to remember that the Lizzie I recall, and the Elizabeth I see, are actually the same person."

She laughed. "Good. If I remember right, you were never too enamored with Lizzie."

"Fishing for compliments?" he asked softly, his voice laced with amusement.

It didn't sit too well with her to have her most private thoughts aired like Monday's laundry. A question like that, she decided, deserved no answer.

He didn't say anything for a moment, for he seemed quite content just to stand there looking at her. Every muscle, every nerve in her body, tensed in awareness of him.

He hadn't changed much over the years that she had been gone. The iron-gray eyes were just as attractive, although when she looked at them now, she rarely saw irritation or astonishment in their liquid depths. His face was just as lean and handsome, his legs were still as long as a ship's mast. But there was one definite change she had noticed, a change that was even more obvious now.

Tavis Mackinnon had never in her entire life looked at her with anything but irritation or amusement. But since her return, she had noticed those looks had been replaced, or at least covered, with one she could only call interested.

Perhaps he was interested—solely because of the change in her, something that raised his curiosity, as if he were speculating as to whether she was genuine or not.

And then again—and she prayed this was the case—his interested look might have been prompted by just that: interest.

She didn't get to speculate any further, for her thoughts were interrupted when he spoke.

"A while ago you said you didn't think I was ever too enamored with you. . . ."

"You weren't," she said flatly. "And don't you go trying to make me think differently. That's the sort of thing that can make a body go crazy."

He smiled. "I don't think I can honestly say I was ever enamored with you. . . . You *were* nothing more than a child, you know. But there was always something—something about you that never let me be quite as angry at you as I led everyone to believe."

If he had come right out and told her he had designed

a ship that could fly, she couldn't have been more astonished. "You could have fooled me," she said.

He smiled again, flooding her soul with sunshine. "Apparently I did just that."

"And you fooled a lot of other people as well," she said. "Like everyone else in Nantucket, I thought you hated the sight of me."

"Hate never entered into things," he said, his voice strangely soft. "You irritated the daylights out of me on occasion, but even then, I'd go home at night and more often than not, I would find myself lying in bed, thinking about something you had done and laughing." He raised a brow at her. "I was always curious to know just how you got the red dye out of your hair."

"It wasn't dye. It was henna. It washed out . . . eventually."

"You see? I do remember things about you."

"But you always seemed so angry."

His hand came up, brushing over the hollow beneath her cheekbone. "Sweet Elizabeth, I had to. How else would I discourage you? You were a child. I was a man full grown. People talk about a man with interests like that," he said, his voice light and teasing. "They won't allow him to come into their homes. They say prayers for his black soul at church. They take their children by the hand whenever he passes. They think he should be locked up."

She knew he was making light with her, but all of this was simply too much for her to absorb quickly. Standing there looking at him, she felt like she had been looking at a black horse all her life, only to discover it was really white.

Before she could think further, she felt his hands, warm on her shoulders. He drew her toward him, nestling her gently against the hard lines of his body, an act that was neither forced nor suggestive. In truth, it struck her more as a token of affection than anything sensual. His chin resting on the top of her head, he spoke to her, and she could feel the vibrations of his words against her cheek which harbored in the curve of his throat.

"Don't be so quick to condemn yourself," he said. "You will never know how much you brightened a world that seemed terribly dull after you were gone."

It was a good thing he was holding her, she decided, for she would have toppled right over, so weak her knees went at the impact of those words.

"After you left, I found myself missing all the attention," he said. "I had, thanks to you, built up quite a reputation . . . and there is nothing so flattering to a man's ego as notoriety. Once you were gone, however, I found my reputation slipping down a notch or two, approaching ordinary . . . which, to a bachelor, has the ring of a death bell to it."

He fell silent after that, and Elizabeth, who was basking in the afterglow of his words, found she wanted more. "Is that all?" she asked, and felt his body shake with laughter.

"You are still an odd little creature," he said. "Odd but fascinating."

"You will have to excuse me if I find all of this a bit much to understand. I've never changed horses midgallop before."

He smiled. "Well, sometimes trying different things can be good for you."

"Did you think of me? When I was gone, I mean."

He laughed. "More than you would believe, I'll wager. I remember one time in particular when I was thinking about you one evening, a year or two after you left, and made a surprising discovery."

"What was that?"

"I found myself thinking about you—the way you were before you left—and how it made me feel like a shy person who had always relied on the talkative people around him to keep up the conversation. But after you were gone, I found I had to do my own talking, that I had no one to keep up my end of it."

"I don't understand."

"What I am saying is, you brought a lot of laughter and adventure into my life. I never realized how much until you were gone and suddenly my life seemed dull and flat."

Elizabeth drew back, looking at him strangely. "Are you telling me that you might have even *liked* me?"

When Tavis looked down at her, his instinct had been, at first, to laugh. But when he looked into her eyes, all the laughter drained out of him.

Although he had held her in his arms for quite some time, he had no intention of kissing her. Her face studied him with such interest, such devotion. It brought back a flood of old memories.

He was suddenly aware of her, not as a memory, not as a child, but as a woman. He could feel the rounded thrust of her pointed breasts against his chest, a curious sensation that was both surprising and disturbing.

He had never kissed Elizabeth before. He did not want to kiss her now, or at least he thought he didn't. A gentle squeeze, a quick peck on the check—these things would serve him better to express the genuine fondness he felt for her. She was a sensitive person and proud. He knew how deeply her past must have scarred her, how cruel it must have been for her to live with her illusion of endless love being held up by Nantucket's finest for dispassionate inspection and thoughtless chatter. Without a doubt, she would be as happy to put the past behind her as he was. Would it make the pain of it easier to bear if she knew he considered her his friend?

He gazed down at her, seeing her lovely eyes, realizing for the first time they weren't just blue, but an odd shade of blue, and ringed with lavender. It had been his intention to give her a chaste peck on the cheek, in friendship.

But when he lowered his head to kiss her, she turned, bringing her mouth against his, touching his lips with her own. The shock of it went through him like the blast from a cannon. He recoiled, jerking his head back.

She was looking up at him, looking into his eyes, her own filling with shame and humiliation, the same expression he had seen in her eyes as a young girl, the same look that had reached out to him even then. Without thinking about what he was doing, without even being conscious that he was moving, he lowered his head again, his body no longer touching hers. With the slow, awkward movements of a blind man, he groped with his mouth until he found hers. A sound seemed to explode within his head, a sound he only heard when a new ship was released from its cradle. In his mind he heard the loud clatter of tumbling keelblocks and a tremendous splash, and suddenly he knew what it meant to have purpose.

The feel of her was no longer a tangled memory, but reality and desire.

From somewhere behind them came the unpassionate sound of giggling. He jerked back at the same time she did, both of them turning to see the bright face of Meg Robinson smiling up at them.

"Doesn't that tickle?"

After that day, Tavis seemed to avoid her completely. Only Becca knew just how hard it was on Elizabeth to see Tavis squiring this woman and that around town. Once, when he had spent several weeks paying court to Harriet Landsbury, Becca came right out and said, "Elizabeth, how can you stand it?"

"Oh, it isn't so difficult really," Elizabeth replied. "I drink lots of strong tea. I take long walks. I read dozens of books, and try to keep my mind occupied on other things. I stay up late until I'm too exhausted to think straight. I watch the two of them together and learn to hate her. Whenever I see her, I scrutinize her appearance and comfort myself with thoughts of her big feet and her horrid taste in men. Whenever I can, I go to the lighthouse to drink a lot of wine and watch the sea gulls soar until I get a crick in my neck. And if that doesn't work, I abandon all attempts to think about him, exhausting myself with cooking or cleaning. As a last resort, I kick his buggy."

"Well, at least the last part isn't hard, since his buggy is always parked in front of the shipping office. Did you notice the change?"

"What change?"

"The one on the sign at their shipping office. Remember it used to say 'Mackinnon, Graham and Mackinnon'?"

Elizabeth nodded. "I also remember that before Tavis and Nick came, their uncle Robert simply called it 'Graham Shipping Interests.' "

"Well, it's now 'Mackinnon and Mackinnon.' "

"Did old Mr. Graham die?"

"No, but he decided he was getting too old to work. He's left here, you know. Moved to Cape Cod to live with Nicholas."

"Why did Nick move to Cape Cod?"

"To be closer to their shipyards. They stopped building ships here years ago. The harbor is too shallow."

"I wonder why Tavis didn't go with them."

"He said it wasn't necessary for him to go, since he's the architect. He told my father once that he couldn't design ships anywhere but in his old office. He must be a creature of habit."

"Maybe he is. He certainly does have some habits he persists in," Elizabeth said, thinking about his determination to stay single.

"You know that since the decline in whaling, there hasn't been much profit in building whalers, so Tavis has been designing other ships. My father said he has ideas that are quite revolutionary. Just think! Tavis could be famous one day."

"I doubt that," Elizabeth said, growing silent, wondering just what changes had been made in the Mackinnon brothers' business since Nick Mackinnon and Robert Graham were no longer present. Did those changes mean Tavis would be leaving? Until now, she had never really been too interested in what Tavis did, as long as it kept him on Nantucket Island. She tried to think back to the time Nicholas and Tavis had first come to Nantucket, but it had been too many years ago, and she had been only eleven and so taken with Tavis that she could think of little else.

Later that afternoon, Elizabeth packed a basket of food for her grandfather and walked out to the lighthouse on Brandt Point. She was in a talking mood and she had a lot of questions she wanted answered. Her grandfather was the only person she knew who would listen.

"Well, blind my eyes if it isn't my Lizzie," Captain Robinson said when he opened the door and saw her standing on the other side. "Come in, come in. I was wondering if you were too busy to pay your old grandfather a visit."

Elizabeth stood on tiptoe and kissed him. "You're never too old and I'm never too busy," she said, seeing the flat faces and odd-colored eyes of Robin and Friar Tuck peering at her from beneath the fringe on the sofa.

"How are you and the cats getting on?" she asked, remembering all too well the day she returned from Boston with Aunt Phoebe's cats—one basket on each arm. The moment she released them in the parlor of her father's house, her sisters, Meg and Sally, were charmed.

"Oh, Lizbeth, did you bring a kitty for me?" Meg asked.

"I brought two," Elizabeth said, "if they'll have you."

But Robin and Tuck must have sensed some family tie between Elizabeth and her sisters, for the moment Meg reached for Tuck, he hissed, scratched her hand, and ran from the room, Robin following close behind.

"I don't think they like her," Sally said. "Or me either."

Elizabeth watched the cats dash from the room and sighed. "Well, Aunt Phoebe did say they were ever foolish cats."

"Those were Aunt Phoebe's cats?" Meg said.

"Yes," Elizabeth said, giving her a hug. "Don't you remember seeing them in Boston?"

"No," Meg said.

Then giving Sally a wink, Elizabeth asked, "Do you remember who Aunt Phoebe was?"

"Of course I do. I've always remembered her. Papa used to tell me all about her," Meg said with a saucy flip of her skirts as she sat down.

Sally looked at Elizabeth. "As you can see, she hasn't outgrown her fondness for stretching the truth."

It took them two days to catch the cats, after discovering only Matt and Asa seemed to pass the cats' muster.

"Maybe we should take them to the lighthouse," Matt said, "since I'm not home enough to take care of them."

"Why don't we send them back to Boston?" Meg said.

"That's an excellent idea," Samuel said. "I don't know why you brought them here, since they obviously haven't taken to you either."

"I brought them because they were Aunt Phoebe's cats and there is no one in Boston to leave them with since I've closed up the house."

Seeing the set look on her father's face, she said, "I'll take them to Grandpa's. At least they seem to approve of him." She knew Asa might not be a lover of cats, but he wouldn't refuse to keep them, knowing they belonged to Aunt Phoebe.

"Rob and Tuck and I get on fine," Asa was saying, "that is, until they spy you . . . then they do the disappearing act. I did learn one thing, though: Long-haired cats and dark clothes don't go too well together."

She laughed, putting the basket on the table and turning to smile as Asa began digging through it.

"They need to be brushed a lot," she said.

"I figured that out. Problem was, I didn't realize you had to wear a bed sheet while you were doing it." He looked toward the sofa where two sets of eyes still peered out. "That's the darnedest thing," he said, "the way they don't like you." His eyes twinkling, he winked at her and said, "Far as I know, those are the only two critters alive that haven't taken a shine to you."

Elizabeth wanted to remind him that it could also be said that Tavis Mackinnon hadn't exactly taken a shine to her either, but she remained silent, storing the things away while Asa put on a kettle of water. When the kettle whistled, she made two cups of tea, carrying them to the table. Sitting across from him, she felt his gaze upon her.

"Is this purely a social call, or do you need to talk?"

She put the cup down and laughed. "I never could fool you, could I?"

"Not too many times. But tell me, what's amiss? You having trouble with Mackinnon already?"

"No, no trouble, Grandpa. I just wanted to find out some things about him."

"What kind of things?"

"About his past. I was awfully young when he and Nick came here, and I wasn't really interested in what they did."

"Well, I can't rightly say I know too much, you understand. Whatever I know, I came by."

"Do you remember why they came here? I know Robert Graham was their uncle, and that must mean he was their mother's brother."

"Yes, that much I do know. After you went to Boston, Robbie Graham used to come out here to the lighthouse to play checkers. Got to know him pretty well."

"Did you ever talk about Tavis?"

His brows went up. "Well now, I wouldn't be much of a grandpa if I let an opportunity like that slip by, now would I?"

Elizabeth smiled. "No, I suppose not."

"According to Robbie, Tavis is one of five brothers—there used to be six, but the oldest brother was killed along with their mother, when Nick and Tavis were just young tykes. Seems their baby sister was taken by the Indians about that time—"

"Indians?"

"Indians," Asa said, "The war-whooping kind, although I don't reckon I know what tribe of Indians it was . . . seeing as how all this happened back in Texas."

"Oh," Elizabeth said. "Go on."

"Well, let me see if I can remember correctly what Robbie said. It seems that Tavis's little sister was kidnapped by the Indians, and the boys' father left his wife and oldest son behind, taking the five younger boys with him to look for his daughter. They didn't find her, of course, and when they returned, they discovered their mother and brother had been killed. Seems the boys' pa left them alone a lot after that, while he roamed the country checking out stories of white children being traded or seen with different bands of Indians. About a year later, the boys got word that their pa had been scalped. After that, the five remaining sons tried to scratch out a living for themselves on the old homestead, but that was nigh on impossible, you see. One by one, they gradually drifted away."

Elizabeth didn't say anything for a moment or two. She was too busy thinking it was no wonder Tavis didn't have strong feelings about marriage and family life, when he had had so little memory of it. At last she shook her head sadly and said, "I know Nick and Tavis came up here, but where did the other three brothers go?"

"I don't rightly know for certain where they are now, mind you. It was some time ago that Robbie told me about them, you see." He paused a minute and rubbed his chin. "Seems I do remember Robbie saying something about two of them starting a sawmill somewhere. . . . California, I think. Twins, I believe he said they were."

"Twins," she repeated, trying to imagine two Tavis Mackinnons. For a moment she found herself wishing there were. It might not be so hopeless if she had two chances, instead of one.

You could also have two rejections, a voice inside her head seemed to say, and she let the idea slide slowly away. "And the other one? What happened to him?"

"Now, that one I remember quite well, simply because it was such a surprise. It seems the Mackinnons were Scots—both their mother and father were born in Scotland. From what Robbie said, the boys' father must have been in line to inherit a title of some sort, and when he died, it passed on down to him."

"What kind of title?"

"A duke, I think it was."

Elizabeth looked aghast. "*Tavis* Mackinnon has a brother that's a Scottish duke?"

Asa nodded. "According to Robbie Graham, he does."

"But Nick and Tavis are the oldest. I know that much. Why didn't they inherit the title?"

"Hold on now. I don't know all there is to know. All I was told is that Tavis and Nicholas earned enough money to buy passage on a ship and that they came up here." He winked at her. "Now, as to what's happened since they came, well, I suspect you know more about that than I do." He paused and gave her a frank look. "You still have your heart set on him, I take it? Nothing has changed?"

Elizabeth looked thoughtful. "No, nothing has changed," she said, "although I sometimes wonder if I don't have more hair than gumption."

She remained silent for a moment, wondering if she was destined to be the biggest fool of all time for loving Tavis the way she did. To get her mind off that, she said, "I wonder why Tavis wasn't interested in building ships like his brother and uncle. What made him decide to design them?"

"It's hard to explain why a man does what he does. Why did I captain a whaler instead of a nice clipper ship?" Asa took a drink of his tea, then looked at Elizabeth with a twinkle in his eye. "Course, if I were to hazard a guess, I'd say I suspect it might have something to do with the fact that Tavis Mackinnon gets seasick."

At that, Elizabeth almost dropped her teacup. "Seasick?" she said, but the word had barely left her mouth when something about it rang familiar. She mulled that over for a minute, seeming to remember her father saying something like that a long time ago—before she went to Boston. "I can't believe a man like Tavis would get seasick. He's very robust and strong."

Asa laughed. "Well, that just goes to show you that a man's stomach can be of a different constitution than the rest of him."

"Have you ever seen a ship Tavis designed . . . one that was built?"

"Why? Are you just curious, or did you think it might sink?"

Elizabeth smiled. "Just curious."

"I've seen one or two. From what I hear and what I read, it would seem the lad has built quite a name for himself. Some folks think of him as being right up there with Donald McKay. I've always heard the Scots had a knack for mixing a dreamer's vision with an engineer's practicality—and since they are both Scots, well . . . it stands to reason."

"You still consider Tavis a Scot, when he was born in America?"

"Well, he's American by all practical standards, you understand, but it's been my impression—after having worked with a good many Scots over the years—that there is something about their blood that seems to withstand diluting. If you ask me, I'd say Tavis Mackinnon is as Scottish as smoked salmon."

"Hmmmm," Elizabeth said. "I've heard the Scots were opportunists—a prideful, poor, prejudiced people prone to resist even when common sense says give in. Maybe that's why Tavis is so stubborn. . . . He comes by it naturally."

With that, Asa threw back his white head and laughed.

"Don't laugh, Grandpa," she said. "I'd wager Tavis Mackinnon is successful not because he was an opportunist, but because he's too *stubborn* to build a ship that would sink."

CHAPTER
❧ SEVEN ❧

Tavis Mackinnon might not be too stubborn to build up a ship that would sink, but he was too stubborn to give up on something he believed in. For several months now he had been working on the plans for a new type of vessel, something that had never been done before—a ship with an iron hull.

Until now, ships had always been of wooden construction, but Tavis, being a bit of an inventor as well as an architect, was working on a new idea—a design for a ship made of oak planks to be covered with iron armor. A ship that could not be sunk with standard cannons.

Several years ago he had his first visions of a golden age at sea; a golden age that would include, not only steam-powered ships, but those made of iron.

His imagination fired by his inventiveness and his love for ship design, Tavis had spent the last three years perfecting his original idea, transforming it from a mist-shrouded fancy into a solid concept, from which emerged a complete set of plans. Like his fellow ship-building Scotsmen in Glasgow, Tavis paid canny attention to detail—something he was becoming quite famous for.

He began work on this new concept soon after he had completed the plans for a ship that would far exceed the famous *Britannia* in character, speed, and safety. With a Scotsman's eye for frugality, he had devised a number of features that would keep the price of construction down, and with some ships now costing over three hundred thousand dollars, this was a godsend. The ship was under construction now, but Tavis rarely thought of it anymore. He was too obsessed with his idea for an ironclad.

"How are the plans on that new design of yours coming along?" Nathaniel asked him one afternoon when he stopped by Tavis's office.

Tavis and his draftsman, a young Scot by the name of Robert McNabb, stood over the drafting table, discussing modifications that might boost the ship's speed. Tavis turned around and waved Nathaniel inside. "Come here, Nathan, and I'll show you."

Nathaniel, with his customary jovial disposition, sauntered to Tavis's side, in a mood to do a little ribbing, and apparently thinking this was the perfect time. After studying the designs for a moment and listening as Tavis talked, telling him of his plans to install ram and slanting casemates made from railroad track over thick oak backing, it was obvious Nathaniel was highly impressed.

"You're telling me that cannon-fire won't penetrate the iron covering?"

"Yes—if we use two-inch iron plating. Right now the navy is using eleven-inch cannons that fire fifteen pounds of powder. It would take a gun capable of firing at least thirty pounds of powder to put a hole in two inches of iron plate."

"How do you know?"

Tavis grinned. "Because I've tested it," he said.

"My God! Where?" Nathaniel asked.

"On the other side of the island."

"I thought you were keeping this a secret."

"I am."

"And no one heard you firing fifteen pounds of powder?"

"Thirty pounds."

"Thirty pounds of powder from a cannon and no one heard you? I don't believe it."

"No one heard it. At least not the night I fired it, they didn't," Tavis said.

"What night was that?"

"Remember that storm we had a couple of weeks back?"

"The big one with all the lightning and—"

"Cannon-fire," Tavis interjected.

"Well, I'll be damned," Nathaniel said, then he threw back his head and laughed. As abruptly as he started, he stopped. "Wait a minute," he said. "I thought you said the navy fired fifteen pounds of powder from eleven-inch cannons."

"They do."

"Then where did you get a cannon to fire thirty pounds?"

"I didn't. I used one of the eleven-inch cannons."

"My God! It could have blown up in your face. You might have been killed."

"But I wasn't," Tavis said, "and now I know it takes thirty pounds of powder to penetrate two inches of iron."

"Tavis, you're not sane. Sane people don't go around doing the things you do."

"And sane people never make any discoveries, either."

"Hang discoveries," Nathaniel said.

Tavis laughed and began rolling up his plans. "That, my friend, is why you are a banker."

"Why? Because I'm sane?"

It was Tavis's turn to throw back his head and laugh. Nathaniel clapped him on the back. "Come on, let's go home. I'll walk with you."

The two of them started off, accompanied by the lonely ringing of a buoy bell that marked the dangerous sandbars hidden in the shoals. They left the wharf area and walked down Main Street, passing the church, the chatter of women and shrieking of children drowning out the sound of buoys and gulls. Glancing to his left, Tavis saw a group of people working in the cemetery.

"Spring cleaning in the graveyard," Nathaniel said. "I wonder what those old biddies would do if one of them unearthed a bone or two."

"Clear out, more than likely," Tavis said.

Nathaniel laughed. "Might be worth burying one out there, just to see how fast they could move," he said, and they both laughed.

They had paused in their speculations beside the wrought-iron fence that encircled the cemetery. Giving Tavis the elbow, Nathaniel said, "Come on. This place gives me the jitters."

But Tavis was reluctant to go. He had seen something that caught and held his attention. Far over in the corner, beneath the squat shape of a fruit tree, he had caught a glimpse of bright golden hair—just a flash of it before the woman twisted it into a coil and covered it with a drab gray bonnet. He hadn't gotten more than a glimpse, but it was enough. There was only one woman he knew of who had hair that color. He looked around the cemetery, seeing only the elderly, the matronly, nothing but widows, spinsters, and married ladies. What was a woman like Elizabeth Robinson doing here?

His curiosity aroused, he turned to Nathaniel. "You go on. I'm going to mosey around here for a spell."

Nathaniel looked at him in that dazed way a man looks when he surfaces after a long dive and doesn't at first connect to the world above. Then he shrugged and said, "Okay. I'll be seeing you."

"Right," Tavis said.

After a few steps, Nathaniel stopped and said, "Are you coming to the Colemans' tonight?"

Tavis was looking off. "Perhaps," was all he said.

Nathaniel followed the line of Tavis's gaze. Seeing nothing but a bunch of somberly clad women, he shrugged and rammed his hands deep into his pockets. A moment later he walked off.

As soon as he departed, Tavis hopped the fence and made his way toward the fruit tree in the back corner of the cemetery, nodding to a few women who paused to stare.

He wondered what he was doing, why he was even bothering to seek her out. He reminded himself of what a pest she had been in the past. Did he want to start up all that trouble again? Then he remembered the way she had looked at the party that night, and he grinned. None of it made much sense, of course, but when had anything he did made sense?

He found her down on her knees in an isolated place where only one marker stood. The headstone was lichen-covered, but it wasn't as old as some of the others, making it easy to read the name. Patience Robinson.

There was no date, no other words, but somehow he figured it was the grave of her mother. He stood quietly behind her, watching the slim, white hands that were bare and pulling weeds. She seemed very alone to him, isolated in a family who did not understand her. He rarely had thoughts such as this about women, and even as he watched her, he wondered what in the hell he was doing here. It was insanity—pure, simple insanity—to think the kind of thoughts he was thinking. Yet the insanity of it seemed to wind around the attraction he felt toward her, forming a single strand of inevitable probability.

He pulled his mind away from that to wonder why she didn't cover her hands. He didn't have time to think about it further, for she must have sensed someone was looking at her and she turned around. Her startled gaze found him.

He came closer, then stopped. Her eyes widened and her mouth dropped open. His first impulse was to throw caution to the wind and pull her into his arms and to kiss that startled mouth before she had a chance to close it. The thought amused him, for he wondered how long it would take for the rest of the women to clear out if he did.

His gaze traveled over her, then came back to rest upon her face. She looked up at him, and what he saw surprised him. There weren't many times when he had looked at her and not seen mischief in her eyes. For a moment he thought she was going to say something. When she didn't, he asked, "Need any help?"

"No ... That is, I'm almost finished," she said.

She was kneeling with her skirts billowed around her,

her cape a gray shadow over the green grass, a small wooden crate with a handle at her side that contained a spade, a few bedding plants, a pair of unused gloves. His gaze traveled past her, over the grassy mound, taking in the neatness of it, seeing the pansies that had been planted next to the marble headstone. "It's a nice headstone. Your mother?"

She nodded. "Yes." She offered no further explanation, nothing about her mother's death, or when, or how young she was when it happened. "My father had the stone made in Boston."

"Do you come here often?"

She looked around her. "This is my first spring cleaning since my return. I hope to come at least once a month . . . just to keep the weeds away."

He looked around the cemetery, seeing some of the women had left. "I've never understood why the Quakers won't allow a stone to mark a grave."

"I would have marked hers even if I was a Quaker."

"It's a good thing you aren't a Quaker, then. You would have been kicked out if you did."

She shrugged. "I doubt it would surprise anyone."

He smiled at that, thinking he had never heard anyone accuse her of being timid, yet he was thinking now that she was just that. He took another step closer, then dropped down to sit on his haunches beside her. When he looked up, his gaze seemed to hold her, for she was still and quiet, and he couldn't help wondering if she was frightened.

He pushed her bonnet back, noticing the way the ribbon caught at her throat. Before she could react, he picked up her hand, holding it in his as he turned it this way and that, looking it over, taking in the smudges, the dirt under her nails, the red welt of a scratch. She tried to pull her hand back, but he held it fast.

"You should wear your gloves," he said. Then bringing her hand up to his lips, he kissed it.

She trembled.

"Are you cold?" he asked.

"No," she said, extracting her hand from his.

"What about the gloves?" he asked, his gaze going to the box where the gloves lay, unused.

"I . . . I can't work in them. I need to feel the dirt, the grass, in order to work it. Wearing gloves is like going outside with a hatbox over your head."

He laughed at the imagery.

"Why are you here?"

He smiled. "Do you really want to know?"

She nodded, then looked away, her hands buried in her skirt.

"Why do you think I came?"

Her eyes were full of answers. "I don't know."

"Obviously it was to be near you."

"Why?"

"Why not?"

"I . . ." She paused, as if searching for something to say.

"I never would have pegged you for someone shy."

"I'm not . . . usually."

"Only around me?"

"It would seem so."

"I wonder why that is."

She laughed, feeling more at ease. "Because you, of all people, know all my ridiculous secrets, my asinine past."

"All your escapades and your capers? Is that what you mean?"

She nodded. "Although I think 'idiocy' would be a better word."

He laughed, fighting back the impulse to drag her into his arms and kiss her until she felt as light-headed as he. Curiosity about her was growing and swelling inside him. She was such an intriguing creature, so different from the young girl he knew before. She was part lady, part siren, part temptress, and all woman. A slow rising warmth suffused him, and he felt a tinge of regret for the conscience that allowed him to pursue her without any deep, amorous feeling, when he knew how she had always felt for him, and knew, too, that it would be best if he left her alone. But when had wisdom ever been an important part of seduction?

"You seem to have put the past behind you," he said at last. "Does that mean you've retired, then?"

She smiled, and looked at him, feeling the same intense shock that she always felt. The gray-blue gaze that stared back at her was warm and so inviting, as enticing as Maxcy's Pond on a hot summer day. His body was hunched over, his hands dangling down between his knees in a relaxed, almost lazy way. The blue in his shirt seemed to steal color from the sky overhead, while the sun left a molten blessing on the black hair that covered his head. How casual he seemed, how at ease, as if this were the sort of thing he did every day, while she was nothing but a tongue-tied, trembling bundle of nerves.

"I suppose it does," she said at last.

"Why?" His blue eyes were inquiring, his head tilted slightly to the left. She couldn't help wondering at his purpose, at the reason he asked so many questions.

"I don't know. Perhaps I outgrew it, like I did my

pinafores." She paused a moment, then said, "Now it's your turn. Why are you here?"

He smiled. "Because you are obviously the most beautiful woman in Nantucket."

She stared at him for a moment, then she put out one hand, and catching him on the shoulder, she pushed, knocking him into a backward sprawl. He was never certain if her laughter was from what he said or the ridiculous picture he made, lying spread-eagled before her.

He looked at her and decided it was the latter, for she seemed to have no inkling of just how lovely she really was, or if she did, it did not matter to her. It simply wasn't part of her value system. It was obvious now, from the way she laughed, that she thought he was teasing her. He knew also that she did not fully understand the real purpose for his interest in her, and more than likely would not understand it, unless he pushed her back on the grass and covered her body with his.

He rolled over and came to a sitting position. "Did no one ever tell you that you were beautiful?"

"A time or two, but aside from the compliment, it has little value. You can't eat it, and it isn't something you can take to the bank."

He realized then that they came from entirely different worlds, that hers was, like that of most people on this island, a practical one, not given to flowery imagery and poetic rapture.

"Has anyone ever kissed you . . . besides me?"

He could see immediately that his words had shocked her, and he hoped she was remembering that day by the pond when he had kissed her.

"That is none of your business."

"Well? What is the answer, my business or not?"

"I've been kissed, yes. More than once."

"Did you enjoy it?"

She stared at him for a long time. A very long time. Then her eyes lowered and she looked down, her hands coming up to pull her cloak together in front of her. Her gaze turned hard, glaring. "As a matter of fact, I did."

A moment later, she came to her feet, as quick and graceful as a doe. "As another matter of fact, this conversation is closed."

He followed her, coming to his feet in time to hear her say, "Good afternoon, Mr. Mackinnon."

He watched her lean over and shakily snatch up her box. He had the feeling more than just her hands were trembling.

He was still looking at her, wondering what she was going to do, when she walked off.

"Elizabeth?"

She kept on walking, making it necessary for him to lope in order to catch up with her. "Good day, Mrs. Coleman. Good afternoon, Mrs. Starbuck. Yes, I believe I'll call it a day, Mrs. Husey. Of course I'll come back tomorrow, Mrs. Longworth," she said, nodding at each woman in turn, and shutting him out completely.

She continued to ignore him until they reached the gate, where she turned hot eyes upon him and hissed, "Will you leave me alone?"

He followed her through the gate and down the street. When they reached the corner, she stopped. "Leave me be," she said.

"And if I can't?"

"They have a word for such as you."

He raised a brow. "Oh? And what word is that?"

"Opportunist," she said, "or obnoxious." Then turning, she left him standing there as she ran across the street.

CHAPTER
❧ EIGHT ❧

On December 20, 1860, Abraham Lincoln was elected president. Following his election—and because he ran on an antislavery platform—South Carolina seceded from the union. Mississippi, Florida, Alabama, Georgia, Louisiana, and Texas followed suit. The country was in a state of unrest now, and under the constant threat of war. Tavis knew the value of the plans for his iron-hulled ship and he tried to keep it a secret, but as secret things often do, word of his revolutionary design soon leaked out. It wasn't long before he was contacted—by agents from the North as well as the South—within weeks of each other.

And therein lay his problem.

While it was Tavis's dream to see his ship built, his feelings of loyalty were mixed. Texas was his home state, and since Texas had seceded, he felt a certain amount of loyalty toward it and the South in general. His brother Alexander still lived in Texas with his wife Katherine and their family. Tavis had no way of knowing what Alex would do if war broke out, but he had a feeling that if it came to the point of needing men, Alex would be one of the first to answer the call.

On the other hand, Nicholas and Tavis had lived in Nantucket for fifteen years, and while Nick and his wife, Tibbie, were, like him, native Texans, the North was now their home. His feelings were divided, and consequently his loyalties. He could not give to one side without hurting the other. He wanted to see this ship built, but not at the cost of lives. Tavis prayed to God he would never have to choose one side over the other. It was his hope to remain neutral.

That hope was never to be, for about the time Tavis was thinking about going to England to show his plans to the English navy, the plans were stolen. Like it or not, Tavis was drawn into the war.

It was uncanny how he had worked all night that fateful day, stopping only when the first golden rays of sun began to creep over the harbor that fanned out beneath the window of his office.

Finding himself weary and exhausted, he stretched and looked out the window, seeing the first rosy-gray hint of morning on the horizon. He hadn't realized until that moment that he had worked straight through the night. Giving his back a slow twist to remove the kinks, he rolled the plans for his ironclad up and placed them in the oiled pouch he always kept them in, storing them in a locked, fire-resistant cabinet.

Once that was done, he turned out the lights, then left for home. He made it halfway down the block before he remembered he had left the keys to his house lying beside the coffee cup on his drafting table.

He returned to his office and opened the door. He started to go inside, then paused. Something was wrong. He knew it the moment he heard the door creak open.

Far across the room, a little, shifty-eyed fellow—the kind who often linger around the docks—was rising from the locked cabinet.

"What the   " Tavis said, his next words frozen in the cold shiver of fear that rippled down his spine. The man stood and turned fully toward him then, a cold smile settling across his hard mouth. *Criminal* was written all over him, from the way he tried to distract Tavis with his grin, to the black eyes that knew no fear. Then Tavis saw it. The oiled pouch in the man's hand. For a moment Tavis just stood there, his gaze locked on the oiled pouch. Then his mind registered, with terrible clarity, just what was happening. He raised his eyes from the oiled pouch to the thief. Then, with a bellow of rage, he blindly charged into the room

The moment Tavis charged, the man whipped out a knife and threw it. Tavis ducked, mere seconds before it would have imbedded itself to the hilt in his chest. While the handle of the knife still vibrated from the wall behind him, the man turned and climbed out an open window, onto the roof, and disappeared.

In a flash Tavis was after him, going out the window, running across the sharply pitched roof, jumping down on a rain barrel, and then sprinting down the wharf, his gaze never leaving the shadowy figure that raced ahead of him.

At the end of the wharf, the man leaped onto a small skiff, where two men waited to row him farther out, to where a sleek ketch waited.

Desperate, Tavis searched for a likely prospect—anything seaworthy enough for him to give chase. His legs were already in motion by the time it registered in his mind that there was one small sloop anchored a few yards from the wharf, one that looked both seaworthy and small enough for him to sail alone. Without wasting a moment, Tavis leaped into a dinghy and rowed himself out to the sloop. A few minutes later, he was aboard and pulling up anchor.

With the anchor hoisted, the sloop gained momentary sternway. Now, Tavis was not your typical sailor, and certainly no lover of the sea. Ships, he knew and loved, and he understood the mechanics of sailing, but he had, for all practical purposes, never done much sailing due to his propensity for seasickness. Thankfully, understanding the mechanics of sailing, and actually sailing, were two different things.

Without giving much thought to what he was about, he brought the wheel hard over and began working the halyard lines. After a few seconds, he heard the snapping pop of the sail as it filled with wind. In a moment she was sheeted home and lying gently over as she slipped forward through the water, rudder balanced against sail pressure.

Only then did he begin to relax, settling back and listening to the rhythmic slap of water against the bow as the small sloop headed for open water through the patchy clumps of early morning fog stubbornly lingering along the surface of the water.

When he rounded the sandbar that guarded Nantucket Harbor, the ketch he followed was far ahead. By the time he reached open sea, Tavis realized immediately that he wasn't making much headway. He looked back, seeing Nantucket was no more than a thin brown strip on the horizon. All about him lay nothing but shimmering swells of gray-green water. Above him, the sails were full of wind; ahead, the bow dipped and rose. It was only his stomach that caused him grave misgivings of what he was about. Feeling weaker by the minute, he gripped the helm and leaned against it as he fought the dizziness.

His head was spinning with seasickness and dizzy spells and the throbbing beginnings of a severe headache. Warring with his insurgent stomach, he kept his eye on the sails of the ketch, grimly gripping the wheel. He was shivering now, groaning as the wind picked up and began whipping around him. The sloop heaved and corkscrewed, rising up, then sinking down. His stomach heaved. His face was cold with perspiration. He swallowed hard against it. It was no use. He knew it. He was going to be sick—and soon.

By now his seasickness had struck full force, and feeling the first queasy ripples of nausea, he turned away, clinging to the railing. Leaning his head over, he vomited in the foaming swells parted by the bow. Finding no comfort, he dropped down, groaning and lowering his head between his legs, leaving the sails to luff under the strong gusting of the wind. Unable to do more than think about the unmanned wheel, he had never known such misery. With another miserable groan, he raised his head to see the mainsail flapping and the jib whipping about.

And if that wasn't enough, the door to the quarters below opened abruptly and a sleep-tousled blond head poked out.

Tavis groaned. What could be more disagreeable than to find himself sick and alone at sea, with none other than the torment of his life, Lizzie Robinson, on board? He would have cursed at the sight of his worst nightmare coming to real life, but he was too sick. All he could do was hang his head over the side and heave.

He wanted nothing more than to be alone, to vomit in sick privacy—anywhere but trembling weakly beneath the gaze of this woman. He vomited again, then leaned against the railing, moaning and blaspheming. Past experience told him all would be well with him in a day or two, that by then the seasickness would pass, and he would be left with only the presence of Lizzie Robinson to torment him.

Overhead the timbers creaked, the sails flapped, the sea rose and fell, everything blending into a nightmare of sounds as he heard her exclaim: "Good God! What are you doing? Are you trying to kill us both?"

Unable to answer her, he pulled himself up, clinging weak and shuddering to the rail as he vomited once again into the churning foam of the sea.

CHAPTER
❧ NINE ❧

If the cold slap of mist-laden fog driven against her face by the wind hadn't jerked her fully out of her sleepy state, the sight of Tavis Mackinnon losing his insides over the side of her sloop would have.

As it was, Elizabeth didn't have much time to think about her surprise at seeing Tavis, for the sound of a luffed and flapping sail made her forget all about him and how he had come to be on her sloop.

Giving her attention to the mess he had made of everything, she secured the helm, then trimmed sail, slacking off a bit to relieve pressure. She was about to bring the sloop about when Tavis, leaning on the railing and looking green-faced, turned his head and said weakly, "Follow that ketch."

The Robinson blood boiled over. Circumstances of past years had so shaped themselves that this brute felt he had a right to commandeer her vessel and give her orders. Who did he think he was? Another Napoleon?

She sent him a look that said what she thought of him and his request.

"Listen to me, dammit! This is important. Whatever you do, don't let it out of your sight."

She stiffened a little at that, but she had no thought of weakening. You could push a Robinson just so far. "Now, you listen to me, Tavis Mackinnon. If you think—"

"I'm sick as a dog or I wouldn't ask it of you. Just do it," he said as he closed his eyes, hanging his head over the side and retching again.

Follow that ketch. A ghastly vision of doing as he asked and finding herself sailing around the Atlantic with a dead man on board rose up in front of her. Then she thought about not doing as he asked, imagining the fury and anger he would turn upon her when they returned to port and he got over his sickness.

Follow that ketch? This was no ordinary request, but then, this was no ordinary man making it. This was Tavis. And he actually wanted her to sail away with him—and that meant there would be no one but the two of them on board. An opportunity is what it was. One she had waited half her life for.

Out of the confusion of her mind, she could almost hear Aunt Phoebe's voice urging her to be, above all things, practical. *Elizabeth, don't be stupid. If Heaven drops a fig, open your mouth.*

Opportunity was ever a strong seducer.

But at the same time, Robinsons were ever honest with themselves. True, Tavis was playing the part of the pirate, appropriating her sloop for his own personal use, and certainly not out of any desire to be near her. Still, she was thinking it might be worth the bother of knowing the way of it, in return for the chance to be with him and in such close circumstances. The more she thought about it, the more she was convinced that the great trick in life is to be dead certain what you want and to not let anyone or anything set you on another course. Right now she was entertaining visions that were tantamount to certainty. Stratagems were always allowed in love and war.

Elizabeth looked at him. His eyes were still closed, and she wondered what he was really doing here, on her sloop—but he didn't look like he was up to a thorough grilling right now, so she decided to let the questions wait.

He was wearing brown cord trousers and a dark blue seaman's coat, his hair was windblown, his face pale and worried. When he opened his eyes to look at her, she felt isolated and cut off from him, and she knew it was because she had been so defiant and hesitant to do as he asked. She felt uneasy, yet he continued to look at her with that supercilious gaze that had always irritated the very life out of her—the same gaze that had, more than once, made her react by doing idiotic things that got her ignored by Nantucket's right-minded.

After staring at her for a moment as if he were thinking that she had become worse as an adult than she had been as a child, he said, "Are you going to help me or not?"

"I might, *if* you tell me why it's so important to you."

He groaned, and for a moment she thought he would be sick again. "I'm too ill now," he said. "I'll explain it all in detail later. Can't you trust me in this?"

In exasperation she was about to point her sloop toward Nantucket, when a strange, weary yearning, a dissatisfaction, seemed to rise within her, asserting itself in a way that made her think of a woman unfulfilled, as one who marries but never has a child. She could return to Nantucket and her dull, dreary life there, or she could do as he asked and follow the call of the unknown, the lure of adventure. Here was a golden opportunity, and one she could not pass up.

It was the fear of nothingness—an empty life that went on and on and on, just as Aunt Phoebe's life had done—that made her reconsider. It was a visionary experience, one that hit her and hit her hard.

She shrugged, holding the sloop on a steady course, then shook her head and spoke to the clouds overhead. "When did I ever show good judgment?" she said, then added, turning to look at him, "If you don't want to turn around and go back—as sick as you are—then it must be terribly important."

"It is important," he said, finishing with a groan, "or I wouldn't ask it of you. Now, will you keep on the tail of that ketch?"

"As long as you keep your promise and tell me why later," she said.

He nodded and, closing his eyes, turned his head away.

There was still a lot of mystery here that needed to be addressed, though she would have to confess that she was quite pleased with the manner in which she had conducted herself during this clash of wills. There had been a time, certainly, when the sudden appearance of Tavis Mackinnon asking anything of her would have been enough to set her heart beating triple-time. But now she had passed through the furnace, and just the sight of him no longer filled her with the desire to do something idiotic. Truly, if she had learned anything, she had learned that a woman who gazes at stars is apt to step in a puddle on the road.

Perhaps she would never know just what it was, precisely, that made her squint her eyes and search the horizon for the sight of sails—and once locating them, choose to follow. Maybe it was the sight of Tavis doubled over with seasickness. Or simply the sight of

Tavis, period. And then, just maybe it was the desperation she sensed in his voice, the emptiness she felt inside herself.

It was later in the afternoon, when the wind had died, that she went below and found a soft cloth and, wetting it, placed it across the back of Tavis's neck. They had sailed most of the day, having kept in the shadow of the ketch. Several hours ago, she had managed to get him below and into her cot. As she looked at him now, he didn't seem any better than he had earlier. She dampened the cloth again, ignoring his blustery words about trying to freeze him to death as she did.

"My, you're certainly testy for someone who looks as green as a fish bladder."

He groaned at her choice of words. "Thank you for the colorful comparison. If I wasn't already puking my guts out, that would certainly do the trick." He didn't say anything else, for at that moment he rolled over onto his side and began to heave, which soon became spasms of retching.

When the heaving subsided, he rolled onto his back and said weakly, "I've never felt so sick. Has anyone ever died from this?"

"I don't think so. Perhaps you could be the first."

"I won't be that lucky," he said. "But if I had a choice, I'd rather go over the side. It's quicker."

"It would serve you right if I did toss you over the side. Of all the bounders . . . I would have never suspected you," she said with much fervor, then shook her head. "I mean, who would have thought it . . . Tavis Mackinnon stealing a sloop? I must say, I am quite surprised."

He shuddered and said, "My mouth is so dry, I feel like I've been eating salt. Could I have some water?"

"No. You'd only throw it up again. It's best to wait until the retching stops."

"You sound awfully optimistic."

"I believe in keeping to the snug side of the ship."

He closed his eyes. She stood over him for a moment, then turning, she climbed up to the deck.

An hour later, he also made his way topside. Apparently he had been thinking about what she had said earlier.

"I wasn't trying to steal anything," he said, coming toward her. "And if I was going to steal a sloop, believe me, it wouldn't have been yours."

She didn't say anything, for at that moment the little color that remained in his cheeks drained away and his face took on a greenish cast. Tavis lunged for the side of the sloop and hung his head over.

"Maybe you should have stayed below."

"I feel worse down there," he said. For the next several minutes he ignored her.

"Are you feeling better?"

"Every time we crest a wave I feel better. Every time we drop between the swells I feel like shit. Where are we? Have you lost sight of the ketch?"

She smiled at his frankness. If she hadn't had so many brothers, her tender ears might have been offended by such talk.

Elizabeth looked out over the water where what remained of the lifting fog shimmered like intermittent puffs of fine gray gunpowder, just making out through the clearing patches of it the sleek, glossy lines of a ketch under full sail. "No, I haven't lost sight of her, although I'll probably be asking myself for the rest of my life why I got involved in this idiocy."

"Why did you?"

"I've always been a woman of impulse and hot-blooded impetuosity. *You* should know that."

"Yes, of all people, *I* should."

She never realized more than at that moment just how far apart they really were. The good Lord knew how much she still loved him, but Tavis Mackinnon's face—when it regarded her—reminded her of a piercing-eyed pirate. The very sight of him always had her doing the outrageous in his presence.

She asked herself why she was doing it again. With a sigh, she turned her gaze toward the ketch. "She's fast and well manned," she said, "with plenty of sail," then giving Tavis a fast glance, she added, "We may be able to gain a little on her, but we won't be able to overtake her."

"I don't care if we overtake her or not," he said, his face turning ashen, "just don't lose sight of her. Whatever you do, keep her in your sight."

Tavis pulled his head back and, turning, dropped down on his haunches, closing his eyes and leaning his head back to rest against the gently curved side of the sloop. "I've never felt so sick in my life."

"Are you sick enough to turn back now, or do you still insist on following her?"

"If you have the ability and the inclination, then do, by all means, follow her. My whole future is at stake."

She gave him a startled look and he sighed, as if preparing himself for a barrage of questions. They never came. For a moment she thought his eyes were going to close, but he continued to look at her in a way that made her conscious of her appearance.

She was wearing her brothers' clothes, an old pair of pants and sweater—things she had thrown on in haste earlier, when she awoke and realized the sloop was moving. She had rushed up on deck at that moment—without so much as brushing her hair. Now she could well imagine how yesterday's braid must look, scraggly and loosely looped at the back of her head.

Elizabeth pushed a few errant hairs out of her face and, giving the mainsail a quick and thorough look, turned her attention to the wheel, bringing the sloop about. Reaching across the wind now, wind abeam, with the mainsail extending out from the sloop at a 45° angle to their direction, she lined the bow up with the ketch in the distance.

At the change in direction, the mainsail grew slack, then bellied out with a rustling snap and the jib filled. Picking up speed, the *Wildest Dreams* began dancing over the waves, and like a cradle, rocked Tavis Mackinnon blissfully to sleep.

Elizabeth kept her eye on the ketch, fearing that Tavis might wake up and find her reneging on her promise. From time to time she would steal a glance at him, finding him still asleep, his position unchanged, then her mind would wander and she would find herself wondering again. *Just why is following that ketch so blasted important?* Several times she came close to waking him so he could go below, but he seemed to be sleeping soundly, and even sleeping on deck was preferable to heaving over the side—something she feared he might start doing again if he woke up. Besides, he did say he felt worse when he was below. She left him be, partly so he could rest, and partly so she could look at him.

His skin was only lightly browned by the sun, an immediate sign to any Nantucketer that he was not a man of the sea. Her gaze dropped to his hands, one lying limp at his side, the other resting across his stomach.

They were smooth and uncallused—another sign that he was no sailor. They were beautiful hands, though, well shaped, with long, tapering fingers that seemed to suggest both strength and sensitivity. As she watched, his body jerked and the fingers of his hand closed, clenching violently before he relaxed. She found her thoughts not so much on his hands now, but on what it would feel like to have them touch her.

The thought of that was like a magnet in her breast. She wanted him.

She wanted to see if his skin was as smooth and warm as she had imagined it, or if it was truly the scent of the sea that was in his hair. She wanted to look at him, to touch him, to stir the indifferent look in his eyes to one of fire.

Last night she had dreamed he was back again, the center of her life, and he was. She swore she would never fall for him again, but when would fools like her ever win? She had always known one look from him would bring her to her knees. And now here she was, as much in love with him as ever, knowing she had long sailed past the point of no return. Would she always be destined for waiting and watching, praying for some sign from him?

"Do you have any idea how much I love you?" she whispered, looking at him, then she closed her eyes against his pull. Everything about her was quiet except for the faint rush of wind through the sails overhead.

"No," she whispered. "I don't think you do."

The clouds were gone and the sun was full out now, making the sails on the ketch easy to see. She leaned her head back, basking in the warmth of the afternoon sun, so welcome now after the morning's chill. She always found peace here, aboard her sloop and feeling at one with the sea, but today she felt it even more. There was a curious stillness within her soul that made her wonder. It was as if the universe was at peace with itself, a sense that God was in His heaven and that all was right with the world. Perhaps that was because of the tranquillity she always felt whenever she sailed, the oneness she felt with the sea.

In spite of her concentration on the ketch, Elizabeth was acutely aware of him, for she had felt his gaze upon her for some time now. Unable to stop herself, she stole a glance in his direction.

He was watching her intently. The way his eyes seemed to roam leisurely over her—it left her shivering and uncertain. He had known her for years and had never given her more than an irritated glance, save for that day at the pond . . . and now. So why the sudden change? Perhaps it was the sight of her in her brothers' clothes—Stephen's brown whipcord britches, Abel's cable-knit sweater, and the too large jacket she had borrowed from Drake's trunk—that made him stare so, and then again, perhaps it was not.

She felt the sun's heat now and removed Drake's jacket. When she glanced back at Tavis, his eyes seemed to hold hers, as if he was searching for the trail of her thoughts. Then, afraid he might really be able to read them, she turned her head away, putting her mind back to what she was doing, leaving him to look or not look.

She did not glance at him again, but she knew he watched her in silence for a while, and she wondered if he was aware of her odd quietness, the serious tone of her thoughts. Was he remembering the way she had looked when she caught him staring at her, the way her eyes seemed to say she was afraid of him—not of the strange mission he had given her, or even the fact that they had taken her small sloop so far out to sea, but of him?

How odd it all was, for here she had spent half her life chasing him, and now that she had him aboard her sloop and entirely at her mercy, she did not know what to do with him. She felt as awkward and tongue-tied as a schoolgirl, wanting desperately to be near him, terrified he might know how much she still cared.

Oh, she was afraid of him, all right, this man who still held her heart.

She heard him stir and glanced back in surprise as she watched him struggle to a sitting position. When their gazes locked, she fought for something to say. "Perhaps you should stay where you are . . . at least until the nausea passes."

He shrugged. "I'm feeling a little better," he said, and leaned back, glancing around the deck as if it were the first time he had seen it. "You said the sloop is yours?" he asked.

"Yes. A birthday gift from my brothers after I returned from Boston."

"What were you doing aboard at such an early hour?"

"I spent the night."

He looked surprised, then his mouth twisted in a smile. "Alone?" he asked.

The Robinson blood boiled again. She knew what sordid thoughts he was thinking, and it angered her, making her voice harsher than she would have liked. She did not want him to know he got under her skin. "I was with Matt," she said. "He is, in case you've forgotten, my brother."

"I know who Matt is. In case you've forgotten, I know all your brothers."

Hot determined eyes met his cool, determined ones. *Stalemate,* a voice inside her head said. She wondered if anyone ever got the best of Tavis.

Not often, the same voice said. Looking away and softening her tone, she went on to explain, "The sloop wasn't new when they bought it, so they gave it to me with a promise of brotherly help in refurbishing the interior and a scraped, freshly painted hull. They finished working on her last week. For the past two days I've been aboard, putting things away and stocking it for a voyage."

"What happened to Matt?"

"He left early this morning to round up more supplies. Before he left, he said he'd be back before lunch."

"Not knowing he'd be in for a surprise."

"He will be worried about me. All of my family will be."

"I know, and for that, I'm sorry."

She didn't say anything else.

"Why were you stocking so many supplies? Were you planning a trip?"

She shook her head. "No, but one can never tell when the opportunity will arise. Take you, for instance. I would have never dreamed you would commandeer my boat and my services . . . as captain and crew," she hastily added, fearing the implications of her words.

He grimaced, as if warring with his insurgent stomach. "Necessity often pushes one to strange limits. The fact of what has happened here is no less strange to me. To the contrary . . ."

He did not get to finish, for another dizzying wave staggered him and churned his stomach. Climbing weakly to his feet, he barely got his head over the side in time. This time it was sheer agony to vomit, for there was nothing left in his stomach. So he stood there, draped like a fallen flag over the railing, heaving his guts out and wishing any other human in the world besides her were there to witness it.

"Why don't you go back below. Maybe this time you'll feel better lying in the cot rather than standing up here."

He was about to decline the offer until his illness finally drove him below. Once there, he staggered toward her cot and fell across it.

He lay there for some time before he could muster the strength to lift his legs from the floor. Feeling weak and chilled, he struggled with the blankets, then pulled them up, closing his eyes with a sickly groan. Each motion of the sloop seemed acutely exaggerated, and he felt her every move as she sailed across the wind, the wooden beams creaking in unison.

He gritted his teeth and fixed his jaw each time his stomach lurched. He watched the lantern overhead sway, and after another bout of dry heaves, he pulled the blankets over his head. The bed was warm. Soothing. It smelled like a woman. For a moment the churning in his stomach eased.

He closed his eyes. He was in her bed. A woman's bed. For a moment he imagined her naked and lying next to him.

His penis stirred.

His stomach heaved.

He couldn't imagine Lizzie Robinson ever stirring anything but his anger, but she had. He was fully hard now. He cursed at the irony of it.

God may have a sense of humor, but Tavis didn't see a damn thing funny about this. If he hadn't felt so nauseated, he would have laughed at the almost idiotic absurdness of it all. Here he was, sick as a dog, heaving his guts out, with his prick stiff as a seaman's wooden leg over the likes of Lizzie Robinson. He closed his eyes and willed his mind to fight its way toward sleep. That, at least, was an escape.

While he slept, Elizabeth managed to close the distance between them and the ketch they chased. The sun was well past its zenith now, but still dancing across the water and warming her considerably.

Some time later, the darkness began to settle about her, and Elizabeth prayed the dim lights she tracked in the distance belonged to the ketch Tavis wanted so desperately to follow.

She wondered about that, trying to imagine what, or who, could be on that ketch, and why it was so important to him to follow it. Remembering the ghastly way he looked when he went below, she knew it would be a while yet before she could satisfy her curiosity. She wondered where the ketch was heading. A studying perusal of the stars overhead told her they were sailing southeast, and she wondered if Bermuda would be their final destination.

She put her coat on, then looked at the lights again, praying they belonged to the ketch. Only morning's light would tell her if she remained true to the task, or if, during the night, some other sloop or ketch had slipped, unnoticed, into her line of vision and drawn her away on a wild-goose chase.

She watched the sun rise over the water the next morning, and found herself wishing her grandfather was here to see it with her. He would find a poem or two as a testimony to the occasion before lapsing into stories about this sunrise or that, fondly recollecting days gone by and the years he spent captaining a whaler.

She closed her eyes, seeing her grandfather's face, whispering a faint "Thank you," telling him she understood now, for it was from him that she had come to understand and love the sea. She felt the trembling nerves of the sloop vibrate, and felt, too, the calluses of her grandfather's warm hands guiding hers upon the wheel. He was her grandfather, but he was also so much more. *Kindred spirits,* she thought.

She removed Drake's jacket and turned to set it down. When she turned back around, she was surprised to find Tavis standing before her.

"Good morning," she said. "How do you feel?" Her gaze swept hastily over him. "You look much better." She smiled then, and added, "Not quite so green."

"Green? Arrrghhh, don't mention that word," he said, looking out over the water and rubbing the stubble on his face. "As to the other," he said, turning back at her, "I feel like my mouth is stuffed with cotton and someone has been bowling with my head. My ribs feel like they're clattering together, and I'm as wobbly-legged as a newborn colt. Other than that, I suppose I feel fine. God, how does one get rid of this wretched taste?"

"There is some tooth powder below. You're welcome to try it."

He nodded. "I'll try anything," he said, but made no move to go below.

"Do you get seasick like that often?" she asked.

"No, because I don't go to sea often, but whenever I do, I get sick . . . every blessed time."

"For a while there, I thought you were at death's door."

"So did I."

She felt self-conscious under his gaze, at a loss for something to say. Nothing came to mind, save asking him why they were following the ketch in the first place. She opened her mouth to ask, but when she glanced up and saw the way he was looking at her, her words caught in her throat.

Her mind went blank.

Logic evaporated faster than the early morning mist in sunshine, leaving her dazed and somewhat confused. She had not imagined, ever, that the object of her adoration would look at her with such a gentle gaze. It went over her like warm hands. His caressing eyes held hers, never wavering. Her breathing grew shallow. Her heartbeat hammered in her throat. Still his gaze held hers, entranced, and shutting out the rest of the world.

It left her speechless and full of imaginings. Gone was her curiosity about the ketch. Gone was every rational thought. His vitality hit her like a cannon blast, setting fire to her imagination and heating up her pent-up desires. Lizzie felt a surge of longing so acute that for a moment she thought she, too, was succumbing to a bout of seasickness.

Her hands clutched the wheel in a death grip. He looked as if he could clearly see the turmoil going on inside her. For a brief moment she thought he might laugh . . . or kiss her. She closed her eyes, imagining the feel of his warm breath, the fire of his mouth as it touched hers. The woman in her greeted this with avid enthusiasm. The lady in her shied away.

She opened her eyes and gave her attention to the wheel now, catching a glimpse of the pristine white sails of the ketch they followed in the distance. She turned the wheel, feeling the rush of power beneath her hands.

"You hold the wheel like it's a part of you," he said.

She laughed. "It felt like a part of me last night," she said, drawing her shoulders together to ease the stiffness. "I found myself lifting my hands away from time to time, just to be certain I wasn't permanently attached to it."

He stepped toward her. "You must be exhausted. Why don't you go below? I'll take over the wheel now."

She felt embarrassed. "I didn't mean . . ."

"I know you didn't, but I'm feeling well enough to stand at the helm."

"I know you must be weak. Would you like anything to eat?"

He grimaced and said, "I don't think I'll be up to food for a while yet. I'll let you know when I feel I can handle it."

He looked at her and their gazes met. Together on this small sloop, their fates temporarily entwined, they both seemed uncomfortable with the shadowy unknown, the future and what it held in store.

They were like two strangers suddenly thrown together. The moment seemed to shimmer around them like a crimson spark, a brightness looking for a way to ignite and burn. And finding none, it would glisten for a brief moment and then go out, leaving nothing behind but a cold, empty darkness.

"Lizzie Robinson," he said softly, speaking her name as though he were hearing it for the first time. "You are full of surprises, aren't you?"

CHAPTER
❦ TEN ❦

A small shaft of fog-gray light settled upon her face and Elizabeth opened her eyes, not knowing, at first glance, just where she was. She looked around the cabin as familiar things began to stamp recognition in her mind. Hearing the groaning and creaking of the sloop, she sat up with a bolt.

She came quickly to her feet and grabbed Drake's jacket before staggering up the steps to the deck, her mind still fuzzy with sleep and her face still showing the pillow streaks on her cheek.

Tavis was still at the wheel, a faint breeze ruffling the ebony shafts of hair that hung to his shoulders. Apparently hearing her stumble on deck, he turned and gave her a quick nod.

"Good afternoon."

"Afternoon," he said.

"Where are we?" she asked.

"I wish to God I knew."

His curtness made her wonder if he'd lost sight of the boat they trailed. Her heart lurched. "The ketch? Have you lost her?"

"No, but I see something that concerns me more."

She came to stand at his side, on her tiptoes, so she could see far out over the gray swells. The glare off the water was great, so she brought her hand up to shield her eyes, seeing a giant, gray shadow that loomed in the distance.

"A frigate?" she asked, understanding now the curtness in his voice, the concern in his gaze.

"That's my guess."

"Whose?"

He looked at the sky. "Southern sympathizers, I'd say, judging from the direction we've been sailing."

"A rendezvous, do you think?"

"More than likely. I doubt those bastards would let something they wanted as bad as my plans be entrusted to a lowly ketch for long."

"Your plans? You mean the designs for one of your ships?"

He nodded. "A very special ship . . . steam-driven and iron-hulled."

"Iron-hulled? I've never heard of such."

"That's precisely why the bastards want it. They know what a ship like that could mean if war is declared."

"But why wouldn't they approach you with an offer before they resorted to stealing it?"

"They did approach me. Several times. As did the United States Navy. I turned them both down."

"Oh, I see," she said, finally understanding just why the ketch was so important to him. She was glad she had followed her instincts and had kept after the ketch, instead of doing what her common sense told her and returning to Nantucket. Because she loved him, anything that was important to him was important to her as well.

She glanced at the two ships. "Do you think they've seen us?"

"Actually, I'm a bit surprised that they haven't brought out their guns before now. They know we're here. And they know *why* we're here." Turning to look at her, he asked, "Question is, why haven't they tried to blow us out of the water?"

"Don't be asking that question yet," she said "There is still plenty of time to get your answer. Perhaps they were waiting for the frigate."

He frowned. "Are you afraid? Do you want to turn back?" he asked, his look turning soft as if he had just at this moment considered the fact that she was a woman and that she might be afraid.

She was still watching the frigate. "It's a little late to be asking me that, isn't it?"

His eyes soft upon her, he said, "It's your sloop. Tell me the truth. Do you want to go back?"

"Would you? Go back, I mean. If you could?"

"Yes, I would. So what's it to be? Shall I turn her around?"

"No."

"Are you certain you don't want to go back?"

"Yes."

Any real lady would have given him an adamant no. Any real lady would have been terrified. Any real lady wouldn't have spent the night on a sloop in the first place

But then, whoever accused Nantucket women of being *real* ladies? Nantucket women were bursting with talent and independence. That small island town may have produced some remarkably interesting men, but it had, in many respects, surpassed itself when it came to women—women like Keziah Coffin, the Revolution profiteer; or Deborah Chase, the 350-pound Goliath who tossed men on the roof and into whale oil vats; or Maria Mitchell, the astronomer; or Lucretia Mott, the antislavery crusader. And herself, of course.

Nantucket was a place where women outnumbered men, four to one; a place of spinsters, widows, and married women who were separated from their husbands for two to five years at a time. Normal home life, as known on the mainland, was nonexistent. There were never enough men to go around, and most of the business of raising a family and educating the children fell upon the female sex.

Women grew up learning to balance whaling account books and to run the family business, which often meant competing with those on the mainland. Nantucket women were homemakers, true, but it was in the financial sense as much as the domestic.

Do you want to go back? Elizabeth guessed there was simply too much salt water mixing with the hot and determined blood sluicing through her veins. The call for adventure was too great. She looked at him, realizing the importance of what he was asking her. *This is why I love him,* she thought, *because there is something in him that calls to the wild in me.* She smiled at him then, and said, "Not on your life. I wouldn't miss this adventure for anything. I'm thinking I'll have a lot of stories to tell my grandchildren."

For a moment he looked as though he might smile. "Lizzie," he said, "if we don't go back, you may not live long enough to have grandchildren. Those are *real* guns on that frigate."

She wanted to tell him that without him, all her hopes

were dead anyway, that without him there would be nothing left but the rippling laugh of someone unseen, the sunshine of sweet memories—a world as empty as a starless night. She wanted to tell him of the dreams she held for them and that it was all her fantasies and more that inspired her to name her sloop *Wildest Dreams*. But she simply looked at him, laughed, and said, "The only way I'd go back is for you to refuse to stop calling me Lizzie."

He seemed surprised, then he gave her a half smile. "Elizabeth," he said. "I remember now. You asked me to call you that once before, I believe."

"Yes. Apparently you forgot."

"It won't happen again."

She nodded. "Then let's do a little tacking and gather up some wind so we can see what that frigate is all about."

The frigate seemed to sail right out of the haze in the distance. She watched as the ketch they followed drew near the frigate, then disappeared behind it. With a wide, sweeping turn, the frigate seemed to huddle close by, hurrying the ketch, like a mother duck, toward port.

She was about to ask Tavis what he thought that meant when he interrupted her thoughts by saying, "That's no ordinary frigate. It's a warship. Even from here I can make out her gunports."

"What do we do now?"

"We keep behind her, of course."

"And then what? What if she puts into port?"

"Then we follow her and notify the authorities of the theft."

Tavis went below to rest while Elizabeth took her place at the helm. She trailed the warship the rest of the day. It was almost dusk when she noticed something odd. To her it seemed as if the warship was getting closer, as if it was coming their way. A moment later she was certain of it. "Tavis!" she called out, and then again, "Tavis, come quick!"

He was on deck in an instant, running toward her while tucking his shirt into his breeches. "What is it?"

"Look," she said, nodding toward the warship. "I think it's getting closer. Do you think they're sailing our way?"

He squinted and said, "You're right. That's exactly what they're doing. They've changed direction. They're coming for us."

"Coming for us?" she repeated slowly, then as it occurred to her just what that meant, she said, "You mean they're going to fire upon us?"

"More than likely," was all he said as he came to take the wheel from her.

She grabbed his sleeve. "Now, wait a minute. I have no intention of finding myself in the middle of a war."

"We aren't at war," he said simply. "At least, not yet."

"We may be if that ship fires upon us."

"If they do, there wouldn't be enough of us left to indicate what happened," he said. "But I don't think they intend anything that severe. It's my guess that they only want to frighten us away."

"Well, if frightening us is what they want, I'd say having a warship with her gunports open and pointing our way is an excellent way to go about it. Following a ketch is one thing ... even trailing the warship. But having a warship trailing *us* is another matter. We're as vulnerable as a bird nest on the ground." A horrible thought began to form in her mind. "You don't mean you think we can outrun them?"

"We might. However, it doesn't matter. I still don't think they intend to do us harm. They'll put a shot or two across our bow, just to scare us."

"Then they're wasting their time," she said. "I'm already scared."

"Then go below."

"Go below?" She threw up her hands. "Oh, this is wonderful. Does that make death easier then? When you don't see it?"

"I told you they won't go that far."

"What if you're wrong? Listen to me, Tavis," she said, poking him in the chest. "I'm all for helping you, you know that. But not if I'm going to have the whole southern armada after me."

He laughed. "There is no southern armada," he said. "Where did you get such an absurd idea?"

"It's not absurd. They have one warship, don't they?"

He nodded.

"Well, have you ever seen just one of anything troublesome?"

"Oh, I don't know. I seem to remember a time I was mighty thankful there was only one of you."

She crossed her arms over her chest and gave him a look that said just what she thought of his comment. "We aren't talking about me. We're talking about warships. Our luck has turned against us, and as my grandfather says, 'When fortune turns against you, even jelly breaks your tooth.' "

He did not say one word, but he did turn toward her, and his look was incredulous. "Only you would find a similarity between warships and jelly."

"Think what you will, but *I'm* neutral," she said, poking her chest, "and I intend to stay that way."

A sudden flash from the warship was followed by a roar of a cannon and a billowing gray cloud of smoke. A split second later the whine of a cannon ball sailed overhead and landed with an insignificant plop as it dropped into the water behind them.

"You aren't neutral now," he said.

"They're firing over our head," she said with so much authority that he actually laughed.

She gave him a questioning look. "They have no intention of hitting us. . . . Isn't that what you said?"

"It is, and as I said, it's only a warning for us to turn back. However, they may change their plans when they find we have no intention of doing so."

"You may not be turning back, but I am," she said. Just then another volley came whining toward them, dropping into the water in front of their bow, so close, it peppered their sails with drops of water.

"They're aiming closer, and I, for one, have no intention of spending the night in Davy Jones's locker."

Elizabeth glanced at the ship, seeing another flash of light, followed by a puff of dark gray smoke. Without a warning, she was shoved to her knees as Tavis grabbed her shoulders with a strong grip and pushed her down before him. A moment later, he covered her body with his, just as she heard another shot whine overhead, followed by a thundering crack that sent vibrations over the sloop.

"They've hit us!" she cried in tones muffled against his chest. "Can you see? Is it bad?"

"No, they shaved the mast, though." She raised her head just as he said, "That was uncomfortably close, but the mast still holds. We need to strike the sails and slack our pace. That should make them decide to leave us be."

"That's the first intelligent thing you've said," she replied, thrusting her head between his ribs and his arm so she could look around.

"Stay down," he said, pushing her head away and rising to his feet.

She obeyed, watching openmouthed as he set to work. The *Wildest Dreams*'s mainsail fluttered down with a whooshing rush of canvas, just after he struck the jib. Immediately she felt the sluggish slackening of pace as the sloop lost direction and began to drift.

Apparently that satisfied the warship, for it turned rapidly away from the course it had off their starboard beam and took up after the ketch. Still drifting, Elizabeth and Tavis watched the towering sails of the warship long after they lost sight of the ketch. When the ship was no more than an insignificant blemish upon the face of the Atlantic, Tavis began to hoist the sails.

"I was beginning to wonder when we would ever start for home," she said.

"Then keep wondering," he replied, "because we aren't going home. At least, not yet."

"What do you mean, we aren't?"

"Just what I said."

When she sputtered her protest, he explained, "Elizabeth, I told you those bastards have my plans, and I intend to get them back."

"Are you insane? Trailing a ketch is one thing. Being blasted out of the water by a warship is another. You can't take on the whole South. It's a hotbed of hostility right now. Everyone is seceding and itching for war." She waved a dismissing hand at him. "I'm sorry this happened, but it's out of your hands now."

"It isn't over until I say it is." He gave her a sympathetic look that seemed to say, *I'm sorry, but that's the way it is,* then he continued, "I don't plan to take on the whole South . . . just a small part of it . . . and I sure as hell can follow them until they put into port."

"And then what? Find yourself in front of a firing squad?"

He gave her a hard look. "They have something that belongs to me, and I intend to get it back if I have to fight my way through five states to do it."

"Oh, this is wonderful, absolutely wonderful. I fancy myself in love with a man for years, only to find out he's a bloody lunatic."

He grinned up at her then. "Fancied yourself in love with me, did you?"

"Oh, be quiet. And don't you go acting so surprised. You and every other fool on Nantucket Island knew it as well as I did, so there's no need to play coy now."

"I would never stoop so low," he said, giving her an appreciative look. "Well, at least this encounter has been a change for us."

"In what way?"

"For one thing, you aren't spying on me from barn rafters or wagon beds." He paused, as if considering something. "You know, we are actually carrying on a normal conversation for once."

"So?"

"So it amazes me."

"What does? That you can converse?"

He laughed. "No, that *you* can. I don't think I ever heard you say more than ten words the entire time I've known you . . . except for that day at . . ."

She knew he was thinking about Saul's Pond, a day he obviously wanted to forget. Mustering her resolve, she told herself she wouldn't give him the satisfaction of knowing her true feelings. She kept her tone light. "You never heard me say anything because you were always too busy running the other way whenever you saw me coming."

"I'm serious. I don't recall you ever talking much . . . before you went to Boston, that is."

"I was always shy around you."

"Shy? You?" He laughed and shook his head. "In speech, perhaps"

"I was shy, and whenever you saw me, you never hung around long enough for me to talk. Blister it, Tavis, you could run faster than a Chesapeake trotter, and you had a way of vanishing into thin air."

When he stopped laughing, he said, "I remember one time when I wasn't fast enough."

She grinned and cocked her head to one side, looking up at him, squinting at the glare of the sun. "Oh? When was that?"

"The time you spied on me, Cole, and Nathan when we were swimming. Got yourself an eyeful, didn't you?" He looked like he wanted to say something more, but he was laughing so hard, he couldn't.

"Go ahead and joke," she said. "It's nice to know I can fill some need, even if it is laughter."

The laughter died and the humor in his eyes vanished as his eyes traveled over her slowly. "Keep sashaying around in front of me wearing those pants, and you may get the chance to fill another one."

"And I'll let you know," she said saucily, "if the idea holds any appeal for me."

Before he could say anything else, she turned away and started below.

"Where are you going?"

"To get something to eat. I hate the thought of dying on an empty stomach."

The next morning the warship sailed into a thick cloak of fog and disappeared. They blindly followed and soon lost sight of the ship. When the fog lifted, neither the warship nor the ketch was in sight. But there was a thin strip of brown land shimmering on the horizon. Tavis immediately took up the telescope. "We're off the coast of Virginia," he said. "And unless I miss my guess, that's Norfolk."

"Do you see the ship or the ketch?"

"No, they were probably headed here, but went farther south under the cover of fog."

She sensed his disappointment and she hated her inadequacy, her inability to think of anything comforting to say. "I'm sorry," she said at last. "I know how you must feel."

"You couldn't possibly know how it feels to lose something you've given your life to," he said, not bothering to look at her.

She thought of how long she had loved him and the hopelessness of it, and before she knew what she was saying, she said, "You're wrong. I do. More than you."

They stood there in silence, he with his loss, she with hers, neither of them reaching out for comfort from the other, neither of them knowing how.

At last she broke the silence and said, "What now?"

"We'll sail into port and I'll try to find out what I can."

It was later that afternoon when they reached Norfolk Harbor, and just as he had said, neither the ketch nor the warship was in sight. Tavis cursed at his luck, telling her to remain on board. "I'll be back as soon as I can," he said.

"I'm coming with you."

"No. I want you to wait here," he said. "You'll only be in the way."

"I want to ride in with you. My family will be worried. I should post a letter to them, telling them I'm all right."

When he gave her an odd look, she said, "I won't tell them anything. I just want to let them know I'm safe, that I'll explain everything when I return. Besides, I need to get more supplies. When we left Nantucket, I had not laid up a full store of water, and our food is lower than I'd like."

"We have enough to last us until we get back," he said.

"Perhaps . . . if we don't encounter any difficulties, but on water, you can never be certain. I would rather have food and water left over than to run out."

He gave her a determined look and opened his mouth to say something more, when she said, "Look, you have commandeered my sloop. The least you can do now is humor me."

"Come on," he said gruffly. "We're wasting time."

CHAPTER
❧ ELEVEN ❧

She was waiting for him at the dinghy when he arrived back at the dock. He looked at the heavy load, then he looked at her. "Don't complain," she said, "I've already taken two aboard."

"You must be planning on a long trip, or else you have an unbridled appetite," he said, climbing on and moving a tin of crackers so he could sit down.

"I believe in being prepared."

"As well as overloaded. You sure this thing will float?"

"Aye, Captain," she said, flashing him a grin. "I'm certain of it."

"You posted your letter, I suppose," he said.

"Yes," she said, then added, "sort of."

"What do you mean, sort of?"

"The postmaster was away, so I left my letter with the proprietor of the store."

"And we wonder why letters go astray," he said.

He rowed them out to the *Wildest Dreams*, and once they had everything aboard, he said, "Why don't you go below and scare up something to eat? I'll take over things up here for a while."

She gave him a skeptical look. "Are you sure you're up to it?"

"It still isn't too late to throw you overboard," he said.

"Or you either," she replied, glancing at the sky. After a moment's study, she said, "I don't like the looks of those clouds. I hope they're gone by morning."

He leaned his head back and stared overhead. "It looks as if we could have a storm on our hands. Maybe you should get some rest. If it gets bad, it may take both of us on deck." The silence stretched thinly, broken only by the sound of water lapping gently against the hull and the distant cry of a gull.

Elizabeth took one last glance at the dark, churning skies, and something cold and frightening seemed to settle in her stomach. Without saying another word, she nodded and went below.

She opened the mahogany door, then paused. The cabin was as dark and gloomy as a whale's belly, reminding her of how far she was from home. She lit the oil lamp overhead, knowing it would fill the cabin with smoke, but needing its light. Even with the lamp lit, the cabin was dim, smelling of oil, stale air, and smoke all intertwined with a musty smell of dampness—but it was comfortable.

For a brief time she stood in the center of the cabin, glancing about her, remembering the way it had looked before Stephen had holystoned her decks and Matt had polished her brass until it was gleaming. She knew her family would be sick with worry and hoped with all her heart that the letter she left behind would get to them so they would know she was all right.

She thought about Sally and Meg, remembering how she had promised Sally that she would help her with her algebra, knowing, too, that Meg would pout for at least two days because Elizabeth wasn't there to teach her how to make rose petal jam.

She removed her coat and busied herself with putting away the supplies. When everything was orderly, she placed a slice of cheese and a hunk of sausage between two slices of bread and took it up to Tavis, placing a tin cup of water near the wheel. He didn't say anything, but simply took the sandwich, looking the bread over from one side to the other, as if he had never seen a slice of bread before.

"You're safe," she said. "They were out of poison."

"I wouldn't put it past you," he grumbled, and took a bite.

"Like I said, you're safe . . . at least for now. I need you to get home."

He took two more bites, eating like he was famished. Remembering how little he had eaten, she supposed he was.

"And then what?" he asked between bites.

You'll go your merry way, pretending, as you've always done, that I don't exist. "I suppose our lives will fall back into the same pattern as before. You going your way, me going mine."

"And never the twain shall meet?" he asked casually, finishing the last bite of bread and sausage.

"Oh, I suppose our paths will cross from time to time. You will nod politely and tip your hat and say something superficial like, 'Good afternoon, Miss Robinson. Strange weather we're having, is it not?' "

She kept her gaze locked on him, like a drowning person clinging desperately to a bit of floating wood. Without saying a word, she felt as if her eyes were speaking for her, asking him to hold her in his arms and tell her he could not forget her any more than he could forget to breathe. He was watching her, and she felt the world was shut away by the strength of his look. She wanted so desperately to put her head against his chest, as if, by doing so, she would hear the steady beat of his heart and know that this feeling was real. But he spoke then, and the magic of the moment slowly slipped away.

"And you?" he asked softly. "What will you do?"

"Me? Why, I'll dip my head ever so slightly and say something equally superficial like, 'Good afternoon to you, Mr. Mackinnon. Yes, it is indeed strange weather. It looks like rain, don't you think?' "

Tavis's blue-gray gaze moved over her slowly from head to foot, returning to her face with a look she could only describe as a sort of reverent admiration. Tavis Mackinnon had rarely looked at her that way. The newness of it, the shock, was an assault upon her feelings that left her bewildered. She felt suddenly uncomfortable and self-conscious.

She looked at him and tried to smile, but the corners of her mouth trembled. Her gaze locked with his, and there was such strength in it, such reassurance, that she felt for a moment as if his eyes were the only thing holding her up, that if he looked away, she would crumble and fall to nothingness.

Oddly, a curious sensitivity seemed to exist between them, a sensibility that seemed to say, no matter what happens, things between us will never be the same.

She did not know why, but the thought of it was unexpected and frightening to her, and she felt a cold shiver that began at her shoulders and traveled downward. Her gaze came back to his to find he was regarding her with an odd look.

Dear God, how had all of this happened? A few days

ago she had been peacefully sleeping on her cot aboard her sloop in Nantucket Harbor. Now she was miles from home in the middle of nowhere, alone and unchaperoned with a man she had always loved, but one she was coming to realize she did not know.

Yet the more she thought about it, the more she wondered if it was Tavis Mackinnon she didn't know, or was it herself? Perhaps Tavis was still the same. Perhaps it was she who had changed, for always before she had looked at him through the eyes of an adoring child. But those were not the thoughts of a child that lingered in her mind now. Was he as aware of it as she? Was that what frightened her?

He handed her the cup, but when she reached for it, he took her hand instead. "You're frightened of me, aren't you?"

She couldn't look at him, so she kept her gaze fastened on the hand that held hers. "I'm not frightened . . . of you."

"Of what, then?"

"Nothing."

"I don't believe you," he said softly. "I don't believe you for a minute." He tugged on her hand. "Come here."

"Why?"

He brought her fingers to his lips, turning the palm upward and pressing his mouth there. "Do I really need to explain it?" he asked, and when she didn't answer, when she refused to look at him, he said, "Why can't you at least look at me?"

"Because I can't. Because I feel like a fool."

"Why?"

She felt as if her words were laden with melancholy, glazed and made heavy because of it. It was difficult for her to express sentiment and feelings to him, of all people. "It seems," she began softly, "that I've spent a great deal of my life being ashamed, or being told I should feel that way. With six older brothers and a well-meaning father, I was never long without hearing someone say, 'Lizzie, you should be ashamed of yourself.' "

"And were you?"

"As much as I could be at such tender years. I always knew I was a disappointment to my father and that at least some of my brothers were indulgent of me because of that."

He smiled. "Now, tell me what you're feeling ashamed of right now."

She shrugged, speaking from her heart. It was one of the most admirable things about her—a totally unselfish giving of both self and thought to others. She had always been one to display her feelings, as he, and everyone in Nantucket, well knew. It would come as no surprise to him to learn she could share her innermost thoughts as well. "What am I ashamed of right now? Of the past, I think. Of my childish infatuation. Of the countless idiotic things I used to do. But mostly I am a trifle embarrassed, knowing you are aware of my feelings, knowing you still look at me as a silly, infatuated child."

"And if I told you I didn't see you that way? What if I told you that whenever I look at you I see a beautiful, desirable woman? What would you say to that?"

Surprised, she could only look at him, at the way his shirt fit his broad shoulders, the way he was gazing down at her with an incredibly rakish air. Against a backdrop of white sail and shimmering ocean he looked every bit the pirate, needing only a blade in his belt, a kerchief on his head, and a golden earring in his ear.

She was certain he would be an indulgent pirate, for there was no evil quality to him, nothing sinister. The thought overwhelmed her so much that her voice trembled when she spoke,

"I would say what you thought didn't really matter, because I know what I feel," she said. Spreading her hand over her breast to indicate her heart, she added, "In here. Some people fear tomorrow, but I'm afraid of yesterday. There is nothing you can do about that, for the past is mirror-clear. In here I would always remember and feel ashamed," she said, indicating her heart again, "and there is nothing you can do about that. Nothing."

"But I can try," he said, taking her other hand in his and drawing her against him. "I can surely try."

The past rose up before her. Her fear made her strong. She snatched her hands away quickly, and turning, she almost ran to the steps that led below, as if, by running away, she could leave the past behind her.

"Elizabeth," he called out, but it was too late. Elizabeth's head had already disappeared through the hatch.

Once below, Elizabeth gripped the main support beam to steady herself and whispered, "I still love him . . . stronger and deeper than before, and that gives him such power, it frightens me." She moved to her cot and sat down upon it, hearing the sound of his name in her mind like the melodious ring of wind whistling through sail.

She lay back, remembering how she had told him everything. She had completely given herself away. Why was she always destined either to behave stupidly or to say something foolish whenever she was around him? She fought the wildest desire to dash back up the stairs and tell him it was all lies. She thought of the years in the past, of all the people who had witnessed her foolishness, her shame, and wondered why she had been so unwise—insane really—to think she could come back and win his love. *He cares little for me,* she thought. *To him I am nothing more than a change in the weather, a squall that diverts his attention for the time being, something that will soon be on its way. Foolish,* she called herself. "Foolish. Foolish. Foolish."

She came to her feet and nibbled a bit of cheese, eating two crackers before deciding she wasn't hungry. With a weary groan, she lay down, not realizing she was near exhaustion until she felt her head on the pillow. She pulled the blanket over her and stretched, burrowing down into the feather ticking. With a solitary sigh, she fell asleep.

She had no idea how long she slept, but she awoke when she felt herself falling. A split second later, she hit the floor with a thud. She opened her eyes to stare up at the oil lamp swinging violently overhead. For a dazed moment she looked around in bewilderment and then she remembered where she was and who she was with. Everything about her seemed in motion, and even from the security of her cabin, she was conscious of the wind. The sloop rose and pitched with each wave, as if it and the sea fought for space. She tried to force her thoughts to deal with things like drift and leeway, but her groggy mind seemed unable to handle such.

A stingy wedge of light sliced down the stairs, and she wondered if it was still very early, or simply dark because of the storm. She fought her way toward the stairs, inching along, feeling her face splashed with water. By the time she reached the deck, she was soaked by hard, driving rain as she made her way over swamped decks thrashed by waves. The sloop rolled and her timber groaned with each icy bath. Shielding her eyes as much as she could from the stinging salt spray, she could barely make out the dark silhouette of Tavis's body holding the wheel.

"We need to get closer to land. The waves there won't be so great," she shouted.

With the lee rail awash, he wrestled with the wheel, and she felt a sense of helplessness as she looked around trying to see where she was needed. Around her the wind blew violently and the waves seemed to race one another to hurl themselves against the sloop. Elizabeth looked up to where the sails strained against the burden of wind. Before she could assess the sail condition, a splintering crack shattered overhead, drowning out even the harsh screaming of the storm. She whipped her head up to see the jagged edge of the mast, watching with a horrified scream as the top half of it toppled forward into the sea, taking most of the mainsail with it.

She lunged for the wheel. "What are you doing?" she shouted. "The mast is gone. You carried too much sail."

"It wasn't too much sail. That shot we took from the warship must have cracked the mast. The wind only finished the job."

"Now what will we do?" she yelled, wondering if he could hear her over the moaning of the wind. Another wave washed over them, and she remembered only a sharp pain in her head before everything went black.

Warm sunlight drenched her face, and Elizabeth opened her eyes. The lion that had roared so ferociously about her now seemed no more than the bleating of a sleepy lamb.

"How do you feel?"

She turned to see Tavis sitting beside her, and realized that her head hurt. Lifting her hand to her temple, she felt a lump. "I hit something."

He nodded. "The wheel. You had me worried," he said softly. "I thought you'd never wake up."

And would you have cared? There were so many things warring within her, things her heart wanted to say to that, deterrents placed by her mind as a safeguard. "Any idea where we are?"

"No. I'm no navigator, and there aren't many charts and maps on board."

"And no sextant," she said.

"And no sextant," he repeated.

For a moment she allowed herself the luxury of just looking at him. She studied the dark, windblown hair, the flawless purity of his bone structure, the brilliance of his eyes, the fullness of his mouth. Her insides quivered. Looking at him cost more than she thought. "I never anticipated I'd be taking such a trip."

He smiled. "Neither did I."

"What do we do now?"

"We drift . . . until someone finds us."

Or we die.

He helped her to her feet. "I'd better go below and survey the damage," she said. "We'll have to start rationing food and water now, since we have no idea how long it will be before someone finds us."

He looked at her oddly.

"What is it?" she asked. "Did the storm rearrange my face? Do I have smudges beneath my eyes?"

"No, you surprise me, that's all."

"In what way?"

"Judging from my experience with women, I would never have figured you for one to take this so calmly."

She snorted, wanting to tell him what he could do

with his experience with women. "Little choice I have about the matter. We are stranded out here with no sail. Common sense tells me no amount of ranting will change that. Now is the time for levelheadedness, not impulsive rashness."

"You're right, of course. So if it's levelheaded we're going to be, I suppose we can use this time to become better acquainted."

"I know you well enough," she said. "And you have no reason to know me better."

"You sure didn't waste any time dismissing that one. Haven't you heard that knowing another's heart and mind always makes a man richer?" he asked.

She didn't respond.

"Once again, you surprise me. Considering the past circumstances, I would have thought you would jump at the chance to spend more time with me."

"Perhaps I've changed my mind," she said in her defense, thinking it was indeed ironic that what he said was exactly what she had always dreamed about, but somehow the reality was not as rosy-hued and rainbow-tinted as the dream. She was no longer a wide-eyed child, and Tavis Mackinnon in the flesh was much more than a starry-eyed child could ever imagine he would be.

Right now he looked very tall and forbidding, his broad shoulders dwarfing the wheel, his words carrying a smooth polish of amusement. Her memory served up only harshly spoken words with a hard ring, words that seemed to be carved from cold metal.

She wanted to inform him with icy dignity that he had waited too long, that she was in love with Harry Beecham, who was everything he was not. She wanted to tell him that Harry Beecham was madly in love with her. But she said nothing, preferring instead to make her way below to survey the damage done by the storm. She made no mention of the mayhem in her heart.

By that evening the *Wildest Dreams* gracefully rode a glassy, moonlit sea, stealing ghostlike over the water, the skeletal remains of her mast and rigging humming with her slow-drifting movement over near invisible waves. Feeling the need for fresh air, and feeling it stronger than her desire to stay away from Tavis, Elizabeth left the brilliance of lamplight in the cabin and sought the darkness above. She saw him immediately, standing at the bow, looking out over the water. She could not see his face, but she knew he was deep in thought. As quietly as possible, she moved to sit on a useless coil of rope he had stacked on deck.

All about her the sky was inky black, surrounding her like a cloak of darkest velvet that glittered with the brilliance of a million stars. *Night, with her train of stars and her great gift of sleep.*

"There's Capella, yellow and high in the northwest," she thought, not knowing she had said it aloud until Tavis spoke.

"If you navigate half as well as you sail, you should be able to figure out where you are," he said, coming to sit down beside her.

"My grandfather taught me to read the stars," she said, searching the sky overhead for familiar constellations. "There wasn't much else to do on those long, lonely nights out on the point."

"I've often wondered what it would be like to live in a lighthouse."

"Lonely," she said, "but Grandpa seems happy enough. I suppose it's because he's so close to the sea."

"You're quite close to him," he said, as if he already knew it for a fact.

"Yes, he is very dear to me. He has taught me much about life, about myself."

"And your aunt?"

Elizabeth smiled. "I thought her the most dreadful old witch I had ever encountered when my father first took me there. Nothing pleased her. We argued a lot. She seemed bent upon one mission, and that was to destroy me. You know, it's almost funny how sometimes when we are feeling most broken, when we are at our lowest point, we begin to see things most clearly."

"She must have been quite a woman."

"She was. Looking back, I can see how she took me apart, stone by stone, until I felt utterly wretched and desolate, then she began to build me back again, showing me my strengths, my ability to become and do whatever I set my mind to. She was the dearest woman, more than a mother, really."

"More than a mother? Is that possible?"

"Yes. A mother, if she loved me, would not have been able to peel away the layers as Aunt Phoebe did. A mother would have felt too protective, too caring. It took a stern constitution and a great deal of internal fortitude to prune me back as she did, grafting a bit here and a little there, as she saw fit."

"And you are stronger because of it," he observed.

"Yes, I am stronger," she said. Afraid to reveal any more of herself to him, she pointed over his shoulder and said, "There's Polaris." When he looked she went on, "See how the stars curve away from it to form Ursa Minor? And those stars lying almost straight below make up Ursa Major."

"And that tells you where we are?"

She laughed. "No. It simply tells you where Ursa Minor and Ursa Major are."

"Imp," he said, and tousled her hair.

"Always," she said, laughing up at him, the laughter dying away when she looked into his eyes. Suddenly her mouth went dry.

"Sometimes I find it hard to believe you're the same person who lost her stuffings at my feet," he said.

"I had hoped you would have forgotten that by now."

He laughed. "Forget? How could I?"

"You could forget me. . . . Why not the silly things I've done?"

"Is that what you believe, that I forgot you?"

"Of course. I was, as you said, an imp."

"That doesn't mean I would forget you, does it?"

"I don't know. What difference does it make now?"

"I'm not sure, but it does. You were gone a long time. . . ."

"Seven years," she interjected.

"I thought it was eight."

That surprised her. "It was *almost* eight—shy of it by a few days."

"A long time at any rate," he said, "but even then, I never completely forgot you. There were times when something would bring you to my mind and I would find myself wondering about you, wondering if you had found anyone else to pester as you did me. On some occasions I was even given to speculate upon your appearance, and I would drift off into imaginings of what the years had done to you, what kind of face and body maturity had given you."

"And?"

"And what?"

"And were your imaginings close?"

"No. Not by a long shot. The reality far outshone my fancy, but the first time I saw you after you returned, I knew who you were."

"Alas," she said, trying to keep her tone light, "and here I had hoped to surprise everyone and take the place by storm."

"Oh, you did that, all right. Cole and Nathan had no inkling as to your identity, and the moment they saw you, they were completely smitten."

"But you knew who I was the instant I walked into the ballroom that night. . . ."

"Wearing a white gown with golden leaves on it, and your hair curled Boston-fancy."

She would have laughed at his description of the white tulle gown embroidered with gold wheat ears if the sharpness of his memory hadn't completely overwhelmed her. "I am surprised you remembered me or my dress at all," she said.

"Not remember you?" he said. "Not even after dancing with you? Or have you forgotten that, Liza?"

It was the first time he had called her Liza. It was the first time he gave her any indication since that day at the pond that he was even aware she existed, and now to tell her that he not only remembered her, but remembered vividly what she wore, how she dressed her hair, and the fact that they had danced—when it was the only time in her whole life that he had ever asked her to dance.

Didn't he see that that dance had been the most precious moment of her life? Could he not see her love for him, even then, written in her eyes? The impact of it overwhelmed her and she turned her head away, terribly afraid that she was too overcome with emotion to do little more than cry.

He caught her chin and turned her face back to him. "You didn't answer me. Did you forget our dance that night?"

"I have never forgotten anything that concerned you," she said. "Not ever. As for our dance, I could have sooner forgotten how to talk."

She felt the hot, burning scald of tears on her face and hated her weakness. "Oh, I wish you wouldn't bring up such things." She looked at him then, shaking her head from side to side as if she saw something that caused her terrible pain. "It isn't fair of you to do this," she said. "What can you possibly hope to gain?"

"The truth," he said softly.

"What difference does truth make now? What do you want? To degrade me more? Can't you leave me with something akin to pride? Do you hate me that much? Is your thirst for revenge so great that you wish to see me humbled at your feet?"

"Maybe there is more to this than you are seeing."

"What?" she almost shrieked. Then doubling up her fists, she said, "Tell me! What else could there be?"

"Have you ever thought that I might begin to care . . . even if just a little?"

"No!" she shouted. "It never occurred to me any more than it occurred to you. Why are you saying this? It's too late. Can't you see that? It's too late!"

"Why? Is there someone else?"

That was like a shower of cold rain that drew all the anger, the anguish, from her, leaving her feeling drained. She didn't say anything.

"Is there?"

She shrugged. "I don't know."

"You don't *know*? What do you mean, you don't

know? How can you not know something like that? There is either another man in your life or there isn't."

"What makes you ask me a question like that?"

"Because I've got two good eyes, dammit! I can see what you look like, and I can feel what looking at a woman like you does to a man. You were in Boston for several years. You can't tell me there wasn't some man with his eye on you during all that time. Now, I repeat, Is there someone else?"

She sighed, a ragged sound. "Yes," she said, thinking it odd, the way he almost seemed angry at her reply.

"I see," he said, "and just how serious is it? Has he asked you to marry him?"

"Yes."

"And?"

"It's all confused in my mind. Aunt Phoebe was ill for so long. There are times when everything during that time seems to bleed together."

"Oh, come now. Surely you can't expect me to believe that a man who has asked you to marry him is someone you can forget so easily."

"I never said that. Harry is still as vivid in my mind as he was the day he came to get Genny and me."

"Who is Genny?"

"Harry's sister. She was my dearest friend in Boston."

"So old Harry fell head over heels for you?"

"He was at Cambridge at the time. When he graduated he came to Boston to go to law school at Harvard."

"And you passed all of that up?"

The way he said it was so comical, she had to laugh. "Yes, all of it ... at least for now," she said, turning suddenly toward him. "But one thing has me curious."

"And what is that?"

"Just why you seem so interested in all of this. Surely anything that has passed between Harry Beecham and myself is of no concern to you whatsoever. Why do you even bother to discuss it?"

He stared off. "I don't know," he said. "I honest to God don't know." Then he looked her square in the eye and said, "But I do know one thing. It makes me madder than hell to think of that son of a bitch putting his hands on you."

Elizabeth was so flabbergasted, all she could do was stare at him, openmouthed and with a look of utter and complete astonishment on her face. Before she could register more than that, he shocked her again by asking, "Do you love him?"

"I love him desperately."

"Liar," he said. "I don't think you love him at all." Both arms came around her. "And I damn well know you have always loved me more than you could ever care for him. Longer, too."

The enchantment of the moment overwhelmed her, as did his words. Never, never in her wildest dreams, would she have thought to ever hear him speak like this. Delight, warm and liquid, flowed through her. Elizabeth's head whirled. Surely no mortal being could stand more bliss, more joy, than this. The moon, high and full and round, must have thought as much, for at that moment it politely slid behind the covering of a cloud.

Tavis brought his face to hers, whispering, coaxing, and she felt herself melting from the onslaught of it. She looked up at him and found nothing but a slightly perplexed and thoughtful look upon his face—and then his eyes closed and she saw the deep etching of desire upon his dear features. The warmth that radiated through her left her feeling sated and drowsy, and she leaned against him quite naturally, like a wet kitten seeking warmth. She felt his kiss in her hair. A moment later his lips were upon hers, moving, fanning fires that had never before been kindled. Her hand came up to slip around his neck, feeling some shock at the cool, slippery feel of his hair.

As if sensing he was losing her, he deepened the kiss. Beneath her chemise she could feel her breasts, their hard points acutely sensitive now as they rose against the simple cotton. He touched her there, with his thumb, and she felt the heat of his touch sear her through layers of fabric.

Suddenly everything that stood between them was a barrier, nothing more than long bindings of fabric that she found uncomfortable. As if sensing this, his hand grew bolder now, coming beneath the heavy sweater to caress her breast, then tugging the fabric until she felt the rush of cool air as her chemise fell open.

Her eyes opened wide as he replaced his hand with his mouth, teasing the swelling fullness to a point that lay somewhere between pleasure and pain. She pulled away in a feeble attempt to allow sanity to come into a brain completely ruled by passion, but he held her hard against him, as if he knew what she was about.

She opened her mouth to protest, but the cry became a moan when he took her words with a deep kiss. His lips parted and he kissed her with a ferocity she had never before seen in him. It was a kiss that was as relentless in its demand as it was coaxing in manner. "Sweet, sweet," he seemed to breathe against her mouth. "I want your sweetness. Let me, Liza. Let me love you, sweet, sweet Liza."

Too soon. Too fast, her mind screamed, and she grew

still. She might have given in to her feelings at that moment. In truth, she might have given in to more than that, if not for something he said, just before he kissed her again. "I'm a man, Elizabeth . . . a man with all the wants and desires of a man. And you are so desirable. I want you so much."

He might be broad at the shoulders and narrow at the hip. He might be the most handsome man she had ever seen. His touch might even be what she had yearned for all her life. But she wasn't something to be used without feeling . . . at least without some feeling other than lust.

The thought wounded her. Deeply. Words of love would have moved her—even gentleness. But not this . . . not this open declaration. Now she did not know which hurt the most: loving him and not having him love her in return, or loving him and knowing he wanted her with no more feeling than he would have for a dockside whore.

Oh yes, she was lovely to look at and nice to hold. But she was also something else. Unavailable.

With a muffled curse, she pushed him away. "Stay away from me."

He drew back and his look was one of regret, and she knew what it was that he regretted . . . that he hadn't been able to consummate his desires before she came to her senses. *These* were her thoughts, so his softly spoken words, when they came, startled and surprised her.

"I can see that I've frightened you. Believe me when I say it was not my intention."

His apology brought her gaze to his, and she looked at him with wide-set eyes filled with dismay. She knew what he was saying and why. *Not his intention?* Those were the last words she expected to hear him say. *Not his intention?* She searched his face for some clue, something that would answer the questions lingering in the back of her mind, but she saw nothing. "I don't believe you."

"I don't blame you. I knew what I was doing. You did not. The fault was entirely with me. It won't happen again."

Not like this, it won't, she thought, then turned away.

CHAPTER
❧ TWELVE ❧

Tavis remained sitting on deck long after Elizabeth had gone below. He leaned back, resting his head against the coil of rope she had sat upon earlier. His hands folded behind his head, he watched the moon burst from behind a cloud with a silvery path of brilliance that seemed to connect heaven to earth. Soon it would be in its first quarter, thin and stingy with its light. But for now it brightened the world below and turned the skeleton of the masts to shadow. His thoughts shifted toward how he could go about setting this thing between himself and Elizabeth right.

It was while he was lying there thinking that Tavis realized although he had known Elizabeth for years, there were precious few times that he had actually spent any time talking to her—and none of them had occurred before she went to Boston.

While it had been a big surprise to find her on board, he would have to admit it was an even bigger surprise to learn that his earlier suspicions had been right—that the Lizzie he had known before and the Elizabeth he was coming to know now were about as similar as substance and shadow.

If he had to pick one thing that had astonished him above all the others, he would have to say it was the fact that she obviously had something in her head all those years besides landing him for a husband.

She was smart, quick-witted, educated, a good cook, and an even better sailor. She had a lot of pride, an even-paced temper, and she knew mathematics and astronomy like he knew the plans for his iron-hulled ship. He couldn't help smiling when he remembered an evening when she had offered to teach him algebra.

"What makes you think I need to learn algebra?" he asked.

"Because you're an architect, and quite frankly, I'm amazed you have managed thus far without stronger mathematical abilities."

He hadn't particularly liked the way she spoke to him any more than he liked knowing when it came to mathematics, she knew more than he did. Feeling just a little put out with her, he had snapped his reply. "I'll get by," he said.

She gave him a look that said it was exactly the kind of response she would have expected from a moron. "That's what Samson said when they told him he'd die of fallen arches."

He had been madder than hell, and he had been about to tell her so when she turned around—prissy as you please—and sashayed down the hatch without giving him so much as a by-your-leave. Looking back on it now, he had to admit time had managed to remove his irritation, leaving nothing but humor in its place.

And now, in spite of himself, he found he was laughing. *That's what Samson said . . .* Did anyone ever get the best of her?

He was a bit amazed at this point to realize that he was actually coming to enjoy her—her quick wit, her infectious chatter, her ready laugh, the adoration he saw in her eyes. In plain English, he enjoyed her company—that in itself being quite a revelation, coming from a man who had spent over a dozen years trying to avoid her.

She was the kind of woman a man could easily be around, for she seemed to know when to talk, when to tease, when to be quiet, and when to give a man some breathing room and a little private time to himself—rare qualities in a woman. As far as physical attributes went, she was fair of face, built the way he liked—ample where it was important, trim and lithe where it was not.

He looked at the moon again, sitting up there a solitary thing, which, in spite of its brightness, looked forlorn and in want of company. Perhaps these thoughts teased him a trifle, for come to think of it, he was feeling a bit lonesome himself. It was obvious just how much he had grown to depend upon her and her sharp mind to brighten the long, lonely days they spent doing nothing but drifting at the mercy of a few fickle breezes.

Those thoughts stirred up a memory of a time when she had tried to rush Mother Nature a bit and had ended up losing her stuffings because of it. What an odd little thing she had been back then, so obviously infatuated with him for years.

He knew she still loved him. He could read it in her eyes. He could also read the pain and hurt that was there when she had left him moments ago. He was no fool. He knew what upset her. She might love him, but she didn't want to be a temporary whim, something he dallied with because there was no one else around to dally with. In one respect she was like the other women he knew. She wanted what all women want. Love. Romance. Marriage. All tied up neatly like a silk noose around a man's neck.

He might be attracted to her. He might desire her. He might even go so far as to say he wanted to bed her. But he wasn't fool enough to call that love. Love being something he knew nothing about. He was, however, man enough to admit he had been wrong to let her think he wanted nothing more than to seduce her.

He came to his feet and looked around him, as if he would find what he was searching for on the deck. He ran his hand through his hair and stared out over the water. He knew what he had to do. He just wasn't certain as to how he should go about it.

After much thought, he decided he could only approach her with honesty. He *had* tried to seduce her. He owed her an apology, at least for that. Instinctively he knew it was up to him to set things right.

A moment later he went below and found her sitting on her cot, bathed in a beam of moonlight that turned her hair to white.

She watched him step down the hatch. He turned toward her as he left the last step. He paused, looking at her, as if he were waiting for her to invite him closer—something he knew she wouldn't do. Her face was moonbeam-pale and streaked with the path of recent tears.

"If you came to finish what you started up there, get out."

His shoulders slumped. She wasn't going to make this easy for him. He felt his body recoil, his muscles grow tense. He was unsure of himself. He was not a man accustomed to apology, and that made him uncertain as to how he should go about it. Because of his discomfort, his first thought was to take the easy way out by charming her, but something told him to keep his charm to himself, knowing that if he didn't, she would tell him to do just that. He looked at her with pleading in his eyes, seeing stubborn refusal in her own. He had been right earlier. Honesty was the only way to go with her. "I came to tell you I'm sorry."

His words had obviously shocked her. Did she think him such an ogre that he couldn't see when he was in the wrong, that he didn't know when it was time to apologize? "I've enjoyed the friendship we've begun," he said. "It was foolish of me to try and push it toward something more."

"You weren't pushing it to anything *more*," she said, emphasizing it in a way that made him understand perfectly what she meant. Then she went on to add, "You were simply and quite frankly seducing me . . . and fool that I was, I was going along with it."

"I was not intentionally seducing you."

"Oh? Was it an accident, then?"

For a moment he simply stared at her, wondering how it was that a woman could take a simple statement and twist it all around a man until she hung him with it. He was feeling inept and bungling again. "It just happened, that's all. No matter what you think, I don't go around with my pants unbuttoned, with only one thought in my mind whenever I see a beautiful woman."

"Ha!" she said, coming up off the bed. "Don't think you can fool me. I've heard all about your escapades . . . your *skill* at seducing."

"Don't believe everything you've heard," he said blandly. "I'm not *that* good."

"That's exactly what I've heard."

They were like two wooden statues for the next two days, each saying as little as possible to the other, each one making a great and obvious effort to stay out of the other's way.

To her, Tavis was stiffly polite. When he did engage her in conversation, it was mostly small talk dealing with the weather, or what he wanted to eat, nothing either of them could speak upon with any genuine emotion.

It gave her plenty of time to think about what had happened between them that evening. By the time she had run to her cabin and thrown herself across her cot, with her heart hammering and her pride pricked, she knew she had made a big mistake. No woman in her right mind would let Tavis Mackinnon slip through her fingers. Especially a woman who claimed she had been in love with him for half her life.

Why did her foolish pride keep getting in the way? And how long was she going to let things go like this? Until they were both dead?

Dead? The thought hit her like a board between the eyes. She had done what she thought was the right thing, and what had it gotten her? Nothing. And if she kept this up, what would it get her? Nothing.

Once again she could hear Aunt Phoebe speaking to her. *Elizabeth Amelia, sometimes I swear you'd rather be right than happy.*

Sitting on her cot, staring at the wall opposite her, Elizabeth made a startling discovery. Seduction didn't just happen all by itself. Both had to want it. Realizing her own culpability made her see things in a different light.

So what are you going to do about it? Wait until it's too late and you're either found or dead?

With a sense of desperation, she knew she was running out of time.

As for Tavis, he was on deck, wondering why Elizabeth was so bullheadedly cordial toward him—in an overly exaggerated way that made him wonder just how long a man could spend on a boat with a woman who behaved like that before he throttled her. Or threw himself overboard.

She prepared their meals, took the helm a fair amount of the time, and generally went out of her way to carry her part. As for communication, she initiated nothing on her own. She talked when he wanted to talk, and she was silent when he was. By the end of two days they were both tense and on edge.

Growing more irritable by the minute, Tavis decided the answer to his previous question was two days. A man could stay on board with a woman for two days before he throttled her or went overboard—then he reminded himself that he could, in fact, throw *her* overboard, and no one would ever be the wiser.

How much longer could he put up with this stiff formality? They were nearing the end of their food and had precious little water left. If someone didn't find them soon, it wouldn't matter. Once he was dead, nothing would matter.

He shook his head, thinking it was strange how the fact that they would be dead in a few days didn't seem to make any difference. She had taken a verbal shot at him in anger, and it had really gotten to him. The thirst for revenge was boiling in every ounce of his red blood.

Normally Tavis was a pretty easygoing fellow, and for that reason he didn't know why it was that Elizabeth's stinging cut bothered him so much—especially considering she had never been anything other than a pain in the arse since he had known her.

That's exactly what I've heard. . . .

He shuddered. Every time those words went through his consciousness, they were like a white-hot iron that seared the word *revenge* across his brain. She had cut him to the quick, and it galled him. Over and over he asked himself, *Why should I be concerned over anything she said?*

He didn't know why. He just was. *Why do I let a comment like that needle me when I know damn well I'm good at whatever I do . . . seducing women included?* He couldn't answer that one either, but her words ate at him nonetheless.

Tavis was leaning against what was left of the mast when Elizabeth came on deck. She didn't look at him, but went straight to the rail and, after scooping herself a bucket of water, began washing her hair. He tried to concentrate on what she was doing, tried to think of her in a different light, but it was no use. He was still struggling with his anger, still feeling like he had eaten scorpions. In his opinion, it was the perfect anger— Aristotle's words on the wall over his drafting table be damned: *Anyone can become angry—that is easy—but to be angry with the right person, to the right degree, at the right time, for the right purpose, and in the right way—this is not easy.*

Well, so much for quotes. He was angry. With the

right person. To the right degree. At the right time. For the right purpose. In the right way. And it damn well was easy!

Whenever he tried to reason himself out of it, he remembered what she had said: *That's exactly what I've heard. . . .* He looked at her, telling himself this was one time she wasn't going to get the best of him. His pump was primed.

She poured the last bucket of salt water over her head and wrapped a towel around it. She turned around. Their gazes locked and the two of them stared at each other for a brief combative second before Elizabeth, looking away, removed the towel and began drying her hair, as if unwilling to acknowledge the growing sense of animosity between them.

There she stood, the picture of innocence, fluffing her long hair this way and that, the perfect image of womanhood, her lush breasts bouncing with each jerky movement. *She's bouncing them on purpose, just to aggravate me,* he thought. *But it won't work. She isn't going to falter me and sidestep the issue with distractions. Nope, it won't work, Lizzie. Not with me.* With a snort of disgust, Tavis turned away. If she wasn't going to use that bed of hers, he sure as hell would.

He went below, lying down on the cot and folding his arms beneath his head, remembering the way she had looked at him before drying her hair. It chafed him— she didn't even acknowledge the friction between them. Well, it was there whether she liked it or not. He gritted his teeth. And she sure as hell would acknowledge it before too damn long. He would see to that, or his name wasn't Robert Tavis Mackinnon.

The longer he lay there, the madder he got, and the madder he got, the sooner he realized that it was one thing to have his pride hurt, but it was another thing entirely to have his lovemaking ridiculed. And by *her* of all people. *Her!* A woman who wouldn't know a good seduction if it bit her on the arse.

"So I'm not that good, am I?" he said to the lamp swinging overhead. Suffer or triumph? That was the question. "Well, I'll show you just how good I am," he said. A moment later, he was coming up off the bed. *I'll show you, all right,* he thought. *What was it Byron wrote? "Pique her and soothe her . . . soon passion crowns thy hopes."*

Or, to express it more eloquently in his own terms, *Any woman is weak and willing when she's seduced by a determined villain.* Lizzie was going to be seduced and well, or he would die trying.

Beware vinegar and sweet wine, and the anger of a peaceable man.

On deck, Elizabeth was still drying her hair, and as usual, she was thinking about Tavis. Perhaps her thoughts were strictly from habit, or perhaps they were prompted by the uncomfortable situation that stretched painfully between them. Whatever the cause, it was a strain emotionally, and once she started thinking about him, she couldn't stop.

It wasn't long until her thoughts began to dwell upon the hopelessness of their situation, the reality that they could very well die here without ever sighting land or being rescued. *Well, it was just as well.* Things weren't easy between them anyway, and the way she looked at it, if she couldn't have Tavis, what was the use in living anyway?

Dead or alive? Either way, he was lost to her.

If she was going to die—and by now she was certain

she was—she didn't want to die with someone who was angry at her. They could at least offer each other comfort at the end.

At that point it also occurred to her that there were a few other things she and Tavis could offer each other besides conversation and comfort. *Well, wasn't that what he tried to do when you promptly doused his amorous fires?*

She put that thought from her mind, telling herself that she wanted to be loved, not seduced—a great thought, actually, *if* they had more time.

What it all came down to was this: She could die an unloved virgin, or she could die a woman unloved, but a woman in the truest sense of the word. Practicality ruled the moment. A mariner must have his eye upon rocks and sands, as well as upon the North Star.

Over and over, from deep within herself, she seemed to hear a still, small voice that was bent upon repeating an infinite number of times, *Lizzie, if you are going to die, you don't want to die an ignorant virgin do you?*

Well, of course she didn't.

She wanted to know what it is like to make love. Who wouldn't? Death was so final, and while it would answer some questions about the hereafter, it would leave a whole lot more unanswered about the present.

There were so many things in life she would be denied in death. Surely God in His infinite mercy could not fault her for wanting to see granted just one last wish: If she was going to die, let it be in Tavis Mackinnon's arms, *after* they made love.

But Tavis didn't look too willing to do much of anything right now. She had galled him with that comment about his masculinity, and now he would barely speak to her. So how could she possibly expect him to make love to her?

Well, she told herself, *there is only one way to find out. He either will or he won't.*

That much was true, but what if he wouldn't? After all, she hadn't exactly fallen into his arms the last time he tried. *I don't know,* she thought, remembering he had hardly spoken to her for two whole days, remembering, too, the hostile way he had looked at her a few minutes ago. She sighed, thinking the least she could do was to try and let him know she had changed her mind.

And if that doesn't work?

Then I'll seduce him, she thought. *I don't want to die a virgin. I don't. I don't.*

In Elizabeth's opinion, dying a virgin was a steeple without bells. It was ignorance without bliss. It was downright stupid. Tavis might not love her, but he wanted her—she knew that much for certain. Next time she was with him, she would not restrain him. Instead, she would give him a free hand, but even as she thought it, she couldn't help wondering, *What will he do with it?*

Elizabeth, ever practical, tried to look at the thing logically, while also ignoring something her grandfather often said: "Elizabeth, you must remember that logic is doing wrong with confidence."

With the logic of a dreamer, she decided there were two factors unquestionably in her favor:

One was the fact that Tavis was, as he had said, a man with a man's desires—this undoubtedly should make him overcome his residual anger.

Secondly, what else was there for him to do on a sloop with no mast, in the middle of the ocean?

She would win him over to her way of thinking. She

was certain of it. And to make sure she did, she would be the picture of sweetness; the epitome of the temptress. Before he knew what happened, Tavis Mackinnon would find himself seduced.

In spite of his foul mood, Tavis found himself grinning at her. Apparently Elizabeth was getting lonesome and remorseful at the same time, for here she came down the stairs, humming a little tune and smiling, drawing to a halt when she saw him on the cot.

"I know you must be hungry," she said pleasantly, and foolishly thinking his grin meant he had forgiven her. He stopped smiling and started to rise. She immediately rushed to his side, placing her hand on his arm. "Oh, don't get up. Rest while I find us something to eat."

He didn't want to appear too easy, however, so he gave her a surly look and said, "I'll think about it." He came to his feet, then climbed up the ladder to the deck.

"Well," Elizabeth said to the empty cabin, "you can't expect to set a hen one day and have chickens the next, now can you?" She sighed and pulled out a tin of potted meat. "Patience, Elizabeth. Patience. He has on his horns, so give him a wide berth."

Overhead, Tavis paced the deck, remembering his earlier decision to show her just how good he was, and concentrating on how this seduction/revenge thing should go. This wasn't just your ordinary seduction. After all, his reputation was at stake here. The way he saw it, cold-blooded seduction required a cold-blooded attitude. After a lifetime of putting up with her escapades and capers, he had something to prove to Elizabeth.

Pique her and soothe her . . . soon passion crowns

thy hopes. He had no idea why that quote kept coming to him, or why it came, but it gave him an idea. It surely did.

He heard her call him, but he purposefully did not go. He was starving, of course, but it was more important to pique her than to eat.

She called his name again. He kept right on pacing. Then he paused. She would be getting piqued by the count of three, or he'd miss his guess. *One . . . two . . . three . . .*

"Are you coming down to eat or not?" a voice boomed out from below.

He grinned and checked his watch. Then he waited a full fifteen minutes before he made his slow descent below.

She was sitting at the small table, thrumming her fingers on the top, and although she was obviously cross, she was doing her damnedest to not look put out. "I waited for you," she said in a cheerful voice that in no way went with the acutely irritated look he had just seen on her face.

"You shouldn't have," he said, wondering why she was obviously forcing herself to be nice.

He sat down.

"Here," she said, shoving the food at him, but when he looked at her, she was smiling. "Eat," was all she said.

He frowned. She wasn't piquing too easy. He'd have to try a little harder. He took a bite and dropped his fork.

"What's wrong?" she asked.

"What are you feeding me? Rat poison?"

He saw her lips go white. A surefire sign of anger if he ever saw one. *I've got her now.*

"It's potted meat," she said in calm, succinct tones before giving him a sweet smile.

"It tastes like cow slobber," he said, knowing he was pushing it to the limit.

She looked like she wanted to hit him, or at least ask him how he knew what cow slobber tasted like. It obviously took a great deal of restraint not to do so.

"If you don't like it, there is a little sausage and crackers left," she said, the words fired off in quick succession that made him think that if they had been bullets, he would be dead about now. "Would you like me to get you some?"

He leaned back and crossed his hands over his middle, exaggerating each word as he spoke. "Oh, I don't rightly know if I do or not. What else have you got?"

Her fists clenched. Her knuckles turned white. But her words were pleasant. "Unfortunately, there isn't much . . . a little cheese, a tin of biscuits, one of canned fruit. . . ."

He blinked. What was the matter with her? Was she dense? Was she raised on gall? Didn't she understand he was being a complete ass? Where was all that pride of hers? Didn't she want to crown him, or at least throw something? She was a woman of action, so where was it? He gave her a nasty look, thinking that would surely pique her. When it didn't, he said hatefully, "Never mind. I'm not hungry." He came to his feet, intentionally scraping the chair on his way up. He grinned. Now she looked ready to throw something.

But instead, she said nicely, "Would you like to talk?"

"Not particularly."

"How about a walk on deck?"

"My thoughts exactly."

She released a pent-up breath and started after him. "I'd rather be alone."

That drew her up short. For a moment she looked as though she might cry. "Why are you being so hateful?"

For the life of him, he didn't know why he persisted with this. It was just one of those things that once it got started, you couldn't find a place to jump off—like riding in a runaway wagon. But instead of telling her that, he cocked his head to one side and said, "Am I?"

"You are, and in case you haven't noticed, I'm *trying* to be nice."

"Don't be," he said. "I can stand anything but nice."

"Well, nice is all that is being offered at the moment."

"Why?"

"Why shouldn't I be nice?"

"Why should you?"

"Are you trying to provoke me?"

"Am I?"

He knew she was gritting her teeth when she said, "Of course not."

"Pity," he said. "Provoked, you might have something that faintly resembled a personality." Turning away, he went topside, thinking, *That ought to do it. She ought to be good and piqued now.*

A few seconds later she came stomping up on deck. He had his back to her, and although he heard her coming like a bull angry enough to tear up an anvil, he didn't turn around. He knew by the sound of things that she was marching toward him like a colonel with his ire up, but her words were anything but peppery.

"It's a lovely night, isn't it?"

His jaw dropped. Words deserted him. Patience to this degree bordered on the lunatic, the absurd. He turned around slowly, to see she had stopped a few feet away from him. Her face was turned in his direction, bathed in the moon's approving light. For a moment he forgot himself. She was lovely. Moonlight adored her face. He would have gone further, but he suddenly realized she was smiling.

Smiling? When he was being so horrible? For a moment he could do nothing but stare at her, dumbfounded. No one could be this dense, this thick-witted. No one.

"What did you say?" he asked stupidly, still trying to sort things out.

"I said, it's a lovely night, isn't it?"

"It was."

"Was?"

"It was, until you came up here."

Apparently that did it, for she clamped her hands on her hips and glared up at him. "What is wrong with you? Why are you treating me like this?"

"Like what?"

"I've tried and tried to be nice to you. . . ."

"Don't be."

"Why not?"

"Because I don't want you to be nice to me. I don't want you to be anything, because I don't want to have anything to do with you. Understand?"

It was at this point that Tavis made an astounding discovery: This business of piquing a woman worked both ways. It had its advantages and its drawbacks. Here he was, doing his damnedest to be horrible in order to provoke her, and the minute he did, he felt lower than a snake's belly. He looked at her, seeing her wreathed in starshine and bathed in moonlight. A breeze lifted the tendrils of hair along her neck, and he thought how vulnerable that slim neck looked.

After all the times he had thought of her as such a pest, an aggravation he would like to rid himself of, he could hardly grasp now that she was, in reality, so much more. The thought of it hit hard enough to make him want to drop his earlier notion of revenge—realizing it for what it was, asinine and typically male. His anger had been a blind thing. Losing his temper was like putting to sea in a storm.

What began with folly ended with repent.

Tavis saw the way her lip quivered and felt his heart contract. He said her name quietly, but she did not respond to it or to the soft look in his eyes. She was looking bewildered, as if she didn't know where she was, like a sea gull blown off its course and driven too far inland. He watched, feeling utterly helpless as a tear fell. One. Then another. He wanted to reach out, to wipe them from the curve of her cheekbone, then bring the taste of them to his mouth. But when he lifted his hand to reach for her, she turned away, running from him. A second later, she was gone.

With agonizing clarity, he realized what he had done. For a long time he stood there, feeling disarmed, not knowing what he should to. Revenge, it seemed, had a sweet taste, but it was far too bitter to swallow.

Well, old boy, you certainly have her piqued now. What's the matter? Isn't it what you wanted?

Not this, he thought. *I didn't want this.*

But you were angry. Think about all those wonderful reasons.

Anger always has a reason, but rarely is it a good one. If only his mouth had stopped when his wisdom did.

He couldn't seem to think about anything right now, save how lovely she had looked only moments ago, smiling up at him, her face bathed in moonlight. And now she was below, rejected and desolate. He couldn't hear her, but he knew she was probably crying her heart out, and the thought of it reached out to him.

She was like an opened flower that draws back into a bud when touched by rain. Only it wasn't rain that touched her. It was pain.

And he was the son of a bitch who caused it. He had been a fool to let his anger be fueled by his pitiful pride. He saw himself as a strutting cock and hated the imagery.

Suddenly he was on his way below, all thought of seduction erased from his mind. Now he was nothing more than a man humbled and brought to his knees.

He was feeling inept and bumbling. He had no experience with the softer emotions. He was out of touch with the things a woman likes and needs. In the end, it was knowing the pain she felt and knowing he had caused it that called out to him, overriding his insecurity. Little did it matter that he was clumsy, in a way that a man is often awkward and clumsy around a woman.

"Elizabeth?" he asked, walking toward the cot and seeing her lying on top of the blanket, wearing a chaste white gown, her hand curled into the pillow that held her head and absorbed her tears.

"G-g-go away."

He came to the cot and sat down beside her, his hand reaching out to stroke the silver coils of her braid. She pushed his hand away. "Leave me alone. Please."

"I want to talk to you," he said, trying to brush the tears from her wet cheek.

She looked at him, and something wrenched inside him, seeing those eyes of hers, shining like a doe's—trapped, vulnerable, and knowing it. She made a small sound of distress and buried her face in the pillow.

A warm, comforting hand ran along her back, touching her bare arm. "You're cold."

She gave a short hiccuping sob. "Yes I am, but I could never be as cold as you."

He covered her with the blanket. "I know you couldn't. You're too nurturing. You care too much. Sometimes that can be a woman's downfall." He sighed, knowing what he needed to say. "This is all my fault. I'm sorry."

She lifted her head and rolled over to face him. "Sorry? You think you can take away the pain of your cruelty by saying you're sorry? Well, it doesn't work that way. Feelings aren't something you can open and close like a door. You treated me like dirt, and for what?" She was crying now. "Tell me, what did I do that made me deserve this?" She shook her head. "All I ever did was love you," she said, looking into his eyes. "Was that so terrible?"

"No," he said, "it wasn't terrible and it wasn't that."

"Then what was it? Tell me. I have a right to at least know."

"I was angry and I let my anger override my good judgment. Anger makes a coward brave," he said. "I'm not making excuses. I know what I did ... well, it was wrong. I'm not normally like that. It has never been my habit to make another person suffer."

He looked off for a moment, as if he were giving his attention to studying the dark shadows cast on the opposite wall by the lamplight striking the support beam. "I don't know what's wrong with me, why I seem to do such crazy things around you."

He looked back at her briefly, then shifted his gaze to her hands, lying pale and stiff on the blanket. "I wish I had the right answers. Some of this, I don't understand myself. My manly pride was wounded because of something you said in anger, and for a while I allowed my mind to be occupied, not with why you might have said it, but what you said. I was obsessed with getting even."

"Well, you certainly got your wish."

"Yes," he said, looking at her, "only now I discover, too late, that it isn't what I wanted at all. My so-called victory has cost me more than you, I think, and brought with it many regrets."

"Is that supposed to make me happy?"

He gave her a sad sort of smile. "No, but it shouldn't make you any angrier." He wiped the wet tear-trails with his thumb. "You're hurt and angry, and you have a right to be."

She remained mute.

His expression changed and he gave her an odd sort of look. He felt a knot form in his stomach that hit him like a fist. He had never been so distracted by her eyes, by the trueness of their color, the deep, faithful blue that leaned toward violet. And right now they were glaring at him. "I find this strange. You are, I think, even more beautiful when you're angry. I wonder why that is. Perhaps it's because a woman is so much more irreproachable when she is as virtuous as she is blameless."

She made a sound of doubt and looked away, lifting her hand to trace the seams in the wooden panels that covered the walls. Matt had painted these, and she tried to hang on to the thought, as if it were a lifeline she could cling to. "Virtuous," she repeated. "Is that what you call a bumbling undesirable too unsophisticated to get herself ravished?"

Her words cut him to the core, but he knew sympathy would send those waiting tears rushing down her cheeks. She had her bit of pride, too. He forced lightness into his voice. "Ravished, is it?" His heart was in his smile. "Are you sure that is the word you meant to use?"

Her hand fell to the blanket, and she turned angry eyes to gaze right at him. "I was trying to seduce you, you bloody idiot."

"Seduce . . . You mean you were being nice because you were trying . . ." His gaze snapped to her lovely face, seeing there what he had been too blind or too angry or too pigheaded to see before. She had made her mind up. Now it all came back to him in a rush of feeling. This was what she had been about.

"You want me to make love to you?"

She nodded.

"Oh, Liza," he said, taking her in his arms. "Don't you know that is what I've been wanting to do all along?"

She was no longer angry, but she was still miffed. "You have a strange way of showing it. From where I stood, it looked like you were close to going over the side, just to get away from me."

"If I wanted to get away from you, I could have tossed *you* over the side," he answered, smiling inwardly at the way she drew up into a stiff little knot. "And I did come damnably close to making love to you the other night . . . and you stopped me, as I recall."

She eyed him narrowly. "Oh, so that's what you called it? I seem to remember a flowery speech you gave me that made you sound like a rutting bastard instead of a man with any finesse at lovemaking. What did you expect me to do?"

"Well, I thought you deserved more than a casual rutting on the deck, no matter how much *I* wanted to. And believe me, I did want to." He laughed and made a pained, groaning sound, remembering the stiff erection he had had for hours afterward. "Painful night it was, too."

"Good," she said, "it couldn't be painful enough to suit me."

He laughed at her innocence and drew her closer, pulling the bed sheets from her body and rolling against her, tossing the blanket over them both.

"What do you think you're doing?"

He scooted toward her, his arm going around her waist. "Getting close to you."

"I don't want you anywhere near me; besides, this bed is too small for two of us to sleep in," she said, giving him a shove. "It's my bed."

"True, but I'm stronger." He rooted back against her, then nuzzled her neck, whispering, "It doesn't really matter. I don't intend to sleep anyway. At least, not yet."

"You know what I meant. I don't want to make love with you . . . not anymore."

"Liza, you don't know what you want, but luckily for both of us, I do. Now, will you be quiet?" He didn't give her a chance to answer, but folded her in his arms, his mouth coming down on hers.

"You think too much. And you talk too much. And for thirteen years you've tried too damn hard." He raised up on one elbow so he could look down at her. "Will you, for once, resist the urge to control things between us and be content to lie back and let nature take its course?"

He could tell by her awed expression that his words couldn't have hit her more precisely if he'd taken up a board and slammed her square between the eyes. In the flash of an instant he read so much in that face. The youthful hopefulness staggered him. The innocent hunger in her eyes cut him to the depths.

She sighed and stretched, feeling wonderful. And why shouldn't she? After all these years of her pursuing him hotly, he was taking control. She wasn't chasing him anymore.

She sighed again. *Let nature take its course. . . . There must be something wrong with me,* she thought. *Any woman who finds a comment like that romantic must be a half-wit.*

She didn't think about anything else, for Tavis put his hand on her breast and nuzzled her neck. Then he moved to her ear, taking the lobe between his teeth. Elizabeth groaned, arching her body closer to him. His mouth was all over her now, smothering her face with kisses. He took her chin between his fingers, tilting her mouth upward, rubbing her lips with his, then kissing her again and again. When she was mindless with sensation after sensation, he rolled away.

She opened her eyes with a start. Before she realized what he was doing, he was removing her nightgown. "Take this off. I want to see you," he said. "I want to see if you're as lovely as in my imagination."

His words went over her like a shiver. A moment later, she was naked. He moved away from her, long enough to turn up the wick of the lamp, then he went back to look at her. Self-conscious now, she made a move to cover herself, picking up a corner of the blanket. "Don't," he said. "You have a beautiful body . . . one that's—" his words caught in his throat at the sight of her "—much too lovely to hide."

She dropped the blanket, turning her face away. A moment later, he was sitting beside her. "Liza, lovely Liza, don't be ashamed. A woman's body is like a temple for a man to worship. It should give a woman a feeling of power to have a man look at her as I look at you."

Power? All she felt was limp. She was mesmerized by him, by the touch of his hand on her, the low, throaty sound of his voice. Everything around her existed in a dream. This was what she had always wanted. It was what she was created for. She should be happy—and she was. But at the same time she had never felt so sharply the agony of a woman's forlornness. That bleak, disheartening feeling that comes from loving someone who doesn't love you in return.

He felt the heat of her tear on his wrist. He drew back, pulling away from her, for suddenly he was aware of a new flame hurling through his loins. This woman, more than any other, frightened him, for her honesty was as threatening to him as it was arousing. He fought his desire for her, but it raged and encircled him, settling in his groin.

He removed his clothes, then he turned back to Elizabeth, putting his arms around her and running his hands over the curve of her back, a blind, stroking motion that was more instinct than caress. He traced the fullness of her breast, burying his face in the cove of her neck. Then, taking her hand in his, he brought her fingers down to touch him.

"Tavis . . ."

"There is no turning back," he said. "We passed that point a long time ago."

His hands traced her spine. She felt the burn of it at the back of her eyes, not because she was afraid, but because she had always known it would be like this. The reality was as perfect as her dream. It did not matter that no one had told her what it would be like, for there could have been no way to describe this feeling. She felt herself grow restless, wanting to touch him, suddenly yearning to know him all over—every mark, every curve, every childhood scar. Like a wave lured to shore, she felt herself drawn to him, sighing at the feel of the heat of his body as he moved over her, putting her beneath him.

It was so strange, really, for she felt like she was in a place she had never been before, yet each road she took, each path she trod, was hauntingly familiar. He taught her things about herself she did not know, seeming to shape her, drawing out responses she didn't know she possessed. When he entered her, she knew peace. At long last, peace.

Even in the delirium of passion, in that moment of incoherent rapture, she felt such an intense peace that the old Elizabeth shattered, and in her place a new one was reborn. Trapped in a miracle, it enfolded her, warm and comfortable, melting her into a marvelous serenity, calm and free, free of wondering, free of questions. She knew. Dear God, for all eternity she knew.

Watching his face above her, she saw her reflection in his eyes. His mouth dropped down to hers and he kissed her, repeatedly, speaking to her in the aftermath of passion.

It was too lovely to end and she clung blindly to him as he pulled back, feeling a new and tender love for him when she felt that wilting part of him withdrawing, so tender in its frailty, so vulnerable and helpless now after the fierceness, the powerful thrusting.

In her heart, which had always loved him, a new wonder was stirred to wakefulness. How beautiful he was, how sensitive, how strong. She took him in her hand and felt power, unspeakable power, life within life. The strange weight of it, the mystery, they were known to her now. Her heart seemed to melt out of her in love and in awe.

She clung to the warm, half-sleepy remoteness of him, her hands brushing over the soft curve of naked haunches, her own mind sharp and crystalline with new knowledge. There had been no force, no deception, no betrayal. There was no pain, no embarrassment, no guilt. It was beautiful in its perfectness, but it was more beautiful because of its honesty.

This was what she had been born for. This was what would stay with her throughout eternity.

He lay against her, limp, sweating, and exhausted, his breathing deep, his hand curled against the curve of her breast. Kissing the top of his head, she held him to her and felt as if she were the richest woman in the world.

"Now I know what love is," she whispered against the soft filaments of his hair. "After years of wandering, it is finally coming home."

CHAPTER
❧ THIRTEEN ❧

It was a warm, sunny day with hardly any breeze at all, a day that drew Elizabeth topside to braid her hair. The ocean was calm and green, the world above so tranquil, it made her yawn and blink her eyes like a drowsy owl. Hardly the image one would have for a time and place to die. But die they would, and soon— for they had eaten the last of their food yesterday, and the final drop of water went this morning.

She let out a breath and closed her eyes, her body melting with the sun's warmth and the rhythm of the sea that moved beneath her like a great lumbering whale. The breeze billowed her skirts around her and left the taste of salt upon her skin. She opened her eyes, seeing the familiar all about her—the bare skeleton of rigging, the splintered mast, the molten glow of sun moving over varnished mahogany rails—and for a moment she wondered what would become of her treasured sloop. Tavis had made love to her, here on these very decks. Here she had come alive. Here she would die.

She didn't know why she woke up this morning and

decided to wear the only dress she had on board, or why it was important to her to wash her hair and braid it, unless she was thinking of dying romantically tragic, like Ophelia. *There's rosemary, that's for remembrance. . . .*

Remembrance. Memories. She had plenty of those. She tied a ribbon on the long braid and tossed it over her shoulder, then leaned forward to hug her knees.

She heard a splash and came to her feet, walking to the rail. Leaning over it, she watched Tavis surface, then throw his head back to sling the water out of his hair. "Come on in," he called out when he saw her. "The water is a little cold at first, but—"

"You get numb quickly, and after that, you are unable to feel anything," she finished with a laugh, jumping back when he splashed her. The water was clear, and from where she stood, she could plainly see he had nothing on. The thought warmed her, bringing back a fragrant wash of memories of the past few days.

He was watching her now, grinning up at her, as if he knew what she was thinking. As she watched, he flipped over on his back, and she giggled, giving him a frank, surveying look which seemed to please him, for he laughed. *Men. They are such immodest creatures.* In truth, they would just as easily show their privates as their faces. She was also thinking how the sight of those privates seemed so natural to her now, natural and nothing to be embarrassed by. It was amazing to her how far she had come in just one week.

It seemed impossible to her in so many ways—that it had been only a week since the night he first made love to her. She counted back, trying to remember how many times she had seen that passionate side of him since then. Twice the first night—it was easy to remember that, for what woman would ever forget the first time? And the second night? Twice again, she was certain. But after that, the days and the lovemaking seemed to melt together into one beautiful moment that shimmered just beyond her reach, impossible to touch, yet sharing its light and beauty, quite like the sunset. She sighed, thinking how glad she was for the chance to really and truly live. For all time she would know that for one glorious moment she had existed in an exalted place, a place of stars. Surely this would send her to Heaven with dry eyes.

The sun went behind a cloud, and a shadow passed over the sloop like the wings of Azrael. She thought about dying and how everything looked different when filtered through the wings of the Angel of Death. How strange it was that she had not known what life really meant until faced with death. Why did it take the presence of death to give life significance?

She had no answer, yet it seemed to matter not. Her heart was glad for the living of the past week. She could not be sad. Her love was too beautiful to be sad, too powerful to cry. It was something not even death could touch.

Feeling her heart would burst with the joy of loving him, she glanced back over the side, anxiously seeking his face and feeling acute disappointment when she saw he was no longer there.

"Looking for me?" he asked.

Startled, she turned quickly around, flooding him with a smile that matched the one in her heart when she saw the way he looked at her—obviously distracted by the sight of her in a dress. Was there any better feeling in the world for a woman than to see the eyes of her beloved drinking in the sight of her like this?

She didn't think so.

"How was your swim?" she asked, feeling her soul hum. It was all she could do to keep from hurling herself at him, to restrain herself from covering every inch of him with exuberant kisses. She loved him. She adored him. She worshiped every part of him, and her heart was bursting with the joy of it. How sad it was that they were out here all alone, when she wanted the whole world to know of her feelings, the delight, the excitement, the pleasure she found in this man. She could stand here forever, simply looking at him. She didn't even try to keep her eyes from dropping to where the sheeting he used to dry himself was tied low about his waist. It would have been useless to try. Just looking at him made her warm all over. She wondered if he could feel the heat.

"That look is still piping from the fire," he said.

Her gaze came back to his face. She laughed. "It must not be too hot," she replied. "Your lips are still blue."

"*All* of me is blue," he said, "but looking at you in that sassy pink dress is warming me considerably."

She almost laughed, but something in his eyes held her, draining the humor from the moment. His eyes were so beautiful and clear, she could see her reflection in them. But it wasn't her reflection that touched her. It was the look of abject and utter desolation in his eyes—a look as bleak as a strip of wind-washed Nantucket beach. She knew what he was thinking. He was blaming himself for what had happened . . . for what was about to happen.

He had not only his own death to reckon with, but hers as well.

"Liza, I want you to know . . ." His voice broke. "If

there was any way I could undo what has happened . . ."

"I know," she said. "I don't hold you at fault. Truly."

"But you should. If I hadn't shanghaied you and commandeered your sloop, you would be at home right now. . . ."

"Shriveling on the vine and wasting my life writing poetry and gazing at stars through telescopes, destined to never know the touch of your hand, the joy of knowing for all time the mystery of lovemaking, the joining of a woman and a man. No, thank you. If I had it to do all over again—"

She didn't get to finish, for he stepped closer and, taking her hand, drew her against him. A second later, he was lifting her into his arms and carrying her away from the bow to a place where a ragged remnant of sail lay waiting like a bed. He stood her on her feet, and when she made a move to lie down, he stopped her. She gave him a puzzled look, but he only grinned and said, "I like the way you look in a dress . . . but I like you better in nothing."

He began removing her clothes. She leaned her head back and closed her eyes, wondering briefly how many times he had done this before, and how many women had felt the same anxiousness to touch him, the same burning ache to be touched by him in return.

When she was naked, he dropped the sheeting around his waist. Before he could draw her down to lie upon the sun-warmed canvas, she went to her knees, putting her arms around his slim loins, drawing him to her. His belly was flat and firm, his phallus heavy and yet delicate in its manliness. "You are beautiful," she said, and took him in her mouth.

"Dear God!" he groaned. Throwing his head back, he

said nothing more, speaking to her with only his hands, which came around to cradle the back of her head.

Nothing was slow after that. Their coupling was fierce and wild. He covered her the moment she released him and lay back, his fingers digging into her hair, angling her head back and kissing her deeply. "A woman is a beautiful thing when there is no hypocrisy, no shame. You are as pure and lovely as truth. I love your wantonness. This time I want to make your body hum," he whispered.

"It's already humming," she said. "A song I don't know all the words to."

"You will," he said, and kissed her mouth again.

He was naked, warm and hard, and she couldn't touch enough, kiss enough, feel enough. She wanted it all. He seemed more than happy to give it to her. His hands on her breasts now, he kissed his way down to her belly, but when she cried out his name, "Tavis," he seemed to sense the urgency in her voice and he came back to her, whispering her name against her mouth and kissing her deeply.

He entered her with one quick, hard thrust. She was so ready for him that on the third thrust, she shuddered. It was fierce and violent and scalding. She loved what came afterward, the pause of peace after the heat of lovemaking, like the sun when it goes down. There was a joining even in lying chastely together, a delicate thing that flowed over her like warm water. For a long time they lay there, neither of them speaking, but she knew that he, like she, was thinking about the time they had left.

After some moments, he spoke. "What are you thinking?"

She opened her eyes, looking at the white puffy

clouds drifting overhead. "I feel as if I'm floating out there somewhere, just beyond the bow," she said, then rolling to her side, she hooked her leg through his and kissed him softly on the mouth. "Is that what it's like to die?" she asked. "You just close your eyes and drift away to a place where nothing is left of you but what you are thinking?"

"I don't know. Like you, I can only guess. They say it's like sleeping."

"But there is some link with sleep," she said. "In sleep you dream. When you awake, you remember it. There is a connection, don't you think?"

He drew his head back and looked down at her with a puzzled frown. "You think I'm some sort of expert?"

"In some things," she said, touching him.

He grinned and kissed her, then lying back, he said, "I suppose you are conscious of things, even in death." He gave her an odd look. Then he kissed her nose and smiled. "I'll tell you what. If I go before you do, I'll try to wait around long enough to let you know."

Her heart skipped a beat and stilled.

If I go before you do . . .

Dear God, she had not considered that—that he might go before her. Her mind was swimming with the reality of it. She had imagined them dead, only now she could see it was a childish sort of imagining at best—something akin to Romeo and Juliet being laid out in a flower-drenched bower, their faces young and tragic in repose.

But now? Now she saw things clearly—clearly and for what they were. Cruel and unfair, surely, but certain. There was no way out, save rescue, and that possibility was so remote that it no longer seemed an alternative. What was certain was the fact that they were on a sloop in the middle of the ocean, sans food, sans water, sans hope. They would die here, and rot here, with scavengers picking the flesh from their bones. There was no glory in that, no element of romantic tragedy to be played out. Yet in spite of it all, in spite of knowing she would die and die horribly, the most difficult thing to accept was the fact that one of them would go first.

Let it be me, she pleaded. *Dear, sweet Christ, please . . . let it be me.*

She looked at him, feeling a strangeness she had never before felt, feeling the power of what had passed between them like a benediction. The warm satisfaction of it ran through her like tongues of fire, licking at her womb. It was too soon. So much had been taken away from them. She should be angry. She should raise her fist and curse God. Yet all her responses were numb. Something flowed out of her, something that made her feel a bit maudlin. She was a woman now, fulfilled and with an instinct for happiness.

It could be so good with him.

She felt lonely now, and isolated, as if part of her had been pried away from him. Sadness seemed to grip her, yet there were no tears in her eyes. The tears were all on the inside. She didn't know what prompted her, or why she did it, but she locked her arms around his neck. It didn't matter. Not really. All that mattered now was the fact that they were both still alive and she needed him, needed his strength, his comfort, the rhythmic rise and fall of his chest, for only then would she get what she needed most. The reassurance that he lived.

She closed her eyes and slept.

She dreamed of a warm summer morning on a sun-drenched street in Nantucket. Judging from the number of birds singing in the tree outside her window and the sound of her sisters playing and laughing in the yard below, she knew it was springtime, that it had to be before she went to Boston.

She dreamed she saw Tavis walking down the street, as he always did, talking to his friends, Cole and Nathaniel. He nodded his head and spoke to every woman he passed, stopping often to do more than merely say "Hello."

She saw herself coming down the street, and when she reached him, mumbling some awkward, childish remark, making a fool of herself and not receiving so much as a recognizing nod for her efforts. She heard, too, the mocking sound of his laughter after she had passed. He had no time to give to her, and took no notice of her mumblings, save for the good laugh it provided him and his friends.

She awoke with a start, realizing her dream was reality, the truth of the relationship between them. How different things might have been if he had not taken her sloop, if they were not faced with the imminence of death.

It wasn't the threat of death or the pain of his ignoring her in the past, or even the loss of something she never really had, that made her cry. It wasn't even her, but something greater than herself, that rose up like a great consuming anguish and wept, sobbing out the soul-wrenching unfairness of it. She was ashamed to feel such a lowly emotion, shamed to her heart that she felt pity for herself. She sobbed out the agony of it.

I am dying, she realized at intervals throughout that night. *Surrounded by water and nothing to drink, floating on a sea of fish and nothing to eat.* The thought made her laugh. *I must be delirious,* she thought. *If I find that funny, I must be.*

She felt Tavis's arms come around her, heard the comforting sound of his voice. "Shhhh," he said. "Try to get some sleep."

"Why?" she asked. "Before long, I can sleep for an eternity."

"Ever the practical one," he said. "Even when faced with death." He pushed her head down. "Close your eyes," he said.

She closed her eyes and drifted.

When she awoke and her mind cleared, she found herself sitting on her cot. The heat was stifling, and she knew that must be what woke her. She dressed and went topside and found Tavis, wearing only his pants, lying in a small scrap of shade. He looked at her, his eyes inviting. She said nothing, but stretched out next to him. From that moment on, they adopted this wordless form of communication, since even to speak seemed to draw precious moisture from their mouths. His belly was sunken. His cheeks, too. His breathing was shallow and rapid. She fitted herself into the crook of his arm and closed her eyes. *I will die here. This is the last time I will lie down. No more will I get up.* The thought slowly drifted from her mind. Her last thought was, *He was right. It is like going to sleep.*

Once she thought she heard voices near her and she was terrified, thinking they were the voices of angels and imagining they had come for her at last. Her soul cried out, *Why hast Thou forsaken me? Why could this cup not pass from me? Oh, giver of life, why could Thou not grant me more time?*

She felt herself lifted, borne up by angels' wings.

"What do you make of it?"

"Dehydration, most probably."

"They look almost like they're sleeping, like they're alive."

"They are alive.... At least this one is."

"And the other one? Is he dead?"

"Close, but still breathing."

Something within Elizabeth told her she was not dead, yet she could not open her eyes. Nor could she speak. She wasn't even certain that she was conscious of anything, save the miracle of voices. She felt her soul cry out, then she slipped into unconsciousness.

She had questioned God, had complained that He had not given her more time, and now she knew she had been spared. She opened her eyes and saw only a pair of gentle blue eyes peering at her from a bearded face as two strong arms raised her head, bringing a cool cup to her lips and cautioning her to sip slowly. She grabbed the hand that felt as gnarled as a tree trunk, and bringing it to her mouth, she kissed it.

"Sleep, lass," a beautiful voice said. "You wilna die now."

She nodded weakly, and still tightly gripping the hand, her heart fluttering with joy, she fell into a deep void of painlessness.

The next time she reached consciousness and saw the blue eyes, she waited for the familiar, but strange-sounding voice. "You look verra much better, lass. There's a wee bit o' color on your puir pale cheeks."

"Who are you?"

"Rob MacGregor. And you have a Scots name as well, Elizabeth Robinson."

"How do you know my name?"

"Your friend told me."

"Tavis?" She rose up so quickly, her head spun.

Rob pushed her back down. "Lie still, lass."

"Tavis . . . He's all right?"

"Aye, he's a huckleberry or two ahead of you, but I wouldna say he was in a holiday humor."

She smiled, feeling weariness close her eyes.

She recovered rapidly over the days it took them to sail to Nantucket. According to Rob, they were on a Canadian ship that had picked them up far south of Bermuda. Of Tavis, she saw little, until the day they were to reach Nantucket.

She stood beside him on deck, scanning the horizon for her first glimpse of home, wondering why they had grown so close while under the sentence of death, only to grow so far apart in life. She glanced at him, seeing the beloved outline of his profile, the sculpted planes of his face. He did not look at her, and in a way she was not sorry, for the times that he had looked at her, there had been a hardness, an aloof quality in his eyes, one laced with the finest edge of remorse. Was he trying to tell her something? Was he sorry for what had passed between them, for the taking of her virginity? Did he want nothing more to do with her? Had nothing changed between them after all?

She opened her mouth to speak, but was interrupted by the loud clanging of bells. A moment later the deck was swarming with hands. She knew the signs, knew they neared their destination. She squinted, bringing her hand up to shield the glare, seeing the hazy outline of Nantucket just ahead.

Home. She would soon be home. She felt herself go limp with relief. She turned toward Tavis, wanting to share her joy, but when her gaze rested upon the place she had seen him last, he was no longer there.

As she watched Nantucket grow closer, she felt a sense of loss. Why did it always happen that whenever she gained one thing, she gave up another?

Her thoughts were interrupted by the sound of someone approaching. A moment later, Tavis reappeared at her side. Without looking at him, she spoke lightly, her gaze fastened on the lighthouse at Brandt Point. "It looks the same, doesn't it? I suppose that it's good to know some things never change."

"Unlike people. Is that what you're saying?"

She looked at him. He was watching her, his gaze unreadable. "I don't know. Do you know someone who has changed?"

He looked off, leaning closer to the rail and resting his arms there. "About what happened, I want you to know that if things had been different, if we had—"

"If," she said, interrupting him because she feared what he was about to say, feared this change in him. "It's such a fickle word, don't you think? So much depends upon it, and yet it's so weak. If. So many conditions. So many stipulations. A word abounding in contingencies. Take now, for instance. So much is riding upon it, so many wishes. And I find it sad. . . . You have your ifs, and I have mine."

"Elizabeth."

She winced at the use of her name. Liza belonged to another time, another place. The old mask was back in place, the old boundaries of behavior had been redrawn, and a world of difference lay between them. *Tavis Mackinnon,* her heart cried out. *You are such a fool. A blind fool.*

Even as her heart hammered out those words, she

knew she did not, would not ever, have him. He was as lost to her as before. What they had shared, whatever was between them—it was all gone now.

But she had the memory. Question was, would it be enough?

The ship sailed around the point, dropping anchor before it reached the sandbar. A moment later Rob was beside her. "We've lowered a rowboat to take you ashore." He looked at her, then at Tavis, then back to her, before adding, "Whenever you're ready."

She felt Tavis's gaze upon her. "Give us a few more minutes," he said.

Elizabeth put a detaining hand on Rob's arm, then turned, giving Tavis a direct look. "Give us a few more minutes for what?"

Before he could reply, she turned back to Rob and said, "Tell the captain I'm ready to go. Now."

Rob nodded, touching his fingers to his cap. As soon as he departed, Elizabeth turned away. A second later, she heard Tavis speak, her heart hammering at the detached tone she detected in his voice. She started to leave, but he took her by the arm.

"If you would wait a minute . . ."

She turned toward him, her gaze searching his. "*If.* There's that word again, wobbly and barely able to stand." Without another sound, she pulled out of his grasp and turned away, leaving him to stand behind her, watching her walk away.

She was already seated in the rowboat, her gaze fastened on the hazy rising slopes of the Wesco Hills in the distance, when he descended the rope ladder, dropping into the rowboat and taking the seat beside her. Soon they were over the sandbar, passing a few members of a small colony of gray seals. Any other time she would have smiled at the antics of these social animals, or found herself wishing she had a pollack or cuttlefish to toss to the large, dark gray male that swam beside them for some distance. But today there were no diversions that held her attention for long—nothing that would take her mind off the fact that she would, in precious few minutes, find herself speechless and facing the questions of her father and her brothers, Stephen and Matt.

As they were rowed toward Straight Wharf, she pulled her gaze away from the playful seals to look upon the ships scattered about the harbor, sitting at anchor. Her heart lifted when she recognized the whaler three of her brothers had been on, knowing they had come home. Unable to forget that day years ago when they had sailed away on what was to be the *Lady Anne*'s final voyage, she was happy for something to put her mind to besides facing the inevitable between herself and Tavis.

"They're back," she thought, not realizing she had said it aloud until Tavis spoke.

"Who is back?"

She did not look at him. "My brothers, Abel and Barret."

"They were on a whaler," he said.

"Yes, the *Lady Anne*," she replied, thinking her other brothers might also have returned to Nantucket because of her disappearance. Her heart went out to her family, knowing a happy occasion had been spoiled by a sad one. *Well, at least my brothers are back. Misery does love company.*

As if reading her thoughts, Tavis said, "I suppose that means your brothers from Maine will also be here."

When she looked at him, he was frowning, deep in

thought. "Yes, I would think my brothers' return would have brought them back, unless my disappearance brought them home first," she said wondering at his frown. "It isn't that far for Drake and Hayden to come. Of course, if the *Lady Anne* has just arrived, they may not have received word."

"Oh, they received it, all right," he said.

That made Elizabeth look up, seeing Tavis with his mouth tightly held, his eyes narrowed and staring ahead. Following the hot trail of that gaze, she looked up to see the beloved faces of her six brothers standing at the end of Straight Wharf.

The closer the rowboat drew, the darker her brothers' faces became.

CHAPTER
❧ FOURTEEN ❧

It was her brother Matt who took Elizabeth's hand as she stepped onto the wharf. A moment later she was crushed against his chest.

"Elizabeth," he said, his voice breaking. "I never thought I'd see you again. What happened? Where were you? Are you all right?" He released her, holding her at arm's length, looking her over and waiting for an answer.

She threw herself at him, her arms going around Matt's middle as she pressed her face against his barrel chest, wanting to feel the strength and security she had felt as a little girl when he carried her about on his shoulders, wanting, too, to pluck several reluctant memories of past times to replace more recent memories that continued to linger in her mind.

But all she felt was an emptiness, an awareness that said, *This isn't Tavis*. "There is so much to tell," she said. "I'm not certain where I should begin. The most important thing is that I'm safe and well . . . and I'm so happy to see all of you again."

She pulled back and looked at her brothers, soon

finding herself surrounded by dear, beloved faces, hugged by each brother in turn. And then, as if someone had given them a cue to do so, they grew suddenly silent and turned in unison to stare at Tavis Mackinnon as he stepped onto the dock, giving the lot of them a nod.

"Mackinnon," Matt said, throwing him an odd but pleasant look, "what are you doing . . ." The pleasant look on Matt's face faded, suddenly turning to one of puzzlement as he looked from Tavis to Elizabeth and back to Tavis.

Elizabeth could almost hear the gears clicking in Matt's head. Matt was no fool. He would be painting a pretty picture of what happened between herself and Tavis about now. The thought made her face flush, and she was glad Tavis was to her back and couldn't see it. "It isn't what you think, Matt," she said, placing a restraining hand on his arm.

Matt looked down at her, his face still wearing that puzzled, on-to-something expression. "What are you talking about? What isn't what I think?" A moment later his expression changed to one of disbelief. Then came what she feared most, a look of slow, simmering rage, the kind that glows white-hot and can't be put out.

"What do you mean, *it isn't what you think*?" Barret asked, stepping forward, his gaze boring into her. "How do you know what we're thinking, Elizabeth?"

Elizabeth braced herself. "I know the lot of you, remember? Even if I didn't, a fool could see it written all over your faces. I know what you're thinking, the questions you want to ask."

"All right. We'll ask them, then. How did you and Mackinnon happen to be on that ship together?" Abel asked.

Elizabeth took a deep breath. "I told you there's too

much to tell, Abel. It's a long story," she said, and seeing how many other people were on the wharf, she added, "and one I would rather speak of in private. Can we go home now? I can tell you what you want to know when we get there."

"I think you better tell us what we want to know here and now," Matt prompted. Turning to look at Tavis, he said, "And I think you better wait right there until she's finished doing it."

"I'm in no hurry," Tavis said.

Elizabeth was watching Tavis, seeing the way his fists clenched, seeing, too, the muscle working in his jaw. She knew, as well, that it was out of respect for her that he kept a lid on his anger; that he refrained from telling Matt that he didn't take orders from him or anyone else. Her heart thumped crazily as she looked at him, for he seemed too distant and too free of her, when she wanted him to be neither.

She felt a bittersweet pain close around her heart. She was home, surrounded by her loved ones, something she thought she would never again see. A few feet from her stood the one man above all whom she longed for, the one man she would have given up all her brothers for. She tried to ignore the premonition she had that said something terrible was about to happen, something that would change forever the course of her life. With a weary heaviness, she looked at Tavis, finding the sight of him as breath-stopping as she ever had, finding she wanted to believe things would be all right between them, that her brothers wouldn't act stupidly and drive him away.

"I have a feeling we aren't going to like what we're about to hear," Barret said, folding his arms over his chest and looking as cross as two sticks.

"I have a feeling you're right," Drake replied.

Elizabeth glanced back at Tavis, recognizing the look of seething anger. Tavis didn't like to be told what to do. But then she looked at the hostile faces of her six brothers and knew it would be best if she started talking, telling them what they wanted to know, right now. "It all started when . . ." she began.

Several minutes later, she finished with, ". . . And that's how we ended up together." One quick glance when she finished, and she saw there was not one pleasant look on any of her brothers' faces.

"He stole your sloop? With you on it?" Matt asked, his voice throbbing with anger. "Without giving a thought to what that might do to you, or to your reputation?" He glared at Tavis. "I'll tell you one thing, Mackinnon, you're a brave bastard, showing your face around here again."

Tavis looked at Elizabeth, then back at Matt. For a moment Elizabeth thought he might not speak, but as he often did, he surprised her.

"I don't think the wharf is the place to discuss this," Tavis said after a long, uncomfortable stretch of silence. "She's been through enough. She doesn't need to be put through this. When you've had a chance to talk to her and see reason, pay me a call. You know where to find me."

With that, Tavis nodded curtly and started to leave.

"I might have thought you a lot of things, Mackinnon, but I never thought you a coward," Matt said.

Elizabeth felt the life drain out of her. Tavis wouldn't take that kind of talk. No man would. But once again, he surprised her. He did not say a word. He simply paused and looked long and hard at Matt, before turning away.

Tavis Mackinnon's refusal to be drawn into any kind
of argument was a bitter brew for her brothers to swallow. Elizabeth knew that. Turning his back on them
without saying a word raised their ire.

Behind her, Elizabeth heard Hayden's curse. Then another angry expletive and the clatter of boots. Hayden,
ever the hothead, lunged for Tavis. He threw his body
at him, hitting Tavis square in the back. Hayden's massive arms went around Tavis's middle, swinging him
around.

Elizabeth cast a pleading look at Stephen, begging vi-
sually with the one brother who thought things through
before reacting, the one brother they always called the
"peacemaker of the family," to intervene.

A second later, Stephen laid a restraining hand on
Hayden's shoulder, giving Elizabeth a reassuring look.

"Hayden . . . now, don't you go jumping to conclusions," Stephen said. "Don't do something you'll regret
later."

Hayden shook off Stephen's hand. His face was scarlet. He was beginning to perspire. The vein in his forehead was prominent now, throbbing with anger. "The
only thing I'll regret later is letting this coward off the
hook. And I'm not jumping at anything . . . but this bastard," he said, and threw a punch.

Tavis ducked just as Drake jumped in the fight and
lunged for Tavis, shouting, "You seduced her, you for-
nicating bastard!"

"You don't know that," Stephen said the moment
Barret stripped off his jacket and jumped into the fight.

Elizabeth gave a frightened yelp and jumped out of
the way as Matt grabbed Tavis by the shoulder and spun
him around with one hand, smashing him in the face
with the other. It was a dandy one that caught Tavis just

below the eye. Tavis staggered backward, then caught his balance. He spun around to face Matt, throwing a punch that busted Abel's bottom lip.

Elizabeth had never seen so much blood. Frantic, she looked around for help.

By this time, quite a crowd had gathered on the dock. Elizabeth glanced at them in helpless frustration, seeing the men were reluctant to look at her. Apparently watching a fight was one thing. Involving oneself in it was another. She didn't know what to do. Five against one was hardly fair, yet she didn't have any inkling how to stop things—although surprisingly, in spite of the blood running out of his mouth and nose, Tavis seemed to be holding his own against such uneven odds.

While her brothers were wild-eyed and spitting with passion, Tavis was a portrait of iron resolve. Even Elizabeth could see that for him, there were no wild punches, for each blow was well aimed and carefully placed.

Oh, how she ached for the chance to fight like this, for it would be a way to rid herself of her own anger and pain. Like the generations of women before her, Elizabeth could only stand and watch as the men bloodied each other, keeping her anger and pain inside.

Never taking her eyes off Tavis, she could see now that his eye was swelling and his brow and lip were cut. Not knowing what else to do, she started toward them, stopping only when Stephen took her arm.

"There is nothing you can do now," he said.

Her gaze riveted on Tavis just as he spit a mouthful of blood onto the wharf, she cried, "I can't let them do this. They'll kill him."

"They'd like to," he said. "But you know they won't. The best thing to do is to let them fight it out."

Another look at Tavis and she wasn't so sure. Elizabeth wriggled away from Stephen's grasp and bolted before he could grab her. "Stop it!" she screamed, running toward the fight.

She doubled up her fists and pounded Matt on the back. "Stop it this minute!" She gave Stephen another beseeching look. A moment later, he began pulling their brothers and Tavis apart.

"Stay the hell out of this, Stephen," Abel said, gasping for breath and wiping blood out of his eyes.

"Enough!" Stephen replied, grabbing Hayden by the collar and yanking him backwards. Hayden took a swing at Stephen. Stephen ducked and gave him a shove. Hayden stumbled backward to the edge of the wharf. Teetering for a moment, he frantically waved his arms, trying to regain his balance. A second later, he fell.

Horrified, Elizabeth saw Hayden go over the side. She brought her hands up to stifle her gasp when she heard the splash.

At that moment, Tavis's friends, Nathaniel and Cole, seemed to come out of nowhere, and joining Stephen, they pulled the remaining four brothers off of Tavis.

"Hold on now! Stop that!" Cole said, his arm around Barret's neck. "What are you trying to do? Stomp him into the wharf?"

Turning toward Elizabeth, Nathaniel asked, "What in God's Heaven is going on here?"

Elizabeth gave him a confused look. She didn't know where to begin.

Turning toward Tavis, Nathaniel grinned. "Hello, friend. Where have you been?"

"The son of a bitch has been out seducing my sister. *That's* where he's been," Drake said.

Nathaniel looked from Tavis to Drake, then back to Tavis. Tavis didn't say anything, but he did take the handkerchief Cole handed him and wiped the blood from his face, dabbing at his torn lip.

"He stole her sloop and kidnapped her," Barret said, breaking Stephen's hold on his neck and pulling the ripped corners of his shirt together. "And if that wasn't enough—"

"Now, we don't know that for certain," Stephen interrupted, receiving an angry scowl from Barret.

Cole started to speak, but Hayden broke in. "How can you say that?" he said, climbing back onto the wharf, the water running from his body tinged a light pink from the dozen bleeding places on his face. "You know what kind of reputation he has. He seduced her. Even he won't deny it, will you, Mackinnon?"

Every head turned to stare at Tavis, but Tavis didn't say a word. Not one. Not that it surprised Elizabeth, considering the condition of his face. He was bleeding a river, and not even the handkerchief Cole handed him could stop the flow. He was staring straight at her with his clothes bloody and ripped, the wind catching his hair and whipping it around in a way that reminded her of when they were on the sloop. His eyes were intense, his mouth stiffly held in his study of her.

"You see?" Abel said. "Look at his face. He's guilty as hell and he knows it."

"Silence doesn't always mean guilt," Cole said.

"Maybe not to you, it don't," Abel said, "but it sure as hell does in my book."

"He seduced her, and we intend to see he doesn't get away with it," Barret said.

"At least not with our sister," Hayden added.

"Why don't we go home and talk this thing over, instead of jumping to conclusions? We don't know for certain what happened," Stephen said.

"The hell we don't! Look at her face," Barret said. "Even now she carries that devil's mark on her neck!" He grabbed Elizabeth, holding her against him. Roughly he yanked her hair aside and pulled her collar down. "See for yourself!" he exclaimed.

Elizabeth felt all heads turn to stare at her, the heat of every gaze fastened on the red mark.

The guilty conscience needs no accuser, and in spite of her efforts, her conscience could not sleep through such thunder. Uncomfortably aware of herself, Elizabeth turned her head away in shame as her hand came up to touch her neck and her face exploded with color.

"You see?" Drake said. Then, turning to Stephen, he said, "Even you can't defend him now."

"Elizabeth," Stephen said, imploringly.

The look on Stephen's face was her undoing. Not even great Neptune himself, with all his great oceans, could wash away her guilt, her shame. To understand would be to forgive, but there would be no understanding now, no forgiveness. They had scented blood. Their appetites would not be appeased until they tasted flesh.

"No," she said, backing away. These were her brothers. Her own flesh and blood was doing this to her. She wished at that moment that she had died out there, that they had not been discovered. Not even dying would have been this bad, this painful. Death would have spared her this. Death would have been a way out. "You don't understand," she said, shaking her head. "None of you understand."

"Then tell us," Stephen said. "Tell us what happened."

One glance at Tavis and her composure crumpled.

Crying now, she said, "Why? So you can take something beautiful and make something sordid out of it? Is that what you want? Look around you. See what you've done. You've shamed me before everyone. Does that make you feel better? Does it make everything all right? Are you satisfied now? Does it give me my virginity back?"

There. She had done it. She had given them what they wanted. She had admitted the truth, not only to them, but to half the people of Nantucket. Strange. She would have thought her confession was what they wanted. But looking at her brothers now, all she could see was shock . . . shock and a look of guilty betrayal.

Robinson men were ever a hotheaded lot, her father often said.

Elizabeth never believed it more than at this moment.

"Elizabeth," Matt said, looking as guilty as the others, with a tone of apology in his voice.

But Elizabeth had already turned and was running down Straight Wharf.

She went straight home, going to her room. Sally and Meg came in, joining her on the bed.

After lying there for a moment, Meg said, "Lizbeth, where is your virtue?"

"Meg!" Sally said.

"What do you mean, where is my virtue?" Elizabeth asked.

"I heard Barret tell Papa that you lost it, so I wanted to know where it was."

"It wasn't lost," Elizabeth said. "It was just misplaced for a while."

"Oh," said Meg. But Sally was laughing so hard, Elizabeth barely heard the reply.

When she had bathed and washed her hair, Elizabeth put on a nice but simple dress. Then she went downstairs to wait, like a queen for her execution, her long, golden braids wound like a crown of thorns about the top of her head.

Elizabeth was waiting for them in the parlor when her brothers walked in an hour later, accompanied by her father. A moment later, Sally and Meg came bouncing into the room.

"Out," Samuel said.

"But we wanted to be with Lizbeth," Sally said.

"I know what you wanted," Samuel said. "You want to get your ears full."

"We can do that anyway," said Meg. "We can hear everything you say through the stovepipe in the kitchen." Sally made an attempt to clap her hand over Meg's overproductive mouth, but she was too late.

Samuel gave them a stern look. "You may both go," he said, "anywhere *but* the kitchen."

"Blabbermouth," Sally said in retreat.

"Sticks and stones," Meg sassed as she followed Sally through the door.

Samuel looked at Elizabeth. She knew he was glad to see her, of course, and she soon found he was more reasonable than her brothers had been—but barely.

After he had asked for, and received, a complete accounting of events, he didn't say anything for a long, long time. Then, when she thought she might scream from the strain of it, he spoke at last. "Do you love him?"

Elizabeth, just at that moment, noticed that Matt was not with the others.

"Elizabeth, do you love him?" her father repeated.

Before she could utter a response to her father's question, she was interrupted.

"Does she love him? Good God," Barret said, throwing his arms in the air and waving them around as he paced the floor. "She's *loved* him since she was eleven years old. *That* isn't the issue here."

"No, it isn't. It's far more important than the issue," Stephen said, looking at each of his brothers. "What's the matter with you? Have you lost your senses? Here you are, your minds set and trying to force our sister into marriage—and you don't think love is the issue?"

Abel turned to Stephen. "She loves him, and we all know it. That's enough for me."

"That is the perfect answer, of course, except for one thing. *You* aren't the one being asked to marry him."

"Will you stop it? Will you all stop talking about me like I'm not here?" she said.

When they paused and turned to look at her, Elizabeth said, "Isn't anyone going to ask *me* what I think about all of this? Doesn't anyone think *I* have a right to be involved in the planning away of my own life?"

"Well?" Stephen asked, giving them all a penetrating look. "Does she have that right?"

"Tell us, then. What do you think, Elizabeth?" her father asked.

"I'll tell you what I think," she said. "I think you're ruining my life with your good intentions." She looked at them again. "It isn't what I think. It's what I know. None of you realize what you've done. I know I don't want to marry him . . . I won't marry him. Not now. Not this way."

"Don't ask her," Abel said. "She doesn't know what she wants."

"And you do?" she asked, giving him such a stare that he looked sheepish and turned his head away.

"We may not know what you want, but we sure as hell know what you need," Barret said.

"And what is that? Marriage?" she questioned, thinking it odd that it was the four married brothers who were the most bent toward forcing her into marriage, while the two bachelors, Stephen and Matt ... well, Stephen was the only one she could truthfully say was on her side. Matt? He was still strangely absent.

"Hell yes, it's marriage," Barret said. "You know yourself that marriage is the only solution to something like this."

"Something like what? A jump to conclusions?" she asked.

"You know what I mean," Barret said, "and you know I have every right to expect the bastard to marry you."

"I don't know that at all. What I do know is, I don't want to marry Tavis. I won't marry him. And no matter how many times you ask me, I'll still say the same thing. You can't force me."

"But I can," Samuel said, rising angrily out of his chair. "You will marry him if I say you will."

Stephen laid a restraining hand on Samuel's sleeve and shook his head.

Samuel looked at Elizabeth, then back at Stephen. With a bewildered expression, he sat back down.

Turning back to her, Stephen said, "I hate to ask you this, but the possibility must be addressed. Elizabeth, there is the chance that you might be carrying his child."

Elizabeth felt weak. The second thing she felt was stupid. *A child,* she thought, then, *You idiot!* With a sick look, she cast a pleading look toward Stephen, who seemed at as great a loss for words as she.

She came slowly to her feet and walked to the window, where she parted the lace curtain and stood looking outside for quite some time. How strange it was that while her world was falling apart in here, everything on the outside was business as usual.

Across the street, Mrs. Mayhew was sweeping her porch, while little Oliver Stretor was chasing his sister, Mandy, down the sidewalk. Mrs. Peterson was cutting her roses and talking to herself as she always did. Abe Folger was speaking to Captain Wyer, who had come home from his last voyage with a wooden leg, while two floors above them, Mrs. Swain was sitting with her ear at her bedroom window, trying her best to hear.

"It doesn't matter," Elizabeth said at last, dropping the lace curtain and slowly turning away. "I don't want to marry a man who doesn't want me."

"He may not want you now, but he sure as hell wanted you then," Hayden said.

"We ought to kill the bastard," Barret said.

"I will if he has her with child," Drake put in.

At that moment, Matthew walked into the room. Like his brothers, his face was bruised and swollen, his shirt splattered with blood. He had a limp when he walked.

"Where have you been?" asked Samuel.

"Planning a wedding," Matt said.

Elizabeth gasped, her hand flying up to her chest. "You didn't."

Matt looked at Elizabeth. He nodded. "I did," he said. "After a fashion."

Elizabeth groaned. "I can't believe you would do this."

"Did he agree?" Drake asked.

Matt nodded.

"You don't think he'll back out?" asked Abel.

"His friends will see to it," Matt said. "At least Nathaniel and Cole ooo reason."

Elizabeth had never been so hurt, so angry. "I can't believe you would do this to me! My own brothers! I thought you loved me."

"We do love you," Stephen said.

She looked at Stephen. "*You* do maybe, but they don't," she said, glaring hotly at the other five.

"There was no other way, Elizabeth," Matt said.

"What do you mean there was no other way?" she screamed. "You could have left things alone. You nearly beat him to death! Wasn't that enough?"

"Why are you protecting him?" asked Barret.

"Because she loves him, you sap," Hayden said. "Any fool could see that."

"We should've killed the bastard," Abel said.

"Why?" Elizabeth shouted, glaring at Abel. "Because he's so much like you?"

Abel had the audacity to look amazed. "Like me?"

"Exactly like you," she said. "Have you forgotten how long it took you to marry? How many women there were before you did?"

Abel didn't seem to be listening, for all he said was, "You think Tavis Mackinnon is like me?"

"Down to a flaw," Elizabeth said.

For some lunatic reason, Abel looked pleased.

Elizabeth glanced at Hayden, who must have noticed the idiotic look as well, for he glanced at Barret and said, "He's right. We should have killed him," he said.

"Is violence and force your answer for everything?" she shouted. "Is that the only way you men can solve

anything? Haven't you ever heard of talking, of understanding and reason?"

"Now, Elizabeth," her father said, "Hayden was only
teasing."

"He wasn't teasing," she said, "and even if he was, *I*
don't find it funny. None of this is anything to tease
about, and you wouldn't find it such a jolly thing to
banter about either if it were your life being manipu-
lated."

Her father tried again. "Now, Elizabeth, calm down
and be sensible."

"Why don't you tell *them* that?" she said, waving her
hand to indicate the lot of them.

Samuel ignored that outburst and went on to say, "By
now, every soul on the island knows what happened between you and Mackinnon, and—"

"Oh yes, they know, all right. And *who* do you think
told them? You did!" she shouted, looking at her brothers. "And you," she said, turning to glare at her father,
"raised them to be stupid enough to behave that way."

"Elizabeth, will you calm down?" Matt said.

"Why? So you can lead me to slaughter like a dazed
sheep? So you can force me into something else?"

"No, so we can talk some sense into that lovely fool
head of yours. If you would think about it for a minute,
you would see that this is the only way," Matt said.

"Why? Because it pleases the five of you?"

"Pleases us? Mackinnon isn't good enough for you,
and we all know it," Drake said.

"Well, you couldn't prove it by me," she said.
"*Something* about him must be pleasing to you. Why
else would you go to such lengths to force us to
marry?"

"We're doing it for you," Matt said. "We have your best interest at heart."

"Heaven help me then," she said, coming to her feet and looking at them, tears running down her face. "He will never forgive me for this. Never." She started from the room.

"Elizabeth," Stephen said.

She shook her head and waved a hand, dismissing the lot of them. "It's too late for that," she said without stopping, without even turning to look at them.

"What if you are with child?" Matt asked.

She stopped and turned around. "That won't make any difference. Not now. You don't know him like I do. If you had stayed out of it. If you had given us just a little time." She laughed harshly, remembering something. "*If,*" she said with a mocking tone. "There's that cursed word again. *If* he loved me. *If* he wanted this marriage. *If* he wanted to make it work. But he doesn't, you see. And he will find a way to let me know it."

Before any of them could speak, Elizabeth ran from the room.

"She'll be all right," Samuel said. "After she's had time to rest and think about it, she'll see what you did was right. Give her a few days and she'll warm to the idea."

"I hope you're right," Matt said.

"Heaven help us if he isn't," Stephen said.

CHAPTER
❧ FIFTEEN ❧

It is a woman's prerogative to change her mind, and Elizabeth did just that.

One month after she swore she would never marry Tavis, she married him.

At first she resisted them all, telling her father and her brothers that she would not marry Tavis Mackinnon. Ever.

When Matt chastened her about her refusal, lightly commenting, "You will change your mind," she informed him that she intended to resist until she drew her last breath. They could order her to marry him, but they could not force her. They could plead, but she would not be swayed. They could bargain, but she would not be bought.

"Nothing will make me marry that man," she said, stomping her foot for emphasis. "Absolutely nothing."

But she was wrong.

There was *one* thing that would make Elizabeth change her mind and marry Tavis Mackinnon.

For two weeks after that horrible day of the fight, Elizabeth thought about what Stephen said. What if she was with child? What would she do? How would she tell Tavis? What would his reaction be?

He would hate her. She was certain of it.

He hates you now, so what difference does it make?

With a dejected sigh, Elizabeth knew, without a doubt, that she was going to have Tavis's child. It wasn't because of any physical sign. It was simply because she had always been a person who had never gotten away with anything. Every little thing she had ever done had, by one way or another, come to light. If she did something to get herself with child, then she was with child. It was as simple as that.

As the weeks passed, and her woman's time had not come, she knew what her brothers dreaded had come to pass. She was going to have a baby.

It was strange how it had come upon her. Since her return to Nantucket, Elizabeth had stayed close to home, letting her sisters, Meg and Sally, do the shopping and errand running, while she remained home, under the pretext of giving the house a thorough spring cleaning.

"But it isn't spring," Meg said, her handsome brown eyes steadily fixed on Elizabeth's face, when Elizabeth used the cleaning as an excuse to send Meg skipping down to Burnell's Store. "It's the beginning of summer. We've already passed the vernal solstice."

The vernal solstice? Elizabeth stared at Meg. Was there going to be another female astronomer in the Robinson family? "All right, summer cleaning then. Does that meet with your educated approval?"

Meg nodded. "Yes, but I know that isn't the *real* reason you want to stay home. You're afraid you might see Tavis . . . and you're worried about what people might say because you lost your virtue."

"Is there anything about my personal affairs that you don't know?"

"Nope," Meg said. "I know everything, because I read your journals while you were away." And with that, she was gone.

After Meg departed, Elizabeth, armed with a worn-out broom and feather duster, set to work. She had no more than started on the parlor when she felt so nauseated, she had to sit down. Fifteen minutes later she was still lying on the parlor sofa when Becca came by.

"What's wrong with you?" Becca asked, coming into the room.

"I don't feel well," Elizabeth said.

"Maybe you should go see Doc."

"I'm not that sick. It's just a queasy feeling in my stomach. It usually passes in half an hour or so."

Becca's brows went up. "Usually? You mean you've had this before?"

"A few times over the last week or so."

Becca's eyes grew large and round. "I think you better go see Doc. Right away."

"Why?"

"Because I think you are carrying Tavis Mackinnon's child, that's why. Have you had your monthly time?"

Elizabeth shot into a sitting position. Her color faded to a paler shade of pale. Her heart was beating triple-time. "Oh Becca," she said. "I could never keep anything from you, could I?"

"Now, will you go to the doctor?"

Elizabeth gave her a look that was, at best, skeptical. "Why? I already know why I'm getting sick, and there isn't anything the doctor can do to change things."

"I still think you should go."

"Would you go? If you were me?"

Becca considered Elizabeth for a moment, then sighed. "No, I suppose I wouldn't," she said and looked helpless. "Well, if you aren't going to the doctor, and you aren't going to marry Tavis, just what are you going to do?"

"I don't know."

"You have to tell your father. You know that, don't you?"

"Yes, I suppose I do." Elizabeth looked forlorn. "I don't want to."

"Neither would I, if I were you."

"Well, at least I don't have to tell him right away."

Becca frowned. "You'll have to tell him before long. You can't keep a baby a secret forever. Your body will tell if you don't."

Elizabeth looked sick.

"You should marry him," Becca said. "Sooner or later, you'll have to."

"I don't want to."

"Fine, but marry him, anyway. You have a baby to think of now."

Elizabeth came to her feet and began pacing. *A baby* . . . "I don't want to marry him this way. It's for all the wrong reasons. He would be furious enough if he is forced to marry me. Can you imagine what it would be like if he found he wasn't just getting a wife, but a wife *and* a baby?"

"Well, he should have thought about that before. You didn't just up and get yourself in this condition all by yourself, you know. He certainly had a hand in it." Becca paused, then laughed. "Well, maybe not a hand, exactly, but—"

Elizabeth threw a sofa pillow at her. "We must be

crazy," she said. "How can we laugh at a time like this?"

"Why shouldn't we?"

Elizabeth turned suddenly serious. "Oh, Becca, what am I going to do? Do you see any way out of this for me?"

"I'll tell you what I think, not that you'll listen to me. What this all boils down to is this: When there's a baby on the way, then getting married is most assuredly the only option," Becca said, then taking Elizabeth's arm, she suggested, "Come on. Let's go for a walk."

"Now?"

"Of course. You don't really want to spend this beautiful day dusting and sweeping this fusty old parlor, do you?"

"No, I don't suppose I do."

Elizabeth looked distressed and stared at her friend. Then she gave an exasperated sigh and sat down, folding her hands over her knees. Becca was right. She didn't want to dust the parlor. She didn't want to go for a walk either. She wanted to stay right here, sitting at home and feeling sorry for herself. She thought about suggesting a game of Rigmarole in the kitchen instead, but one look at Becca said Becca had decided Elizabeth should go for a walk, and knowing Becca as she did, she knew she would settle for no substitutions. It was take a walk, or else.

Shortly after Elizabeth and Becca finished their walk, Elizabeth started for home. She was only a block from her house when she decided to pay her grandfather a visit. She needed someone to talk to, someone who understood.

Her walk with Becca hadn't solved anything. As far

as marriage to Tavis went, she was as solidly against it as ever. Yet the prospect of bearing a child out of wedlock didn't hold much appeal for her either. Nothing, she decided, could be as painful as indecision.

Unless it was making the wrong choice.

Turning down the street, she made her way toward the lighthouse. Soon she was walking along the sandy, winding path, between tenacious clumps of poverty grass and slim spears of beach grass, passing the halfway mark, where a massive whale jawbone lay bleaching in the sun. Overhead, gulls drifted and screeched in a clear, cloudless sky; below, sand-colored grasshoppers stirred in response to her intrusion. Black ducks were feeding in the marshy shallows, while farther inland, bayberry and beach plum hugged the dunes, as if determined to hold them in place.

When the path broke from behind a dune to reveal the lighthouse, Elizabeth saw her grandfather was sitting outside in a chair that was gradually forming to his shape, reading a newspaper and soaking up the sun.

Asa looked up to stare at her, leaning forward, his hat shading his eyes from the sun. But even then, Elizabeth could see that he knew. Strange as it seemed, somehow, someway, he knew.

That fact hurt her more than if her father, her brothers, even the whole of Nantucket Island, knew. Of all people, she wanted her grandfather to think her perfect. Of all people, her grandfather knew she wasn't.

Of all people, she knew her grandfather would be the one to understand. Perhaps that was why she had refused to tell him, for by doing so, she was punishing herself, hoping she could chasten away her guilt.

She felt the sharp points of his eyes upon her like two pinpricks, peering at her in his squinted way. She stood still where she was, staring at him, feeling how simply looking at him and knowing he knew made her heart quicken.

"Hello, Grandpa. You look like you're having a relaxing day," Elizabeth said.

Asa put down his newspaper. "At my age, every day is a relaxing one," he said, the eyes that had pricked her earlier becoming softer.

"Well, out with it," Asa said. "What kind of trouble are we into now?"

She smiled at him. "I'm surprised you ask, since you already know."

He smiled back at her but didn't say anything.

"How did you know?"

"Your absence told me," he said. "You haven't been out to see your old grandpa in a while."

"I was too ashamed to face you."

"Did you think I would stop loving you?"

She shook her head, remembering how she had always wanted to see her grandfather's blue eyes gleam with pride. For once, she felt at a loss to put her feelings into words, but even she knew there was nothing that would ever make this dear man stop loving her. She looked into his face, seeing the same understanding, the same love, she had always seen there. "We've always been kindred spirits, you and I," she said, coming to stand in front of him and feeling the presence of that secret, wordless sort of love that had always existed between them.

"You want to talk about it?"

Elizabeth felt a huge lump in her throat. No one could bring her to the verge of tears like her grandfather could. She wished she could roll back time, that she could be a little girl again. Life was so simple back then—back when her grandfather's knee seemed as wide as the Atlantic and just as able to buoy her up. Overcome with the emotion of what she was feeling, all she could do was nod.

Asa said, "I know it's difficult talking about something when all the words seem to clump together in your throat. But remaining silent won't ease the pain none. You're in a quandary because you don't know what to do." His look was full of understanding. "None of this is going the way you hoped, is it?"

"No," she said. "It isn't. I love Tavis. For all of my life I thought there would be nothing better than to be married to him, but now I find I was wrong. There is something better than marriage, Grandpa. It's love."

"And if you can't have his love, you don't want the rest of him? Is that it?"

"Yes, I suppose it is, but the way you say it . . . well, it makes it sound like some kind of business proposition. All or nothing."

"There will always be those who would agree with at least part of that statement. In many ways marriage is a business proposition."

"But there is so much more."

"And you don't think you could have that with Mackinnon?"

"Not if he is forced to marry me. I need time, Grandpa. I know he could fall in love with me. If only we had more time."

"And time is the one thing you don't have," Asa said, shaking his head sadly. "You can't put this off much longer. As much as it pains me to say this, you must make up your mind, and soon. You haven't forgotten the wee one, have you?"

Elizabeth nodded, her voice breaking while she

blinked back tears. "I ... I suppose I have been too caught up in my own misery to think about anything else." She dropped down beside him, resting her hands upon his knees. "Oh, Grandpa, why must life be so miserable?"

"Misery isn't a permanent thing, you know."

"I'm afraid this misery will be."

"Didn't you tell me once that your aunt Phoebe said you were a Brewster, through and through, and that Brewster women were independent and strong-willed?"

Elizabeth nodded.

"What she didn't tell you is that Brewster women are traditionally stubborn, traditionally opinionated, and traditionally inclined toward misfortune ... which they traditionally get themselves out of. Eventually."

Elizabeth sighed. "I wish I had taken more after the Robinsons."

Asa stroked Elizabeth's bright head. "Misfortunes come to everyone, even the Robinsons—and they are as varied as plumage. No one escapes."

"I know, but right now my own predicament is enough. I cannot worry about another's misfortune when I am so miserable."

"Don't lose courage," he said, patting her hand. "My grandfather always told me, 'A torch may point toward the ground, but its flame will soar upward.' You've faced difficult situations before and never let them get the best of you."

"I don't know if I can go through this ... a forced marriage, a child born too soon. Everyone will know my shame."

"They know it already."

"It is too much, Grandpa. Too much."

"There is only one thing greater than misfortune, and

that is not being able to bear it. You are made of sterner stuff, Elizabeth."

She shook her head. "I used to think so, but this time I don't know. This time I feel I've been handed something too big . . . even for me to handle."

"You're young, and you're strong," Asa said.

"And I'm a Brewster, but even Brewsters can feel shame," Elizabeth said absently, as if shame were something she could put on like a wool shawl.

"Shame is an ornament to the young," he said. "You'll grow out of it."

Elizabeth gave him a doubtful look. "Grow out of it? Where did you hear that?"

"Aristotle, I believe."

Her look turned skeptical. "I didn't know you read Aristotle."

He smiled. "How else do you think I'll get all that wisdom that is supposed to come with old age?"

She knew what he was doing, and she loved him all the more for it. She tried to smile at his levity, but her heart was too heavy to be lifted. Sorrow is a serious thing and a burden that cannot be dispelled.

She felt the fight drain out of her. She sighed, as if by that one sigh she had released her last bit of resistance. She looked at her grandfather. "I know what you're thinking."

"You do?"

"Yes. You look as if you knew what I would decide a long time ago," she said.

"I knew you would make the right decision, whatever it was," Asa said. "You've always been a resourceful girl. And you've never been one to bear your problems by hiding them."

"Maybe not, but I'd like to know just where it's written that I have to hold a candle to them."

Asa looked for a moment as if he would laugh. "In your heart, I would imagine . . . since that's where most of your troubles start," he said.

Elizabeth sighed and made a forlorn sound, lying her head on Asa's lap, feeling the strength flow into her from those gnarled old hands as they stroked her head.

"Would it be so bad," Asa asked, "being married to Tavis? I remember there was a time when you believed that everything had its rainbow, its ray of hope . . . if you only believed."

"I don't know if I believe that anymore. It's been a long, long time since I've seen a rainbow," she said.

Her words seemed to surprise him. She saw the deep lines of concern etched upon his beloved face. That added another scrap to the mountain of guilt she already carried. She didn't want to cause her grandfather grief. She tried to give him a cheerful look, but it failed miserably.

"You aren't giving up, are you? Where's your faith, Elizabeth? You have your whole future ahead of you, and you have a choice. You can marry Tavis, or you can refuse. Not many people have options like that in their life. The way I see it, this is a time for careful consideration, not a time for going around with your spirits as heavy as a lead log. You have always found something good in everything. Why don't you try that with Mackinnon? Look on the bright side. Search for the rainbow, Elizabeth. It's been there all along."

She looked at her grandfather, feeling the heavy sadness that had engulfed her for the past few days fade away. "You could persuade a wolf to turn mad," she said, looking off, wondering what it was about talking with him like this that always made things seem better. She couldn't help the sudden turn in her spirits, which had lifted toward optimistic.

That was one her grandfather missed. Brewster women were traditionally known for sudden bursts of optimism in the midst of oppression.

"Strange as it may seem, I feel better."

"You've made up your mind, then?"

"I don't think I ever had a choice—not when I look at it as being a case of the lesser of two evils. Living with Tavis and knowing he doesn't love me will be hard. But losing him altogether will be even harder. I love him, Grandpa. How could I bear to give him up and keep his baby? You were right, you know, there are worse things than misfortune."

She kissed her grandfather on the cheek. "For whatever reason, I've decided the baby should have a father, and his father's name."

"So you've decided to tell him about the child?"

"No. I've decided to marry him . . . if *he* is willing, but I won't tell him about the baby. If Tavis agrees to marry me, it will be for his own reasons. I won't use the baby to force him. I don't want him to use that against me. I don't want it to be a reason for him to hate his own child."

"You don't think your brothers are trying to force him?"

"Of course they are, but it won't do them any good. They *might* persuade him, but I don't think they'll ever force him," she said. "It's getting late. I'd better go tell Papa and my obstinate brothers."

"That should make the lot of them happy," her grandfather said.

"And drunk," Elizabeth replied, leaning over to hand

Asa his newspaper. "You should stick to Aristotle," she said, "for I may need your wisdom again, although I can't say you exactly told me what I wanted to hear."

"I can live with that, as long as I know I told you what you *needed* to hear." Giving her a soft look, he said, "Regardless, it was done in love."

She nodded. "I know, but sometimes knowing that is what often makes it so difficult," she said. Turning away, she started up the path.

CHAPTER
❧ SIXTEEN ❧

Tavis cursed and kicked the front door shut the moment the last of Elizabeth's brothers passed through it.

He was trapped and he didn't like it. He had never felt so helpless in all his life. He was backed into a corner. Boxed in. And there was no way out. He didn't take too kindly to force. Especially when it was directed toward him, and most especially when it concerned marriage.

If he had to be honest with himself, he would have to say that the thing that irritated him the most was knowing that in spite of his anger toward Elizabeth and her brothers, he was guilty—at least in part. He was the one with experience. He'd known what he was doing. Even though Elizabeth had been an eager participant, he couldn't blame her, not completely. A fault willingly committed deserved no pardon. He knew that. But knowing it didn't make it any easier to swallow.

He poured himself a healthy shot of rum and stood looking down at the glass in his hand. He could refuse, of course. There was no way in hell her brothers or anyone else could force him into marriage. But there was something about an out-and-out refusal that didn't sit right with him. There would be no solace in rum tonight, for rum would not comfort him. Not this time.

This time he needed something more. He wanted to strike out, to hurt something, as if it would lessen his own pain. Something inside him seemed to snap. The glass in his hand shattered. His hand was cut, the rum burned like fire—yet it did little to reconcile him to his fate. He needed some way to vent his anger, his frustration, both at himself and at the situation he found himself in.

Elizabeth. Her name pounded with each beat of blood against his temples. Her vision danced in the blurred recesses of his mind. Her name clung to him like the fumes of liquor on his breath. He might not throw caution to the wind and dismiss this marriage her brothers insisted upon, but no one could do a thing about it if Elizabeth were the one to refuse.

He tossed the remains of the shattered glass across the room, and vividly cursed Samuel Robinson and all of his get. From their hands he had been dealt nothing but misery. Even now, a month later, his body ached in a dozen places from the beating they had given him. He figured it would be a long time before he could crawl out of bed in the morning without experiencing pain.

But the worst pain of all was knowing that he was being forced into marriage, and that he could do absolutely nothing about it—because, deep within him, he knew he was more guilty than she.

After kicking the door and cursing the Robinsons to high Heaven, Tavis settled down somewhat, his outburst of anger giving way to a more dangerous emotion. Feeling completely detached, he told himself to be reasonable. His first task would be to go to Elizabeth. She was, after all, his fiancée now, so there was nothing further to be gained by avoiding her.

He paid a call to her house, only to be informed by her sister Sally that Elizabeth had left an hour ago to take a basket of bread and cakes to their grandfather, out on Brandt Point.

Wasting no time, Tavis hurried toward the lighthouse. When he reached the whale's jawbone, he pulled off the path that led across the marsh to wait, his mind fertile with what he wanted to say to her, the reasons he would give to convince her to call this whole absurd thing off.

He waited for over an hour before she came along. It was dusk, and although it had been a warm day, it was turning cooler now, a brisk wind blowing in over the water. As Elizabeth drew even with him, she pulled her cape more closely about her, her head bent as her feet skimmed along the path.

Tavis stepped out, directly into her way. She gasped and drew up, her eyes wide with surprise, growing apprehensive when recognition dawned. "Tavis," was all she said, speaking in a startled, breathy way, for she did not believe, at first, what she saw towering before her.

He stared at her for a moment, as if memories of their time together on the sloop, or some other similar feeling, had risen up before him. Yet he seemed to force the return of his cool, formal stiffness. "It's only been a month," he said, seeing the way she looked at him, as if he were a stranger to her, "and not so long that you should have forgotten what I look like."

"No, I haven't forgotten," she said. "You startled me, that's all." She paused, giving him a look that said she had, just at that moment, realized this was no social call. "What are you doing here?"

"Waiting for you, obviously."

Elizabeth shivered, as if a cold, driving wind had passed through her. "Why?"

"Why?" His look turned dark. Hateful. "We are to be married, are we not?" Her shocked expression seemed to anger him. "Oh, come now, at least be honest about this. Your honesty was always one of the things I admired about you. You wanted this, and now you have your wish. But be careful when you get it. It may not be what you wanted after all."

She stared at him, disbelief, humiliation, and resignation churning inside her. Her father's warning that he had decided to force this marriage, the threats of her brothers to pay Tavis a call, were apparently no longer warnings, or idle threats. What she had feared, and feared most in this world, had come to pass—in spite of her holding the fact that she carried Tavis's child from them.

For weeks now it had been her biggest nightmare . . . that she would, at last, get what she wanted and become Tavis Mackinnon's wife, only to lose all hope of ever having him love her. Was this to be her punishment, then? To be married to a man who could not stand the sight of her? Surely this is how Tantalus felt.

In spite of her turmoil, she also knew what he must feel. He was as much a victim of manipulation as she. Because of this, she forced herself to endure. There was pitiable little dignity she could muster, in the face of what had happened, but she was able to persevere, scraping together a minuscule amount by holding the image of her unborn child in front of her.

Tavis was angry and full of vengeance, but he wasn't a cruel, vindictive sort of man who would spend his life bent on revenge. Her best course of action was levelheadedness. He might not ever come to love her, but in time, they could have a tolerable marriage. Becoming angry would serve no purpose here.

It was difficult to remain calm and collected beneath his piercing dark stare and cool, detached manner. She would soon be his wife and completely at his mercy. Burning with humiliation, she faced him, studying him closely, allowing her gaze to go slowly over him, looking for any telltale marks left by her brothers' beating. "You are looking . . ." *No, he isn't looking well at all. His face still shows the marks of his beating. He's lost weight. The fire has gone out of his eyes.* "I'm sorry about what happened."

His gaze lingered on her for a moment, then traveled the length of her, pausing at the point where her cape drew apart over the fullness of her breasts. "The beating, you mean?"

She nodded, knowing he saw the way she winced at his choice of words, and knowing that he must have found some satisfaction in that, for he said, "And it was a beating. . . . Have no doubts about that."

"I know. I was there," she said. "Are you well?" She looked straight into his eyes, as if, by doing so, she could see the truth of his words written there.

"Well enough," he said. "Although I'm surprised you ask about me now. It was some time ago," he said.

"I wanted to come . . . to see how you were, but my brothers forbade it," she said.

"You have a way of minding your brothers when it suits you, I see." Then he seemed to dismiss the thought. "It is just as well. There was nothing you could have done."

An uncontrollable shiver caught her and she drew her cloak more tightly about her body. The desolateness of the windswept moor behind her leached into her bones. "Still—"

He cut her off. "If you want to set things right, call off this brotherly performance and put a stop to this travesty."

"I can't," she said.

"Can't, or won't?"

"What would you have me do, Tavis? Defy my father and my brothers? Turn myself into an outcast and live in a hovel on the beach? You aren't the only person being punished by this forced situation, you know. You aren't the only one to be considered." The moment she said those last words, her heart stilled. She prayed he would take no notice of what she had said, that he would find no hint of their child in her foolish and hastily spoken words.

She released a long-held breath when he said. "No, but you, unlike me, are getting what you wanted."

"And what is that? A false marriage? A husband who cannot stand the sight of me? Just how long must I pay for a childhood fantasy? I am a woman now. Long ago I put such foolishness behind me." Hoping he saw the honesty in her eyes, she said, "I never wanted this. Truly."

"That's not what you said when we were out there together," he said, knowing full well she still loved him, had always loved him. "You may change your story now, but your feelings for me haven't changed."

"You seem to be talking all around it, afraid to say what you are thinking. Are you speaking of love, Tavis? Are you so afraid of it that you cannot even say the word?"

Their gaze met for a moment, then, as if to taunt her,

he spoke hatefully. "Call it *love*, if you like. Whatever the term, I would have thought you had more pride."

She faced him with nothing separating them but cool air. With a boldness she thought bordered on madness, she stood tall and looked at him squarely. "Pride has nothing to do with it. I am being forced as much as you. If you have a problem with that, take it up with my brothers or my father."

He looked surprised, and raising one brow, he spoke, the hostility gone from his words. "You know as well as I how much good that would do."

"Then I suggest you do as I have done, and try to make the most of it."

"Resign myself to this marriage? Is that what you are saying?"

"Yes."

He had the cruelty to laugh. "And I suppose that should come with convincing myself that I care about you, at least enough to give this marriage a try . . . that I desire you, and other marriages have started with less."

Too embarrassed and humiliated to try anything else, she told herself to rely on her honesty—which had always served her well before now. "I am not pinning any hopes on that. Once the wedding is over, you can go to the Devil, for all I care," she said, hating herself at that moment, hating the hypocrisy that made her feel justified.

She was fighting back tears now. Their gazes locked, and she could barely stand the strain of it, for the fury in his look, the guilt she was feeling. Her heart aching for reasons she tried to ignore, she said, "Now, get out of my way."

She shouldered around him, but he put his hand out. Taking her arm, he stopped her.

She turned on him, her eyes hot and flashing. "Let go of me. You may be forced to marry me, but you don't own me."

"Well, at least I know you can be goaded. For a while I thought you had no backbone."

"Oh, I have backbone, all right. Unlike you, I simply know when to use it. Now, if you are finished humiliating me, I need to be on my way."

"And if I'm not?"

She felt as if someone had pulled the world out from beneath her. She was falling. Falling. "There is no reason for us to stand out here like this. I *know* how you feel. Heaven knows you've told me often enough."

"And what about you, Elizabeth? How do you feel about all of this? Have you nothing more to say?"

"I have nothing further to say except if I were you and I found this entire thing as repugnant as you seem to, then I would do whatever I had to do to see that it did not take place."

"I've done everything I could, save jilting you at the altar."

"And there you have it," she said softly. "The one irrevocable way out. If you don't want to marry me, Mackinnon, you can always skip the ceremony and stay home."

"Even I'm not that big a bastard."

"There was a time I would have believed that, but now I'm not so certain," she said, picking up her skirts and hurrying away from him.

"*You* would be the one who would do well to stay away from the ceremony," he called after her. "Otherwise, you may get your damned marriage, but you'll never have a husband. I can promise you that. You will have my name, Elizabeth, and my name only."

His words jerked her to a halt. She stood there for a moment, her arms wrapped around her middle, her eyes closed. "That is all I want," she whispered into the wind, then quickening her steps, she hurried away.

She ran all the way to the lighthouse. Asa looked up when she ran through the door, then closed it behind her. Leaning back against the door, Elizabeth closed her eyes and breathed deeply to catch her breath.

"You look like you've had a run-in with the Devil," he said.

"I have," she replied, and without saying anything more, she went into the kitchen.

A few minutes later she returned. Asa looked up. "You going out again?"

"I'm going to Saul's Pond," she said. "I need to gather some grass for a new broom." When Asa gave her a look that said he didn't believe a word she said, she added, "But mostly, I need to cool off."

"You sure do," Asa said, "but I'm not certain the pond will do it."

Elizabeth gave him a quick glance, then went outside.

The day was warm and quiet, except for the occasional cry of a gull overhead. She took the overgrown path toward the pond, picking her way around silvery gray clumps of dusty miller and thick dunes of goldenrod, her skirts brushing the faded purple blooms of beach pea, her slippers stepping between tussock mats of beach grass.

She left the dunes, cutting across one of the few hilly parts of the island, through what was once pastureland, walking along a broken-down split-rail fence that would be the last sign of civilization for some time. Soon she reached the pond that lay surrounded by low hills and fields of wildflowers. The pond itself was surrounded by thick masses of thatch grass that rose from the soggy mud and sand.

Gathering her skirts and tucking them up, she waded into the thick grass, which danced to the subtle caress of a gentle breeze. She began gathering handfuls of it to make a new broom. When she had enough grass, she made her way back toward shore. Bogging down in the mud, she lost her balance and fell, flat on her face. For a moment she was tempted to simply lie there, as if by doing so the world would somehow pass her by. But Elizabeth was ever a doer, and lying down and taking life's licks had never been her way. With an oath that would have done a sailor proud, she struggled to stand.

Once she reached dry land, she looked at the muddy state of her dress, deciding the mud would stain the pale yellow dress if she allowed it to dry.

It felt a little awkward to be removing her dress outside, in broad daylight, but convincing herself there was no one to watch, save the gulls and small animals that frequented the pond, she removed it anyway. The mud had soaked through to the drawstring top of her chemise, but she decided against removing that, too. She could rinse it in the pond along with her dress.

She waded out into the clear water of the pond, washing the mud from her dress, ducking down to her neck in the cool water to rub the bodice of her chemise. Deciding both her chemise and dress were as clean as she could get them without soap, she waded back to the shallows, avoiding the marshy spot where she had fallen before.

She spread her dress on the grass, while turning in to the wind to dry her chemise. She stood there, plucking at the fabric, pulling its transparency away from her skin, as she found herself thinking about the wildflowers and how pretty a bouquet of partridgeberry, lady's slipper, sea lavender, and cattails would look in the parlor. As her line of vision moved from flower to flower, sweeping over the glassy surface of the pond, she realized she was staring at the reflection of a man in the water.

He was standing with his back to the sun, his body no more than a dark silhouette. Raising her hand to shade her eyes, she could not make out the features of the man, but it didn't seem to matter. Something in her heart told her who he was.

After his confrontation with Elizabeth, Tavis stood beside the whale's jawbone, watching her run away. Long after she was gone, he remained where he was, staring at the place he had seen her last.

The day was quiet, except for the occasional shriek of a gull overhead, the lonely cry of a field lark echoing across the moors. She had been gone for some time when he started up the path toward town, then paused. He wasn't ready to go back to civilization.

Right now he wanted to be alone. He needed to walk awhile, needed time to come to grips with the snowballing of events in his life. He needed time to think.

With that in mind, he turned and walked away from the lighthouse, going in the opposite direction. He cut across the dunes and moorland, spread with a rough tapestry of bearberry, low-lying blueberry bushes and gnarled scrub oaks, and the ever-present heather. When he reached the beach, he turned toward Madaket, paying no attention to the jetsam and flotsam along the shores, or the wide variety of turret shells, moon snails, white quahogs, and sea urchins he routinely stepped over.

His mind was on more important things.

He stopped for a while to look out over the water, his hands rammed deep into his pockets, his gaze taking in nothing but a solitary stretch of ocean. He was puzzled over his anger.

Although he couldn't call himself in love with Elizabeth, he knew he had come to care for her. Why was he so dead-set against the marriage?

There were worse women he could marry. He knew that. So what was it about all of this that got under his skin? He reviewed the obvious reasons, other than his outright objection to being forced, her behavior in the past, the fact he did not love her, and such. Even then he came up with nothing to fuel such deep-seated resentment and anger. He thought about her, the way she was with him on the sloop. There was nothing there that caused the hackles on the back of his neck to rise. Then he thought about the night he had first seen her, after her return, the night at the dance. Immediately he felt his neck hairs bristle. Then it hit him.

His mind rolled back to that night, seeing her in her white gown, remembering his conversation with her as vividly as if it were taking place right now.

It still won't work. You aren't going to snare me, no matter what tactics you employ, he'd said.

If all I wanted was to snare you, Tavis Mackinnon, I could do it easily enough . . . if I set my mind to it.

Give it up. I'm a confirmed bachelor. You'll never win. Never. Whatever it was that they taught you in Boston, it wasn't enough to lure me into marriage. Give it up, Elizabeth. You can't win. Admit it.

I admit nothing. And don't keep throwing that chal-

lenge into my face, or I might surprise you and take you up on it. You aren't dealing with a besotted child anymore. . . . *If I wanted you, Tavis Mackinnon, and it didn't matter how I got you, I could do it. You would do well to remember that.*

Oh, he remembered it, all right. Problem was, it was a little late for hindsight now. That she had outwitted and outfoxed him burned like a brand in his belly. He had never thought it would come to this, that her childish infatuation would lead to the cold and calculating ways of a woman bent upon marriage at any cost.

Well, she had gotten her wish. She would be his wife. But that was all she would get. He would see to that.

Ready to go back now, he cut across the moors, heading toward the road that led into town, passing Saul's Pond on the way. He saw her almost immediately, a shimmer of formless substance, a faceless image bathed in summer's palpitating light.

He paused to look at her, his eyes soon adjusting to the glare of solar rays which touched her with unabashed freedom; a goddess in linen and curves, caressed by sunshine, queen of the out-of-doors.

She stood still as a rock, facing the sun, which was doing a pretty remarkable job in illuminating everything that quivered, showing him just what lay beneath the thin white linen of her petticoats and chemise. He had seen her naked before, of course, but there was something erotic about seeing her body revealed to him through a gossamer-thin layer of creamy wet linen.

A gust of wind revealed the curve of her breasts, and when his gaze dropped lower, he knew the role of shadow as an accent to heighten a man's arousal. His body hardened in response. The forbidden quality, the

disturbing warm, earthy colors of her, the almost vapor-
ous character, all had a latent effect upon him.

Then she looked up, as if sensing his presence. She
stared at him for some time, a hazy reality without an
outline, then she turned away.

A moment later she was pulling on her dress. Soon
she was gone.

Cursing her and the painful hardness in his groin, he
turned away, and unfastening his pants, spilled his seed
in the grass, cursing her, hating her, vowing he would
get even. He looked down at his penis lying flaccid in
his hand. His desire was spent, his erection gone, he
swore he could easily forget her. But even then, he
knew somewhere in the innermost part of him that
he could not completely forget. A fragmentary vision,
she left him the spectator, when he knew deep within
the soul of him that he wanted to be so much more.

They were married three days later in a quiet ceremony in the parlor of Elizabeth's home with only her
immediate family and Becca present. Tavis was there,
of course, in body at least, along with his friends
Nathaniel and Cole.

"I thought your brother Nicholas would be here,"
Samuel said to Tavis, his attempt to make conversation
painfully obvious.

"Nick wasn't invited," Tavis said coldly. "I prefer to
keep my family out of this," he added, and then turned
away.

"Hostile bastard, isn't he?" Drake whispered to Matt.

"We said he had to marry Elizabeth," Matt whispered
back. "We didn't say he had to like it."

"It's a good thing," Barret said, "because he looks
anything but happy."

As if sensing the tension in the room and succumbing to it himself, the Reverend Mr. Phipps cleared his throat and said, "If the parties will gather before me, we will commence."

One last pleading look toward her brothers, and Elizabeth found herself hugged by a tearful Becca. "It will all work out. I know it will. Don't be sad, Elizabeth. Not on your wedding day."

Feeling Tavis's arm brush hers as he stepped forward to stand beside her, Elizabeth turned toward him in a blind panic, nausea burning at the back of her throat. *Dear God, don't let me get sick now. Not here. Not in front of him.*

"My, my, you aren't looking well, my dear. Don't tell me you've had a change of heart," he said. "Could it be that this hasn't turned out to be the rosy occasion you had planned?"

"I don't feel well," she said.

"Then we must hurry," Tavis said stiffly. Then to the minister, "If you would be so kind, Reverend Phipps."

Elizabeth stood as still and as full of feeling as a wooden statue, listening to the stammering words uttered by the minister, feeling their hollow echo in the emptiness of her heart. Nausea gripped her stomach. Her heart beat in irregular flutters. Her face felt warm. Her fingers were cold. She had never been more miserable.

At last she stole a look at him, only to find him standing cold as stone, his face a frozen mask, his lips white and tightly held.

"Dearly beloved . . ."

Liar, Elizabeth thought, looking up and catching a glimpse of Becca's stricken face.

"We are gathered together . . ."

So absorbed had Elizabeth been with Becca's stricken look that she was barely conscious that Tavis was sliding a ring on her finger.

"I now pronounce you man and wife."

The impact of those words hit her full force. *I now pronounce you man and wife.* She was Tavis Mackinnon's wife.

Stupidly Elizabeth looked down at the thin gold circlet that lay on the fourth finger of her left hand, feeling its unbearably heavy weight upon her heart.

"What God has joined together, let no man put asunder."

You can't put asunder something that is already asunder, Elizabeth thought, just as she felt Tavis Mackinnon's cold mouth lightly brush her own.

"Well, you have what you wanted, love. You wanted me so desperately, you would stop at nothing to get it," he whispered against her ear.

She tried to pull back, but he held her fast.

"What is it that drives you?" he said. "Where does it come from ... this determination I see written across your beautiful face? If I didn't know better, I'd swear you made love to me just to get what you wanted."

"Did it ever occur to you that in making that mistake when we were together, I might have punished myself even more?" she whispered back. "That my life might be just as ruined as yours? Maybe more."

"No," he said. "It hasn't."

She closed her eyes, forcing herself not to cry here in front of everyone. When her composure slipped back into place, she opened her eyes, meeting his accusatory ones.

Her mind filled with dread. A dark, deep depression settled about her. It wasn't so much from the knowledge that she was married to a man who did not love her, or even the fact that she was going to have his child, who would be born months too soon. It was from the recurrent feeling that she had, in solving one problem, created another one of far greater consequence.

CHAPTER
❧ SEVENTEEN ❧

There were two things that Elizabeth would always remember about her wedding. One was the fact she carried no flowers and wore an old dress. The other was the look on Tavis Mackinnon's face after they signed their names in the registry.

His eyes were cold, glittering with anger. And yet deep in their blue depths she had caught a glimmer of another emotion, one she could only call regret. She knew then that she would die an old woman with that look still hammering in her mind, hammering with each beat of her heart.

Did he hate her so much? Was he determined to be so unhappy? Would he never find it in his heart to forgive and forget?

She squeezed her eyes, but it was a wasted effort against the hot flow of tears too long held back. What hurt so much wasn't even the fact that her husband hated her, but the fact that Nathaniel, in trying to be kind, had given her such false hope.

Shortly after signing the register, Nathaniel had

kissed Elizabeth on the cheek. "Go easy on him, Elizabeth. Tavis cares for you. More than you think."

Sitting on the bed in her husband's home, Elizabeth picked at the white satin ribbons on her nightgown while she cried herself out, thinking of what might have been. Of all the things she imagined she might be doing on her wedding night, all this thinking and crying was not among them.

She looked around the strange room, finding comfort in its barrenness. She was glad she was in this room. It lacked pretense. It was bare and cold. As bare as her hopes. As cold as her husband's stare. She tried to imagine her life if she hadn't carried this child, but the truth of what she had done was too great. For her there would always be the reminder, the child. There would be no escape. Not now.

"If there is no escape, then I will make the most of it. There have been greater tragedies." *Put your mind to something else, Elizabeth.*

It was one of the most endearing things about her, this ability she had to put misfortune from her mind and to lighten her mood. A moment later she was wishing she had had the forethought to bring a book with her. At least she would have something to do on her wedding night. She thought about all the books Tavis had in his study downstairs, deciding against going down there to get one. What would she do if she ran into him?

That, she knew, was an odd thing to be thinking, and a strange way to start off a marriage. *Well, nothing about this marriage has been normal.*

She folded her arms and looked around the room . . . the *guest* room. Strange, she didn't feel even as welcome as a guest. She didn't feel welcome at all. She sighed. Perhaps this was all a mistake.

She thought of the child she carried and knew she had done the right thing. The child. Her child. Hers and Tavis's. She tried to imagine a little girl and how she would look. She refused to think it would be a boy. She would not give him that much satisfaction. A girl would be hers. All hers. Soon she would call her daughter by her name, no longer referring to her as *the child*. But for now it was still the child, for in truth, the child she carried felt no more a part of her than the man she had married.

She spread her fingers over the flat stomach, trying to imagine it bloated with child. She tried to imagine the child. How large was she now? Was her heart beating? What would be the color of her hair? And eyes? Would they be the same blue-gray as her father's? She tried to think how ridiculous she must look, sitting in the middle of this enormous bed, her hands spread over her stomach, a silly grin on her face.

A grin? When she was supposed to be sad?

It occurred to her then that in spite of Tavis's anger and rejection, in spite of the shame, in spite of the wedge driven between herself and her family, she was happy. She was going to have a baby. A beautiful, tiny child. A little girl. A little human being. How foolish she had been to think of the child as not a part of her, for in truth, it was as much a part of her as the heart that pounded wildly beneath her breast.

She was going to have her baby. Proudly. And she was going to have her book to read, too. Tavis would have to deal with his own problems. She wasn't going to start this marriage out by hiding in her room.

Feeling the strength of a hundred Brewster women

behind her, she sprang from the bed, pulling her dressing gown on as she headed for the door. A moment later, she was going down a dimly lit stairway and opening the door to Tavis's study.

What she saw on the other side surprised her.

"Oh," she said, stopping quickly. "I didn't knock. . . . I thought you were asleep. I didn't know anyone was in here." She did not retreat, nor did she step farther into the room, but simply stood her ground, looking up at him, wariness in her eyes.

His brows narrowed and he straightened up from the sheaf of papers that he had been sifting through on his desk. Tavis regarded her with bold disrespect, not endeavoring to conceal either his surprise at seeing her or the fact that she interested him, in a vulgar sort of way. It made her feel dirty. Used. Cheap. It was the first time in her life she could ever remember wishing she had been born a boy. She had never wanted to punch anyone as much as she wanted to punch out Tavis Mackinnon.

"What are you doing here, Elizabeth?"

"I came for a book."

He glanced at the bookcases. "Be my guest, although I doubt you will find much to suit your reading tastes. Most of my books are nautical in nature, dealing with the architecture and design of—"

"I know what you do, Tavis."

The stiff-lipped, angry look was still there, only now his face was tinged red. She was surprised to find that it did not please her as immensely as she thought to goad him. It was then that she noticed he had changed out of his wedding suit, that there were two bags on the floor, next to his chair. A third, smaller leather case lay on his desk, filled with papers. Her heart stilled.

"You are leaving?"

"Yes."

"Why?"

"I think you know why."

"You are running away." *And leaving me to deal with this all alone.*

"Call it what you will. It doesn't matter."

"Why are you doing this? Can't we reach some sort of compromise? Can't you find another way to deal with your anger besides taking it out on me? Surely you must know I did everything I could to prevent this marriage."

He gave her a direct stare. "But in the end, you gave in, didn't you?"

She looked down at her hands. "I had to."

"Had to or wanted to. What's the difference?" he asked, never taking his gaze from her face.

"There were . . ." She caught herself. She had been about to say "complications," but she changed her mind. "I had my reasons," she said.

"Reasons. My, what a tidy little word. And convenient. *Reasons.* It sounds like a neat little square of carpet to sweep all your selfishness under. I may be running away, but at least I'm not hiding behind sham pretense."

"I hoped—"

"I know what you hoped, Elizabeth. I've known it for years. But it's time for you to face a few simple facts. I do not love you. I never have. I never will. While I'm gone, why don't you try to find someplace to tuck those facts? That way you can take them out and look at them from time to time, then you won't have to listen to me saying them again."

"You're coming back?" For a moment she found herself envious of him, of his being a man. How lucky to be able to pack a bag and walk away from responsibility, to stuff one's entire existence into a leather bag.

"I'll be back ... eventually," he said, not offering more. He stuffed another stack of papers into the leather case, then slammed it closed. He turned to stare at her fully, his anger, his dismissal of her, still so obvious.

She stared at him, unable to believe what was happening. She saw the near-empty bottle on the desk, the full glass beside it. That, at least, explained his hard looks, the callous treatment—both things she knew not to be indicative of him, of the way he was. Tavis might be a lot of things, but he wasn't cruel.

His gaze followed hers, then he looked from the bottle to her. He sighed then, as if reading her thoughts, and while not changing his mind, at least trying to remove some of the sting from it. His features softened.

"It isn't the rum and it isn't just you," he said at last. "I'm going to Washington, D.C. I'll be working with the navy, designing ships for them that I hope will make those damn southerners sorry they ever heard of the plans for my ironclad."

"With hate and vengeance as your driving force, you'll probably succeed," she said, not missing the surprised look on his face. Obviously her reaction surprised him. What had he expected? Tears? For her to throw things? Did he have the audacity to think that she would beg him to stay? *Not bloody likely. Go to your precious navy. Get your revenge. Run away from the best thing that ever happened to you.* For just a moment she felt as if she might cry. Not for the hurt and pain she felt at his desertion, but because of his stupid blindness.

I could have made you so happy.

"Well," she said, gaining control of herself, "I wish you well, Tavis Mackinnon."

He looked as though he wanted to say something more, but he turned instead, to gaze out the window into the darkness beyond.

When he turned back to look at her, his resolve had returned. "I've left instructions with Mr. Blaysdale at the bank. He has set up an account for you. If there is anything you need—"

"I won't be needing anything that my family cannot provide," she said.

"I am not sending you home, Elizabeth. Regardless of the feelings involved, you are my wife. I will shoulder the responsibility of providing for you."

Financially, perhaps. But what about the other things, Tavis? Where do I go when I'm frightened, or sad? Who do I call when the baby's time comes? Who will comfort me and give me the things a woman needs from a man? Have you relegated those tasks to Mr. Blaysdale, or have you simply ignored that I might be a woman, a woman with needs?

He picked up a packet. "I've put Nick and Tibbie's address in here, as well as the address for the Department of the Navy. They will know how to get in touch with me. . . ."

"I won't be needing your brother or the navy."

"Why are you being so hard?"

"Why are you?"

"Oh, come now. What do you expect? This isn't a normal marriage, and don't try to pretend it is."

"That's not the problem here and you know it."

His gray-blue gaze rested on her sardonically. "Do you know something I don't?"

"I know you're a fool, Tavis Mackinnon. I know that

running away makes you feel safe. I know it won't solve anything. There will come a time . . ."

She had almost broken and told him there would come a time when he would discover he had a child and that he would regret then that he had left her to go through all of it alone. She caught herself. It would serve no purpose to tell him, to use the child to hold him to her. There had been enough wrong reasons used to influence things between them. There was no need to add one more.

If he stayed, it had to be because he wanted to.

It was obvious to her that she had broken his skin, that she had pricked him, gone beneath his armor, and crept inside with the truth.

"You don't make any sense," he said.

"Don't I? Are you so certain?" She smiled. "I can see you are waiting . . . waiting for me to tell you, but I don't think I'm going to. I'm not going to make it easy for you, Tavis, but rest assured your day of reckoning will come. Never you fear. It will come, and when it does, you would give your soul to have back the things you threw away. Only then it will be too late."

"Elizabeth, what—"

"Go on!" she said, waving her hand at him. "Go to Washington. I want you to. I don't want you here anymore. I want you out of my life. Do you hear? There is nothing here for you anymore." She paused, taking a deep breath. "Don't worry. I'm not going to preach you a sermon. I won't tell you how much I could have loved you and how well. I won't mention the things I could have given you. The one precious thing you deny by turning away. But never doubt that you'll realize them one day. You're the most fascinating man I've ever met.

And the most stupid. You throw my feelings in the dirt and then walk over them. But I'll have my day. One day you'll come to your senses. One day you'll return and the scales will fall from your eyes. One day you'll decide you want me. And then it will be my turn to use you, to punish you as you have punished me with your own weakness."

She shook her head. "It's amazing, the things one will do for love. One day," she said, speaking slowly, calmly, "one day I will make you sell yourself like a feathered whore to have me, and don't you ever doubt it."

She wanted to hit him for the way he smiled his disbelief. "You can try," he said smugly. "You sure as hell can try. But you forget one thing here, Elizabeth. I know myself better than you do."

"Do you?" she asked, then she stepped out of the door's way. "We will see, then, won't we? Time will tell, as they say."

"Time is something I have plenty of," he said. "More time than you, I would suspect."

"Time, unforgiving time . . . the wisest counselor of all. How long will it be, Tavis, before time begins to eat away at your old delusions? You may think you have more time than me, but you're wrong. I am accustomed to waiting, Tavis. I've wasted half of my life waiting. But don't expect me to do it again."

Even drunk and blind with anger, he was a compelling man, an unlikely combination of the familiar and the unknown. She had known him all her life. She had lain beneath him and conceived his child. But she did not know him. Not completely. Tavis, she had always seen as such a formidable figure of a man, a man who was always in control, one who made all the right decisions. Before, he had existed on a plane somewhere between God and mortal man. Now she saw him as he was. A man confused and vulnerable, a man as blind and capable of making mistakes as any other.

She studied him, a lonely figure absently clutching his leather case, reminding her of a little boy who has packed his belongings to run away, then hesitates, hoping someone stronger will keep him from going.

Well, she was stronger and she knew it now. She would prove it by not doing the one thing he wanted. She wouldn't stop him. He had started this irreconcilable conflict. It was up to him to finish it. "God speed you, then," she said, before looking away.

For just a brief moment, she thought she saw disappointment sweep across his features. But it was gone so quickly, she convinced herself she was mistaken. There would be no disappointment, no regret. He made his decision to do what he wanted. He was happy to get away.

When she looked back at him, he nodded and picked up his bags. Then he said, "As you say, time will tell."

A moment later, he was through the door, his footsteps echoing down the hall.

"Naught treads so silent as a fool," she whispered to an empty room, then she closed the door.

CHAPTER
❧ EIGHTEEN ❧

Tavis wrapped his hands around the back of his waist and squeezed, straightening his body to a full, upright position. For six hours he had been leaning over the drafting table without a break. It had been well worth the effort, and the seven months he had spent on it.

What lay before him now was the final drawing for the construction of *Old Glory.*

With *Old Glory*, Tavis far exceeded his original expectations. She would be no beauty, but she was revolutionary. Nothing had ever been built like her before. Over sixty inventions for her had already been patented.

Looking over the plans, he kept a mental note of the things that made her so exceptional. She had minimal exposure above the waterline, and thus, would be difficult to hit, and if a hit did occur, she was well protected, with over five inches of armor plate in the hull and two inches in the deck. She boasted two revolving turrets, fore and aft, that contained four eleven-inch smoothbore cannons. The turrets themselves were covered with eight inches of armor. She was steam-powered and fast, and what impressed the navy was the fact she was so maneuverable—and five knots faster than any warship afloat.

The door opened, and Captain Edward Pennybaker poked his blond head in. "They're ready for you now," he said. "The secretary has just come in."

"I'll be there in a minute," Tavis said, and began rolling up his plans.

The presentation went smoothly, and by the time the secretary of the navy had departed, the designs had been approved with no further changes. Tavis walked down the long, deserted hallway, thinking his ship was now a reality. According to the secretary of the navy, construction on her would begin immediately.

Somewhere down the hall, he heard a door close, followed by the throaty sound of a woman's laughter. He was transported to another time, another place, seeing Elizabeth standing at the bow, her long hair drying in the breeze, the sun as brilliant as fire behind her. He felt a yearning so strong, his knees buckled.

In the beginning of his assignment here, when his days were filled with meetings and his nights with late-hour drawing, it was easy to forget her, to harbor the anger and resentment that had driven him here in the first place. But as the weeks faded into months, his memories of her and their brief time together on the sloop began to torment him. He began to focus on her, as if, by doing so, he could escape the grueling monotony of hours bent over a drafting table, the endless discussions with the secretary of the navy.

His mind became his escape, where he relived, with slow precision, every moment that he had spent with her, giving vivid detail to her, recalling the way she looked, the clothes she wore, the sound of her voice, the touch of her hand. And at night, when he lay in his bed unable to sleep, he would take himself in his hand, not really touching himself, but making love to her, over and over in his mind, allowing his body to release its own pressures in the only way it knew how.

When it became too much for him, when the separation from her grew to haunt him and keep him from his work, when the desire to return to her became too great, he announced his plans to leave.

"Mr. Mackinnon," the secretary said, coming to his feet. "In case you have forgotten, you have an agreement with the United States Navy. While I do understand your predicament—being a . . . *harrumph!* . . . married man myself—I must put my country and my obligation to the Naval Department first. We are at war, sir. We need your ironclad and we need it soon. Many will be called upon to sacrifice themselves for the cause of freedom. You are only one of the first."

"Are you telling me that I can't go? That I cannot return home?"

"If that is the way you choose to phrase it, yes. I cannot give you permission to leave the job you have agreed to do."

"Then I will go without your permission."

"If you do, I will have you arrested." Then giving Tavis a look that said the secretary knew what Tavis was thinking, he added, "I have already taken the liberty of assigning an aide-de-camp to you."

"A watchdog, you mean."

"I like you, Mackinnon, and any other time I wouldn't feel compelled to take such measures. But this is a time of war. I must put my job, and yours, first. You will not be allowed to leave Washington until the plans are finalized. Then you must go to Portsmouth, to oversee the building of *Old Glory.*"

Tavis cursed vividly, and the secretary paused.

"I promise you the moment she is built, the moment your obligation is finished, I will personally see to it that the fastest vessel the navy has at its disposal will take you home. It isn't much, I know, but it is, under the circumstances, the best that I can do."

Tavis heard his name called, but he couldn't respond. For a twinkling of time he was blinded, as if he had been staring too long into the sun. He shook his head, clearing the memories of Elizabeth, the secretary's words, from his head.

A moment later Captain Pennybaker caught up to him. Clapping a hand on Tavis's shoulder, Edward said, "Why don't you accept a commission?"

Turning a dazed expression toward him, Tavis could only mutter, "What?"

"They're waiting for you to change your mind. They still want you to accept that commission."

"I thought we settled that issue once and for all the last time we discussed it," Tavis said.

"We did, but you can't blame me for trying."

Tavis raised his brows. "Did the secretary put you up to this?"

Edward laughed. "Doesn't he always? Yes, sir, Mr. Secretary. I'll speak to him straightaway, Mr. Secretary. Yes, Mr. Secretary, I will make it a point to ask Mr. Mackinnon why he is being so confounded stubborn. No, Mr. Secretary, I don't know why he prefers to remain a civilian."

"I'll tell you why," Tavis said. "Because I don't like the way the navy tries to own a man, the way they took control of my life. I never intended to stay here this long. I . . ." He paused, realizing he was opening up old wounds, that he was speaking of things Edward could do nothing about. "Because I like my freedom."

"Freedom?" Edward repeated, sounding surprised. "Are you thinking about taking a trip?"

Elizabeth bathed in sunlight leaped before his eyes. "I may be," Tavis said.

Captain Pennybaker had been taught to show no surprise, no emotion, so the look he gave Tavis was a bland one. "Really? And to where?"

"Home."

"Nantucket, isn't it?"

"Yes."

"Hmmm," Edward said, giving him a sideways look. "I never noticed signs of homesickness in you before."

"They were there," Tavis said. "Like you said, you just didn't notice them. But don't worry about my escaping your clutches. The secretary knows all about me, my reasons for wanting to go home."

Edward grinned. "This homesickness wouldn't have a name, would it?"

Elizabeth, Tavis thought, then dismissed it from his mind. "You ask too many questions," he said, then turning down another corridor, he walked toward the door, hearing the soft tread of his aide-de-camp, his watchdog, coming up behind him.

Once he reached the door, he looked back at his aide. "You might as well stop lurking in my shadow. You can be my watchdog just as easily up here."

"My orders are to follow you, sir," the aide said. "Where are we off to?"

"I'm going home," Tavis said. "I don't know about you."

Once he was outside, Tavis decided to walk home instead of hiring a carriage. He turned up the collar of his coat to ward off the chill of damp wind, and walked up Pennsylvania Avenue. He wished he were going home, back to his real home. Back to Elizabeth and Nantucket. But that option was closed to him for now. He'd have to settle for his tiny box of a home on Pennsylvania Avenue.

After a year of drawing and redrawing plans, *Old Glory* was now a reality. In less than one week he would be in Portsmouth, Virginia, and for the next several months it would be his home.

Home. Nantucket was home. Elizabeth was home. Never had the two of them seemed so far away.

His thoughts spun backward until they stopped, as they always did, upon his wife. "Elizabeth, Elizabeth," he said helplessly, seeing in his mind's eye the beauty of her face as it had been that night he left, when she turned her gaze to him.

Never would he forget the impact of those eyes, or the way they overflowed with love, with nothing held back. At first he had been too angry to give her or her looks much thought, but as time passed and the initial anger and feelings of vindication had faded, he began to see in her things he had either never seen or was too blind to see. *Things would have been so different,* he thought, *if it weren't for this never-ending war.*

He climbed the steps to his simple brownstone, and unlocking the door, he went inside. He did not light a lamp, but stepped to the bed and lay down. Folding his arms behind his head, he picked up his thoughts where he left off.

He wondered how she was doing, and was reminded of the many letters he had written to her, letters stuffed in his drawers, letters that he never mailed. He thought about the few he had sent and wondered if she had received them, or had she simply decided not to answer them?

Thinking about that, he knew he could not blame her. He had left her, after all. On her wedding night. The truth, the cruelty, of it ate at him. There was nothing worse, he decided, than coming home to an empty bed every night and knowing it was all your own damn fault. "Stupid son of a bitch," he said, feeling he was just that. But what really hurt was knowing that it was quite possible that things would never mend, that Elizabeth had never been further from him than she was at this moment.

Maybe I should write again. Maybe I should tell her how I feel. Maybe then she would write me back.

And maybe she won't. Thinking about her made him feel his inadequacy more keenly, for there was little doubt that she had picked up the pieces of her life and was going on without him. What was he afraid of?

Her strength and determination were always the things he most admired about her. If anyone had the strength to overcome what had happened, Elizabeth did. She had always loved him. He could not imagine there being a time when she would not.

He had visions of his house decorated, of every lamp lit and glowing for a party. He closed his eyes, imagining her standing at the top of the staircase, wearing an exquisite gown—the kind the important ladies here in Washington wore. For months now he had felt the desire to go back, to see her, to tell her . . .

He opened his eyes. To tell her what? His fist pounded the bed in frustration. He didn't know. He did not know what to say.

Perhaps that was what held him back. That and the navy and this damn, unreasonable war.

He sighed, feeling older than his years. Old and incredibly weary. He was exhausted, and yet things here with his ship had barely begun. He felt lost, uncertain. Oarless and without a rudder. But he knew his life would go on, flowing in a rhythmic, endless cycle that would take him to Portsmouth and see his ship built. Spring would come, and summer, then fall, and at last he would be finished with the task that had occupied so much of his life. *Old Glory* would be finished.

And then what?

Building *Old Glory* and all the hectic weeks it took were a busy time for him. Every line drawn on paper meant a board nailed or a sheet of iron that had to be cut, its surface riveted in place. It meant long hours watching massive live oak timbers being hefted and locked into place, and fighting sawdust carried by gusts of wind that settled in his eyes. It meant instructing and guiding the use of a steam-hoist, an innovation he had promoted to move the heaviest timbers and sheets of iron.

Old Glory. She would be the finest fighting vessel in the world. As if sensing his pride, the men quickly went about the business of constructing his dream from thick planks of teak rising from a keep of solid rock elm, breaking records with their performance.

The exterior sheathing was bolted to iron ribs. Everything was geared to the perfect production of the perfect warship. There were diagonal tie plates and horizontal stringer plates to reinforce the exterior sheathing, and this ironwork was capable of bearing a stress of twenty tons per square inch.

Although he did not do any of the actual shipbuilding, the work of the ship's architect never ended. Tavis was known about the shipyards for being everywhere at once—making sure wood had been mature when cut, measuring the impregnation of metallic salts in which the wood had been soaked to prevent dry rot, and making certain it had been properly dried in the sun.

He was known as the bantam rooster Scot with a keen, domineering eye, whether he was marking a frame with chalk for a better curve or gauging the camber of a newly laid deck to insure it would drain but not be dangerously steep when wet.

Tavis was such a perfectionist that one of the workers was heard to say, "I don't think he will ever build a ship that comes up to his own ideal."

To which Tavis replied, "I think you're right. I won't."

He knew he was hard to please, a perfectionist. He knew nothing in his life had been completely satisfactory, that he had always wanted just a little something more. And then he thought of Elizabeth. Try as he might, he could not imagine another woman at all.

Then there came the day, at last, when the last timber had been put in place and the last rivet hammered home. Officers and dignitaries of the navy gathered with the secretary of the navy to observe the occasion of launching *Old Glory*.

On the platform, Tavis listened to the speeches, standing to give a few quips of his own when introduced. But, strangely enough, when he sat back down, it wasn't the other speeches he thought about, or even the launching of his lifelong dream. All his thoughts were on Elizabeth.

It still puzzled him—besides making him nervous as hell whenever he thought about returning—that she had not answered any of his letters. He knew she was hurt over his leaving, but he had hoped his letters had shown her he wasn't angry.

At last, when the dogshores holding *Old Glory* in place were knocked away from tallow-greased skids, she eased into the water, making a loud splash. Whistles blew. The dignitaries cheered. Everyone speculated on how the war would be over before it really started.

CHAPTER
❧ NINETEEN ❧

The fire hit Nantucket quickly, ravaging three houses, the Robinsons' and one on each side of theirs, before it was brought under control.

Standing in the street in front of her home with her grandfather, Elizabeth turned her head away as they carried out the first of three bodies.

No, her mind screamed. *It isn't happening. It isn't possible. Not Sally and Meg. Not my papa.*

The world around her seemed to spin away from her and she saw Meg's shining face the way it had been the day she proudly announced she had read Elizabeth's journals. Meg would never read her journals again. She would never read anything. She would never come into Elizabeth's room in the middle of a thunderstorm and ask if she could sleep with her, telling her she was afraid. And Sally would never borrow Elizabeth's locket, or put another rip in her best cape. There would be no more evenings when Sally would lie across Elizabeth's bed, asking her how a body knew when she was in love. No more would she hear Samuel Robinson say, "Lizzie, child of mine, what am I going to do with you?"

The constable, Mr. Whittaker, stopped in front of Elizabeth and her grandfather, placing his hand on Asa Robinson's shoulder.

"I'm sorry as I can be, Asa. There was nothing we could do. The house was engulfed in flames by the time we got here."

As he turned away, Mr. Whittaker nodded at Elizabeth and brought his fingers up to the brim of his hat. She wanted to nod, to acknowledge his respects, but she didn't seem to have control over her own body. Grief had her in its grip now, and she felt the earth opening up beneath her feet.

She looked away, her gaze resting on the three bodies covered with sheets. Before she realized what was happening, one of the men gathered to help walked between two of the bodies, his foot catching on the sheet, yanking it back.

Until now, Elizabeth had only thought in terms of her grief and her loss, of the pain her loved ones must have suffered. She had not considered what the ravages of a fire would do to a human being.

For a moment she simply stared at the charred black thing, bent and grotesquely misshapen, its back arched upward, the burned, clawing hands that seemed to grasp at nothing.

Reality and denial surfaced. Her gaze took in the other two sheeted forms, both smaller than the incinerated black form. She did not want to accept what she was seeing. This hideous monstrosity with its arms flung apart could not be her father.

Papa . . . A wrenching sickness rose in her throat. The world spun around her and she heard the loud buzzing in her ears. For a stricken moment, she turned toward her grandfather, her hands reaching out to him, beseeching—much as the grotesquely charred hands in front of her did. She could not reach him. He was too far away. She tried to call out to him, but no words came out. Down, down, down, she fell, into a silent darkness that had no light, no way out.

Even before she opened her eyes, she knew she was in the widow Peterson's house. Mrs. Peterson had lived across the street from the Robinsons since long before Elizabeth was born, so it was easy for her to recognize Mrs. Peterson's squeaky little voice, even before she opened her eyes and saw the unmistakable yellow roses on the wall.

"Poor little mite. Lost almost all her family in one swipe. It doesn't seem fair, does it, Captain? . . . Course, I know it grieves you, too, losing your son and two granddaughters that way. But grief seems so much sadder, so much harder, on the young, I think," Mrs. Peterson said. "Do you think she'll be all right, Captain? Want me to send for Doc?"

Elizabeth felt her grandfather's warm hand across her brow.

"She's just fainted. The shock of it was too much, that and . . ." Asa's voice broke, and Elizabeth felt his pain. She fought to reach him.

A moment later a chair scraped, and Elizabeth opened her eyes, seeing her grandfather's dark superfine coat.

Asa looked at her, tears welling in his eyes. When he spoke, his voice was wobbly. "If you don't mind staying with her for a minute, Mrs. Peterson, I'll bring my gig around."

During the ride home and for days afterward, Elizabeth felt as if she lived in an artificial world, like a specimen people observed under a glass. People came and went. Meals were prepared. Night followed day. And just as it had always done, the great light at the top of the stairs warned ships from harm.

And still the pain would not go away.

How does one deal with grief? she wondered. What could she do to make the loss, the pain of missing them so much, go away? Death was so sudden. So final. And it was the finality of it that she found so difficult to deal with. Never in her whole life could she remember a time when there wasn't something she could do to change things. Some little thing she could do to alter the course of events. But there was nothing she could do now. Death was final. Irrevocable. It was the helplessness, the goddamn helplessness, of it that ate at her.

"It's too much," she told her grandfather the night before the funeral. They were both sitting at the kitchen table, neither of them drinking the coffee that sat in front of them.

The room was quiet. Not even the steady *tick . . . tick . . . tick . . .* of the clock on the mantel could be heard. Her grandfather, tears on his face, tried to persuade her to eat, but Elizabeth could not. She couldn't do much of anything, save sit there in still, silent shock, wondering why it was that she could not weep, when it came so easily to others.

She glanced up at her grandfather, wishing she could go to him as she had when she was younger, that she could climb into his lap and let him rock her as if she were a baby. She remembered the familiar smell of his wool seaman coat, the security of lying her head on his barrel chest, the safety of being held so snugly in his strong arms.

She did not know which was stronger, the pain of not

being able to go back or the agony of remembering. Love and losses. Her life was nothing more than love and losses. *Why is it that everything I love is taken away?*

She found it strange how the mind works, for suddenly her thoughts were not on her grandfather's comforting arms but on the comforting arms of another. Without making a conscious effort to do so, her mind settled upon Tavis. She thought about the letters he had written to her, and her own letters—the ones she wrote to him. The letters she had written telling him about the baby. The letters she had torn up and thrown away.

He was nothing more than another loss, another person she had loved and watched slip away. She did not feel bad that she had not mailed any of the letters she had written him. He had turned his back on her and left. He didn't deserve to know about his child.

The day of the funeral came, the sun not daring to show its face, the clouds hanging low, the world misty and damp as if the very heavens themselves could not get over their gloom.

She looked at her mother's grave, remembering a sunny day not so long ago when she had knelt here, planting flowers and pulling weeds, never dreaming she was preparing a place for three more members of her family. *Soon,* she thought. *Soon Mama will have company and she won't be so lonely. It's just Grandpa and I left in Nantucket now.*

Then glancing at her grandfather, she couldn't help wondering just how long it would be before he, too, was taken away.

Elizabeth stood at her grandfather's side, watching the crystalline tears slip down his weathered old face.

There had been so many losses in both their lives. *Why?* she wondered, turning her eyes to Heaven, as if she could find her answer written there.

Why? Why? Why?

But there were no answers. Not in Heaven. Not in her heart. Only cold, hard reality stared her in the face. She looked at the tears on Asa's face and wondered why it was that her grandfather could grieve and still she could not. She wanted to cry. She wanted to. She wanted to scream and cry out the unfairness of it all.

There were too many things left undone, too many words not yet said. *Oh, Papa, I did forgive you, I did,* she whispered, remembering how her father had asked her to forgive him for forcing her to marry Tavis and how she had coldly refused to answer him, how she had given him her back and turned away.

So many things had been changed because of her anger.

In anger she had left Tavis's house. In anger she had refused to move back home, preferring instead to move to the lighthouse with her grandfather.

She remembered the day Sally and Meg had come out to the lighthouse, begging her to come home, and how she had hugged them and cried, but in the end, she had sent them away, too.

And now they were gone, the three of them: her father, Sally and Meg. *Losses. Life is nothing but losses.*

She dropped her head to her grandfather's shoulder, seeing her brothers gathered around them, their faces so somber and grave. They grieved, as did she, but they had other lives now, and none of them had chosen Nantucket as the place they wanted to stay. They would return to their homes, leaving the memory of sorrow and pain behind them.

Elizabeth and her grandfather, and the child that would be born any day, would be left alone here.

She stared woodenly as the last spade of dirt was patted in place, allowing her gaze to travel up to the marker over Meg's grave. Meg was only fifteen. She had never even been kissed. She thought about Sally and the marriage to Jared Sherburne that would never take place. She looked at Jared, looking so lost and overcome with grief. It wasn't fair. *Why not me?* her heart cried out. *Why not me?*

I have nothing left in the world, she thought, *nothing but Grandpa and the babe.* But even then, knowing she had a reason to go on, she wondered if she could hang on to the thin fine line that kept her from insanity, if those two people—one old and near the end of his days, one yet unborn who would announce his arrival any day—would be enough to keep her overwhelming grief at bay.

They were the last to leave the cemetery. As they walked slowly from the four graves in the corner, she was conscious of hardly thinking of Tavis at all. *If life were an acorn, I would be holding only the shell. How strange life is; how strange that one grief can drive away another.*

Emptiness. All is emptiness.

CHAPTER
❧ TWENTY ❧

The day Tavis returned to Nantucket, it had been two and a half years since he had left. For days now he had been experiencing an overwhelming desire to see her, to simply spend some time looking at Elizabeth, drinking in the sight of her, taking in the changes that time and maturity had made.

As he made his way from the wharf toward his house, he couldn't help wondering what her reaction would be. His anger had died a long time ago, most of it replaced by guilt. Guilt over the way he had left her. Guilt over his inability to return before now. Oddly enough, he was even feeling a little guilt over the fact that she had not written to him, had not answered one of his letters. He knew what her lack of correspondence meant: He had hurt her and hurt her deeply.

He crossed Main Street, waving at a few faces he knew, his thoughts never leaving her. Why should they? They hadn't left her for over two years. During all that time, he had perpetuated his illusions, nurtured them even, tucking them away to protect, much as he did the plans for his ships. In his mind he had seen this moment of his return so many times, seen the way she would be standing at the kitchen window, how she would turn and notice him, her eyes lighting up at the sight of him, giving him the same adoring, worshipful looks she had given him as a child. Then she would be turning to run to him, throwing her arms around him, not a child now, but a woman with a woman's breasts, a woman's body. For some time now he had known he would never be free of her, for there was something about her, a oneness of mind and spirit, that had drawn him, a oneness whose pull he had never been free of, would never be free of.

He turned down Centre Street—his street—and suddenly the old apprehensions, the old fears, began to eat at him. What if it was too late? What if he had waited too long to return? What if it had taken him too long to remove the blinders from his eyes, blinders that hadn't allowed him to see her, really see her, as the woman she was, not the child? He was a grown man, ten years her senior. She was a young woman, still in her twenties, still in her prime. But of the two of them, he was by far the more irresponsible, the more immature.

He was on the same block as his house now, and with each step that drew him closer, his apprehensions grew. *Liza ... Liza ... what have I done to you? How could I have been so cruel? You never did anything more than love me, while I dashed all your hopes, watching them fall about you, then crushing them beneath my feet when I walked away.*

He paused in front of his house, his heart hammering, his palms sweating. Only a few feet separated him from her now, a few feet and one thin door.

Suddenly all the things he wanted to say to her, all

the words he had rehearsed for so long, vanished into thin air.

He closed the gate behind him and stood looking at the house for a moment, feeling unsure of himself and awkward, groping like a blind thing for some semblance of control. His mind was blank. Panic leached into his bones. He tried to decide if there was anything more pathetic than a man who has lost his confidence and is reduced to nothing more than a bumbling, inadequate fool. Vulnerability settled around him like a hair shirt.

The old Greek Revival house on Centre Street looked the same—clapboard walls, pilasters at the corners, and deep entablatures on the flanks. The fence still tied into the stoop railings the way it always did, and the front door still looked as if it needed a coat of paint. Everything on the outside looked exactly as it had almost three years ago when he left.

As he climbed the front steps to the door, Tavis paused. He couldn't help wondering what changes Elizabeth had made on the inside.

It was early yet, only a quarter past nine. He supposed the housekeeper would still be around, since he had left enough money with his banker to pay her wages for at least five years. He put his key into the lock and opened the door, stepping inside the entry, noticing it was still as sparse as ever, with nothing more than a hall chair and the umbrella stand that had always been next to the door. Still it was holding only one umbrella. His.

He entered the parlor, turning up the oil lamp on the tripod table, somewhat surprised to find it in its usual place, next to the door. Beside the table, the Chippendale chair had the same blue needlepoint cushion he remembered, and the rosewood sofa table was where it had always been, directly in front of the sofa. The Turkish ottoman stood in its customary place, in front of his favorite leather chair.

The room was exactly as he had left it, and even to his unpracticed eye, seemed untouched. He dropped his coat in the chair as he hurried from the room, going into the dining room. Finding it also as he had left it, he went upstairs.

The bedroom would be the one room no woman could use without leaving some reminder of herself about, but once again, he found the room exactly as it had always been—cozy, comfortable, and decidedly masculine. There were no frilly curtains—the kind women like—at the windows, no bright counterpane covered the bed. There were no slippers on the floor, no cotton gown or wrapper thrown about. He looked at the dressing table, seeing only his silver monogrammed jewelry case, a small miniature of his parents, and a tortoiseshell brush and comb that had belonged to his mother.

Of all the things he had seen since he entered his house, it was the sight of this dressing table that bothered him the most. That and the fact that the room had that unused, museum smell to it, when it should have smelled of lilac water and lavender. He felt his fists clench at his sides. "Son of a bitch!" he said, and went to inspect the rest of the house.

He found the housekeeper, Mrs. Chadwick, in the kitchen. "Where is my wife?" he asked upon entering.

Mrs. Chadwick jumped a mile and slapped her hand to her chest. "Lord have mercy! You scared the daylights out of me," she said, giving him a frightened look. "Why, Mr. Mackinnon, how nice to have you back. You should have written me you were coming. I would have aired the place out good and proper."

"Where is Elizabeth?"

"Why, I don't know. Did you try the lighthouse?"

"No, I came here first. Considering the time of day, I was expecting her to be home."

"Oh, she didn't tell you, then?"

"Tell me what?"

"That she doesn't live here. The day you left, she moved her things out to the lighthouse on Brandt Point. I suspected the poor thing was so lonesome after you left that she wanted to be with her grandpa. She's been living out there in the lighthouse with Captain Robinson ever since." She paused, her face suddenly turning grave. "I suppose you don't know about what happened," she said, shaking her head sadly. "About her loss."

His heart hammered in his chest. "What loss?"

"Oh, it was such a tragic thing," she said. "Such a tragic, tragic loss. Old Captain Robinson hasn't been the same since it happened."

"Since what happened?"

"Why, the fire," she said, shaking her head sadly. "The Robinson house and two others . . . burned to the ground, they did. Killed Samuel and Elizabeth's two sisters."

Tavis pulled out a chair and sat down, his body too shocked to do more than that simple act. "When did this all happen?" he asked, his mind still dazed.

"Right after you left. Not more than seven or eight months later, as I recollect."

Before Tavis could fully understand what had happened and what it meant, before he could completely absorb his shock and regret, Mrs. Chadwick gave him a strange look.

"If you didn't know about the fire," she said, "then I don't suppose you knew ... about ... the ... babe."

Fragments of exploding light seemed to shatter within his brain. "What babe?" he said in cold, well-pronounced tones.

Mrs. Chadwick was looking very uncomfortable and she began fanning her face with a pot holder. "Oh, dear me. I should've kept my big mouth shut, that's what I should have done." Then giving him a sickly sheepish look, she said, "Mr. Mackinnon, please don't be asking me anything else. I just come here two or three times a week to air out the place and dust. I don't know anything about nothing."

"You mentioned a babe. Whose?"

"Please," she said, wringing her hands. "Go out to the lighthouse and speak to your wife. Get your answers from her. I don't feel it's my place to tell you any more than what you want to know about the condition of your house."

"This house and everything in it can fall to perdition, for all I care," Tavis said. Without another word, he turned away, walking quickly from the room.

It didn't take him long to reach the lighthouse, passing the whale's jawbone, walking up the sandy path, stepping over puddles, his mind more intent upon what he would say than on where he was going.

Over and over in his mind, the shocking news he had heard kept repeating itself. *The Lord giveth and the Lord taketh away.* Elizabeth had lost her father and two sisters. She had been given a child. *Blessed be the name of the Lord.*

How could he comfort her? What could he say to let

her know he, of all people, understood her loss? His mind spun backward, remembering the time when he was just a boy, and how the loss of his brother and sister had come about the same time he lost both of his parents. Oh yes, he understood loss, all right. He knew the despair, the pain, the relentless agony. It came back to him swiftly. He could feel the emotion on the inside, but he couldn't find a way to tell her.

He looked up then, seeing the lighthouse and seeing Captain Robinson standing at the water's edge, a little boy, not more than two or so, standing at his side. As he drew closer, Captain Robinson looked up. Seeing his grandfather distracted, the boy, too, glanced at Tavis. The moment he looked at the boy's face, he knew the child was his son.

It was like looking into a mirror that went back in time. He was no doubt a Mackinnon, through and through. From the intense blue eyes to the black curly hair. There wasn't a hint of Elizabeth in him. It was both uplifting and disheartening, and it left Tavis feeling as if he had been handed something, only to have it taken away.

Realizing the child was his brought a new question to the forefront. Why hadn't she written him about the child? What did she hope to gain by keeping something like this from him? Then he remembered the night he left, when she came to the library. He had asked her why she hadn't refused to marry him, why she had persisted with the notion. With a clenching in his belly, he remembered his cruel words, his insult.

But in the end you gave in, didn't you?
I had to.
Had to or wanted to? What's the difference?
There were . . . I had my reasons.

His step faltered, and for a moment he felt as if he could not go on. *How much more?* he wondered. *How much more guilt must I bear?*

The boy was holding a boat. Tavis looked at Captain Robinson and nodded. "Captain," he said, shaking Asa's hand.

"Well, you came back," Asa said. "Just like I knew you would."

"Was there any doubt?" Tavis asked, his gaze on the boy.

"To some folks there was," Asa said. "Are you back for good?"

"Yes," Tavis said, "and judging from the changes in things, I think it's a good thing I am."

Asa looked at the boy.

Tavis did, too. "Hello," he said, dropping down to a crouch.

The boy didn't speak and he didn't take his eyes off Tavis, staring at him thoughtfully, then glancing suspiciously at his grandfather.

"That's a pretty sailboat. Did you make it?" Tavis asked.

The boy looked down at the sailboat in his hands, and Tavis caught a glimpse of the long lashes, the sunlit gloss of his ebony hair. Giving Tavis a shy look, he shook his head and pointed at his grandfather. "No," he said, the sound of it strong and sure, as if it was a word he used often.

Tavis smiled and came to his feet, his hand reaching out to ruffle the boy's hair. Something shattered inside him the moment he touched the child, the moment his hand felt the silky strands of his son's hair. His son. He glanced down again, feeling the undeniable urge to take the boy into his arms, knowing it was too soon.

"Is she in the house?" he asked Asa.

"She was in the kitchen a moment ago," Asa replied.

Tavis glanced toward the house, realizing now that he had double the reasons to work this thing out between them, double the reasons to feel the loss if he did not.

It had been raining for a solid week, but today the drizzle and rain began to clear, leaving the sky splotchy and dotted with innocent-looking clouds. Peering through the lifting grayness into a yard that would soon be sun-warmed and bright, Elizabeth watched her grandfather take two-year-old Willie out to sail his boat. Willie was walking beside Asa, jumping puddles. He jumped three of them, then landed smack in the middle of the fourth.

Elizabeth laughed at that, then looked away, feeling happy and contented, delighted that at last the sun was out. She glanced in the direction of town. Out of the mist that lifted in the distance she saw him come.

Elizabeth didn't know how long she had been standing there at the window watching her grandfather and her son. She stood with one hand holding back the worn edge of lace curtain, staring across the sandy stretch of yard, to the overturned hull of a rowboat and past it where a little boy ran along the shore, tugging on a piece of string and dragging a miniature sailboat behind him.

She had not been thinking of him when she first looked out the window, but before long, her thoughts, as they always did, turned to Tavis. Her thoughts of him were always like this, coming unexpectedly and lingering for a spell, before wandering off again, much in the same manner that Tavis had done.

For some time now she had been standing at the win

dow, staring at her grandfather and Willie, and then she thought she heard the sound of Tavis's voice. It came to her from somewhere above, from somewhere beyond the endless circle of stairs that wound around and around until it reached the top, where the lanterns and the large reflectors lay.

Elizabeth . . . Elizabeth . . . Elizabeth

His words were only a wordless echo in her head.

How strange it was, funny even, how many times she would think of him being there, hearing his voice, only to realize it was all in her head. There had been many times in those first few months before Willie was born that she had heard that same voice. Gradually the pain of losing him had begun to fade. Then Becca had married Nathaniel Starbuck's younger brother, Jason, and they moved away to New Bedford. A short while later, her father and sisters had died in that fire, and the whole world seemed to fall away from her, leaving behind only a great, groaning sadness.

It had been—what?—close to two years now since that horrible day of the fire, yet not a day went by that she didn't recall the tragedy, that she didn't relive the pain. Her gaze went to her grandfather. He had aged so much in the past two years. There had been so many losses in his life, but unlike her, he didn't seem to be able to pick up and go on. He seemed to be waiting for something, and each time the thought came to her, it was followed by the same answer.

Death.

Many times Asa had told her it should have been him who was taken in that fire, that he had lived his life and had no real reason to go on, that Samuel was younger with more responsibilities.

"It wasn't supposed to happen this way," he said. "People aren't supposed to bury their children."

Two nights ago, when he had said that same exact thing again, Elizabeth had pointed out that he did have a reason to go on, that he had herself and Willie. "Aren't we reason enough?"

To which he replied, "You're both young . . . and strong. You'll make it whether I'm around or not." Then his eyes took on that far-off cast and he lost himself in the thoughts of his past. "I never wanted to come back," he said. "I never wanted to die like this, old and broken, watching those I love go before me. How much better if I had died at the hands of a whale, or dashed upon the rocks during a great storm." And then he looked at her sadly and said, "It's hard on a man to watch his life slip away a little each day, to watch his friends and family pass on and being left behind with nothing more to think about than when it will be his turn."

"Perhaps God spared you because He knew I would need you. Oh, Grandpa, don't you see, I couldn't have made it without you?"

"Perhaps," he said, staring out the window toward the sea he loved so well. "But you don't need me anymore, and sometimes I get the strongest feeling that it's time."

"Don't talk that way. Willie and I do need you. We do."

He did not turn to look at her. "Well, I'm still here, my bones creaking and my mind wandering, so you mustn't fret. Sometimes I feel it calling to me, calling me to come back."

"Calling to you? You mean whaling?"

"No," he said, staring out over the gray expanse o

water again. "The sea. I think she feels that she's been cheated. The sea doesn't like to give up her dead."

"Then she will have to live with it. You're fine and fit and no longer at sea. You have a lot of life in you yet."

"I don't know," he said, not looking at her but continuing to stare at the water as if he were talking to it, and in a way, she supposed he was. "We still have a rendezvous," he said, "the sea and I."

"Your sea-rover days are over now. No more rendezvous with the sea or anything else more taxing than taking Willie out to play with his sailboat."

Elizabeth cleared her throat, and the memory of that day faded away. What was it about that conversation with her grandfather that kept lingering in her mind? Why could she not let it go?

Suddenly she became conscious of an encroaching dryness in her mouth and throat, of a near-painful thrumming of her heart. She swallowed, feeling her breathing come more quickly, becoming light-headed. Suddenly she realized what she had been staring at.

Out of the distance where the path wound along the point from town, and the sand and sky seemed to melt into shades of watercolor blue, she saw him coming. For an insane moment she seemed to lose track of time, and for the life of her she couldn't fathom if she had been watching him for the briefest second or for the longest while.

A long time ago she had loved this man. She had married him. She had borne him a son. There had been a time, even after Willie's birth, that the passion for him was still alive within her, a living, burning thing. But the passion had died, replaced by a newer, fresher grief, and along with it came the hope that he would never come back. There was no anger in Elizabeth now, no bitterness. She was simply Elizabeth Mackinnon, quiet and sweet, a woman as devoted to her grandfather and her son as she was to the study of astronomy, content to live out her days in the lighthouse out on Brandt Point, with a backbone of iron.

She supposed she owed much of this to her son, her sweet, chubby-fingered Willie. She remembered so vividly what she had said to Becca the day he was born. "Tavis I will never have, but I can have his child. This is a part of him that will always belong to me, a part he can never take back. There is a purpose in my life after all. I suppose that has been the worst thing about loving someone who doesn't love you in return. You have no purpose."

Her gaze went back to the man walking up the path. Tavis Mackinnon, the man who left her with a child in her belly and no purpose.

Her knees went suddenly weak. He was dressed much the same as he always was, brown pants, a dark blue seaman coat with the collar turned up. What little of his face she could see was not as deeply tanned as she remembered, but somehow she knew the blue-gray eyes would still be capable of reducing her to a quivering heap.

Her heart in her throat, she watched him approach, seeing the way he stopped for a moment where Willie and her grandfather were sailing Willie's boat. He nodded to Asa and shook his hand, then turned toward Willie, speaking as he did so. She saw her grandfather nod, and Tavis dropped down in a crouch, asking Willie a question. He smiled when Willie shook his head and pointed at his grandfather. Tavis ruffled the hair on Willie's head, then rising to stand, he exchanged a few more words with her grandfather. She was already feeling the wild pounding of her heart when her grandfather nodded toward the house.

No . . . no . . . send him away. Don't tell him I'm here. I don't want to see him. . . .

The moment Tavis turned away from her grandfather and Willie, the congenial look left his face. With purposeful strides, he crossed the sandy yard. It did not take a wise person to see he was upset, angry. She watched until he drew too close to the door for her to see anymore, then she held her breath, waiting for his knock. A moment later she heard the door open, then close.

She heard his footsteps going about the house, searching for her. She was still standing at the kitchen window, too afraid to move, when she heard him walk into the room. For a moment she stood there, still clutching the dish towel in her hands, then with a deep breath, she turned to face him. "So you've come back," was all she said.

Emotion leapt like flames in his eyes. "Was there ever any doubt that I would return?" he said, not bothering to hide the hint of sadness in his voice.

"More times than not," she said, letting her voice drift off to nothing. She wanted to be strong and resist, to show him he wasn't the only one who could be cold and uncaring, but she knew she didn't convey it in the way she would have liked.

He, however, had no trouble letting her know the direction of his thoughts. "I wish so many things between us had been different," he said. "I wish you had told me about the boy."

With as much defiance as she could muster, she said, "Why? What difference could it have possibly made, save to make you angrier at me, to make you hate me more?"

"I was angry, yes, but I never hated you. I would think the birth of my child would be something I had a right to know. You could have at least written to me or answered one of my letters. I left you instructions on how to reach me if you needed to."

"Oh yes, you did, didn't you? You left instructions for the way your money was to be spent and as to how your house was to be cared for, but you forgot one thing. You never mentioned your wife."

He persisted. She should have told him, and he would keep on saying it. "You should have answered my letters. You should have told me I had a son."

"Why? If you didn't care about your wife, what makes you think I would believe you would care about the son I bore you?"

He didn't say anything for a moment, remembering his earlier thoughts, the night she said, *I had my reasons.*

"Did you know about the baby before? Is that why you let your family push you into this?"

"Yes."

Something seemed to register in his mind. At first his look was incredulous, then his entire being seemed to relax. "It was a mistake. Things would have been different. I may be a lot of things, but I wouldn't have turned my back on you."

"How was I supposed to know that? You were angry enough at the time. I thought telling you was the worst thing I could have done. I wanted you to get used to the idea of having a wife before you had to deal with becoming a father. I had no way of knowing you intended to leave the day we were married."

At least he had the decency to look a bit sheepish. "If I had known," he said softly, "I would have stayed."

She lifted her chin and looked at him directly. "If you had stayed, I would have told you."

He started to speak, but she cut him off. "It doesn't matter. None of this matters. As far as I'm concerned, you gave up your rights when you abandoned me, and as you can see, I was able to have Willie without your help."

"Willie . . . is that what you named him?"

Her immediate response was to take advantage of his distraction and to level him with a broadside, but she never said the things that would have delivered it. Perhaps that was because what was in her heart was so very different from what was in her mind. Perhaps it was because from the first moment she had seen him, she had known she stilled longed to be Tavis Mackinnon's wife in every sense of the word. "Willie is what we call him. It's short for William . . . William Tavis."

"You named him Tavis after me?"

"He is your son. Do you object?"

"No. Of course not. To the contrary, it's just that . . . well, it surprises me."

"Why should it? He's your son, your firstborn and the one to bear your name. I would never deny him that any more than I would hold your being his father against him."

He stared at her. She met his gaze unflinchingly. Slowly the hard, angry look left his eyes and he relaxed. "This is hardly the welcome I expected. For some reason, I thought you would be angry with me."

"I was, but my anger went shortly after Willie was born. I don't want my hate to poison Willie's life. Besides, I really don't have time to fan the flames of my grudges. Faith! I never knew being a mother could keep one so busy," she said, hoping the lightness would hide the heaviness of her pain.

For a moment she thought he might smile, but his face remained impassive. Her attempt at levity hadn't fooled him. "Mrs. Chadwick said you moved out of the house right after I left."

"The next day, to be exact."

"Why?"

"I would think the reasons I left would be obvious. I can't believe you don't know why. Actually, it wasn't such a difficult decision to reach. It was more than apparent to me that you didn't want me, or our marriage. Under the circumstances, I thought it best. By that time, I wanted nothing more to do with you or anything that belonged to you."

For a moment it was a standoff, and they eyed each other from across the distance that separated them, both convinced they were right, neither of them willing to give in. After a few seconds, he sighed. She saw the disappointment in his face, but in spite of it, he gave her a wry smile.

"You've changed," he said.

"I'm a mother now."

Suddenly she realized he really had expected to find her happily ensconced in his house and waiting for him. *Oh, God, now he wants to have a go at this marriage. Why? Why now, when I've only begun to make a life for myself?* "Motherhood has changed me," she said, then added, "That, and tragedy."

His face softened. "I heard about Samuel and your sisters. I'm sorry . . . very sorry." He paused, feeling more guilt, more insecurity. "I should have been here for you."

"Yes, you should have been, but you weren't, and all the wishing in the world won't change that. Things are different now. You abandoned me, and for almost three years I had to learn how to deal with losses and grief. You made your decisions and you stood by them. They hurt me. You hurt me. The pain of it doesn't go away simply because you decide to walk back into my life and offer your apology."

"I know that," he said. "But just the same, I want you to know how sorry I am. I know what a loss like that can do."

She knew he was thinking about the deaths of parents, brother, and sister in his own family, but his losses were a long time ago and the wounds were healed over, while hers were still fresh. She looked off. "Yes," she said, "losses are very hard to bear, and I've had many. Sometimes I think that there must be someone sitting up there listening for us to count our blessings, just so they know where to start when it comes time to take them all away." She looked him straight in the eye. "Don't think I'll let you take Willie away. I'll kill you first." She looked outside, where her grandfather and Willie stood. "I have nothing left except Willie and that dear old man out there. Losing my father and my sisters almost killed him. I'll not have him suffer any more grief." She looked back at her grandfather, keeping her gaze fastened upon him as she gave him warning. "Stay away from him. Stay away from me. When I hurt, it causes him pain."

"I didn't come back to hurt you, Liza."

She flinched at the use of her name, remembering all too well the times aboard her sloop and the occasions he had used it. "I don't know why you bothered to come back at all. And don't call me Liza. It is an endearment. Something we both know I am not."

He continued to stare at her, as if something deep in her violet gaze had moved him. At that moment she heard Willie's voice and turned, seeing him coming toward the lighthouse, tugging her grandfather's hand.

"It's lunchtime. I was just about to feed William," she said, picking up a bowl from the cabinet behind her. She felt his eyes boring into her back as she went to the stove and ladled up a bowl of thick clam chowder. She placed it on the table, where she had set two places. She ladled up a larger bowl for her grandfather and placed it across the table from the other one.

"I want to talk to you, Elizabeth, and I'll do it, in front of them if need be."

She heard the door open. Her heart turned to ice. At last she said, "We can talk in the other room."

He followed her into the main room of the house. He jerked to a halt. What he saw there made him lose all composure. *This* was what had been missing at his house on Centre Street. *This* is what he had expected when he unlocked the door. *This* is what she had deprived him of. He closed his eyes as if fighting something and doubled his fists at his sides.

When he opened them, he looked around the room. All about him lay signs of life, the homey clutter that bore the patina of love and use. His gaze went immediately to a table scattered with the tools of a carver's trade, curling bits of wood and sawdust falling over the side and scattered about the floor. On its top lay Noah' ark, complete with its menagerie of wooden animals.

His heart wrenched.

It was a cheerful room, crammed with an abundance of books and child-sized furniture, and scattered with toys. Even with only himself and Elizabeth inside, it was noisy and crowded, echoing its many functions. Here was the center of life. Here a child was fed and romped in boisterous play. Here he was soothed with a lullaby and rocked to sleep by the fire. Here all his cuts and bumps were lovingly attended and the hurts all kissed away. Everywhere he looked, toys lay— sailboats, a ball, toy soldiers, a rocking horse, circus animals, a spinning top. A copy of *Child's Easy Reading Book* lay on a miniature Windsor chair, and for a moment his gaze rested on a copy of *Higgledy, Piggledy, My Black Hen.*

Overcome with the impact, he shut his eyes, but even then, the reality of what was missing in his life haunted him. Even with his eyes closed, he could tell the difference. Here the smells of home wrapped themselves around him. Here the aromas of roses and talcum and something simmering in the kitchen reached out to him. Here is where he wanted to be, not back there, in his house, where the place smelled of darkness and disuse, like a trunk that is packed with memories and taken down to air once a year.

"Mama . . . Mama . . . hurt . . . Willie's hurt."

Tavis jerked his head around at the sound of his son's voice, catching sight of him running through the door, holding his finger. Elizabeth was beside him in an instant.

"What happened to you, Willie?" she asked, the softness, the love, in her voice shattering Tavis.

"Clamshell," Willie said. "Hurt."

"Hasn't Mama told you not to play with clamshells?

They're sharp, Willie. They cut your finger, don't they?"

Willie nodded and held up his finger. "Cut Willie. See?"

Tavis watched Elizabeth as she took Willie by the hand and led him to the window, where a medicine box sat on the sill. "Okay, Willie my boy, let me have your finger."

Willie thrust out his finger, and Tavis watched Elizabeth wipe the drops of blood away. *Flesh of my flesh, bone of my bone, blood of my blood.* It was all he could do to keep from going to them, from taking his son in his arms and feeling his soft weight for the first time.

She kissed his chubby finger, and Tavis drank in the scene, remembering something from long ago, something his own mother had said. *God couldn't be everywhere, Tavis. That's why He made mothers.*

He watched her tend to his son. There had been so many failures, so many losses between them, but there was one thing that he could see, one thing that would remain indelible and indestructible, something that was the strongest bond upon the earth: the bond between mother and child.

He looked at Willie's face, seeing the adoration etched upon his miniature features, seeing, too, the way he rubbed the fabric of her sleeve between his thumb and forefinger, as if somehow even her clothes felt different from anyone else's. It wasn't so much the things that she did that created the difference, it was simply the fact of being near her that made him feel better.

Feeling like his heart was bleeding in a dozen places, he watched her apply ointment. Finally she gave the boy a hug and said, "Now give me a kiss, Willie boy, and tell me if it feels better."

Willie came up on his toes and threw his arms around Elizabeth's neck, giving her three kisses upon the cheek. "Feels better," he said, and when he finished, he gave her a look that said, *My mother, who can do anything, fixed it.*

"All right, now off with you," she said, giving his britches a dusting. "Go finish your chowder before it gets cold."

Tavis watched Willie run from the room, much in the same manner that he had entered it, remembering he had read once that a house without a woman was like a body without a soul. He had never understood the meaning of those words until today, until he had walked into his own home, expecting . . .

What? What had he expected? He shook his head. He didn't know. God help him, he did not know. But the moment he stepped into this room, he had known. Everywhere around him were signs of living, loving, and life.

The aching need to belong reached out to him. "I want you to come home," he said, unable to feel much more than the desire to have her with him, the desire to have a purpose, an anchor in life. Something to fill the void. Something to keep him from feeling the pilgrim in his own home.

"I am home," she said, feeling acutely the strain he was under.

"You know what I mean," he said solemnly.

She gave him a direct look. "No, Tavis, I don't. Home is right where I am, where I feel comfortable, where my needs are met. *This* is where my heart is. *This* is where I am going to stay."

"You're my wife. . . ."

"I've known that for quite some time. It surprises me, though, that it took you almost three years to realize it."

"Elizabeth—"

He never got to finish what he was going to say, for Willie's voice called out from the other room. "Mama?"

She glanced toward the kitchen. "I'll be there in just a minute," she said, looking quickly back at Tavis and giving him a dismissing look.

"You're busy," he said. "I'd better go."

"Yes, Willie is at the age that he gets frustrated whenever he wants me and I'm not around."

"I can understand that," he said, remembering how many times he felt that way himself.

She seemed to ignore the way he looked at her, to ignore what he was saying, what she must know he was feeling.

She walked him to the door, reaching her hand out to open it. She turned to him; the tension he had noticed about her eyes earlier was now gone. "I'm glad you know. It's one less thing I have to worry about," she said, then gave a short, sad sound that was part sigh, part laugh. "I used to lie awake at night imagining this moment, trying to think what we would say to each other, how I would tell you about Willie . . . what you would say, that is, if you ever came back."

He reached for the door, turning to face her, his hand resting on the handle. "If it makes you feel any better, I've thought about this moment a lot myself. Not that I imagined I would have a son, but . . ."

He paused briefly, then went on, "Most of the time I just thought about the changes in the house, the hundred or so little ways a woman's presence changes things, the uncanny way a woman has of making a house into a home. Not that I didn't do a lot of thinking about you and the things I would say to you." His eyes never left her face. "It seems we both painted some mighty unrealistic pictures."

"Yes, it would seem we did." She glanced back toward the kitchen, and then she spoke, her voice lighter and carrying a tone of finality. "We can't change all that's happened, Tavis. What is done stays done. But we can change the pictures we paint from here on out."

"And what kind do you see yourself painting . . . now?"

Her expression hardened. "Realistic ones. We've both changed, Tavis. Things aren't the same. We can't go back. And even if we could, I wouldn't want to."

"Is this a polite way of telling me that you have no intention of being my wife?"

"What I am saying is, I won't move into your house simply because I am your wife."

"I see," he said, releasing the door and turning away.

She watched him go. "No, I don't think you do," she said to his retreating back. "But then, you never did."

CHAPTER
❧ TWENTY-ONE ❧

She had not planned to go to town that day, for there was no valid reason for her to do so. But it had been an emotional week for her, and seeing the way her grandfather and Willie avoided her, she knew she had been overly cross. She had been cooped up too long. She needed to stretch her legs, to feel the salt air filling her lungs. A walk to town was more than it seemed. It was for her at least, a release.

Up early that morning, she left Willie with her grandfather. After checking a list she had concocted she slipped a basket over her arm and set off. A short while later, she was walking across the moors, rich this time of year with Scotch broom, heather, beach plum, bayberry, and holly. A gull cried out, then she was surrounded by nothing but silence and the eternal out-of-doors.

She had no more than stepped upon the cobblestone streets that ran through town when she saw him coming up the road riding a fancy black horse that pranced and danced sideways. They made a pretty picture, the two of them did, the horse unlike any she had seen on the island, and Tavis looking better than three holidays come together. She glanced down at her old rose-gray dress and felt suddenly overwhelmed with the possibility of meeting him. With a quick step, she was off the road and crouching behind a cascade of pink roses that draped over Mrs. Coleman's fence.

He was headed for the lighthouse, she was certain of that much, and for a moment she felt the tugging urge—was it her mothering instinct?—to rush back there. She felt uncomfortable with the idea that he would be with Willie when she wasn't around. But she knew she didn't have the right to keep him from his son, and Willie had a right to know his father. Perhaps it was better this way. Perhaps they could work out some arrangement for her to be away whenever he came to visit Willie.

After he and his prancing horse had passed, she made her way back to the road and, quickening her pace, hurried into town.

"Tavis came while you were gone," her grandfather said when she returned home.

She heaved the basket onto the kitchen table and began unpacking her purchases. "I know. I saw him on my way into town."

"Funny," Asa said. "He didn't mention having seen you."

"He didn't. I saw him coming," she said. Then giving him a guilty look, she added, "I hid until he was past."

Asa gave her a penetrating stare. "Hiding from him now, are you?"

"I'm not hiding . . . at least not the way you think. I didn't want to see him, that's all." She opened the sack of sugar and scooped some into a bowl before putting the sack away. She glanced around. "Where is Willie?"

"Asleep."

She nodded. "Did Tavis stay long?"

"About an hour."

"Did he take Willie out?"

"Took him for a ride on his horse and promised to get him a pony of his own."

"A pony? Humph! Willie is too young for a pony. That would be pure foolishness to buy him a pony when he can barely walk."

"Well, maybe Tavis isn't as wise as you are," Asa said.

She gave him a quick, hard look, but didn't say anything, noticing he did not seem put off.

"He seems to be quite taken with Willie. . . . Of course, he spent most of his time asking about you," Asa went on to say. "I suspect that is why he didn't tarry too long when he took Willie outside."

She turned a shocked expression upon him. "Questions about me?" She placed two jars of honey on the table and sat down. "I don't know what kinds of questions he could be asking about me. He knows enough already. More than he'd like, or I'll miss my guess."

"I take it you don't believe a body can change."

She ignored her grandfather's words and began sifting through the silverware that was sitting in a crock on the table. "What kinds of questions was he asking?"

Asa's white brows rose and his eyes had a merry twinkle. "Oh, general things mostly."

She stopped, holding a knife suspended in midair as she looked at him squarely. She put the knife into the crock. "What general things, Grandpa?"

"Things like what you do for entertainment. Do yo

go to parties much? Did you have a rough time of it when the baby was born? Do I think you'd ever be favorable to moving back into town?"

"Not into *his* house, I wouldn't," she said, slamming her hands down on the table and rising to her feet.

Asa watched her pace the floor for a spell, then he said, "You know it would be the best thing for Willie ... for the two of you to agree to live as a family." When she glared at him, he said, "I know you still have a raw place from the way he left you, but he's had time to cool down and get over his anger at being forced into marriage. From what he said, he never planned on being gone more than a month or two. I think he wants to try."

"A month or two? I find that hard to believe ... especially when I remember he was gone two and a half years."

"And if it wasn't his fault? If he wanted to come back, but couldn't? What would you say to that?"

"If he wanted to come back bad enough, he would have found a way."

"Even if it meant he would be arrested?"

"Don't tell me things like that," she said. "If he wants me to know, he can tell me." She stood at the kitchen window now, hugging herself and staring out at the water. "You know I've always wanted to be married to Tavis, but I don't want it simply because it's the best thing to do, and I don't want it because he's filled your head with a bunch of excuses. He left me. It's a cold, hard fact, but it's true. He left me and I suffered for it. For nearly three years. If Tavis has decided he wants me, he's a little late. If he wants things to be different between us, he is going to have to do more than hint. I've chased him for over half of my life. I'm through doing that now. I won't go back to him because it's easy, or right . . . not even for Willie. The only reason I would consider it is if I knew without a doubt that Tavis's feelings for me have changed. I can take his anger, even his need for revenge, but I cannot tolerate his indifference. I want his love, or I want no part of him. Every time I think about moving back into his house, I remember the way he left me. He doesn't want me. He wants Willie. I wish he would leave us both alone and go back to wherever it was that he was building those precious ships of his. If I have to, I'll take Willie and I'll move to Boston."

"Well, you know I'm the last person in the world to force you to do anything. I always was a soft touch for a lass with your color eyes."

She turned, but her steady gaze didn't seem to bother him.

"I still think you should consider what he asks. The three of us have been happy here, I know, but nothing lasts. I could go tomorrow—"

She started to speak.

"No, don't say anything," he said. "Just let me finish. You know this can never be a permanent home for you and Willie, and no matter how many times you cover your ears when I try to speak of it, I won't be here forever. I'm old, Elizabeth. And I'm ready to go. When that day comes, you and Willie will have to go, too. You know they'll get someone else to keep the lighthouse."

"When that day comes, I'll take Willie and go to Boston. I still have Aunt Phoebe's house."

For a long time the two of them stood there, each one staring at the other. At last she could see that he seemed to dismiss the subject. She knew he had when he said,

"Tavis wants to take Willie to the sheepshearing next week."

She was glad for the opportunity to talk about something else. She knew it was childish of her to expect her grandfather to live forever, but they were all she had, that old man and the little boy. They were all that mattered in her life, all she wanted to think about—until now. Now she had something else to think about. Now she realized just how raw her feelings for Tavis still were, just how much his rejection still hurt. "What did you tell him?"

"I told him the truth. That you planned to take Willie with you to the shearing . . . at least for a while."

"Is that all?"

"Nope. I told him that you had hired Mrs. Morrison to stay with Willie after that."

She nodded. "What did he say then?"

"Nothing. He did ask if you planned on staying for the dance. And before you ask me, I told him *we* always stayed for the dance and that I saw no reason to do differently just because he was back."

Elizabeth laughed.

"Did I say something funny?"

"No, it's just that I was thinking much the same thing when I was in town. What you told Tavis . . . well, that's the same thing I was thinking. It's what I thought, and it's what I've decided to do . . . go on with my life just as I've always done."

Asa watched her put a kettle of water on to boil, thinking how many times he had seen her do just that, and how many of those times she had been wearing that same faded rose dress. His mind went back to the time she had come home from Boston and how smart she looked then, wearing the latest fancy dresses and catching the eye of every man from fifteen to fifty in Nantucket. He remembered, too, the way she had given every single one of those beautiful dresses away after she had Willie, and how she had told him that part of her life was over.

Leaving her in the kitchen, Asa ambled through the doorway. The more he thought about it, the more he was convinced that Elizabeth tried to make herself look matronly and dowdy, that it was her way of feeling safe and just a little persecuted—not that he blamed her for the persecuted bit. She had been through a lot, and if feeling persecuted was the worst thing that had come out of it, well, he'd have to say she'd come out pretty good. But even then, her looking dowdy hadn't always worked, for there were plenty of times he could remember some fellah or the other trying to catch her eye.

Asa knew all the women in town would be squiring new party dresses the night of the sheepshearing dance. He thought about the meager selection of dresses remaining in Elizabeth's trunk, and decided then and there it was high time she had a new frock. His thoughts turned to the burning pain in his stomach that never seemed to let up. His days were numbered. He didn't have much time. With a resigned sigh, he eased himself into his rocking chair and lit his pipe. A moment later he decided he would sashay into town tomorrow and pay a visit to Mrs. Schultz's dress shop.

The next morning Asa, exclaiming he was out of tobacco, announced he was going into town.

"You should have told me, Grandpa. I was in town only yesterday. I could've gotten it for you."

"I know, but I forgot. My old mind isn't as sharp as it once was."

Elizabeth gave him a thoughtful look. "It's still sharp," she said, "when you want it to be."

Asa laughed and gave her a peck on the cheek, then he took himself into Nantucket, going directly to Mrs. Schultz's. He hadn't expected to see three women he knew when he stepped inside, so he gave a start of surprise.

"Mornin', ladies," he said, tipping his hat. While the women responded, he cogitated for a moment as to whether he should leave and come back another time, but Alice Schultz was looking like she was about to burst forth with a question.

"Why, Captain Robinson, this is indeed a surprise. We don't see much of you in town, and I cannot ever remember a time when you graced my shop. Are you certain you're in the right place?"

If the way he felt was any indication, he wasn't. He stammered for a moment, nodding at two of the ladies as they left. At last he said, "I came to buy Elizabeth a dress for the shearing dance next week."

"Oh, how lovely, and how thoughtful of you. You know, I was just remarking to Mrs. Patterson the other day as to how we see so little of Elizabeth, and how she never seems to wear any of those beautiful dresses she brought with her from Boston a few years back. Now, why don't you sit down right there in that chair, Captain, and let me show you what I have. You know," she said as she began rummaging through bolts of fabric, "I think I saw something that just came in last week. . . . Yes, here it is, a brand-new bolt of lavender silk. With those eyes of hers, and her coloring . . . well, I can't tell you how much I think of Elizabeth each time I look at this. Has her name written all over it, wouldn't you say, Mabel?"

Mabel Starbuck nodded her head in agreement. "Written all over it, just as you said."

Asa paid for the fabric, instructing Mrs. Schultz to do it up in some way fancy enough to do Elizabeth justice.

To which Mrs. Schultz replied, "It will be a pleasure, Captain. A pure pleasure."

After Asa left, Mrs. Schultz looked at Mabel. "What a dear, sweet man. He's so protective of that granddaughter of his."

"He must not be too protective—not if he's ordering a new dress for her. You know as well as I do, Alice, that Tavis Mackinnon is back in town," Mabel said.

"So I've heard," Mrs. Schultz said. "I've also heard—just rumor, mind you—that the shoe is definitely on the other foot this time."

"Why, whatever do you mean?"

"Well, I got this from a very *reliable* source, mind you. And according to *the source*, Tavis has been making a near nuisance of himself. Out at the lighthouse. Under the pretext of seeing little Willie, of course."

"Of course," said Mabel, scooting closer. "What else did you hear?"

"Only that Elizabeth is too levelheaded to repeat *past mistakes*, if you get my meaning, and that she is being a perfect angel about allowing him to spend time with Willie," Alice said.

"Has he asked her to live with him as his wife?"

"No one knows for certain, but it's speculated that he hasn't come right out and put the question to her. If you ask me, he's doing the right thing by making a place for himself with his son."

"Then why would Captain Robinson be in here ordering her a fancy dress?" asked Mabel.

Alice didn't even have to think about that for a minute. "The way I see it, there are two possible reasons. He either wants Elizabeth to look so stunning that Tavis will press his case a little harder, or he wants someone else to."

"Let's hope Tavis takes the bait first. He doesn't strike me as the kind to take too kindly to someone else prowling around his property."

"Exactly. Either way, it's a good way to make Tavis stake his claim publicly," Alice said.

"Upon my word!" Mabel said, her corset creaking with the effort. "I do believe Captain Robinson is a sly old goat."

"Wise men grow wiser with age," Alice said.

"Oh, this is so romantic," Mabel said. "I can't wait until the dance. I wouldn't miss seeing this for the world. I'm going to Mr. Starbuck's office straightaway, and tell him we must be there early."

Mabel started for the door, stopped, and turned around. "Alice, you must outdo yourself on that dress. Do you hear? You simply must." Turning around, she made her way to the door, talking as she opened it. "This is so exciting. Now, I must tell Aurelia ... and Sukey ... and Emily, too. And I know Harriet would never forgive me if I didn't let her know. Let me see ... I have my sewing circle on Tuesday, and the Ladies' Altar Guild on Wednesday. Thursday I can tell the ladies while we're quilting at Jemima Fitzpatrick's. Oh dear, who shall I tell on Friday?" With that, Mabel stepped out onto the street, still talking, but her words were cut off by the click of the door.

For a long time after Mabel left, Alice stood in the main room of her tiny shop, her gaze resting on the shimmering bolt of lavender cloth that was shot with silver. Her brow narrowed in thought. A moment later she turned and hurried to her desk, where she began taking out fashion book after fashion book, flipping through the pages. On the third book she turned to a page near the middle, and sat back with a satisfied smile. "This is it!" she said with some satisfaction. "If this doesn't rival anything done by Monsieur Worth, I'll eat my hat." And with that, she took the bolt of lavender cloth, and after hanging the closed sign on her door, Alice Schultz set to work.

Sheepshearing day came quickly, and by the time it arrived, Asa was feeling fidgety. Since he had picked the dress up in town yesterday, he had opened and closed the brown paper it was wrapped in at least twenty times.

He looked at the dress again, rubbing his chin. He still couldn't get over the way Alice Schultz fluttered around him like an anxious mother hen, giving him last-minute instructions. "Don't let her see the dress until just before the dance, when it's too late for any adjustments. And whatever you do, don't let her talk you out of her wearing it. I know Elizabeth. One look at this dress and she will balk."

Alice stopped talking and looked at Asa. "Listen to me go on, will you? You know better than I how to handle this. Above all things Elizabeth wouldn't want to disappoint you." She smiled. "This may be easier than we thought. She would wear a flour sack if it came from you."

With that, Asa and Alice both laughed. He wasn't much of a judge of women's finery and all of that—having spent so many years on a whaler and away from women—but if his poor old tired eyes were any judge at all, Elizabeth, wearing this dress, would outshine them all and pop out a few eyes in the doing of it.

The sheepshearing was an annual event, and one everyone turned out for. There were three sheepshearing pens on the island—two of them located on the North Cliff at Maxcy's Pond and Washing Pond, the third on the south shore, east of Miacomet Pond. On the day of the shearing, Willie, Elizabeth, and Asa set out early for Maxcy's Pond.

By the time they arrived, sails had already been stretched over the framework of the pens to provide shade, while other sails were smoothed across the sandy ground to catch the fleece. Everyone in Nantucket gathered at one pond or the other, and it seemed to Elizabeth that most of Nantucket's residents had chosen to come to Maxcy's Pond.

While shearing time was quite a social occasion for most of the residents of Nantucket, it was grueling work for the men who did it. Bending forward with a sheep squeezed between his knees, a shearer would move his shears quickly over the length of the sheep's body, shaving the fleece close to the loose, wrinkly skin with as few cuts as possible. Once the fleece was removed, the sheep were dipped and turned out. It was hot, filthy, dusty, fly-infested work, and for the life of her, Elizabeth could never understand why the whole of Nantucket turned out in such force for it.

Willie, watching it all with avid interest, could not be still. After two hours of holding his wiggling, squirming body, Elizabeth was almost relieved to see Tavis approach.

"I've been looking for you," he said, giving Willie's cheek a pat. "I wasn't sure in which pen I'd find all of you, so I visited all three of them. I might have known you'd be at the last one."

He paused, taking in the sight of Eliza's beautiful face—dampened with sweat, it might be, and streaked with dust, too, but to him, it was still the face he most wanted to see. "Here," he said, reaching for Willie, who went readily into his arms, "let me have him for a while."

"Gladly," Elizabeth said. "He's still going strong, but he's worn both me and Grandpa out."

"Come on, Willie. Wanna ride piggyback?"

Willie squealed, and Elizabeth couldn't help smiling at his delight when Tavis hoisted him onto his back. She laughed outright when Willie clamped his hands over Tavis's eyes.

"Willie, move your hands. Your father can't see."

Willie moved his hands, and the moment he did, Tavis's gaze met hers. She knew what he was thinking. She shrugged. "Well, you are his father, aren't you? Did you think I would deny it?"

"No, but I never thought I'd hear you attest to the fact in front of me."

"That just shows how little you know me," she said with a light, flippant air.

"Well, I'm doing my damnedest to rectify that," he said, "and meeting a powerful lot of resistance, I might add."

"What did you expect?" she asked. Then, without waiting for an answer, she turned and flipped her skirts out of the way. "Bring him back when you're worn-out."

"I will." Willie's hands gripped his father's throat in a choking hold. When Tavis spoke, his words came out in a strangled garble. "Come on, Willie my boy, let's see how long it takes you to wear me down." And with that, they were off.

Three hours later, when Elizabeth came across Tavis and Willie, they were both worn out. One look at Willie's heavy eyes and she knew he was almost asleep.

"Let me have him," she said. "Mrs. Morrison should be at the lighthouse by now. She's agreed to stay with him until after the dance."

Tavis's gaze moved over her, trailing down the length of her and back up. In spite of the warm look, a cold emptiness still stood between them. She was sorry for it. It had been much easier when he was gone. Now they were forced to be in each other's company, and it was bitterly uncomfortable.

He was looking at her oddly, as if knowing her thoughts. "I'll take him there for you."

"No! I . . . There are some things I need to tell Mrs. Morrison, and I have to change for tonight."

"Then I'll take you both home."

He looked tired, but not too tired to argue the point, so she relented. "All right."

He had a buggy nearby. He helped Elizabeth in, then handed her Willie, who was fast asleep by now. Climbing in beside her, he took up the reins, but he never gave the horse the command to go. She glanced up at him, and their eyes met and held. Nothing within her seemed to be doing what it ought. This was Tavis, playing the role of husband and father at last, so why couldn't she respond? Why wasn't she laughing and chatting gaily, showing him the truth, that she was so much in love with him and so utterly glad to see him that nothing else mattered? This was Tavis. He was all she'd ever wanted out of life. Hadn't she spent the past two and a half years trying to pick up the pieces he had shattered when he left? Hadn't she worked so hard to get him out of, if not her heart, at least her mind? Goddamn him. Goddamn him to eternal hell! Why did he have to come back, sliding so easily into a husbandly role when she was finally getting him out of her thoughts, her life? Already she felt the old magic casting its spell on her. She didn't want to make a fool of herself over him again. She didn't.

Stunned, inwardly swearing, and very, very angry, she sat there, stiff as a stovepipe, wondering how long she could fight this attentive side of him. *Go. Get out of my life. Don't come back here like this, looking better than I remember, stirring my heart with new, fragrant hopes.*

"If you don't want folks to be speculating on how long it will be before Willie has a little brother, you'd better stop looking at me like that," he said. "People around here might get the wrong idea. They might be thinking we're in love."

For the life of her, she couldn't think of anything to say. The moment seemed to linger, uncomfortably personal. To break it, she shifted Willie's sleepy weight, cradling him in her arms with his face against her breast.

She felt his eyes on her, but she did not look up.

"You'll never know," he said, "just how many times I've pictured you like that since I discovered we had a son."

"You've seen me hold him before," she said, intentionally keeping her voice cold, impersonal.

"Not like that. Not like I imagined you would hold him when you were feeding him."

She knew he was intensely curious, fascinated even with the fact that he had a child—had one, and yet the

fact did not seem to satisfy him. Was he feeling left
out? Did he miss the things that went along with having
a child? Did he regret he did not see her with her belly
swollen, with her breasts growing large and heavy in
readiness? What would he do, she wondered, if she told
him how many times she thought of him during those
long months after Willie's birth, and how many times
ust the thought of him had made her milk leak from her
breasts?

"Why do you mention things like that? What do you
expect me to say? If you feel you missed something, if
ou feel left out, you can only blame yourself. I'm not
he one who left, you know."

"I know," he said softly. "That's the hardest part."

With very little encouragement she knew she would
ry. "I don't know what you want, what you expect of
ne," she said, feeling too uncomfortable with her
houghts to remain silent.

Why did he have to go and agree with her? Didn't he
now he made this all so much harder? Didn't he under-
and that she needed her anger to keep him away? She
anted to be angry with him. She did. She wanted to
unish him for the things she had suffered, to make him
el the losses, the pain, as acutely as she had. But talk-
g to her the way he had . . . agreeing with her, of all
ings—she didn't know how to handle it. It made her
el soft inside. It made her want to reach out to him, to
aw him against her. It made her feel like a woman,
ith a woman's desires and needs. She wanted him to
ke her in his arms and hold her while she shared with
m the joy of those moments, while she told him of
illie's birth, and how lonely she had been, how lonely
e still was.

He slapped the reins, and the gelding started up the

sandy road. "Then that makes two of us, because I sure as hell don't know what I want either. I only know that for some strange reason I had it in my head that you'd be there, in my house, waiting for me, and when you weren't, it made me feel angry enough to . . ." He shook his head. "That's when I realized I didn't have any right to be angry, that anger was something only you had a right to feel."

"Why did you come back? No. Don't answer that. Tell me why you left."

He looked down at the reins lying loosely in his hands. "Anger, I suppose. Not just at you, but at a lot of things. I have always been able to handle almost anything, save the feeling I was backed into a corner. Even as a child, I never liked to be held down. Of course that's the very thing my brothers would do . . . hold me down and tickle me until I was on the verge of tears. It's funny how the mind works sometimes, for to my way of thinking it didn't make any difference whether I was merely boxed in, or if someone held me down. Both made me feel helpless, and it's that helpless feeling that I can't stand. For as long as I can remember I've always had the feeling I would go insane from just feeling helpless. I know that probably sounds like I already have, but I can't help it. Bad luck or misfortune I can handle, but when there is no way out, I get a little crazy." He looked at her. "I know this probably doesn't make any sense to you. Why should it? It doesn't make any sense to me. But getting back to your question. I suppose I left because there were too many things coming together in my life at that point, too many things I had no control over. It was the helpless feeling that got to me the most. Those Confederate bastards who stole my plans started it. I was already frustrated with the feeling of being forced to accept something I couldn't change. My designs were gone, and I felt helpless to do anything about it. And then we came back, and before I could deal with being forced to give up my plans, I was forced into marriage."

"I know," she said softly. "And for that I'm sorry."

"It wasn't your fault," he said. The look in his eyes . . . it went straight to her soul.

"What started out there . . . on your boat. It was good, I think. If we had been left alone, if I'd had time to come to grips with my loss, I think things would have been different for us. Contrary to the way it looks now, I'm not really such a bastard. I just made some bad choices. After that, things just seemed to get out of my control."

"I heard. Grandpa told me that you had no intention of being gone so long, that you wanted to come back."

"Did he tell you why I didn't?"

"No," she said. "I didn't want him to."

"I see."

He stopped talking after that. For a while they rode along in silence, then suddenly he guided the horse off the road and onto the rutted path that led to the lighthouse. "You asked me why I came back," he said. "I suppose you think it was solely because my mission was finished, that my ship was built."

"Wasn't it?"

"Yes, partly, I suppose, but something like that is never finished. They wanted me to continue, to work on another design, one that would modify some of the things done in the first one."

"Then why didn't you stay?"

His look was direct, heart-thumping direct. She had trouble breathing. "I think you know why," he said,

pulling the gelding to a halt. She noticed then that they
had reached the lighthouse. She glanced at him, waiting
for him to jump down, to come around and help her
out.

"I came back," he said, "because you had been on
my mind a hell of a lot more than I would have thought
There is something about you, Liza, something that go
a hold of me and wouldn't let go."

"Then perhaps you're the one who needs to let go,"
she said.

He didn't seem to hear her, for he went on, talkin,
just as he had before. "Call it Scots stubbornness. Cal
it foolishness. Hell, call it anything you like, but knov
too, that thoughts about you were there long before
decided to come back."

She turned her face to him and opened her mouth
about to say something, but he put his fingers over he
mouth and kissed her softly. "I came back," he sai
"because I couldn't forget the way you were on th
boat. Most of the time I didn't even realize that I w;
missing you." He drew her closer, careful not to wal
Willie as he kissed her face lightly.

The awkward feeling was leaving her, and gradual
she remembered just why it was that she had loved th
man so much and for so long. He was still kissing h
face, brushing her lips with his. It had been so long. S
almost forgot what it was like to be kissed. For a m
ment she lost herself in the feel of it, her mind goi
back to past times and old feelings.

Willie stirred and her mind leaped forward. T
wasn't the past. It was now. All he thought he had to
was come back after nearly three years and she'd ju
at the chance to be his wife. It didn't work that w

Not for her. If he wanted her, he would have to do more. She had been seduced by this man once.

She pulled back. "I have to go in. Thank you for the ride."

"I'll wait and drive you back to the dance."

"No ... That is, you don't need to. Grandpa is coming back for me."

He nodded, but she could tell by the way he held his mouth that he wasn't too happy about it. "I'll see you at the dance, then," he said.

She didn't answer him.

He was down in a second, and coming around the buggy for her, and doing as he had before, he took Willie from her, helping her down. A moment later she stepped inside the house. "Thank you again," she said.

Mrs. Morrison was standing at the door when she came in. She took Willie—who did not even wake up—to his room, but Elizabeth simply remained as she was. For the longest time she stood with her back against the door, feeling as if she couldn't move. After some time her hand came up to touch her mouth. It was hard to tell which was shaking more: her fingers or her knees.

Later that evening, after Mrs. Morrison bathed and dressed Willie for bed, Asa unwrapped the dress. Carrying it on his arm, he knocked on Elizabeth's door. Elizabeth was still in her wrapper, hanging her head out the window to dry her hair. Hearing the knock, she jerked back too rapidly and bumped her head.

The moment she opened the door, Elizabeth's eyes went to the dress and she forgot all about the bump on her head. "Oh, Grandpa, what have you done?" she asked, taking the dress from him and holding it up against her as she danced in front of the mirror.

About that time Willie came dashing into the room to tell her good night. "Look at Mama's new dress, William. Isn't it lovely? See how it shines like stars?"

"Pretty," Willie said, coming to hug both Elizabeth and the dress.

Looking back at Asa, she exclaimed, "Grandpa, it's lovely, but you shouldn't—"

"Mind your manners, gal, and thank me properly."

Giving him a hug and a quick kiss, she said, "It is much too fine for me."

"Why? Because someone might look at you in it?"

"Yes," she said. "And we both know that is just the sort of thing I don't need. I'm still a married woman."

"That's no reason to hide behind drab, dowdy dresses all your life. Besides, there's nothing wrong with giving that long-lost husband of yours a good and proper eyeful. Now, please your old grandpa and promise me you'll wear it to the dance tonight."

"I promise," she said. "But I don't know why."

"Come on, Willie, my boy. Let's me and you go see what kind of mischief we can get into."

After they had gone, Elizabeth held the dress in front of her again, a frown lining her face. This dress couldn't be for her. It was a queen's dress, or at least the dress of a fairy princess, for truly, she had never seen anything quite like it. It was a *Tarietane* dress of flounced lavender *poult-de-soie* shot with silver and trimmed with embroidered cluny lace edged with bands of silver ribbon. The bodice was low, edged with ruffles and silver ribbon. The ruffled sleeves were of sheer lavender gauze, capped, and centered with bunches of silver-dusted grapes.

It was too much dress for her; she knew that much. *Well, no matter,* she thought, remembering the way her grandfather's eyes twinkled so merrily when he handed the gown to her. There was no way on earth she would disappoint that dear old man. She glanced at the dress again. It was a fairy dress, all right, for surely it must have been spun by spiders from purple shadows and moonbeams.

After dressing her hair, Elizabeth put on the new gown, borrowing the cluster of silver-dusted grapes pinned to the waist and using them in her hair. Then she looked at herself in the mirror. As soon as she did, she gasped at the sight of herself. This couldn't be her.

When she decided it was, indeed, her own reflection she was staring at, her first reaction was to take the dress right off. She had been right. This *was* too much dress for her. She frowned. It was too much dress for anyone in Nantucket—or anyone in her right mind, for that matter.

There was little doubt that this was a woman's dress that showed off a woman's body. The color. The fabric. It was an illusion. It was quite simple, yet it defied description. It made her feel pretty. It made her feel desirable. It made her feel confident. It made her feel like a woman.

A dress like this belonged at Napoleon's coronation, or at least the president's inaugural ball. The thought of wearing it terrified her. The thought of not wearing it would break her grandfather's heart.

Because of the mild weather, the dance was held out of doors in a pavilion, where the dancing had already begun. Tavis stood to one side, listening to Nathaniel and Cole discuss the young, eligible women. "Why don't you two get married? Then you won't have to go through this every time there's a dance," he said.

"Get married?" Nathaniel said. "Why? So we can be like you, stand on the sidelines with a jealous glare for every man that walks by? Ease up, old man. She's not even here yet."

Tavis was about to say something when he was distracted by a ripple of conversation, a stirring among the guests near the entrance that seemed to settle over the dance like a sudden thundercloud. The orchestra still played. People still danced. But something was drawing a lot of attention.

His gaze flicked back to the entrance. Standing in a pool of warm lantern light was a woman in a shimmering lavender gown. He had only one word for the way that gown fit her and the way it seemed to know her body, and that was *damp*. He felt a tightness in his throat, but it was moving lower.

"My God," Cole said. "Would you look at that."

"If I had to describe a first-rate entrance, that would be about it," Nathaniel said. "All I can say is, if you don't do something to set things right between the two of you and do it fast, someone else is going to steal her away. A woman who looks like that ought to be outlawed."

"That dress should be outlawed," Tavis said like a low-pitched growl, his words barely audible through his gritted teeth.

As she stepped farther into the pavilion, the crowd around her seemed to shrink away. For several seconds Tavis felt immobile, vaguely aware that there were people around him, but feeling they and the world were frozen in place and silent.

She stepped out of the entrance into the full light of an overhead lantern, and a muffled gasp rose from several of the guests. He could almost feel the tremor of shock as it passed through the crowd. He felt as if the sun had come out from behind a cloud, as if he had been watching as a beautiful butterfly had suddenly emerged, right before his eyes, from a drab chrysalis. She was throat-catchingly lovely in her dress of shimmering lavender cloth, and yet there was something almost theatrical, something so exotic, about her that Tavis fully expected to hear a blast of trumpets heralding her arrival. He wouldn't have been more surprised to see a naked Nubian, or even a herd of elephants parade by, followed by dancing bears, or even Cleopatra rolled out on her carpet before a roaring crowd. She was the embodiment of summer, an idol, an Amazon priestess, a medieval princess, an Elizabethan queen. And there was nothing, absolutely nothing, about her that spoke to the fact that she was any man's wife.

"I wondered how long she would pine for him," a voice nearby said.

"Looks to me like you don't have to wonder any longer. If I was going to hazard a guess, I'd say she stopped pining tonight," a second voice said.

"She must be telling him that she has no intention of taking him back or becoming his wife," another voice said.

"She is already my wife," Tavis said like a snarl. The moment he turned around, the three women gasped, mumbled their apologies, and fled.

Tavis advanced. The crowd went silent around him. He stopped in front of her, seeing the way her eyes sparkled like jewels that were fastened upon him. For a moment he did not know what to say, and once a thought came to him, how to begin. This was a side of her he had never seen before. She was so sure of herself, so graceful and poised—rather like a sleek, magnificent cat, mysterious, half-wild, and untamed. He knew he must look like a fool, standing there before her, awkward as a schoolboy and decidedly furious, unable to find a way to say anything.

Suddenly she dropped into a low curtsy before him, then rising, she began to laugh. It was a rich sound. Thick. Evocative. It made him randy as hell. It was a laugh he had never heard before. It was one he would never forget. Before he could speak, she spun around in front of him.

"What in the hell do you think you're doing?" he whispered.

"Why, I've come to show you what you threw away."

The sudden shock of her frankness left him stunned. "I haven't thrown anything away, and even if I did, you didn't have to tell the whole of Nantucket."

"But they all know, so what does it hurt?"

"What are you trying to prove?"

"That I'm a little more than you bargained for. That I have value and worth. That I'm not some inexpensive trinket that was pawned off on you by a vagabond Gypsy peddler at a country fair. That I'm a diamond in the rough. A treasure in disguise. A pearl of great price." She paused, and looking straight at him, she said, "That you don't own me."

He glanced around, seeing the wash of astonished faces that stared at them. He wanted to own her. Every silvery thread. Every golden hair. Every overexposed inch of skin. He took her arm, guiding her away, his fingers digging into her flesh. "You happen to be my goddamn wife."

"Am I supposed to be grateful that you remembered?"

He glared at her. "Why don't you stop putting on such a performance?"

"Why don't you?"

"I'm not."

"Are you so certain?"

He looked at her hard, trying to understand what she meant.

"You've put on quite a performance since you've returned, playing the role of the dutiful and attentive husband. Everyone in town knows exactly how many times you've come to the lighthouse to see Willie. They are all speculating as to how long it will be before you have me in line."

Her words seemed to have a softening effect upon him. "We are becoming a spectacle," he said, taking her arm and escorting her to the dance floor.

"We always were a spectacle," she said.

"It's what people expect of us, so why not give them a real show?"

He was still holding her arm and she resisted, but he was insistent.

"Let me go."

"My darling Liza, I've been trying to let you go since the day I married you. But I can't, and now I find I no longer want to."

She smiled and spoke to two ladies they passed, then tugged on her arm. He held her fast, and leaning low, he whispered, "You might as well get used to the idea of being my wife."

"I'll give it some thought," she said.

"You'd do well to give it more than that," he said, but Elizabeth simply smiled.

He took her into his arms and they joined the other dancers. "Did you sleep with anyone?" she asked.

He stumbled, but caught himself. "What did you say?"

"I asked you if you slept with anyone."

It was obvious to her that it pleased him that she had inquired after his behavior.

"Did you?" he asked.

"Of course." She smiled at him. "Dozens."

"Good," he said. "Then one more won't make any difference." He pulled her closer.

She looked up. In the lantern light his was a stranger's face. She suddenly felt terrified of him, of what he could do to her. Until now, until this moment, it had all been a game to her, but seeing him like this, a tall stiffly polite man with smoldering eyes, she was undone. She felt herself whirling around the dance floor the lanterns coming together like ribbons of light. Time was suspended and she felt herself lost somewhere between the past and present. She closed her eyes and felt his pull, the feel of his body moving against hers. He held her so tightly that her body moved as if it were part of his. She could feel the fabric of her dress rustle against the cloth of his coat, and feel, too, the muscle of his arms, as if his body were speaking to her in a language her mind was incapable of understanding.

This time it was Elizabeth who stumbled.

She felt him take her hand. She opened her eyes to see they were leaving the dance floor. Where was he taking her? Had she pushed him too far? She couldn't see his face, but she knew from the way he moved, the tightness of the hand that held hers, the rapid cadence of his walk, that he had some purpose in mind. This was, after all, no mindless stroll. She could feel the warm brush of his breath in her hair, the way the faint aroma of vetiver teased her nose. Vaguely she was aware of people around them as they passed, yet she seemed too removed from it all to notice.

Suddenly the lanterns were behind them, and the music and laughter in the night seemed to vanish. All signs of life had simply drained away, and she, too, felt empty and afraid. She glanced up at him, but his face was hidden in shadow. A moment later she felt herself swept into his arms, felt his lips in her hair.

"I've wanted to do this since the day I came back," he whispered. "I've been haunted by the memory of you, the feel of you in my arms. I thought the memory had served me so well, but now I can see it pales when compared to the real thing."

The world seemed to fall away from her and she felt herself being sucked into a black void. *Too easy,* her mind screamed. *It's all too easy and too fast.* She felt herself pulling back, felt herself groping in the darkness as if searching for her person.

Sensing her withdrawal and knowing she was fighting him, he found her lips with his. Her heart pounded furiously, then seemed to still completely. An aching silence surrounded her. She felt her only connection to the earth at all was the feel of his arms around her, the warmth of his breath in her hair, the smell that was so uniquely him. There was no reality now. Her only reality was this man, this mouth, these arms like iron bands around her. "Tavis . . ."

"Don't say anything," he said. "You've won, you know. I want you. So badly that I'll do whatever it takes to have you."

"Are you trying to tell me you love me?"

"Love? I don't know if that is what I feel or not. I

want you. Isn't that enough? I've thought about you until I thought I would go insane. I want you to come back to my house ... you and Willie. I want us to be a family."

"How different we are," she said. "You want a lot of things. I only want one."

"What is that?"

To hear you say you love me. She pulled away from him. "Of all the things that have happened between us, the one that hurts the most is that you have to ask."

He jerked back as if he had been bitten. His gaze riveted on her lovely shattered face, he searched his mind for something he could say, something to hold her here before he lost her. But all he could think about was the way she felt in his arms, the way her body seemed to dissolve and become fluid, a warm melting softness he wanted to lose himself in. Why couldn't he say the things she wanted to hear? Why couldn't he handle himself around her? Before he could answer, she jerked away from him.

"Leave me alone, Tavis. I've changed my mind. I don't even want to be your wife anymore."

A second later, she was gone.

CHAPTER
❧ TWENTY-TWO ❧

The burning in his stomach woke him and Asa opened his eyes, looking around the room, wondering, for just a moment, where he was. He had been dreaming again, about a time when the wharfs of Nantucket were swarming with ships and barks, a time when tall-masted, storm-weary square-riggers pierced the sky. For a moment it had all been so real, down to the smell of whale oil that called out to him. He sniffed the air, smelling only the residue of the fish chowder Elizabeth had fed him for lunch just before she and Willie went into town.

The pain came again, sharper this time, and he winced, thinking it strange the way the past comes back to a person through the sense of smell. He closed his eyes, remembering the savory aroma of barrels of whale oil stacked on the wharf mingling with the salty tang of their protective seaweed covering. He remembered how, even now, the wharfs retained the stains where whale oil had seeped through the wooden staves so many years ago—and on a warm day, if the humidity was right, how you could still catch a whiff of the strong smell. Like the odor of the mignonette pressed between the pages of the family Bible, it recalled a past that meant nothing to the future.

The pain was more intense now, and the memories, too. Salt water ran in his veins, his heart hummed with the cry of a Chinaman on a junket, the piercing shriek of Malay pirates, the song of beautiful black-eyed girls on flower-scented islands.

Then the memory vanished, and all that remained was the pain. Pain had become his constant companion of late. It had been two years now since he had noticed the first symptoms, the dyspepsia, the prolonged pain and later the tendency to vomit, the passing of blood.

He came to his feet, feeling wobbly as a newborn colt as he left the chair rocking to and fro behind him. His insides were on fire now. He knew his time had come, knew that the envenomed teeth that had been eating at him would never be satisfied. He was dying. He had known it for some time. The burning in his belly was unbearable. Only the coolness of the sea offered respite, and she called to him.

Moments later he was outside.

It was a good day to die. The sun was hidden behind a gray, misty haze. A strong wind was blowing. The water looked cold and choppy, with a thin, white line of foam that capped even the smallest waves. In spite of the intense pain, Asa paused and glanced overhead. It looked like snow—impossible this time of year. Yet all about him the world was cold, dreary, and inhospitable. Even the water's surface seemed antagonistic and violently protesting against any would-be intrusion.

He would not be put off. Soon he would be free from pain and sorrow. Soon he would have his final rest. Soon he would leave the angry world above and enter

Neptune's peaceful abode below. There everything would be cool and green and silent, with no hint of the churning turmoil above. The sea would receive him.

It was a good day to die.

Moving to the water's edge, he pushed the dory into the water, remembering he had forgotten his hat. For a moment he paused, thinking. He always wore his hat. He turned, gazing back at the lighthouse, feeling its tug. He saw Robin and Tuck meowing at him from the doorway, and remembering how those cats had never liked Elizabeth, he felt the need to go back.

But the call of the sea was strong, too strong, luring him with its promising call. *Come to me . . . Come . . .*

The cats ran toward him, but he picked up some seashells and threw them, driving Tuck and Robin away.

He climbed into the dory and took up the oars, the wind whipping the fine thin strands of long, white hair about his face. And then, much to his surprise, the world around him grew quiet, and for a moment there seemed to be an end of his long journey into pain.

He saw snatches from his past that came into his mind like fleeting glimpses of passing ships. Suddenly a new strength rose within him. He heard the snap of reefed sails overhead, heard the cry of *Whale!* The sport of it sang in his blood as vast as the swells of the all-knowing sea. Forward, ever forward, in pursuit of the monster of the deep. Around him the dark water swirled and beat against the dory, driving it ahead.

From out of its churning water he heard the cries of the headsmen and harpooners, the sound fading, driven away by the knife-edge pain that chewed at his bowels. He could see her now, a gleaming white ghost of a ship, full-rigged and under sail, running before the wind.

"Wait," he called. "Wait."

Closer she came, and closer still, and the fire in his belly was like a living, burning coal from hell. He felt himself drifting. The pain was becoming unbearable, yet his mind was strangely sharp and at peace. From out of the foam that surrounded him came the strains of a hymn he had sung at Bethel, so very long ago.

> *The ribs and terrors in the whale,*
> *Arched over me a dismal gloom.*
> *While all God's sunlit waves rolled by,*
> *And left me deepening down to doom.*
>
> *I saw the opening maw of hell,*
> *With endless pains and sorrows there;*
> *Which none but they that feel can tell—*
> *Oh, I was plunging to despair.*
>
> *In black distress, I called my God,*
> *When I could scarce believe Him mine,*
> *He bowed His ear to my complaints—*
> *No more the whale did me confine.*
>
> *With speed He flew to my relief,*
> *As on a radiant dolphin borne,*
> *Awful, yet bright, as lightning shone*
> *The face of my Deliverer God.*
>
> *My song forever shall record*
> *That terrible, that joyful hour;*
> *I give the glory to my God,*
> *His all the mercy and the power.*

And the waters of the deep closed over him, and he knew the pain of this life would touch Asa Robinson no more.

The moment she walked into the lighthouse and saw Robin and Tuck run out to greet her, she knew something was wrong. There was an eerie silence that hung about the rooms, a chill that permeated the air. Immediately Elizabeth released Willie's hand and removed his coat. Then she picked up the cats, feeling the hairs at the nape of her neck prickle, heard, too, the moaning wail of wind whipping around the lighthouse tower. Outside, the waves crashed against the land, as if the sea were applauding her victory.

"Grandpa?" She came more fully into the front room now, Willie hanging on to her skirt, and saw her grandfather's pipe in the ashtray, his captain's hat lying on the table. She felt easier now. He wouldn't leave without his hat. She put the cats down.

"Grandpa, where are you?"

Nothing but silence answered her.

Taking Willie into the kitchen, she put him into his feeding chair, giving him two crackers. Then she ran through the rooms calling her grandfather, screaming out his name, hearing only the echo of her own voice answering in return.

She ran back into the kitchen. Willie was crying now. She picked him up, soothing him for a moment, then bundling him up again into his coat, she carried him outside.

"Grandpa, can you hear me?" she called, feeling the wind drive her words back into her mouth. "Grandpa? Can you hear me?"

But only the wind responded.

And then she noticed it, the missing dory.

He's gone fishing was her mind's logical reasoning, and for a moment her heart accepted it, and she turned away. But then a horrible awareness seemed to freeze the very blood that ran through her veins. With shimmering clarity she could see Asa's captain's hat lying on the table. *Grandpa never goes anywhere without his hat. He wouldn't leave without his hat.*

Not unless he knew he was not coming back.

The moment the thought struck her, she was running back to the lighthouse. Putting Willie on the floor and handing him a toy, she told him, "Stay there. I'll be right back."

Fear blazed in her heart. She ran through the door, heading for the stairs that circled their way to the top. She ran up the stairs like a cat until her head poked up through the middle of the floor of the large round room. The great light sat still and unblinking. Exhausted and breathless from the exertion, she ran to the glass and searched the angry tossing waves. Just about the time she was ready to give up, she saw him, a mane of white shaggy hair against the backdrop of a dark and churning sea. Without a moment to waste, she ran down the stairs, grabbed Willie, and ran back to the buggy she had used only minutes before.

A short while later she pulled the racing horse to a stop in front of Tavis's house. Barely taking the time to yank Willie from the seat beside her, she raced up the steps and began pounding on the door.

Tavis opened the door, his gaze going to the terrified face standing before him. "I need your boat," she said. "Where do you keep it?"

"Down at the wharf, but why—"

"Grandpa," she said, running down the steps and heading for the buggy.

Without taking time to think, Tavis was off the porch and running after her, taking her by the arm and whirling her around to face him. "Elizabeth, what the—"

"Let me go!" she screamed. "I don't have time to talk. It's a matter of life and death."

"Whose?" he said calmly, taking Willie from her. "Whose life is in danger?"

"My grandfather's," she said, collapsing against him and pounding his chest. "The sea will take him, Tavis. It was what he wanted. Don't you understand? He wants to die. He wants to!"

"Liza, this could be a wild-goose chase. He might not be out in his boat at all."

"I saw him!" she screamed, pounding his chest. Willie began to cry. "I saw him from the top of the lighthouse. Why can't you understand what I'm saying? He's gone out there to die. I know it." She stood there clutching his sleeves, her face turned up to his.

There was something about her eyes; perhaps it was the stark terror, or the soul-wrenching look of urgency, that made him know whatever she felt was right. "I'm coming with you," he said. "Let me take Willie inside," he said, stooping over to pick the boy up. "He can stay with Mrs. Chadwick."

She stood beside the front gate, shivering, dreadful fears chasing each other through her mind. "I have to find my grandfather. I don't have time to take care of you when you get seasick."

"The only way you're going at all is if I come along."

A few minutes later they were racing along the wharf, then climbing into a small skiff, Tavis fighting the choppy waters as he rowed them out a way before raising the small sail.

The sky was a deeper gray now, the wind blowing up clouds heavily laden with rain that began to fall. Elizabeth could see nothing around her except Tavis and falling sheets of water. Again and again her gaze raked the never-ending swells, searching, praying, begging for a glimpse of him before it was too late. *He wants to die,* her mind kept repeating like a litany. *He wants to die.*

Please . . . Please, God, don't let him die. He's all I have. Wet-lashed, she turned her head back and gazed at the sky. *Is this all there is? Nothing but pain and more pain? You said You never gave us more pain than we can bear. Well, I can't bear this. I can't. And still it comes. Another loss. Another period of grieving. Another grave beside the four I hold so dear. When will it end? When will I be whole again? When will I have my sanity back?*

Her legs ached. She was chilled to the bone. She hadn't eaten all day and she felt dizzy. The air was quite cold now, and she wondered how long they could stay out here like this, in their summer clothes, before their clothes began to turn icy.

Tavis's expression turned grave. At last he said, "Perhaps he's gone back. It will be dark soon."

She turned furious eyes upon him. "Can't you understand anything?" she screamed. "He won't be going back. Not ever. He wanted it this way. He wants to die out here . . . at the hands of the sea."

Suddenly a small boat seemed to sail out of nowhere into the misty grayness. "There," Tavis shouted. " think I see it."

Elizabeth looked, watching the faint gray outline of small dory riding the crest of a great green swell, an the hope began to die in her. She felt as if she wer

turning into a creature carved from stone that could feel
neither despair nor happiness.

There was no way to put her sorrow into words. It
was finished. She did not look at the dory as they ap-
proached. She knew it would be empty.

Sadness did not touch her at first. Her memory had
stored too many things that seemed anxious to be recalled
in great haste. As she sat on the hard wooden seat, the
rain hitting her in pelting sheets, she remembered her
grandfather. Only when Tavis spoke did reality hit her,
and looking up at him, the vision of happier times grew
dim, as faded as last winter's withered leaves.

"I'm sorry," Tavis said, his voice sounding far away.
"There was nothing you could have done. It was what
he wanted." He guided the boat into a turn.

She grabbed his arm. "What do you think you're
doing?"

He looked surprised. "I'm turning back. There is nothing more that we can do, and the weather is getting
worse."

It was the first time she looked at her grandfather's
dory. "I won't leave his boat out here."

Tavis gave her a pleading look. "There is a storm
coming, and if we don't get back, we may not make it
at all."

"I won't leave without his dory, and I will never forgive you if you make me."

With a loud curse, Tavis made a wide turn, sailing close
to the dory. He gave her a pained look, and she knew he
was feeling the first weakening spasms of seasickness.

"Here, you take the helm," he said. "I'll try to catch
hold of the rope."

After three tries and three misses, she knew Tavis
was feeling worse. On the fourth try, he threw one leg

over the side, and leaning forward, was able to grab the dory's rope. He had no more than secured it with a knot when his face turned a ghastly green, and she knew immediately that it was a wave of nausea that hit him, preventing him from drawing his leg back into the boat. Holding his position for a moment, he seemed to be waiting for the nausea to pass. She leaned forward, trying to reach him.

A split second later a wave crashed against the dory, driving it with a shattering crash against the skiff, crushing Tavis's leg between the two.

With a groan, Tavis fell back into the boat. A second later, Elizabeth saw his ashen face, the shattered leg, the blood washing over her skirts.

Two hours later, she sat in the doctor's office, waiting for someone to come out and tell her that she had suffered yet another loss.

Outside, it was raining. Inside, the room was damp, inhospitable, and dark, with only a small lamp burning on the table beside her. The room was warm. Stifling. Her body was exhausted. She kept trying to think about her grandfather, but all she could think about was Tavis. And in a way it seemed right to her. Tavis was alive, at least for now. And it seemed the right thing to do, to worry for him, knowing she could grieve for her grandfather later.

Her eyes felt heavy. The heat seemed to choke the breath from her. She felt exhausted, haggard, old. A moment later her head bobbed and her eyes closed.

"Mrs. Mackinnon?"

Elizabeth's head snapped up. She saw the blood on the doctor's clothes.

"Is he still alive?"

"Yes, but he's taken a turn for the worse. The leg is hopelessly shattered. It will have to come off."

It will have to come off. She came to her feet. Enough was enough. This was one loss she would not suffer. "Don't touch his leg."

"Mrs. Mackinnon, you don't understand—"

"No, you are the one who doesn't understand. You will not touch his leg," she said.

"Then I can't help him."

Elizabeth headed for the door to the room where Tavis had been taken.

"Where are you going?"

"I'm going to see my husband, then I'm going to find someone to take us to Boston."

"Then you'll lose him. He'll be dead before you reach Boston," Doc said.

"If you take his leg, I'll lose him anyway. He won't want to live without his leg."

She went into the tiny room. It was unbearably hot and smelled of blood. Moving to Tavis's bedside, she saw his leg was still there and it had been bandaged and the blood was seeping through it to pool on the sheets below.

She turned, seeing the doctor standing in the doorway. "Do you have any opium?"

"I've given him some already."

She turned to look down at Tavis, seeing the pale face, the perspiration that dotted across his forehead and over his lip. He groaned and his lids fluttered. For a moment she thought he would open his eyes. "He's still restless. Can you give him some more? I'm taking him to Boston. It would be easier if he slept all the way."

The doctor didn't say anything, but when she continued to stare at him, he shrugged and turned away. "I'll give him another dose, then. But I think you're making a big mistake."

"The biggest mistake I made was wasting too much time in bringing him back here. Have him ready. I'll return as soon as I can."

A few minutes later, Elizabeth had located Nathaniel and Cole, who made the arrangements for the fastest sailboat they could borrow. An hour later they had Tavis aboard and they were under sail.

Elizabeth sat beside the small cot, studying Tavis's face, bathing the beads of sweat as soon as they appeared, giving him small doses of opium when he was restless.

"You won't lose your leg," she whispered, then gently brushed the hair back from his face. With one finger she traced the shape of his brow, the line of his nose. Then she followed the line of his mouth, leaning forward to kiss him. His skin was hot and damp. Beneath her other hand, his chest rose and fell beneath the blankets. One hand rested on top of the blanket. She picked it up and held it in her own. It, too, was warm, but dry. It lay lax and unresponsive as she began tracing the shape of his fingers, kissing each one after she inspected it.

She thought about that hand touching her, causing her so much joy, and she felt tears burning in her eyes. "You won't lose your leg," she whispered again, bringing his hand up to press against her cheek. "This is one loss I'm going to cheat them out of."

She leaned back in the chair, still holding his hand. She had loved him for so long, an eternity, it seemed. Her love for him had been like a flower that grew on the other side of the fence—one that she could not see and yet its fragrant scent reached out and surrounded her.

CHAPTER
❧ TWENTY-THREE ❧

Tavis opened one eye, saw a strange man standing over him, and promptly closed it. He knew he was dead. Then he felt the stabbing pain in his leg and he wished he were.

He opened both eyes this time, and stared at the man in the white coat. "Who are you?" he asked.

The man smiled. "I'm Dr. Carver."

Tavis groaned. "God, I hope not."

Dr. Carver laughed. "You still have your sense of humor. That's a good sign."

"It may be a good sign, but I feel like hell."

"But you do *feel*, Mr. Mackinnon. That in itself is a blessing."

Tavis groaned as he shifted his position, looking at the pristine white walls behind Dr. Carver, the bare table beside his bed. "Where am I?"

"Boston. Massachusetts General Hospital."

"Boston? . . . How in the . . . how did I get here?"

"I brought you," a familiar voice from the other side of the room said.

Tavis turned his head to see Elizabeth sitting on the

other side of the bed. His shocked gaze traveled over her, drinking in the sight of the slender female figure wearing rose-gray silk trimmed in black velvet. In spite of the tired look in her eyes, the paleness of her skin, he thought she was the loveliest thing he had ever seen. He felt as if he were spinning through space, going back in time when the image of the pale beauty before him blurred and transformed itself into another image, one of an unforgettable young girl—flamboyant hoyden one minute, sober as a judge the next, turning theatrical enough to dye her hair red, so down-to-earth that she would spy on him swimming naked and tell him he didn't have anything she hadn't seen before. He had witnessed so many sides to her, from the oddest witch of a child to the most outlandish comic. He had been hounded by her as a young girl, known her as a woman, could not forget her as the mother of his child. Wherever she went, she brought shades of fantasy and poetry into the dreary lives of Nantucketers—a world still influenced by their former devotion to whaling, and the plain and serviceable way of life begun so long ago by the Quakers.

Never had he met a woman like her, one capable of turning life's trials and disappointments into melodramatic capers, using all the drama of the romance novels she read to console herself.

It occurred to him then that perhaps she had developed that strangeness for living an inner life of fancy as an escape from a dull and painful outer life. It was the first time he wondered, really wondered, what it had been like for her, growing up with no mother in a household dominated by older men and younger women. He thought about the losses in her life and wondered if he would be yet another, for the message she had been giving him of late was one of rejection. And yet she obviously cared enough to bring him to Boston. Why?

"*You* brought me here?" he asked.

"Yes," she said, "with the help of Nathaniel and Cole."

"Where are they?"

She smiled. "They were as cross as two sticks. After a few days, I told them it was either them or me."

He seemed puzzled. "This feels so strange. I don't remember anything. Not being on a boat. Not coming here. Nothing."

"She kept you laced with opium," Dr. Carver said.

"Why did you bring me up here?"

"The doctor in Nantucket was going to remove your leg."

Tavis recoiled and his body jerked in response. Dr. Carver placed a restraining hand against his shoulder. "Easy. You haven't lost anything, except a little weight and a lot of blood."

His strength expended, his body exhausted, Tavis leaned back, his head falling against the pillows. Too tired to speak, he closed his eyes, his mind bursting with the thoughts he could not express.

A moment later Dr. Carver said, "I'll be going home now, Mrs. Mackinnon. I'll be back to see you and check on our patient in the morning."

"Thank you, Dr. Carver. I'll be here," Elizabeth said.

Tavis heard the sound of Dr. Carver's retreating footsteps, but for the life of him he could not open his eyes.

The room grew quiet. He wondered what she was doing, but he couldn't seem to make his body obey the urge to look at her. "Thank you," he whispered, his eyes still closed. "I wouldn't have wanted to live without my leg."

"I know," she said, speaking softly. "That's why I brought you here."

"You should have left me in Nantucket. They would have sawed off my leg and you would have been rid of me."

She looked at his pale face, the sunken hollows of his cheeks. "I'll never be rid of you," she said, rising to her feet.

He struggled to open his eyes. "Elizabeth . . ."

He felt her restraining hand on his arm. "Don't talk anymore now. You need your rest."

His hand groped and found hers. Squeezing it tightly against his chest, he asked, "Are you leaving?"

She smoothed the hair back from his forehead. "Only long enough to find something to eat, then I'll be back."

"Where is Willie?"

Her heart lurched. "I left him in Nantucket. I had to leave him at your house. He's with Mrs. Chadwick."

He was thinking of the losses in her life, knowing how hard it was for her to leave their son. He thought of her grandfather, knowing that in spite of her grief she had not deserted him. "I'm sorry," he said.

"So am I," she said. "For a lot of things. Now, try to sleep."

Elizabeth left, hiring a hack to take her to her aunt' house so she could bathe and eat.

The house looked like it belonged to someone's ol aunt, she thought when she walked into the entry, for was a house that wore the burden of time gracefull with a sort of lavender-and-old-lace dignity.

Stepping farther into the room, she was greeted b

the lingering residue of the musty smell that had first greeted her when she came here over a week ago. She paused in the center of the room, expecting, for a moment, to see Aunt Phoebe sitting in her rocker, the hasty departure of Robin and Tuck.

"Is that you, Mrs. Mackinnon?"

At the sound of that voice, Elizabeth gave a start. She removed the pins from her hat, then pulled it off her head as she answered. "It's me, Mrs. Willoughby."

A second later Mrs. Willoughby appeared in the doorway. "Oh, you poor dear. You look exhausted. Do you want me to heat some water for a nice hot bath?"

"A hot bath sounds like just what I need. The hotter the better. I don't know why it is that being around a hospital all day makes me feel so dirty."

"Why don't you come on into the dining room? I have dinner ready. That way, you can eat while I prepare your bath and turn down your bed."

"I won't be staying the night. I'm going back to the hospital."

"Not tonight again, surely." Mrs. Willoughby gave her a motherly look.

"I have to go back."

"You can't go on much longer like you've been going. Young or not. It's all going to catch up with you. Mark my word. It'll catch up with you."

"Sometimes I feel like it already has," Elizabeth said. "But my husband is conscious and talking. I thought that since this was the first night that he's awake and alert, I should be there. Tomorrow night I'll let you turn down my bed. I promise."

After dinner and the hot bath, when she was feeling definitely better, she returned to the hospital. Tavis was still sleeping when she entered the room, but fitfully. She removed her gloves, turned up the bedside lamp and placed a hand on his forehead. His skin fel warm, but she attributed that to the fact that she had jus come in from the outside, where it was cold enough t snow.

She stood beside his bed, looking down at him studying the hand that lay across his stomach. The fin gers were long and lean, curled inward in a way that re minded her of the way Willie's fingers looked when h was asleep. Willie was so like his father—the sam black hair, the slender feet, the way he would tip hi head to one side and look at her when she talked. *Ho many times,* she wondered? How many times had sh held her son and thought of her husband? How man times had she looked at Willie and seen the man sh loved?

You are so much like your son.

But the dark shading of hair on the tops of his finge and hand that turned darker on his arm was not mindf of a child. Without being conscious she was doing s she allowed her gaze to move to his chest, following t narrow tapering of fine black hair that disappeared b neath the sheet riding low on his belly.

Her gaze went to his bandaged leg that lay on top the sheet, lingering for a moment on the strip of sk that lay between where the bandage ended and t twisted sheet tucked beneath his legs began. Flames desire shot through her, even as she was reminded how much and how long she had loved this man. S remembered, too, thinking as a child, all those ye: ago, that God had promised him to her simply beca the first time she had seen him there had been a ra bow arched over him. She shook her head sadly. If

had been promised to her, something had gone awry. He
was her husband, but she had never felt more estranged
from another human being in her life.

She knew he did not belong to her, that he was as lost
to her as all the others: her mother, father, sisters, Aunt
Phoebe, her grandfather. Becca even. But she had
Willie. Perhaps their loss was the price she had to pay
to have him.

Tavis tried to turn over, mumbling something, then
rolling back to the same position he was in before. She
touched his head again. He was much warmer than before. That worried her. She remembered an earlier conversation with Dr. Carver, just a few days ago, right
after he operated on Tavis's leg.

"Will he be all right?" she'd asked.

"It was bad, but it wasn't as bad as I first thought.
There were two major breaks in the leg, a lot of damage
to the surrounding skin and muscle." Dr. Carver peered
at her over the top of his spectacles. "The wound was
filled with bits of bone, wood splinters, wadding, bits of
clothing. Cleaning all of that out is what took so long."

"What now?"

"Now we worry about foul corruption. Infection.
Even gangrene."

At the mention of that dreaded word, Elizabeth felt
weak.

Dr. Carver went on. "There is a doctor in Glasgow,
Dr. Joseph Lister, who noticed that broken bones over
which the skin was never broken usually heal without
complication. But fractures where bones are exposed
through breaks in the skin commonly develop infections
and pus."

He removed his glasses. "We know something happens, but we don't know what it is. It might be some-

thing invisible in the air . . . something that Lister calls disease dust. But we know precious more than that. Le me assure you, Mrs. Mackinnon, that whatever we do we won't use Dr. James's Fever Powder."

Elizabeth poured water into a basin beside the bec and dipped a cloth in it, then folding it, she placed it o Tavis's forehead. An hour later he began shaking an thrashing in the bed. She sat on the bed next to him an tried to hold him down, and finding she was unable to she used her body for the added weight she needec leaning across him, pressing him back to the bed as sh cradled him in her arms.

He was so hot and his body trembled so violently tha she was afraid. She began talking to him, telling hi how they would take Willie on picnics on the beac soon, and how much he had to live for.

"Don't give up," she whispered, pressing kisses his dry, burning forehead. She looked down into h fever-flushed face, thinking how familiar he looked her and how strange. It had been so long since she ha lain with this man, since she had felt his body wi hers.

It occurred to her that even during the years th were apart, she never thought about his dying, and nc that he was back, the threat seemed all too real.

She buried her face against his neck, telling him hc much he meant to her and how she would never forgi him if he died. "I won't let you go," she said. "I wo let you off that easily. You owe me, Tavis Mackinnc You owe me a good fight, and I intend to see that I it. I won't let you go. Do you hear me? I won't."

She was not certain how long she lay there with body slanted over his, but by the time he quieted, was stiff and sore with a pricking numbness in her arm. Releasing him, she sat upright, placing a hand at the small of her back and groaning as she thought about how she felt like an old woman. Certain she would hear her bones creak with age, she made her way off the bed and back to her chair.

For a long time she sat there, regarding him with an undiminished interest. There were so many memories he evoked, but it wasn't the memories that held her.

Something had changed between them. Something had changed within her. Even now, this very minute, she could feel it, a living, growing thing, capable of consuming, of destroying her. She had held herself back, and just when she thought herself immune, the change in her began.

It wasn't fair. Not now, not when she was just beginning to live with her emptiness.

She wanted to be angry, to make him look different from the man she had loved on her sloop. "Don't make me fall in love with you all over again," she said, aware, even as the words were uttered, of the idiocy of the remark. She was already realizing that after all the years of telling herself that she no longer cared, she had always loved him, that she had never loved him more than she did right now.

To break the flood of unwelcome thought, she stood, taking the cloth from his head and rinsing it again. But when she withdrew the cloth, she found she was looking strangely at him, her gaze on his mouth, the cloth forgotten in her hand, the water from it running over her fingers and slowly dripping to the floor.

Those very lips had kissed her, she recalled, then found herself repulsed at the thought. How could she? He was sick. Maybe dying. What had she turned into? Shaking herself out of her daze, she put the cloth on

his head, then returned to her chair. For the rest of the
night, she sat at his bedside, changing the cloth a
fifteen-minute intervals. In spite of all her efforts and
the all-night vigil, when Dr. Carver came by the nex
morning, the fever was worse.

For three days he lay burning with fever and talking
out of his head ... mostly shipbuilding jargon and in
structions to those who apparently had worked for him
but occasionally Elizabeth was certain she heard him
mention her name. Once, when Dr. Carver was in, she
expressed concern over Tavis's lack of appetite.

"I'm an avid follower of Graves. I believe in feeding
a fever. Stuff him full, Mrs. Mackinnon. And when he
can't eat another bite, give him some more."

Elizabeth did as Dr. Carver suggested. Every time
Tavis opened his mouth, she had a spoon there, and
when he didn't open it, she forced the handle of a spoon
between his teeth and poured food down his throat.

At last, his fever broke.

She had been sitting beside him, knitting a cab
sweater for Willie, when she heard him speak.
thought you were an angel."

Her eyes opened wide and her gaze flew to him, see
ing his eyes were open and clear. All at once she w
weeping, the tears coming with an overflowing abun
dance that not even the wool on Willie's new sweat
could absorb. She cried as if there were nothing else
do, not anything in the world, but to cry out her troubl
which were deep and inexhaustible.

"I call you an angel and you cry," he said. "I ha
never understood you. I know now I never will. Bu
doesn't matter. I want you, and for me, that is enoug

But it wasn't enough for her. It never would be. T

misery of it made her cry harder. A moment later she sprang to her feet and ran from the room.

Half an hour later she returned, her face washed, her eyes dry, and without saying a word, she moved to her chair beside his bed and took up her knitting, as if nothing at all had happened.

The next afternoon she was shoving food down his throat when he said, "No more. I'm full."

Remembering Dr. Carver's words, she shoved another mouthful at him. A second later, Tavis slapped the spoon out of her hand and grumbled something about how much she enjoyed torturing a man. Elizabeth dropped down into her chair and laughed, knowing his crotchety behavior was indeed, as Dr. Carver said before, a good sign.

She took him home, to her aunt's house, two days later. It had been three weeks since his accident, three weeks since her grandfather died.

At first, things between them went smoothly, for Tavis was still recuperating and confined to bed, but gradually his strength and color began to return, and by the end of that first week, Dr. Carver said he could walk with the aid of crutches. That is when the trouble began.

Tavis confined to his bed was one thing. Tavis mobile and hobbling about the house was another. Even then, things were tolerable during the day, for Mrs. Willoughby was there, and whenever the tension between herself and Tavis was stretched too thin, Elizabeth would simply make the excuse that Mrs. Willoughby needed her and disappear.

The evenings were the hardest, when Mrs. Willoughby would leave shortly after dinner.

Tavis was never ready to retire early, and when Eliz-

abeth announced her plans to, he would make it known
he wanted her company.

It was two weeks later that Elizabeth, after bidding
Mrs. Willoughby good night, went into the music room
where Tavis sat, his leg elevated on a footstool. He had
been unusually cranky today, and Elizabeth was feeling
she couldn't take much more of his temper without losing some of her own control. As a diversion, she carried
her knitting with her.

She sat in the rocking chair nearest the fire, and after
adding two fresh logs, settled back to knit, her needles
clicking in harmony with the slow, rhythmic creak of
the rocker. After a few minutes, he snapped irritably at
her for all the "infernal noise" she was making. She
stopped rocking.

She didn't look up and she didn't say anything, but
she knew he was giving her a hostile look, one that
dared her to respond to his provoking. She began working the sleeve, counting her stitches, not because she
needed to, but because it took her mind off things.

"Elizabeth?"

Her head snapped up to find him looking at her with
a guilty, shamefaced expression that reminded her so
much of one she had seen a million times on Willie. He
even made an attempt to smile.

"I suppose I should say I'm sorry," he said. "When
you become so irritable and cross that you can't stand
to be around yourself, you begin to understand how others must feel. Nothing seems to be functioning right,
not even my brain. If I don't eat, you're poking food
me. If I eat, I get nauseated. I've had dysentery for over
a week. My armpits are so sore from those goddam
crutches that every time I pick them up, I can't decide
if I want to use them or hurl them into Boston Harbor

He sighed and then said, "It isn't you, Elizabeth. I know what you've done for me, how much I owe you."

"It was my fault that your leg—"

"Don't say that. It wasn't your fault. I was the one who insisted on going with you. You had no other choice."

She smiled. "A woman always has another choice," she said lightly, her tone turning serious once more when she said, "But don't be forgetting *I* was the one who insisted on bringing Grandpa's dory."

"I had almost forgotten about that. Did you make it back with the dory in tow?"

"Yes, thanks to you."

"You have more than repaid me," he said, and she nodded, giving her attention back to her knitting.

She stopped counting stitches and began thinking about the weeks they had spent here in Boston. It was odd, really, how you never really know a person until you play nursemaid to him.

How different living with a man was from the collection of girlhood memories. There was nothing heart-thumpingly romantic about having a man tell you his armpits were sore, or that he had been plagued with dysentery for days. And yet there was an odd sort of closeness that she felt whenever he said such. The thought of it almost made her smile.

She went on with her knitting, not bothering to look up again until the fire had died down, and when she did look, it was to see Tavis with his head dropped backward in sleep. Now those blue eyes of his were closed. Those I-know-what-you're-thinking, those I-know-what-you-look-like-under-that-dress, eyes that made her so uncomfortable. She studied him, the way his mouth was open slightly, the slow rise and fall of his chest.

She put her knitting down and rose, placing another log on the fire, then turned to look at him from across the room. He was still sleeping, with his mouth slightly open. Just like Willie.

So like Willie, she thought. *When he's asleep, he is so much like his son.*

She was never certain just when her thoughts stopped being thoughts and started becoming spoken words. "This all feels so strange, you know . . . our being together at last, and yet we have never been farther apart. I still love you. I always will. I always have. I remember when I was a little girl and I would lie in my bed at night, looking at the stars through the window and thinking that you were out there somewhere looking at those very same stars. Somehow that made me feel connected to you."

She turned away from him and stood staring into the fire. "Maybe this is all my fault. Maybe I've wished and prayed myself into a situation I can't get out of." She felt her eyes burn and she closed them, bringing her fingers up to massage the tightness that throbbed at her temples. "Dear God, I did want you, but not this way. What can I do? How can I undo what's been done?"

Now she could see back through the long years that she had loved him, watching herself peeking at him through the potted palms at the Starbucks' house, enraptured with the sight of the handsome young man with the grayest, the bluest, knock-me-down-dead eyes she had ever seen.

She saw clearly now that he was only a childhood fancy, an infatuation that should have lasted no longer than her love for dolls. But she had persisted, past reason, past good sense even, to the point of obsession. He had never loved her, never given her any reason to hope he ever would. If he had ever given her even the tiniest hope, one look, one small token that she could keep locked in her box of treasures, she might have had a reason.

But he had given her nothing but years of rejection, indifferent looks, and cold shoulders. And then she understood. Their problem did not lie in the fact that Tavis did not love her. It was because of the different plans they each had for him. Was it too late to give him his life, his freedom back? Was it too late to return what she had stolen?

She turned away from the fire, but when her gaze encountered him, she stopped dead.

He watched her from across the room, his eyes dark, almost brooding, and oddly unsettling. She wanted to tell herself that he had just awakened that he had not heard her wild rambling, but she knew in her heart that was not true. She had poured her heart out, and he had been awake.

"So you heard," she said.

"Elizabeth . . ."

"No, don't say anything. Please. You heard what I said. You might as well hear the rest of it."

"You don't have to say it."

"I know I don't, but it makes me feel better. There re too many things inside my head right now, too many urdens that my heart carries. I know what a fool I vas," she said, feeling as bitter as the words implied. "I vas a fool, and now I have to pay for my foolish mistkes. I finally got what I wanted. You married me. And ow that I'm married to you, I don't want to be."

"I'll make it up to you," he said. "I want us to be together."

"Oh, I know that. I remember you said you wanted

me, wanted us to be a family, but what else could you say? We're married. We have a child. We have all the trappings of marriage but none of the substance." She sighed, shaking her head slowly. "At least you're trying to do the right thing. At least you have some sense of honor. While all I have is the memory of a forced marriage and a husband who does not love me."

She dropped her hands to her sides and thought about her life. She had prayed for the cleansing of tears, but none came. Some things were too deep for tears, just as some things were too late. Sometime, someway, she would know what to do. For now she could only wait until he was better. Then they would go home.

An odd sort of peace settled between them after that, with Tavis controlling his crabbed humor and Elizabeth giving him more of her time. Her goal, her only goal now, was to have him on his feet and dismissed by Dr. Carver as soon as possible. She wanted to go home, back to Nantucket, back to Willie, back to . . . what?

She had not thought about that until now, for she had been too occupied with his injury and recovery to think much beyond that point. There was nothing for her in Nantucket. There was no reason for her to remain there any longer. Her parents were gone, and her sisters and Grandpa, too. Her brothers were all married now and off sailing or fighting for the Union. All she had in the world was Willie.

Willie and Aunt Phoebe's house in Boston.

She remembered the day Aunt Phoebe had told her she was leaving her the house and how she couldn't for the life of her convince Aunt Phoebe that she had no need of it. "A body always needs a place to come home to," Phoebe had said. "Promise me you'll keep it."

It occurred to her then that Aunt Phoebe had given her more than just a house. She had given her a way out of the tangle of things between herself and Tavis. She had given her a way to start over.

It was so simple, really, once she thought about it. She knew now what she was going to do. Her mind was made up.

Once they reached Nantucket, once she had him back home, she would see Tavis for the last time. Then she would gather up her son and return immediately to Boston.

She didn't know what would happen after that, but she knew it was the right thing to do. She could not live in the same town with Tavis after this. She could not bear to see him look at her, or to hear him speak to her, when there was no love in either. She thought about never seeing him again and knew the pain of it would always be with her. She had loved him as a child. She had loved him as a woman. Both times she had lost.

It was enough.

The night before they were to leave, she couldn't sleep. There were too many thoughts of going home, too many thoughts of taking her son and leaving. Once again this old house would know the loneliness of a woman living without the comforting presence of a man. But at least she would not live with fear and despair as she had done before when he had left her. She had made her mind up. She did not want to rethink those things again. She would have a new life soon. It was all she wanted now—breathing space. A place to rest and heal. A place to go to lick her wounds. A future for Willie.

But first things first. Right now she needed her sleep. But sleep eluded her.

She sat up in bed and, dropping her feet over the side, put them into her slippers. Taking her dressing gown from the end of the bed, she tied the sash as she walked toward the door. There was some port wine in the library. Perhaps a glass of it was what she needed.

Her mind occupied with other things, she made her way downstairs, not really conscious she was opening the library door until she blinked from the brightness of the desk lamp striking her in the eyes. With an open-mouthed expression, she stood in the doorway staring at the brilliance of light and the face on the other side of the room that it illuminated. He was sitting behind the desk, writing what looked to be a letter. Her gaze strayed to the crutches propped against the side of the desk.

He looked up.

"What are you doing down here?" she asked.

He replied, "What are you doing out of bed?"

"I couldn't sleep," she said. "I thought a glass of port . . ."

His gaze went to the decanter of port sitting on the table between them. He nodded at the port. "It probably would help," he said, then smiling, he added, "Although I know something else that would work much better. And there would be no bad feeling in the morning."

She knew what he was referring to. That he would make light with her using something sexual left her feeling unsure of herself. She said the first thing that came into her mind.

"It might not leave me feeling badly, it would only leave me feeling shamed."

He frowned. "Shamed, is it? There was a time you

didn't feel that way. I hope there will be a time when you won't again."

She looked at him, her face etched with emotion. "That was a long time ago. Things are different between us now. We can't go back."

"I don't want to go back," he said. "I want to go forward ... from this day forward."

"You sound like you're reciting poetry," she said.

"I'm talking about reality."

She sighed. "What is real and what isn't?" She looked off. "I don't know the answer to that. I remember telling Aunt Phoebe once that I felt as if there were so many people inside of me that perhaps that was why I had so many names. Elizabeth, Eliza, Liza, Lizzie. I told her that perhaps I should settle for just one name, or if I were only one person, I wouldn't be so complicated."

"You aren't complicated. You're just confused, and it's partly my fault. I haven't been a very good husband to you. All I am asking is for the chance to try again."

"I may not be complicated," she said, "but complicated is the way I feel things are ... between us." She looked down at her hands, twisting the ring on her finger. "Perhaps I am confused. Who wouldn't be? You want me, you don't want me. You want to be married, you don't want to be married. You hope never to lay eyes on me again. You can't go another day without seeing me."

Then she glanced up, looking at him, square in the eyes. "Honestly, Tavis, sometimes I feel just like a chameleon that landed on a Scottish plaid."

For a moment he just sat there watching her, blinking his eyes like a great, wise owl, and then, as if he understood what she had said at last, he gave her a whimsical look, then threw back his head and laughed. "You might be a lot of different people, but if you were just one, you wouldn't be half as interesting," he said.

She smiled. "That's exactly what Aunt Phoebe said."

"Well?" he said, looking at her with a tender look. "You managed to live with her, didn't you?"

She didn't say anything. She couldn't seem to connect her thoughts with any words. Nothing seemed to be working right, nothing seemed to register in her mind, save the desire to be with him once more, the need to be loved by him one last time before she let him slip away.

Desire coiled like a snake around her, making her feel giddy and strange. She let her gaze move over him, studying him in depth.

His smile was crooked, carrying a wealth of meaning all sensual, all beckoning, just as he did with his finger that called her to him.

"Come here," he said.

"Why?"

"Because I want you to."

"Why?"

"You have a lot of questions," he said.

"I need a lot of answers," she replied.

"You aren't going to make this easy for me, are you?"

"Why should I? You never made it easy for me."

"All right. I want you to come here because I want you to. I want to hold you, Elizabeth," he said, coming to his feet and putting his crutches beneath his arms. "I want to hold you and keep on holding you until you stop fighting me."

A terrible fear seized her and she turned, intending to flee. He put a crutch out to stop her, and she gasped the contact of his body pressing against her from behind.

"Don't go," he whispered into her ear, and the repercussion of it rippled over her.

She froze, closing her eyes against the sensation. His crutches clattered to the floor. His arms came around her, his hands cupping her breasts. The humming vibration of her sloop running before the wind filled her ears. Her legs were as weak as a newborn's. She laid her head back, feeling his lips touching the side of her throat where it curved down to her shoulder. Shivers of pleasure rippled over her. "Why are you doing this?"

"I don't know," he said softly, nuzzling her ear with his mouth. "Do you want me to stop?"

Helplessly she said, "Yes."

He inhaled deeply and buried his face in her hair, his arms holding her more tightly, pulling her more closely against his body, which seemed fiery with hunger. His hands loosed her buttons, sliding inside and going beneath the linen of her chemise. She gasped as he whispered sweet rhythms in her ear, matching their cadence with the motion of his hands. "It isn't easy to let you go," he said.

She felt the shock of cold air where only a moment before there had been the warmest of hands. A peculiar tension crept over her, one she didn't understand. Her muscles felt tense and ready. She could feel the blood surging through her heart. Without looking at him again, she moved to the decanter and poured herself a glass.

"I think I should drink it in my room," she said, not looking at him and turning away.

"I wonder," he said.

She turned to look at him. "What?"

"Earlier you said we couldn't go back," he said. "
simply said, I wonder."

"It's no wonder," she said flatly. "It's a known fact.'

Then she hurried through the door, closing it firml
behind her.

The port helped her go to sleep, but it was a restles
sort of sleep where she tossed and turned and foun
herself glancing in the direction of the draperies, look
ing for the signs of dawn's first light.

She heard a noise and opened her eyes, staring at
halo of mellow light coming from the candle he held
his hand. She scooted back against the head of the be
coming to a sitting position, staring through the dar
ness that separated them, seeing the way the light cou
not penetrate the hollows on his face.

There was nothing to be afraid of, she knew that, y
her heart pounded furiously in her chest. She could n
speak. She could only stare at him, aware of the painf
drumming of her heart, the way her breathing was sh;
low and difficult.

Suddenly she realized that the man standing the
leaning on his crutches, with nothing on but a lig
woolen robe that revealed a bare chest, was the m
whom so many women wanted. He had taught many
them the things they wanted to know.

Tavis Mackinnon.

He was her husband. He had loved many women. I
had made them cry out his name. He had done the sa
to her. He had made love to her. He had made her
out his name. He could do so again. He could make I
do anything . . . crawl on her hands and knees throu
snowbanks if he wanted to. He could even make her
out again.

The thought terrified her. "What do you want? What are you doing . . ."

She didn't finish the sentence.

She watched him come, stepping farther into the room, walking slowly, coming to the end of the bed and standing there, his gaze fixed on her face, his eyes telling her that he knew she knew why he had come.

"Elizabeth . . ."

"No," she said. "I don't—"

"Know what you want," he finished.

She rolled from the bed, her gaze on the dressing gown that lay on the chair across the room, behind him. She started for it, then stopped, looking into his face. Not more than three feet separated them now. Absently she watched him step closer, watching the way the candle seemed to light up half his body.

Moving the candle to his left hand, he reached out with his right and, using one finger, traced the fullness of her breast, lingering for a tingling moment as he circled her nipple, then, still using that one finger, he pushed the straps down, over her shoulders. First the left. Then the right.

She felt a draft of cool air swirl around her as the gown dropped around her waist, felt, too, her body warm considerably when his hand closed firmly over her breast.

Catching her nipple between his forefinger and thumb, he stared into her face. "Now tell me what you were afraid of. Tell me what you knew was going to happen. What you are as powerless as I to stop."

She was still staring up into his face. She did not say anything, but she saw the way he looked at her when her tongue came out to moisten the dryness that seemed to silence her lips.

"Tell me," he asked, caressing her again. Harder "What were you afraid of down there?"

"That you would make love to me," she whispered

She felt his arm come around her as he drew her int his arms. "Are you sure that was it?" he asked as he le her to the bed. "Or were you afraid you would let me?"

"Both," she said, feeling her back touch the mat tress, and a moment later, his nakedness as he covere her.

"Make love to me, Tavis."

"Damn right," he said, and she knew he meant it.

His arms came around her as he looked down at he He kissed her, holding her jaw between his finger forcing her lips open wider. His tongue was inside h mouth now, and the feel of it drove her hands up an around his neck. Part of her was shocked, but part her was overrun by excitement and desire to have hi do the things to her his eyes had promised in the librar

"Damn," he groaned, and she knew it was caused pain in his leg. She tried to roll away, but he held h fast. "I'm not in that much pain," he said. "I'll tell y when it gets unbearable."

He kissed her again and again, rubbing his mou over hers until she thought she would scream wi wanting. This was so much harder than it had been b fore.

Before, she was a naive girl. Now she was a woma a woman with a woman's needs and a memory th served her too well. She knew what it was like to loved by this man. She remembered what it felt like have his mouth on her, what it felt like to be kiss where no other man had kissed. She felt a throbbing tween her legs.

The memory of it made her want him to kiss

there again. She opened her legs, feeling his response, feeling him groan as he began to kiss his way across her face and then began to travel lower, kissing his way down.

It was more than she could stand. She heard herself whisper his name and then she was arching against him, wanting him, wanting the feel of his mouth. Her body shuddered when he put his tongue where his lips had been. Her body became a living flame, a fire that fed on the ache within her, then turning white-hot, the flame leapt high, her body became molten. When the flame died down, leaving nothing behind but the afterglow, she sighed, feeling as if her soul had been purified by fire.

"I knew you needed that, but I never thought you'd admit you wanted it," he said.

"Hmmmmm ... You wanted it, too," she said, her hand coming out to close around him.

He was hard. Good and hard.

"You still want it," she whispered.

"You're damn right I do," he said, and rolled over her. He winced and rolled onto his back. "The mind is willing, and my prick, too, but this damn leg of mine ..."

"I seem to remember," she said, rolling on top of him, "that there is another way."

She straddled his hips, feeling him slide inside.

"God," he groaned. "If your memory was any better, I'd be a dead man."

She laughed, and her hair came unbound, falling down over them. She saw him like a vision beneath her. The lamplight tinted his skin with a golden glow, the heated flush of desire adding a ruddy hue to his cheeks. His eyes were looking at her with such intensity, and she felt the burning enchantment of it and knew then that once would never be enough. *I love you. I'll always love you.*

His skin beneath her had grown warm, and she stirred against the sensation of his hard body pressing against her, opening herself to him, feeling whole and complete when she felt him come inside. It was all so achingly new; everything about it was so shatteringly poignant, a bitterness laced with sweet. It was everything she remembered. It was like her first time. It was the substance of a million and one imaginings. It was far, far better than any of her dreams. Knowing she was only making it harder for herself to let him go, she made love to him, permitting herself, just this once, the unrestrained pleasure of her hands on his body, her hips moving in perfect rhythm with his.

"Love me," he whispered, the sound of his words sending a warmth surging through her veins.

"I do," she whispered, losing herself in a stormy sea of desire and confusion laced with a wild, wild yearning.

A shudder raced over him, and then another. A second later, she felt her own shattering response.

Her mind slowly surfaced from the valley of desire and she stared down into his eyes, feeling their hypnotic pull. His eyes were smoky and liquid, looking at her in a way that made her want him again.

He must have read it in her expression, for at that moment he rolled over, putting her beneath him.

"Your leg . . ."

"To hell with my leg," he said.

This time, when Tavis made love to his wife, he took his own sweet time, lingering with her for hours, holding himself back, teaching her about him, about herself,

Each time her body shuddered, she thought it more powerful than the first.

Dawn was chasing the shadows away when Tavis loved her for the last time, then cradling her in his arms, he fell into a deep sleep.

She lay tangled against him. Then when she knew he would sleep for some time, she eased herself away from him, slowly pulling the long skeins of her hair from beneath him. She inched her way across the bed, feeling a soreness, a stiffness, in her body that was unfamiliar. Her feet on the floor now, she stood, moving silently around the bed, finding her gown.

She went to the table beside the bed, intending to turn the lamp off, but when she looked down at him, seeing the smooth muscles of his back, the inky blackness of his hair against the pillow, she paused. She gave full vent to her desire to look at him, allowing her gaze to roam over him at her leisure.

No sheet or blanket covered him, so there was no part of him that was left to her imagination. He was a splendid-looking man. His skin was smooth and naturally golden in color, his legs long and perfectly muscled, his buttocks firm, high, and round.

The sun was full up now, streaming into the room through the windows, spreading its warmth over the carpets on the floor. As she had done for Willie so many times, she drew the blanket over him, smoothing the tousled hair back from his face as she kissed him.

"I will always love you," she whispered, then, as she turned off the lamp, she found herself thinking that her love for him was a lot like that lamp.

Burning brightly in a sun-filled room, it was hardly noticed.

CHAPTER
❧ TWENTY-FOUR ❧

Elizabeth stood beside Tavis on Nantucket's Straig
Wharf, watching him step forward—with a slight lim
that was so familiar to her now—to shake hands wi
the ship's captain.

She watched him pause, absently rubbing his leg, a
she found herself wondering if it would ever cease
pain him.

He had almost lost his leg because of her. While s
couldn't undo the pain and suffering he had go
through, she had, by taking him to Boston, given hi
his leg back.

She watched him, studying his every move as if s
were committing it to memory. He was walking with
barely noticeable limp now. In time she hoped that, t
would pass. He was whole again, and soon he'd be
good as new. With an uplifting sense of satisfaction, s
realized she had done what she set out to do. Her he
aching for a loss that was to come, she realized th
was no reason for her to drag things out. It was time
her to go.

"Tavis! Tavis Mackinnon! Is that you?" a voice called out.

Tavis and Elizabeth turned to see the smiling face of Nathaniel as he hurried down the wharf.

When he reached them, he grabbed Tavis in a bear hug. "Aren't you a sight for sore eyes," he said, giving Tavis the once-over. "You look good as new."

Tavis grinned. "Another month and I will be," he said.

Elizabeth watched them for a moment, then seeing Captain Burroughs turn away, she caught him on the sleeve, detaining him.

"One moment, Captain."

Captain Burroughs turned toward her, bringing his fingers to his hat. "Mrs. Mackinnon. Is there something else I can do for you?"

Her gaze flicked over to Tavis. Finding him deep in conversation with Nathaniel, she gave her attention to the captain. "Yes," she said. "I was wondering . . . well, you see, I wanted to know when you would be returning to Boston."

He gave her a curious look. "Why, I'll be returning day after tomorrow, ma'am."

"If there is room, I would like to book passage to Boston." She ignored the speculative look.

"Passage for just one?"

"For two," she said. "For myself and my son."

Captain Burroughs gave her a puzzled look this time, his gaze going quickly to Tavis and back to her again. "It would be a pleasure to have you on board again, Mrs. Mackinnon . . . both you and your son. I'll give your name to the first mate. You should have your things here and ready to load by a quarter past eight tomorrow. We sail with the tide on Wednesday."

"I'll be here. Thank you, Captain."

"My pleasure, ma'am," he said, touching his hat. "Good day to you."

She watched him depart, then turned around. She was greeted by the openmouthed stare of Nathaniel Starbuck and the shocked expression on her husband's face.

"What was that all about?" Tavis asked.

"I'm going back to Boston."

"Whatever for?"

"I think you know the answer to that," she said.

"Humor me," he said. "Tell me why you're leaving."

"Oh, Tavis, must we go into all of this again?"

"Yes, you're damn right we must. I want to know why in the hell you're leaving. I thought that after the other night . . . well, that things were better between us, that things would be different."

She felt the warm spread of heat across her face at the mention of the other night. She kept her gaze on him, feeling too timid to look at Nathaniel. "I'm giving you your freedom, Tavis. It's what you've always wanted. I'm taking Willie back to Boston with me. I want to start a new life for us."

"Why?"

She looked at him, seeing that Tavis's eyes held a heat, a hunger, that any woman would give ten years of of her life for. But heat and hunger weren't the same as love.

"Elizabeth," he said. "Please tell me why."

"Because this marriage between us is all wrong. It's been wrong from the very start. No. Please don't say anything. Let me finish. I know this is all my fault. You were as much a victim of my childhood fancy as I was. You may think you've come to care for the woman, but we both know you could never accept the child. That why it won't work. Because I'm both people. Don't you see that? I am both people. I always have been. I always will be."

At that moment, if there had been any way she could have gotten Willie and left Nantucket Island, she would have run from him without ever looking back.

"And if I don't want my freedom?"

Elizabeth looked at him and felt suddenly tired, so tired that she didn't even care if Nathaniel Starbuck and half of Nantucket could hear her. What was there to hear anyway? Her feelings for Tavis and his lack of feeling for her had been common knowledge for years. If the truth were known, probably no one wanted to hear it again. If they stumbled out to the wharf and saw the two of them here, they would clamp their hands over their ears and go running for cover. Sometimes things could be discussed too much, talked to death. Perhaps that was why she felt so weak, so lifeless.

"Elizabeth, will you answer me? What if I told you I didn't want to be free, that I wanted you?"

"I would say it didn't matter. Not anymore. I spent so much of my life chasing you, Tavis Mackinnon, that I never had a chance to live in quiet repose. I am going to do that now. I'm tired. I want nothing more than to raise my son in peace. Leave me be."

It was a clear day, and warm for this early in March. She felt the sun heat her back as she started up the wharf, not going more than a few steps when Tavis's hand on her arm stopped her.

"You're being a complete fool."

"And you should know all about fools," she said. You've been one often enough."

"Only over you," he said softly. "But now it seems it s your turn. You're being the foolish one now."

She gave a sad sound, one that lay somewhere between a sigh and a derisive laugh. "I think you're probably right. I spent so much of my life entranced with being a wife to you that I didn't even realize that the man I wanted to be a wife to wanted nothing to do with me."

"I think you should give yourself more time to think about this," he said.

She shook her head. "I had weeks to do that in Boston."

"I want you to stay."

"I'm sure you do . . . for Willie."

"It's not just for Willie, dammit. I'm asking for a chance," he said. "It's a little hard learning to be a husband and a father at the same time, but I'm willing to try. If you are."

"Well, I'm not," she said.

"Then stay anyway. You'll get used to the idea."

"No."

He looked down at her face, recognizing the stubborn set, and why shouldn't he? He had seen that resigned determined look often enough. He had seen it for years when she peeked at him from behind buildings and out of trees, when she had asked him to marry her when she was twelve, and the time she had dyed her hair that hideous shade of red.

"Why not?" he asked.

"Because we would be nothing more than two miserable people huddled together in the same house—two miserable people who didn't love each other, with nothing to do but spend the rest of their lives, each one blaming the other for all their misfortune and misery."

"Dammit! Stop being so stubborn. You're my wife! It's a cold, hard fact, and your leaving won't change that." The moment the words escaped him, he saw they were futile. She was leaving him. Her mind was made up. She would take their son and go away. His heart beat frantically, and he wondered if he could die from the pain of it.

What's wrong? his mind screamed. *What is wrong?*

And then it came to him. Clear. Sharp. Concise.

He wasn't looking at her as a woman. He was still seeing her as the child. He had married her out of force, and even when he had been away from her all those years he was in Washington and Portsmouth, he hadn't seen himself as married to Elizabeth the woman, he had seen himself shackled with a child.

It was the child who had always been with him, the child who held him fascinated, even now. From that first time he had glimpsed her, she held a special attraction for him. He had found amusement in her antics, tucked the memory of them away in his mind, only to fling them back in her face whenever Elizabeth, the woman, got too close.

The child, he understood, but it was the woman who made him afraid.

He realized now that he had made love to her on the sloop, not out of desire for her as a woman, but because of the idolizing of the child. He had granted her lifelong wish for him to love her with the casual sort of ease one would give worn-out clothing to a servant who had long admired it.

And even then, she had loved him.

What can I do? How can I show her I realize my foolishness? How can I possibly make up for what I've done, for what I've taken from her? He looked down at her face. *Oh, Elizabeth, what have I done? How could I have been so blind, so stupidly blind? You grew tired of waiting. You outgrew a childish dream. While I remained the same.*

"Stay with me," he said, feeling too lost, too desperate, to think of anything more. He noticed the way she seemed conscious, almost embarrassed, that others gathered on the wharf might hear them.

Suddenly he threw back his head and bellowed loudly. "Stay with me and be my wife, Elizabeth."

There must have been close to a hundred people on the wharf and gathered around it by now, and all of them were turned to watch—a gathering Elizabeth obviously did not like.

But Lizzie would.

With all the romantic zeal of Sir Lancelot, Tavis painfully went down on one knee, holding his folded hands up to her in entreaty. "I know I hurt you," he said. "I know it's all my fault for going away." He was almost shouting now. "I should have never left you in the first place. Don't leave. Stay with me."

"Stay with him, Elizabeth," a woman called out.

"Give Willie a good home," shouted another.

Her face turned red as the sumac bushes in October. "Will you stop shouting?" she asked, giving his sleeve a yank and trying to drag him to his feet. Barely whispering now, she leaned closer. "Will you get up? You're being a complete ass. Everyone is looking at you."

He grinned. "Do you really want to go to Boston? Are you certain you want to live in that musty old house with just you and Willie?" he shouted.

He was gaining momentum now. This was turning into a real performance. Worse, he was certain, than any she had ever been guilty of.

"I want you to be my wife," he said, "and I know you want to be. You're just too stubborn."

"Tavis, get up!" she hissed.

"You won't be sorry. I'll make it up to you. I'll work hard. I'll build you a new house. I'll name a ship after you. I'll give you all my money. I'll swear off alcohol."

"You rarely drink," she said.

"Then I'll swear off anything you ask."

"Will you stop making a spectacle of yourself?"

"That, too," he said. Then grinning at her, he added, "And if you want me to stop making a spectacle of myself in front of the whole of Nantucket, then just say yes!"

She narrowed one eye and looked at him, her gaze speculative. "Are you drunk?" she asked.

"No, of course not."

"You should be," she said, pushing her way around him. "Leave me be, Tavis. I wouldn't marry you if I had to."

"You don't have to," he called after her. "We're already married."

"I mean if I had it to do over again," she said without breaking stride and without turning back.

He hobbled after her, catching her and taking her by the arm. "Leave me be, Tavis," she said, and then turning toward him, she placed both hands on his chest and shoved.

Tavis went over the side, hitting the water with a tremendous splash.

A second later, she was swallowed up into the crowd on the wharf.

Going to the side of the wharf, Nathaniel looked down at Tavis, giving him a hand up.

"Why didn't you tell her what she wanted to hear?" he asked.

"And what is that?" Tavis replied.

"That you love her. That's the one thing a woman, any woman, wants to hear."

Tavis gave him a thoughtful look. "Love?" Tavis said, wondering if someone like him could ever know what love was. Was that what was missing here? Is that what she wanted, really wanted?

He had cared for his parents, certainly, but was that love? He spent his life designing ships, but was that love? Elizabeth touched him in a way no other woman had, but was that love?

He did not know. He shook his head sadly, wondering why he seemed to be the only person who did not know.

"Why don't you go find someone else to pester and leave me alone," Tavis said, giving Nathaniel a dismissing look. "I don't feel like company right now. Especially your meddlesome company."

"All right," Nathaniel said. "Go suffer all by yourself. Although I think the whole thing is completely unnecessary. I don't know why you can't see something as plain as your love for her."

"Nathan," Tavis said like a warning, "will you stay the hell out of this?"

Seeing Tavis's angry scowl, Nathaniel held up his hands and began backing away. "Okay . . . okay . . . I can see from your utter misery, from your eagerness to make a fool of yourself over her, and from your thoroughly sour disposition that this is the real thing."

It began to rain, a light spring shower, the kind that appear suddenly and then go almost as quickly as they came. Elizabeth left the wharf, walking toward Tavis's house like a woman in a hurry. She was going to pick up Willie.

She hadn't given much thought to where she would take him, to where they would spend the next two nights and day. She only knew she wanted to get him away from Mrs. Chadwick before Tavis got there.

Then she would think about where they were going to stay.

Five minutes later, she was knocking on the door. Mrs. Chadwick didn't answer. She knocked again. Still no answer. Elizabeth was about to knock a third time when a voice behind her said, "Here, let me unlock the door for you."

Her shoulders drooped in defeat. "I don't need your help," she said. "I just came to get Willie."

"I know why you came," Tavis said, jabbing his key into the lock and pushing the door open. "Apparently he isn't here."

She gazed into the darkened interior. "I'll just gather up Willie's things while I'm here. I'll find him and Mrs. Chadwick later. It's a small island. They can't have gone very far," she said, stepping into the house, feeling a sudden panic when she heard the door shut behind her.

The house was dark and chilly. She drew her cape about her. She had never felt so alone, so friendless, so scared.

"Elizabeth, I am begging you not to do this. I am begging you to stay."

She stopped and looked straight into his face, her gaze searching his. "Do you love me, Tavis?"

He looked at her, seeing the pride, the agony, the fear, etched on her face. He saw so many faces when he looked at her—the face of the child, the young girl, the woman, the wife, the mother.

He thought about the past, remembering a young girl

who lost her stuffings at his feet, saw, too, the woman she had been when they were alone together on he sloop. He saw the stunned, hurt face of the wife as h told her he was leaving her on their wedding night, an would never forget the face of the mother the day h came back to learn she had borne his son. He though about her losses, and his, knowing they both would suf fer yet another loss if he could not answer yes.

"Do I love you?" he said, looking at her with intens feeling in his eyes. "Honest to God, Elizabeth, I don know how to answer that. I'm not sure I know wha love is."

He saw the light fade from her eyes, and he knew I had this one chance and this one chance only. "I kno the thought of you fills me with warmth, while your a sence is as cold as ice. I admire your strength, your lo alty, your honesty. I remember the first time I ever sa you. You were a little girl ... ten or so ... walki down Straight Wharf with your grandfather. I was lea ing the ship with my brother Nick when I looked up a saw you. There was something about you, even the that called out to me. How else would I remember vividly that day?"

She didn't answer him.

"I remember a lot of other things," he said. "Like way we made love and how one week in your ar ruined me for any other woman—enough that I mained celibate during all the years that I was away know the thought of spending the rest of my life w you floods my soul with sunlight, while the thought losing you leaves me in the darkness ... babbling, b ging, and blind. I know you fill my every wak thought, and at night, my dreams all go your wa know that when I look at you I feel close to bursting side, but when I try to speak of my feelings, I feel like I'm filled with a ball of tangled twine. I know that if you leave me, I'll never be free of you, for you've awakened my soul and you'll come back to me in my dreams."

He stepped closer to her, picking up her hands and holding them in his. "If these things are love, then yes, I love you."

He put his arms around her. "Give me your fire and your craziness, give me your strength and your love. Child of passion, mother of my child, bend your will to mine."

She looked at him and suddenly she couldn't understand why she had ever wanted to leave him. She didn't care if he didn't love her. She didn't care about anything except the reality of his being the first thing she saw every morning and the last thing she saw each night.

"Don't you understand what I'm saying? I want you. Forever. I want you to be the mother of my—" he paused, thinking they already had one child "—other children."

She crossed her arms and looked at him with the deepest scowl. "And just how many do you have?"

He laughed, taking her in his arms. "Only one . . . so far."

He began kissing her throat, her face. "Come here, Lizzie, and make love to me. I'm anxious to start working on the rest of them."

She melted against him, soft and infinitely tender, laying her head against the love-warmed strength of his chest, and closing her eyes, she saw the face of her grandfather.

Thank you, she said, *for giving me hope.*

She opened her eyes, thinking there were stars sprin
kled about her head, and scattered at her feet. *I am*
child again; my joy holds me fast.

And suddenly she knew she was where she had al
ways wanted to be. This was her man; her home, he
little slice of paradise. She looked around the sma
room, seeing the Persian carpet, the Dutch clock on th
overmantel, the teapot, the window draped in cranberr
damask.

Outside, it had stopped raining, and the world la
sun-warmed and drowsy. A comfortable sense of peac
filled her as she felt the love in those arms that held he
saw the world she held so dear, saw the rickety wago
that passed down the street, saw the rain-soaked shi
gles on rooftops as gray as a Quaker's bonnet, the th
curl of smoke coming from a dozen chimneys, and s
saw, too, the rainbow that stretched itself like a sm
over it all, a promise of what was to come.

And who is to say? Heaven only knows. Perha
their family did begin to grow that very night.

❧ EPILOGUE ❧

Elizabeth had been in labor all afternoon, giving birth to her sixth son. Tavis knew it would be a son, of course, for Elizabeth had never given him a daughter. She knew how he felt about girls.

The thought of having one of his own left him terrified. After all, girls took after their mothers, did they not?

It never failed in all the times he had sat down here in the parlor—waiting for the housekeeper or the doctor to tell him Elizabeth was fine and that he was a father again—that his mind would drift backwards, remembering a time, so long ago, when a blond-headed imp by the name of Lizzie Robinson had made his life a living hell.

As he drew up the memories one by one, reliving the escapades, shaking his head at her capers, he would always pause, thinking just how lucky he had been, having five strapping sons, how thankful he was that God had never seen fit to bless him with a daughter. He never ceased, whenever he thought about this, to think how much empathy he had for Samuel Robinson. For he couldn't help wondering, if he had a daughter, if he would be able to be as good a father.

Upstairs, he could hear the sounds of his two younger sons in the nursery, giving their nurse, old Dolly Clare yet another reason to drink half of her cough elixir before retiring. Aside from that, the house was pretty quiet now, since Willie and the two brothers who had followed him were off at school.

He thought his happiness complete when the housekeeper, Mrs. Forrester, poked her head into the library and said, "Mrs. Mackinnon and the baby are both doing fine. Just fine."

Tavis breathed a sigh of relief. *Another baby,* he thought. "Well, it looks like I'm the proud father of another son," he said.

He looked at his old friend Nathaniel Starbuck just as Nathaniel said, "But, Tavis, she didn't say what the baby was. There's always the chance that it might be a girl, you know."

Tavis's chest swelled with pride. "It's a boy," he said. "They're always boys."

Nathaniel grinned. "You don't always get what you order. Tell me, just what would you do if you had a girl, Tavis? Give her back?"

Tavis laughed. "If she looked anything like Elizabeth, I would," he said, for a girl who looked like Elizabeth would grow up to act like her. And as far as Tavis was concerned, that was reason enough to never, ever—no matter how many times he thought about what a beautiful child Elizabeth had been—order up a daughter.

It was Nathaniel's turn to laugh. He clapped Tavis on the back. "What's the matter, old man? You afraid of history repeating itself?"

That was exactly what he was afraid of. "It would be my luck," Tavis said.

"Well, you've said you've got yourself a son, so I'd say this is a call for a celebration," Nathaniel said. "Want me to pour you a drink?"

Tavis nodded. Before he could say anything more, Mrs. Forrester was back again, poking her head through the door again.

"I was so excited, I plumb forgot to tell you," she said. "It's a girl ... and a pretty little thing, too—with blond curly hair. If you ask me, I'd say she's the spitting image of her mother."

Tavis looked at Nathaniel. "Make that two," he said.

Upstairs in the bedroom, Elizabeth heard the most charming sound in the world—the low, rumbling laugh of her husband when he heard she had given him a daughter. Biting her lip against another pain, she heard Dr. Montgomery tell her to push.

Mrs. Forrester was standing beside the bed, holding Elizabeth's hand. "What do you think he'll say if it's another girl?" she asked.

"Heaven knows," Elizabeth said, groaning as she bore down with yet another pain.

A moment later, another baby was placed in her arms. She cuddled the two babies against her, thinking that of all the things Tavis had given her, it was through her children that she felt most blessed. She thought about the shock he must be feeling now, the apprehensions he always had about having a daughter. But even then, she knew he would come to love his daughter as much as he loved her.

Her mind skimmed, like sunlight over water, back through the many memories of her past and how she

had always loved one man and one man only. She fe
her heart cry out to all the daughters and granddaugl
ters that were to come, her legacy.

I can never wish you greater happiness than this.

She looked down at the slumbering babes in h
arms, thinking sons were the anchors of a mother's li
but a daughter was her double. Her double. Elizabe
smiled at the thought, her heart going out to Tavi
What would he do when Mrs. Forrester told him s
had given birth to yet another babe?

Another daughter?

Dear Reader,

I always knew, when I came up with the idea of writing five books about five brothers from Texas, that there would come a time when I finished the last book, a time when I wrote what I've come to think of as the last of the Mackinnons. Only I never knew it would be so difficult to let them go. How do you say good-bye to characters you have lived with for so long, characters who have become very, very real? Working with the Mackinnons was like having children. One day they were little and playing around my feet. The next day they were grown and gone.

I can only hope these five books have been as special for you to read as they were for me to create. There will be other characters and other books, but the Mackinnons will always be there, like the memory of first love.

Being one who always believed every ending was a beginning somewhere else, I move on, to a new beginning. It is late now, and I am sitting alone in the dark with the ghostly presence of all the characters who have come before haunting me. I wait, my thoughts suspended, like the tightly furled petals of a bud. Perhaps, when I sit down again to write, they will have opened into full bloom— or already I feel the first stirring of a few new companions.

* * *

Friendship and romance may fail us. Our children grow up and leave. But the characters who have been given life in a book are indestructible. They live on. . . .

Elaine Coffman

P.O. Box 8300-561
Dallas, Texas 75205-8300

Also by

ELAINE COFFMAN.

Published by Fawcett Books.
Available at your local bookstore.